Praise for Gena Showalter

"I love this world and these alpha males—this is Gena Showalter at her best!"
— J. R. Ward, #1 *New York Times* bestselling author

"Sexy paranormal romance at its hottest! The Gods of War series is my new obsession."
— Christine Feehan, #1 *New York Times* bestselling author

"Violence and passion infuse Gena Showalter's thrilling new world of gods and war. Hold on for a wild ride!"
— Nalini Singh, *New York Times* bestselling author

"Gena Showalter's attention to detail, innovative play on mythology, and sexy alpha male heroes come together seamlessly to create a world so vivid and engrossing that I never want it to end."
— Mandy M. Roth, *New York Times* bestselling author

"A new and stunningly brilliant sexy paranormal romance series by the talented Gena Showalter. I couldn't put it down!"
— Michelle M. Pillow, *New York Times* bestselling author

"One of the premier authors of paranormal romance."
— Kresley Cole, #1 *New York Times* bestselling author

"Gena Showalter never fails to dazzle."
— Jeaniene Frost, *New York Times* bestselling author

"The Showalter name on a book means guaranteed entertainment."
— *RT Book Reviews*

"Gena Showalter is a romantic genius."
— *San Francisco Book Review*

GENA SHOWALTER

FROST AND FLAME

HQN™

ISBN-13: 978-1-335-50504-0

Frost and Flame

Copyright © 2019 by Gena Showalter

Recycling programs for this product may not exist in your area.

To Michele Bidelspach. Our first book together.
I look forward to many more!

FROST AND FLAME

Once upon a time, kings and queens from across the galaxies searched for new worlds to inhabit, and other species to rule. These greedy royals sent armed legions into battle. Millions died, the newly discovered planets destroyed. While the heartless monarchs thrilled as they watched these bloodthirsty battles, they inherited little more than wastelands.

Wanting to continue their games *and* master new worlds, they agreed to a contest—the All War. Each sovereign would send one warrior to any newly discovered territory. Their *best* warrior. That territory would be their playground...and their battlefield. One champion would take everything, and all losers would die.

Throughout the centuries, one unspoken edict has remained the same. *Do not fall in love with a local.*

"Love? Never again. My heart is made of vengeance and hate."

—Bane of Adwaeweth

"I've warred with fibromyalgia and lupus for years. Tame some big, bad beasty-boy? Watch me."

—Nola Lee

PROLOGUE

The Realm of Adwaeweth
1026 AA (After Alliance)

BANE OF ADWAEWETH ignored his instincts to dominate his woman—always he ignored his instincts—and rolled to his back, the expected position for an Adwaewethian male. Not just expected, but enforced by law.

Would the pleasure be greater on top? Bane had broached the subject with Meredith once, only once, but she'd had no interest, so he'd dropped it. Most days, he told himself he didn't care. Some days he believed it.

Bathed in candlelight, Meredith rose to her knees, straddled him and sank down on his throbbing erection. The pleasure!

Head tipping backward, spine arching, Meredith moaned with rapture and began to ride him. Sweat glistened on her golden skin, and desire hooded her golden eyes. *So beautiful.* So strong and brave.

Meredith was the love of his life. Not too long ago, they'd recited vows in front of royals and peers alike, forever binding their futures. *Only in death shall we part.*

When she braced her hands on his calves and whipped her hips, his mind blanked…only to come back to life with a single thought. *More.* Releasing a strangled groan, he clasped her waist to control her motions. Up and down. Faster. Harder. Just the way she liked.

"Bane. It's so good." Short flaxen curls danced around her gorgeous face.

Harder still. Faster and faster. She loved his ferocity. But then, he'd always gravitated to warrior women. The ones courageous enough to rush into battle at his side.

Meredith offered more than physical resilience, though. A treasure inside and out, she had become his only refuge in a brutal, bloody eternity.

A shrill voice suddenly blasted through his mind. —*Stop what you're doing and come to Hivetta. Shirtless! I might as well enjoy the view as we discuss queendom business. And hurry!*—

Bane jerked. Only one person ever communicated with him via telepathy. Queen Aveline the Great, chosen by fate and imbued with preternatural powers. *My master and tormentor.*

Like all queens and princesses in the ruling class, Aveline could speak telepathically with her people, heal swiftly and teleport; she also had a special power all her own: the ability to drain a life force with only a touch.

Meredith continued to ride him, unaware of his distraction.

He replied to the queen, *I'm busy. Can this wait an hour?* Foolish question. He knew Aveline well. They'd been childhood sweethearts, until the once kind and considerate royal had grown into a cruel and selfish queen. Now, her impatience knew no bounds. *Or thirty—twenty—ten minutes, just ten.*

He didn't wish to leave his wife unsatisfied.

—*You have five minutes. Fail to appear before me, and I'll make your bride a widow. Ticktock.*—

Aveline never uttered empty threats.

In his four centuries of life, Bane had watched six different princesses ascend to power. No matter how sweet the female, something dark and insidious always infected her during the coronation ceremony, a violent process known as the Blood Rite. Swirling golden runes would appear on her skin, an eternal brand that somehow torched anything good and right, creating an entitled, self-indulgent, intemperate entity with no moral compass.

"I'm sorry, love," he grated, already losing his...edge. "I must go. The queen has commanded my presence."

"What?" Meredith beat her fists against his chest. "You can't leave me like this."

"I won't." He reached between their bodies, pressed the pad of his thumb against her clitoris and brought her to a swift climax. As her inner walls squeezed his length, he gritted his teeth and wheeled her to the side, and withdrew from paradise. What remained of his pleasure dovetailed into agony. "I'm sorry," he repeated, jumping from bed to wrangle his erection behind a pair of black leathers.

She sagged onto the mattress and grinned. "My poor baby. You'll never fit that thing inside your pants." The grin ebbed. With a tilt of her chin, she motioned to his shaft. "Aveline has the worst timing."

"Aveline has the worst *everything*."

Muffled voices drifted through the walls, a chorus of laughter following. Right now, Bane and Meredith lived in the army barracks next door to Hivetta, the royal palace, where jagged crystal walls were set in a honeycomb pattern.

Over the years, Hivetta had become the beating heart of the entire realm—and a prison rather than a home.

A few weeks ago, he'd purchased land outside city limits, where he'd begun building Meredith's dream home. A place to raise their children, if ever they were blessed in such a way.

"When I return, we'll pick up where we left off, and I'll give you another orgasm." He sat at the edge of the bed to pull on his boots.

"Unacceptable." Meredith pressed her bare breasts against his back and rested her chin on his shoulder. "You'll give me *two* orgasms—to start."

He chuckled, though his amusement faded fast. A countdown clock had begun racing inside his head. *Tick-tock. Ticktock.*

She ran his earlobe between her teeth. "If I could challenge Aveline on your behalf, and win, I would."

"I know." But, if she dared try, Bane would be forced to retaliate against *her*. Nothing broke the mystical bond between an Adwaewethian warrior and his queen, not even love for another.

A queen had absolute control over her men, as well as the beasts that lived inside them. *Literal* beasts who despised everything but death. A dark scourge the warriors battled physically, mentally and emotionally every minute of every day, with two exceptions. Sex, and the nearness of a royal.

Right on cue, a familiar roar of protest sounded inside his head. The beast didn't like that he would soon be leaving a willing partner. Any partner. Beasts weren't picky, and they were never satisfied.

I know the feeling. All his life, Bane had felt incomplete. He'd thought, hoped, his marriage would fix him, but…

More roars. Louder. Bane breathed deeply, filling his lungs in an effort to remain calm. Whenever a host lost control of his temper, he lost control period, the beast overtaking and changing him. He would grow in height and girth, horns sprouting from his head, spikes protruding from his spine, claws blooming at the ends of his fingers. Scales as hard as steel would cover his skin, and his teeth would sharpen into enameled daggers. He would kill with abandon and glee, the taste of blood ambrosial, screams of pain like music.

"What do you think Aveline the Greatly Terrible wants from you?" Meredith asked, drawing him from his musings.

Ticktock. "Most likely she'll command me to murder someone who's offended her." And Bane would do it without hesitation. He would do anything she requested; no matter how despicable, her command was his duty. Physically, he *couldn't* disobey her.

At the reminder, fury burned through him.

"We must find a way to sever the queen's hold over you," Meredith said.

"As awful as it is, as much as I despise it, a link with a royal is necessary." A fact difficult to understand for the beastless. They couldn't comprehend the constant tug-of-war between man and monster, or the balance created by the royals.

Meredith heaved a sigh. "I'll help you, whoever she orders you to kill."

"One of the countless reasons I love you." He gave his lovely wife a swift kiss, then sprinted from the barracks as if his feet were on fire.

A warrior stepped into his path, but he easily dodged. With forty-nine seconds to spare, he flew into the throne room and stopped beneath the dais, where he jutted his chin, squared his shoulders and braced his legs apart.

The beast went quiet.

The scent of candle wax and honeysuckle filled his nostrils. Honeysuckle—a scent exuded by every Adwaewethian queen and princess.

Hate honeysuckle!

Light glowed from a chandelier as big as his bedchamber, reflecting off a solid gold floor. On the walls hung portraits of past queens. Seated upon a throne of amethyst and crystal, Aveline raked her amber gaze over him before unveiling a cold smile.

"As delicious as I remember," she purred. "I approve."

Just a piece of meat to her. Once, she'd looked at him with love and affection, even adoration. She'd held his hand, and kissed his knuckles, and rested her head on his shoulder, content to just be with him.

Like all royals, she possessed a deceptively delicate appearance, with flawless golden skin, hair as pale as moonbeams, and irises the shade of a sunrise his toosensitive eyes had only ever seen in pictures. Faint golden runes etched her flesh in swirling designs. A sheer pink gown molded to her every perfect curve: full breasts, cinched waist and flared hips. Peekaboo slits in the skirt provided a glimpse of thigh when she shifted.

For those who preferred their women to look as fragile as glass, Aveline was a vison of loveliness—on the outside. On the inside, however, she was rotten to the core, greedy and corrupt, and Bane despised her with every fiber of his being. To be fair, he despised all Adwaewethian royals so vehemently.

When Aveline made no effort to start the conversation she'd insisted on having, he cut off a curse. "You summoned?"

"Leaving your new wife was…hard, I see."

Quite. White-hot lust still flowed through his veins. "Why am I here, Aveline?"

She waved a dainty hand, dismissing the guards who stood behind her. Mount and Micah, brothers known for their vicious natures.

Micah blew him a kiss. Mount winked.

The moment the doors closed behind the males, Aveline said, "You're here because you have something my other elite warriors do not. A reason to win quickly."

Suspicions danced through his thoughts, and his fingers curled, desperate to hold a weapon. "Do not say—"

"The All War Alliance has discovered another realm," she interjected. "A vast world known as Terra, with climates and terrains for every preference. There are oceans, mountains, flatlands, forests, deserts and so much more."

Suspicions confirmed. Dread and aggression surged. "I've already done my duty for Adwaeweth, Hivetta and even you, winning two new worlds." In return, he'd gained scars, nightmares and a deep distrust for others. "I have earned my retirement."

"In one week, you will journey to this new realm," she continued, merciless. "You will act as my representative and fight in the next All War. You will win Terra."

Throughout the galaxies, there were thousands of other-worlds, realms and dimensions. Homes to different species, immortals and creatures of lore. As these worlds had vied for domination, wars had erupted, leaders eager to gain more territories and slaves. The more territories and slaves, the greater the likelihood of winning the next war, and the next. But, in the process, many of those other-worlds, realms and dimensions had been destroyed, rendered uninhabitable. In a bid to save future worlds, leaders formed the All War Alliance, and birthed the All Wars.

Each participating realm sent a representative to the newly discovered land, where they battled to the death. The whole planet became a gladiator-type arena. But there were problems.

As more and more planets were found, more and more representatives were sent to fight. And, because scribes kept records, prospective combatants were able to learn from the mistakes of their predecessors, becoming harder to kill. The result? A single All War could last decades rather than days.

Bane's second All War had taken thirty-three years. By the time he'd returned home, his betrothed—Princess Aveline—had been crowned queen and decided she didn't want him anymore.

At the time, he'd been devastated. He'd loved her dearly, had missed her with every fiber of his being. Then he'd noticed the changes in her personality and rejoiced, thinking, *Dodged a bullet.*

If Aveline ordered another warrior to pursue Meredith during Bane's absence...

Fury morphed into white hot rage as corrosive as acid while raw panic hollowed out his chest. Another problem: Bane used sex to control his beast, bedding Meredith twice a day. At least! If he journeyed to Terra, he would have to go weeks, years, *decades* without a lover. He would rather die than betray her.

"In this war, my combatant will be at a terrible disadvantage," Aveline said, unconcerned about the brutal storm brewing inside him. "The Terran sun is brighter than most, and shines for longer periods of time. With our sensitivity to light, measures must be taken."

"Why not fight this battle yourself?" he snapped, his blood like fuel, every cell a blazing match. "Are you too weak? Too cowardly?"

Tone brittle, she told him, "Careful. I can make you cut out your own tongue."

"I'll grow a new one in a matter of days."

"Good point. I'll cut out Meredith's tongue instead."

Damn her. The price was too steep.

"Judging by your shell-shocked expression, you're done protesting." She smirked. "My trackers discovered Terra a year ago. I portaled in a contingent of breeders, with orders to seduce the strongest, most influential males. Most wove themselves into the fabric of society seamlessly, and many are already pregnant with a Terran-Adwaewethian mongrel. Perhaps my next crop of warriors will be able to walk in sunlight without being weakened or blinded."

He ground his molars. Mongrel, a derogatory name for an Adwaewethian hybrid. "Failure to report the discovery of a new realm is a chargeable offense, but sneaking your citizens onto it…that is a crime punishable by death." And not just for the queen. The High Council would send an army of Enforcers to Adwaeweth with a single objective: *kill everyone*.

Enforcers were trained as assassins, their numbers incalculable. Both males and females, all given to the High Council as children as payment for entering an All War. Adwaeweth would be reduced to a cautionary tale.

Aveline disregarded his statement, saying, "But I

digress. I do not know which breeders are carrying a royal."

Whenever Adwaewethians procreated with another race, they created a new colony, producing a handful of princesses, who would one day have the option to become queen. If they survived the Blood Rite. If more than one princess survived, the two would battle to the death.

Bane knew what was coming next and swallowed a curse.

"When a royal is born," Aveline said, "you will kill her, and preserve her heart."

Yes. That. The curse escaped, along with a dozen others. When a queen ate the heart of her enemy, she strengthened exponentially...for a time. "You would have me murder an infant?"

"Aw. Does my wittle beastie have a conscience?" She dismissed the idea with another wave of her hand, as if his "sensibilities" had no bearing on the situation. "We cannot allow a princess to become a queen. The moment she does, the mongrel beasts will awaken, and the High Council will discover what we've done."

"What *you* and your insatiable greed have done. You have placed our people—"

"*My* people," she insisted.

"—in grave danger." She had placed *Meredith* in grave danger. Yes, his wife could take care of herself, but he would tolerate no unnecessary risks to her well-being. He'd lost too much already. His parents, both of his brothers and his only sister.

Perhaps he should find another full-blooded Adwaewethian princess willing to challenge Aveline, and help *her* assume the crown. *Were* there others? Aveline had killed so many.

As soon as he found one, his connection to Aveline would weaken and he could form a bond with another royal. But why bother? He would be subjected to the whims of another capricious bitch just as bad as Aveline. Or worse!

When would the terrible cycle end?

"I won't kill a child," he grated. "Pick someone else." Pretty words. The woman could make him do anything, and they both knew it. Although, forcing him to anything, especially war, would be unwise. Unwilling and unmotivated representatives faced a higher likelihood of defeat.

Irritation twisted her features. "You refuse to win Terra?"

"I do."

Aveline tsked-tsked. "Never has a male been so ungrateful for the life I have granted him. I suppose you need an incentive to leave, and a better incentive to return swiftly. Very well. I'm happy to provide one. No matter what transpires, you will not transform into your beast, Bane. That's an order."

She snapped her fingers. To the left of the dais, a pair of double doors opened. Micah entered, dragging a chained prisoner behind him. She wore a pale blue nightgown. One Bane recognized.

A roar exploded from him, echoing throughout the chamber. Meredith! Their gazes met, fury crackling in her golden irises—fury tinged with fear, and it gutted him.

Like him, she'd been raised a soldier. Fear had been beaten out of her. The fact that she felt it now…

Desperation launched him up the dais stairs.

Aveline's eyes narrowed. "Stop. Kneel."

Just. Like. That. Only a few steps from his destination, he stopped and dropped to his knees. Upon impact, his kneecaps cracked. Fury and fear burned through him, every panting breath flaying his lungs. He fought with every ounce of his considerable strength, but he could not stand.

Micah smiled, smug and superior, as he pushed Meredith to her knees in a mimic of Bane. The bastard had always enjoyed the suffering of others.

"My darling Micah," Aveline said. "Be a dear, and make the girl bleed."

"No!" Bane shouted, willing his beast to emerge despite the queen's command. Alas, the beast refused to try; he might hate Aveline, but he bore Meredith no love, either, only tolerating her for sex. Sex, the fiend believed, could be found anywhere, anytime, by fair means or foul.

Micah slid his gaze to Bane. Smile widening, the bastard struck. Meredith's head whipped to the side, her lip splitting. A crimson river trickled down her chin.

"No!" Bane strained so fiercely he dislocated both shoulders. Searing pain shot through him, but he didn't care and didn't halt.

"Whatever she wants—" His wife spit out a mouthful of blood, then lifted her head high. "Don't you dare give it to her, Bane."

Though his vision blurred, he met Aveline's stare. "Do not do this. Please." He told himself she wouldn't dare. They no longer loved each other, true, but they had history. In this, she would capitulate. She must.

"You give me no choice," she replied, as ruthless as ever. "I must remove your desire to remain here."

"If you kill her, I'll have no incentive to win your war." Though he longed to look to Meredith again, he kept his gaze leveled on Aveline. "I will gladly give my life on Terra, and you will lose the All War."

She smiled, the gears clearly rotating in her mind. "My answer is…no. You'll do everything you can to win the All War, if only to return and seek revenge against me."

Realization: she might actually…do this. Panic returned and redoubled, clawing at him. "I'm begging you, Aveline. Do not do this."

"Silly Bane. It's as good as done." She nodded to Micah.

The bastard maneuvered behind Meredith, then fisted her hair to tilt back her head and expose her vulnerable neck.

"I will go," Bane rushed out. "I will kill the hybrid princess and win Terra. You have my word."

"Too late." Aveline stood, the action as fluid as water, and glided closer to Meredith. She stopped a mere whisper away.

He fought, fought so hard. A sizzling tear streamed down his cheek. "Please, Aveline."

"I love you, Bane." Meredith tried to smile, but a sob escaped. "May we meet again in the hereafter."

"You cry for each other. Pathetic." Lacking any kind of gentleness, Aveline cupped Meredith's cheek.

Bane bellowed curse after curse. *Calm down. Think!* Words began to rush from him. "Do you remember when we were children, Aveline? You wanted a rose from the queen's private garden. I snuck in and stole it for you, earning twenty lashes. Yet I bore the pain with pride, for I'd made you smile. You said you'd never forget, that you'd always be in my debt."

"Oh, yes. About that. I lied," she said, not bothering to glance in his direction.

New curses burst from him.

Meredith struggled…at first. Then black lines—death lines—branched over her face, beginning where Aveline's hands rested, and she stilled, utterly subdued. Blood leaked from her eyes and poured from her nostrils.

Fresh tears streaked down his cheeks. The Touch of Death. Aveline's unique ability in action.

As his precious wife gasped for breath she couldn't catch, her mouth flailing open and closed, blood painted her teeth and dribbled down her chin. Still he fought. *Get to her! Just have to get to her, and she'll be all right.* He would transfuse her with his blood. Every drop, if necessary. His life for hers. A worthy sacrifice. Muscles and tendons tore, the pain excruciating. Stars winked through his vision. And yet, the compulsion to remain in place never wavered.

Then Meredith's head lulled forward, her body going lax.

"No!" Was she de—gone?

Aveline punched a fist through his wife's chest cavity, ripping out her heart. Micah released her body, and Meredith crashed to the floor, the pop of breaking bones ringing out.

She was. She was gone. Dead. Guilt, grief and betrayal stabbed Bane, leaving his heart in ruins. Meredith was dead, and Aveline had done it. The woman he'd once loved, once planned to wed, had killed the woman he did love and had wed. She'd treated their shared history like garbage. Treated *Bane* as nothing. Less than nothing.

The queen met his gaze, grinned and bit into his wife's heart. As she closed her eyes, savoring the influx of strength, he threw back his head and shouted to the rafters until his lungs threatened to collapse.

"Be quiet," Aveline snapped.

Helpless to obey, panting, he dropped his hands to his sides and sagged to his haunches. He'd failed his precious wife, and he didn't…he couldn't…

The queen finished off the organ and approached him, just as graceful as before. With two fingers under his chin, she forced his attention up. "Do you wish to strike at me, warrior?" Blood stained her teeth.

"I do." Rage blistered him, the need to lash out stronger than ever before, her every inhalation an unforgivable offense. He would give *anything* to strike at her. And, if he couldn't end her himself, he would find another way.

Or another queen.

Forget the toxic cycle. Bane would serve *anyone* but Aveline.

Even the princesses on Terra, whoever they happened to be. When one came of age, he would be able to pick her from a crowd of thousands. He would find and protect her until he won the All War. Just before Aveline arrived to claim her prize, he would perform the Blood Rite, awakening hybrids. The High Council would assume *Bane* had sired them during his years of combat, which was perfectly legal.

The new queen could fight and kill Aveline.

Ramifications? Yes. He wouldn't be the one to deliver the deathblow.

Did it matter? One way or another, Aveline had to die.

Hope kindled, a flame in need of fuel. "You're right," he said, glaring. "I'll go to Terra, and I'll win the war. One day, my smiling face will be the last thing you see before a sword is driven into your black heart."

She patted his cheek and smiled, pleased. "I look forward to your attempt."

CHAPTER ONE

How to melt his icy exterior!
   —Nola Lee, *Oklahoma Love Match Magazine*

AD 701, human timeline
103rd All War, Month 2
Terra

KILL. NO MERCY.

On the trail of his next target, Bane skulked through a Terran jungle. Sweat drenched him, draining his strength, but a rush of adrenaline kept him going, feeding his ravenous muscles. Massive trees abounded, their interwoven limbs forming a leafy canopy, blocking the sun's too-harsh rays. A blessing and a curse. Those gnarled limbs also placed intractable walls in his path, slowing his progress.

Hurry! As he maneuvered around another tangle of vegetation, menace accompanied his every step. He did his best to remain in the shadows. Monkeys watched him from the trees, wary and frightened. Did they sense a predator greater than themselves?

An ever-present fury clung to him like a second skin, worsened by the sweltering heat and thick veil of humidity. Beneath his fury, the need for vengeance remained unflinching. A lifeline. His only friend. *Maintain your focus. Do not think of Meredith.*

Gloriously strong Meredith.

He bit his tongue, tasting blood, and forced his mind on the hunt at hand.

He carried no weapons; he had no need. *I am* the weapon. His target owned a mystical sword known as The Blood Drinker, able to cause unfixable wounds. To strike at Aveline with such a blade…to hear her screams…to watch her writhe in agony…

I must have it! According to one of three All War rules, each combatant was allowed to bring a single item from home. Thirty-nine warriors meant thirty-nine weapons to claim. To activate a weapon, you had to kill its owner. Since Bane had known he could steal from combatants as well as native dwellers known as vikings, he'd brought a pair of goggles to protect his eyes.

So far, he'd killed a single soldier, winning a dagger able to turn its handler into mist. But the beast had burst from its cage, and shredded the metal like paper.

Today, he would kill a male named Valor, acquiring and activating The Blood Drinker.

Bane would have to remove Valor's head or heart, or burn his body to ash. The only ways to end a combatant. Even the fire-breathers like Bane could be burned, one blaze not always equal to another.

When he came upon a wall of gnarled limbs, he traced a fingertip over the Rifters on his left hand. Every combatant owned Rifters, three crystal rings able to create a one-minute portal anywhere within the Terran realm. As the rings vibrated, he waved in the direction of the limbs. Two layers of air split apart, creating a doorway through the obstacle.

Animals and insects created the perfect soundtrack as he walked to the other side. Birds squawked, frogs croaked and locusts buzzed. A jungle cat roared. The beast shoved an answering roar past his lips, the animalistic sound echoing from the trees. The rest of the forest went silent, and he paused to listen for any sign of his enemy's approach.

Nothing. *Inhale, exhale. Good, that's good.*

Beneath the scent of earth and foliage, Bane picked up his target's distinctive musk. So close! Anticipation drove him forward. Soon, the morning sun would rise, putting him at a major disadvantage.

Kill the combatant, return to my mountain lair.

He yearned for the day he could slay *every* combatant and return to Adwaeweth. First, he had to find a Terran princess, ensure she reached her eighteenth birthday and train her to fight. Which meant the All War had to motor on, even if he had to start *saving* combatants. Therefore, he would contain the beast, however necessary. Even if he had to obtain a lover.

Denial screeched inside his mind. He would rather die an agonizing death than touch another woman. But he would rather live with endless guilt than give Aveline what she desired.

I will avenge you, sweet Meredith. Nothing and no one will stop me.

Enough! Ignore the grief. Forge ahead.

Hushed voices drifted from a short distance away. He froze, listening more carefully. Two speakers—his target and another male with a deep tenor. Another combatant. One who'd brought an elaborate suit of armor with retractable spikes that ripped through flesh and bone as easily as melted butter.

Anticipation spiking once again, he stalked around a tree. Closing in…

Behind him, a twig snapped. He ducked and spun, and a sword was swinging over his head with an ominous *whoosh—the* sword. The one he wanted more than his next breath. *Hello, Valor.*

"Voice projection," Bane said. "Nice trick." Staying low, he flowed with his momentum and kicked Valor's ankles together.

The warrior dropped, but swiftly rolled to his feet.

Movement to the left. Another warrior approached—a male named Malaki. He jumped from a tree while clinging to a vine, swinging, swooping… The spikes in his armor slashed Bane from cheek to navel, shearing off hanks of muscle. Searing pain. Tides of blood pouring from the open wounds.

The beast snarled and beat at his skull, wanting out of its cage.

Calm. Steady. Both opponents were tall and packed with strength, yet they were no match for Bane, even with the beast under lock and key.

"Did you think we'd make this easy for you, beast?" Malaki landed on his feet, the grille of his helmet splattered with bits of Bane's face.

Valor grinned with cold calculation. "You murdered my brother during an All War." He lifted his sword, the metal glinting in a beam of sunlight. "Today, I avenge him."

Morning had arrived.

Both males spoke in their native languages. Languages Bane had never learned. Because of the translator embedded in his brain, he interpreted every word. They had translators, too, and understood when he answered in Adwaewethish. "I'm sure your brother was a worthy adversary," he said. "For others."

A dark scowl replaced Valor's grin, the taunt hitting its mark. The time for words had ended. With a ragged war cry, the male lunged and swung his sword. Target: Bane's throat.

He dodged, and a savage dance ensued. He punched, kicked, blocked and clawed, went high, went low. The two allies worked together in a constant flow of motion. When one man attacked, the other adjusted his position, preparing to deliver the next blow.

Bane deflected a particularly nasty blow, then slammed his palms against Malaki's armor. The spikes embedded in his hands, as hoped. Despite the pain, he tossed the male into a tree. The trunk split, shards of bark volleying in every direction. Leaves rained down, beams of sunlight spotlighting Bane. He hissed.

Eyes stinging, his skin blistering, he slashed, punched and kicked to herd the pair into a shadowed alcove. When Malaki's armor grazed his gut, his intestines spilled out. A flare of pain. Dizziness. The beast protested, razing more of his control as he put himself back together.

Valor thrust the sword at Bane, but Bane jumped up and latched on to a hanging vine. He soared overhead, landed directly behind the bastard and kicked him into Malaki's path. The two collided, the armor doing its job, skinning one side of Valor's chest.

Valor wailed in agony, and Malaki staggered back, his features contorting with horror.

In a quick one, two motion, Bane swung to Valor a second time, cupped the man's forehead and jaw—and twisted. Valor went limp, his spine severed.

Down but not out. *Must remove the head or heart before he heals.*

"You'll pay for that," Malaki snarled, diving into him.

They careened backward, those metal spikes nicking an internal organ or two. More pain, more blood. When they hit the ground, the spikes cut deeper, earning more protests from the beast.

Careful. If the beast shredded the sword and the armor…

But "careful" got him pinned to the ground, with Malaki's knees digging into his shoulders. The warrior raised a gauntleted fist, ready to whale, but Bane acted fast, slamming his knees into his back, unseating him. The punch landed in the dirt.

The other man struggled to regain his balance. Bane slid out from underneath him, turned and kicked. A mistake. Valor had healed—and snuck up behind him.

Pain ricocheted through Bane's shoulder, the blade going in one side and coming out the other. His vision blurred.

Valor hopes to kill me, to deny me the right to avenge my wife. He dies today. Now!

Rage overtook Bane. Blood screamed in his ears, his heart thudding against his ribs. Finally, the beast broke free. Bones elongated. His gums burned, his teeth lengthening and sharpening. Flesh hardened, dark green scales sprouting from his pores. Darkness eclipsed his mind.

He heard anguished wails in the distance…

Pleas for mercy…

Pop. Whoosh. Thump. Then, silence.

When next he blinked, carnage surrounded him. An ocean of blood soaked the ground, body parts scattered here, there, everywhere. Bits of skin and muscle dangled from tree limbs. Pieces of Malaki's indestructible armor lay on the mossy grass. Damn it! The sword...where was Valor's sword? There! The hilt had sustained some damage, but the blade itself remained intact.

Heaving a sigh of relief, Bane labored to his feet. A sharp ache drew his attention to his shoulder, near the tree of life tattoo on his chest. A tattoo every combatant possessed. The mystical ink infiltrated their blood, allowing an Enforcer to track their every move.

The wound caused by The Blood Drinker hadn't healed, the cut just as raw and red as before. He massaged his nape. There had to be a way to reverse the damage.

Think! A combatant carried a sword with healing properties. Another owned a magic wand able to manipulate energy. Perhaps one of the two could mend the unmendable.

Very well. Bane had his next targets. Once he'd completed his tasks, he would end Aveline's tyranny at long last...

Then, I will join you, my darling Meredith. We will be together again.

103rd All War, Month 5
Somewhere in the Arctic Circle
Assembly of Combatants

FOR THE PAST three months, Bane had kept his mind on his goals, burying his grief beneath layers of seething hatred for Aveline. Somehow, he'd held the beast at bay *without* the aid of a lover. He hadn't killed anyone else, or destroyed any more weapons. Of course, that meant he hadn't won the healing sword or magic wand, either.

Another mistake on Bane's part.

Minutes ago, the Assembly of Combatants kicked off. A mandatory roll call. Soon after, an army of vikings had attacked the combatants in droves.

Now, the remaining twenty-five combatants worked together. Immortals against humans, the immortals trapped inside an icy mountain valley, unable to leave until the conclusion of the meeting. Yet, their assailants could move in and out at will.

Metal clashed against metal, the scent of blood permeating the frigid breeze. Grunts, groans and bellows echoed, the battle as savage as the terrain. Above, streaks of green and purple lit up the night sky.

Ignoring the throbbing pain in his stitched shoulder, Bane swiped up a discarded sword and lopped off a mortal's head. Since battling Valor, the wound in his shoulder had only worsened. Blood loss winded him far too easily, and slowed his reflexes.

Footsteps. Challengers approached at a clipped pace. The beast roared, enraged, thirsty for blood and hungry for flesh. As usual.

Calm, steady. If Bane transformed, he would slaughter the vikings, yes, but also the combatants, winning the war before he'd found the Terran princess. If that happened, he would remain bound to Aveline.

Unacceptable! Her downfall trumped *everything.* Right now, the vikings were obstacles in his path. Obstacles got mowed down.

Bane twisted and lurched. He ripped out one man's throat with his teeth, and punched into the other man's chest cavity, removing his heart. An action that pained his own heart, reminding him of the worst day of his existence.

Inner shake. Blank your mind. Another viking raced toward him, an ax raised and ready. But, just before they collided, an arrow pierced the man's eye, and he dropped.

"Thank you," he grumbled.

Emberelle of Loandria nodded and pivoted to unleash a volley of arrows upon the mortals outside the circle.

Usually she fought with a viking sword. She must have known she'd need a different method today. Possible. From home, she'd brought a metal band that fit over her forehead and allowed her to read the minds of anyone around her. Early on, she'd won a pair of wrist cuffs that might or might not grant the wearer the ability to time travel. Weapons Bane could utilize.

He placed her at the top of his hit list. *Find the princess, make my kills.*

When the skylights brightened, reflecting off the ice, his eyes burned and watered. He cursed. He'd left his goggles in his lair, knowing there would be a battle at the assembly's conclusion; there was *always* a battle after an assembly. In the chaos, weapons were often lost, stolen or destroyed.

Should have risked it.

Another mortal approached, brandishing an ax, and the beast fought harder for release, sending a lance of pain through his temples. Bane blocked the human's swing, spun and clawed out his trachea.

Behind him, a war cry sounded. Again, he spun and blocked—a plunging seax this time. Bane rammed his claws through the male's torso, ripping out his intestines.

No time to rest. The next challenger arrived. In a

(literal) snap, Bane ripped off his arms—and used them as clubs.

A horn erupted, blaring through the mountains. The vikings went still before rushing backward, forming a circle around the combatants, remaining outside the strike zone.

A male wearing a horned helmet split from the group and stalked closer. Blood smeared his tanned skin, scars marred one side of his face and a thick black beard covered his jaw. He wore leather, fur and sheepskin, and held a long staff with a bulbous tip. The Rod of Clima.

Bane stiffened. The Rod belonged to a combatant named Cannon. Had the viking killed him? If so… The viking had joined the All War.

Immortals drew together, watching as two soldiers dragged a decapitated body forward. Someone else pitched the head. It rolled, rolled… Oh, yes. Cannon was dead.

Hisses of fury blended with shouted threats, combatants throwing themselves against the invisible wall that trapped them inside the clearing, only to bounce back.

"When I rip off your dick, even your future children will scream."

"Should I cut off your head, remove your heart or burn you to death? Who am I kidding? I'll do all three."

"I'll enjoy making you rest in pieces, you son of a bitch."

Bane remained in place, the beast busy tearing through his skull. *Deep breath in. Out. Maintain control. In, out.*

The helmeted male lifted the Rod and announced, "You invaded our land and killed our men, because you did not fear us. I am Erik the Widow Maker, and I will teach you the error of your ways." He slammed the tip of the Rod into the ice.

A brutal arctic wind erupted, howling and blustering, the ground shaking. Between one blink and another, ice grew over Bane's feet, up his calves. Higher, higher.

Ice grew over *all* of the combatants.

Horrified, Bane battled for freedom…to no avail. *Trapped. Helpless. My fight over?*

No! He hadn't used his final weapon.

Bane stopped fighting the beast, and the transformation begun. Muscles and bones—

Nothing. The beast remained trapped as well, the ice unbreakable as it spread. Over his waist, his shoulders. Panic decimated what remained of his calm. None of the combatants escaped. Then, the ice covered his face.

I am…defeated?

I failed Meredith?

No. No! He *refused* to accept defeat. He would escape. He would find the Terran princess, win the All War and oversee the Blood Rite, finally severing his bond to Aveline. Aveline would come to Terra to claim the planet and then…oh, yes, *then* he would have his vengeance, die in peace and rejoin the love of his life.

CHAPTER TWO

You've got to tease to please!

Present Day
Strawberry Valley, Oklahoma

MAGNOLIA "NOLA" LEE swallowed a cocktail of medications, readjusted the mound of covers piled atop her and settled more comfortably in bed. Well, not *more* comfortably. Not really. Her entire body ached, her fingers looked like sausages, fatigue rode her like she was a horse and her every nerve ending sizzled, mini-bolts of lightning zapping her again and again. And again.

It—never—ended. Disease wrecked *everything.* Romantic relationships. Friendships. Goals. Fun. She'd only ever wanted to be a normal girl, with a normal life. *But nooooo.* Early on, she was diagnosed with lupus. After going into remission, fibromyalgia decided to come and play.

This was day too-many of a major flare-up, the pain too much. She felt like she was being poked with a thousand acid-drenched needles. Fatigue, foggy brain and insomnia continued to worsen. Basically, the party never stopped. She wished she had a medical marijuana card, but her pain management doctor considered it "unnecessary," leaving her at the mercy of opioids.

Joke's on me. Opioids had no mercy.

She'd already taken the maximum dose, but the pills had barely dulled the pain. If not for her upcoming vacation with her foster sister, Valerina London—Vale—she would have pulled the covers over her head and sobbed in the dark. Now, at least, she had a reason to get up in the morning.

"Which one of these dresses do you want to take on our trip?" Vale emerged from the walk-in closet, tall and willowy, with pale white skin and bicolored hair, half the color of snow, half the color of midnight. Thick dark slashes rimmed her hazel eyes; the tattooed liner gave her a perma-smoky look and the best Resting Bitch Face ever.

In one hand, Vale held a red dress with more cutouts than material. In the other hand, she held a conservative black dress usually wore to funerals. "The one that says *my body is a wonderland, and there's a price for admission,*" she said. "Or the one that says *come near me, and I'll remove your testicles with the power of my mind.*"

Nola chuckled. "You've met me, right? Wonderland. Obvi." Once upon a time, she'd longed to fall in love and become someone's wonderland. She'd had crushes, she'd flirted and she'd dated. For some reason, she'd vomited every time she'd tried to be intimate. Ultimately, she'd given up on love, relationships and romance, instead focusing on getting healthy and making money for her trip.

Well, she'd *mostly* given up on love. A few years ago, she'd started dreaming about a gorgeous man with golden everything, and the muscle mass of a hulk. No other man had ever measured up.

A breathy sigh escaped. Her golden god never called her the "Asian chick" or "the living sex doll,

Korean edition." He never lied to her, or stole money from her purse. He only ever referred to her as "princess," and asked—demanded—she find him in Russia. The Khibiny Mountains, to be exact. His presence had become a nightly comfort, and dang if she wasn't halfway in like with him already. Maybe because he wasn't real, so he would never die?

Her parents—dead. Her favorite doctor—dead. Carrie, the world's greatest foster mom in history—dead. Other foster moms and dads, foster siblings, caseworkers, friends had died metaphorically, leaving her in their dust. So far, Vale was the only exception.

"Excellent choice." Vale gave her a thumbs-up. "Carrie didn't raise a fool."

With a wink and a grin, Nola said, "But if she did, it'd be you."

Vale snorted. "You are such a meme queen. Just be sure to carry wet wipes in your purse, in case people drool on you when they see you in the dress."

"In case? Please," she retorted, playing along. "It's as good as done."

"Ohhh. I like this confident side of you. Sick or not, you are a prize among prizes."

Was she, though? What did she have to offer? A house filled of "treasures" she'd hoarded—pretty glass shards, buttons and coins she'd found in the street; junk to anyone else. A mountain of medical bills. Refusal to ever have children and pass on this terrible disease. An inability to leave her bed for long periods of time. Any man she loved would ultimately become a caregiver and have to bathe and change her in bed. No, thanks.

But she kept her lips zipped, camouflaging her inner

pain. Vale battled too many burdens already and didn't need to worry about Nola's mental health, too.

"You know, a trial reveals a person's true character," Vale said as she strode back into the closet. After insisting Nola conserve her strength, she'd started packing for both of them. "Before you invested too much time and energy into a relationship, you discovered just how badly a potential love interest sucked. That's priceless intel, baby."

Well, Vale wasn't wrong. Whenever Nola had decided to ignore the initial onset of nausea and forge ahead with a guy, he'd either treated her like spun glass sure to break, or worse, like a hypochondriac who'd exaggerated her symptoms for sympathy. The last guy had even made her doubt *herself.* And she couldn't not tell a man about her array of health problems; he had a right to know what he was getting into.

"You think *everyone* sucks," she reminded her sister.

"Yeah. Because I'm, like, supersmart."

True. "Well, onward and upward for us both." When they returned from vacation, they planned to buckle down and open a gourmet donut shop as fifty-fifty partners. Vale would do the paperwork and interact with suppliers; Nola would bake and interact with customers.

Baking wasn't her great passion—what was?—but she had a major talent for it, thanks to Carrie. Plus, she'd happily do anything with Vale.

—*Where are you, princess? Come. Find me.*—

Nola jolted. The deep, husky voice belonged to her golden god, and doubled as a sexual caress. But how the heck had a dream man spoken inside her head while she was awake?

Was he a delusion caused by her plethora of medications, maybe? But which one(s)? And why now? Nothing new had been added to her regime.

She should probably call her doctor. Okay, she should *definitely* call, and she would. Upon her return. He'd tell her to cancel the trip—again.

No way, no how.

First, she and Vale planned to visit Jukkasjärvi, Sweden, to tour ice castles, go dog sledding and view the northern lights. Then, they'd travel to Russia to get their hike on.

Nola's heart rate spiked. She didn't know why she felt like she had to get to Russia, just because a dream man commanded it; she only knew the need never faded, only ever grew.

So badly, she wanted to discuss the golden god with Vale. But, whenever she tried, something odd happened. The words died on her tongue—literally!—and she experienced selective mutism.

An internal warning? Maybe. Or maybe it was some sort of undiagnosed mental disorder. Either way, the golden god's nocturnal existence remained a secret, a sense of urgency growing. *Hurry! Must get there.*

Tomorrow, no matter how bad she felt, she would board the plane and hide her pain; Vale would never know, would never suggest they put their plans on hold until she felt better.

Bottom line: nothing would stop Nola. She'd scrimped, scraped and saved every extra penny, forgoing college while working two jobs, even when pain and fatigue plagued her.

For job number one, she sold baked goods to employees around town. For job two, she wrote a how-to column, dishing out romantic advice for *Oklahoma Love Match*. Oh, the irony.

Crap! "I forgot to write this week's article."

"Chuck it in the fuck it bucket," Vale called. "The time for work is over, and the time for play has come."

If only she *could* chuck it. "I promised my boss I wouldn't leave him high and dry, so I've got to draft something up." Call her old-fashioned, but Nola believed your word was your bond. When she made a promise, she kept it, always.

"What's this one about?"

"How to win any man you desire." Her boss always picked the subject matter, and Nola usually had fun researching the answer.

"Two words—*get naked*. There. Done." Vale peeked her head from the doorway. "Does that mean I get 50 percent of the profits?"

A laugh slipped from her. "Sorry, but the electric company gets 100 percent of the profits."

"Boo. Hiss."

"Ready for another meme from the queen?" she asked her sister. "How do you make millions as a writer of articles? You start off as a billionaire."

Vale howled with amusement.

—*I need you, princess. You know where I am. Come find me.*—

Nola gulped. The daytime delusion had just doubled down and jacked up the volume. Which meant the need to reach Russia jacked up, as well.

She wondered…what if her golden god was actually real?

What, like some gorgeous blond guy had the ability to speak telepathically? No. Not possible. Would she make the trip and search for him, anyway, just in case? Yes. Except, a new fear took root.

Would she have anything else to live for when she returned?

MIRACLE OF MIRACLES, Nola strengthened as soon as she reached Sweden. Her pains faded, the sense of fatigue vanished and she started resting well, her brain free of fog. While she no longer dreamed about the golden god, he continued to speak inside her mind with an increasingly snarly tone. She'd heard:

—*Please, take your time, princess. I don't mind being tortured for another thirteen hundred years.*—

—*Useless royals.*—

—*Do you* want *someone else to rule your world?*—

Every day she endured a new mental tug-of-war. He couldn't be real, but he had to be real, but he couldn't be, but he had to be. On the plus side, his aphrodisiac voice kept her body in a state of sexual arousal without a hint of sickness, no matter how often he complained, and she loved and hated the wonderful, terrible sensations.

Nola had tried to respond to him, and failed. Clearly. Not once had he ever answered her questions.

What's your name?

Why did you stop showing up in my dreams?

Will you do a striptease for me?

She wanted to enjoy every day, hour, minute in Sweden, but every day, hour, minute, the desire to reach Russia magnified, until urgency ruled her thoughts.

Finally, though, the day, hour, minute arrived. She and Vale rented a car and hit the road, with Vale at the wheel, and Nola in charge of navigation.

Now, *excitement* ruled her. *Golden god—GG—here I come!*

"You are practically foaming at the mouth," Vale said with a little laugh. "What's going on?"

Selective mutism wouldn't let her spill the truth, so she'd have to approach this a different way. As Carrie used to say, *If you can't go up, go down. If you can't go down, go around. If you can't go around, kick that mofo to the ground.*

"I have a weird question." While Nola loved to read romance novels in her spare time—she might have given up on love, but baby, she sure did like to read about others taking the plunge—Vale watched sci-fi movies and went gaga for all things supernatural.

"Shoot," Vale said. "You know you can ask me anything, any time."

Here goes. "Do you believe telepathy is possible?"

"Oh, absolutely," Vale responded without missing a beat. "I believe there's a grain of truth in every myth, legend and ability, and that we can do anything we can imagine."

"Why do we have no irrefutable proof of... I don't know, aliens or something?" Wait. What if people with supernatural abilities *couldn't* admit the truth? What if they experienced, say, selective mutism? "Let me rephrase. If superpowers are real, why aren't mutants taking over the world?"

"Maybe we are." Vale wiggled her brows. "I mean, I don't want to brag, but I have the power to make grown men cry."

Nola snickered.

"What brought this on?" her sister asked.

Tell her. Open your mouth, say the words. Simple,

easy. She opened her mouth…but no sound emerged. Dang it! In the end, she shrugged and said, "How awesome would it be to go through a fast-cure drive-through to order a healing and a side of Hulk-smash strength?"

"Dude! Yes!"

As they lapsed into silence, a sinister presence seemed to awaken inside her mind and whisper, *Forget healing and strength. Order the ability to kill with a glance.*

Kill with a glance? What? Where had *that* come from?

Chills crept down Nola's spine. For a moment, she felt like her body wasn't her own and some previously unknown dark side had overtaken her. Who was she kidding? She'd never felt like her body belonged to her.

Reeling, she sank deeper into her seat and peered out the window. Mountains with rocky plateaus, a plethora of lush trees and a babbling brook. She could almost smell crisp pine and dew-kissed wildflowers. Unfortunately, the breathtaking view failed to calm her.

—*Find me, princess. I need you.*—

Mmm, his voice. So sexy! But dang it! He was a figment of her imagination and the source of her predicament. Why did he calm her?

Soon, she and Vale would reach their destination and go on the hike. Nola would look for GG. Once she'd proven he wasn't real, she could finally lay him to rest and move on with her life.

And sob.

THE HIKE DIDN'T go as planned.

Nola and Vale stood in a picturesque valley, taking pictures. Their guide remained nearby. So far, there'd been no sign of GG. Of course.

Suddenly, a sense of weightlessness hit her, the world going dark. She blinked, and light came back. Only, their little threesome wasn't in the valley anymore. They were in a wasteland, surrounded by a sea of snow, fierce winds howling.

"What just happened?" Nola had to shout to be heard.

"I don't know," Vale shouted back, her voice tinged with fear.

Their guide raced around, frantic, shrieking in Russian.

Though Nola wore a fleece jacket, hat and gloves, hiking pants and trekking boots, the frigid temperature chilled her to the bone. "Look!" She pointed to a spot up ahead. "Footprints." Help could be nearby.

They followed those footprints to a small cabin, with an already lit hearth. Thank goodness! Heat!

Once they got inside, the guide stole a coat and boots and went out to check the perimeter for signs of life.

As warmth washed over her, Nola sank to her knees, overcome by relief. But where was the owner?

I could really use your help, GG.

"My phone is dead." Vale plopped down beside her. "How about yours?"

"Dead."

"Crap! We forgot to bring a charger. No worries, though. The guide will come back with the cabin's owner, and all will be well."

But fourteen worry-filled days passed, and neither the guide nor the owner ever came back.

Early on, Nola and Vale had raided the pantry. They'd eaten conservatively, but the limited food supply dwindled fast. So did her medication.

Nola dreaded the coming withdrawal. The aches

and pains, the flop sweat, the constant shivers. Muscle spasms. Feeling like she'd come down with a nuclear flu. Crying over everything and nothing. Vomiting and diarrhea would be a forgone conclusion. *Yay me.*

On the fifteenth day, Vale said, "If we stay, we die slowly. If we leave, we'll find help or die quickly."

"If I'm going down, I'm going down swinging." No way Nola would stay here and watch her wonderfully vibrant sister starve to death. And what about GG? The search could begin again!

Stop! Just stop. He isn't real, and you know it. You're only setting yourself up for disappointment.

"Then it's settled." Vale squeezed her hand, pulling her from her musings, and offered her a sad smile. "We head out in the morning."

Nola tossed and turned that night, desperate to hear GG's voice. Alas. He'd ceased all communication.

Because I'm taking less medication than usual.

Tears welled. So, he'd been a product of her medicines all along, just as part of her had feared.

When morning came, she put on a brave face and donned the survival gear they found in the closet. They packed two backpacks with essentials and set out, and it didn't take long for hypothermia to set in. Her teeth chattered uncontrollably, an earthquake in her jaw. Despite goggles and a full face mask, her nose and lungs burned every time she inhaled.

But, through it all, instinct urged her to turn here, go there. Then, a miracle happened. As the sun set, silvery moonlight falling over the terrain, Vale discovered a large cavern tucked inside a hill of ice. They had to climb twenty feet to get inside, but...*worth it.* Even as Nola's knees buckled, that instinct shouted, *Yes! He's near.*

Uh, what the what? No way! Just no way.

"Stay there. I'll get us warm." Vale extracted logs and matches from a backpack and built a fire, then used climbing rope to create a hanging-line for their wet clothes.

"Thank you, thank you, a thousand times thank you." Nola removed her hat, goggles and face mask, even the gloves. Delicious warmth licked each newly exposed patch of skin.

She scanned the cavern, finding carved images on the far wall, featuring a horned monster and a headless corpse. *Nice.* "Is that ice graffiti?"

"Let's find out." Vale stripped out of her gear and crossed to the other side of the cave. Her jaw dropped, excitement radiating from her. "Someone has to live here, or at least visit upon occasion. We could be close to civilization. I'll look around for more clues."

"Be careful." Whoever had carved those images might be a wee bit…disturbed.

"I'd rather be armed and ready instead." Vale winked, palmed a climbing ax and disappeared around a corner.

—*I sense you, princess. You are close. Get closer. I've waited so long.*—

His voice! She'd heard it again, and it was sexier than ever, all smoke and sensuality, heating her blood. Her belly quivered. *Just a figment of your imagination. Manage your excitement.*

She tried to stand, but her legs refused to support her weight. Frustrated by her weakness, she banged her fist into the ice.

Helpless? Me? No! She would eat something, and regain a bit of her lost energy.

She trembled as she extracted a small copper pot from

a pack, as well as the last can of fermented herring. *Do not gag.* Beggars couldn't be choosers. As a baker extraordinaire, Nola would utilize the one skill she possessed in this type of situation: turning an unpalatable dish into something that wouldn't murder anyone's taste buds.

After bringing a chunk of ice to a boil, she readied the fish. Another five…ten minutes passed, but her sister never returned.

Nola choked down a couple of bites and finally called, "Vale?"

No response. Her ears twitched, picking up other noises. Whispers…cracking ice… Foreboding skittered down her spine. Had something happened to Vale?

Nola drew from a hidden reservoir of strength, and lumbered to unsteady legs.

Putting one foot in front of the other required great effort, but somehow she did it. Step. Step. Step. Tremble. Step. Step. She snaked around a corner, entering a larger chamber, with a higher ceiling and over twenty pillars of ice, all cracked. Vale stood on the other side, staring at one of those pillars as if it held the secrets of the universe.

Voice drenched with relief, GG said, —*There you are. Come closer, princess. Let me get a good look at you.*—

Wait. He was *here* here? He wasn't a figment of her imagination? Hope rippled through her, as glorious as a warm summer's day. *Where are you?*

An invisible rope seemed to wrap around her middle, drawing her deeper into the room. Deeper still, bypassing pillar after pillar.

Instinct spoke up again, saying, *Not this one. Not that one. No. No again. Yes! This one.*

She stopped and gasped, her hand fluttering over her

heart. The pillar...it... She squinted and edged closer. There was a man inside it. An honest to goodness man, shockingly lifelike, glaring at her through the ice. He wore a black shirt, black leather pants and combat boots...just like the golden god she'd seen in her dreams. But more importantly, he had the golden god's face.

I'm not delusional. Her heart pounded, and her skin heated. But, but...how was this possible?

Did it matter? She'd felt his presence for so long, now here she stood, inches away. It was fantastical. Shocking. All she could do was marvel. He *was* real, and he *was* here, and he exuded primitive animal magnetism.

She thought, *Perhaps I gave up on romance too soon.*

He was big—huge—both tall and muscular. The most powerful male she'd ever beheld, and the most beautiful, golden from head to toe. While he had long, thick lashes, and soft, plush lips, a broad jaw and strong chin gave him a hard edge.

A realization hit her, something that should have computed already, and her heart began to race. He'd spoken to her. That meant he was alive. But he couldn't freaking be alive. He was encased in ice.

"Vale!" she squeaked. "Are *people* trapped in here?" *Can't be real, can't be real. I must be wrong.*

"Nah. They're statues," Vale replied with an easy tone. "Some kind of tourist attraction, I think. Men and women will come from all over the world to view these frozen sexcakes."

"Statues. Yeah, that makes sense." A relief. A disappointment. A...mistake? "Statues" didn't explain the golden god. Of course, Nola couldn't talk about her experiences, so she forced a laugh. Maybe, if she laughed enough, she'd begin to find the situation humorous. "But sexcakes? That isn't the word I'd use."

"Why, Nola Lee. You'd rather call them life-size lady-boner figurines? Well, good call. I like that description better. Take a gander at this one." Vale hiked her thumb at a dark-haired man with blue eyes. "Grade A filet."

Were *all* the males alive, haunting people's dreams?

—*You are everything I expected.*—

Was that *disdain* she heard in his tone? Yeah. Must be. An answering disdain shone in his eyes.

Her chest tightened.

Had he hoped to torment someone prettier? Someone stronger? Was he disappointed in her? Well, so what! She was disappointed in him for being too foolish to recognize her amazing amazingness…buried underneath her layers of disease, weakness and addiction.

She was a delight, dang it! Honest, kind and fiercely loyal. Rare qualities in this Dumpster fire of a world. She had so much love to give!

"Sexcakes is absolutely right." She pointed to another dark-haired warrior. "I just made eye contact with this one, and I'm pretty sure I'm pregnant. With twins."

Vale approached, her hazel eyes wide and dazed, her pupils blown. Well. She wasn't as blasé as she'd sounded.

—*He is nothing to you. Nothing! I am everything.*—

He was…jealous? Nola rejoiced at the possibility.

She met his gaze through the blur of ice, about to smile. Then a new sense of foreboding stormed through her, stronger than ever. "I don't know why I'm feeling the things I'm feeling, or what's real and what isn't," she whispered, "but I have a sinking suspicion something terrible is about to happen to us both."

CHAPTER THREE

What to do when your dishy dreamboat is also an assassin

AT LAST! THIRTEEN HUNDRED years of confinement. Thirteen hundred years of listening to the beast throw a temper tantrum. If the fiend wasn't sighing, he growled; if he wasn't growling, he roared. Always he enjoyed kicking and clawing at Bane's skull, leaving him half-mad, his patience forever eroded.

Nothing but a broken shell, the cracks filled with grief and fury.

Worth it. The Terran royal had arrived. The woman Bane planned to use mercilessly to avenge Meredith's death and destroy Aveline.

Something terrible is about to happen to us both.

Something terrible had already happened. One look at her, and Bane had wanted to bed her.

Me? Bed a queen? He'd rather die. And he would tell her so, just as soon as he found the strength to look away. *Such exquisite beauty.* She stole his breath, sucking the air out of his lungs.

I can admire an object without "wanting" it sexually, damn it. And yes, he considered her an object. A means to an end. Besides that, she was too delicate for his tastes. Too fragile. The slightest gust of wind might cause her to shatter. Had she ever wielded a sword? Probably not. *As useless as the other royals.*

During his endless imprisonment, Bane had trained his gaze to see past the ice. Now, he slowly perused Nolalee's slight frame, absorbing every detail.

She had lovely skin as pale and flawless as porcelain, a rarity among Adwaewethians, even the hybrids. Other rarities included dark eyes with pinpricks of light, reminiscent of a starry night sky, and hair so black and shimmery the strands appeared cobalt. But the crowning glory of her physical beauty—bloodred, rosebud lips. The kind of lips a man yearned to have all over his body.

The hybrids would be utterly enraptured by their queen, willingly—foolishly—risking their lives to fulfill her every ridiculous whim. Not Bane. He knew what the hybrids did not. One day, one day soon, she would become a monster, the same change Aveline underwent. The same change *every* queen underwent.

"How many statues are here?" the future queen asked. The cadence of her voice...so soft, so soothing.

Bane's beast went quiet, his head his own for the first time in centuries. A tidal wave of relief flooded him, drowning out the other female's reply—the one named Vale.

As he basked, he rolled her name through his mind. Nolalee. Princess Nolalee. Queen Nolalee...soon.

Escape the ice and cart the Terran princess to safety. Kill a combatant named Zion, and claim his magic wand. Use the wand to heal my shoulder. Attend the next Assembly of Combatants, slay everyone. Perform Nolalee's Blood Rite. Kill Aveline. Join Meredith.

Why continue on? Never again would he allow himself to fall in love. He would not marry, or start a family.

Would not give anyone authority over him. Would not serve another malicious queen.

Obviously, time had not healed Bane's inner wounds. Every day, the desire to mete revenge threw another log on the fires of his rage. *Will take* everything *from Aveline, the way she took everything from me.* He lived for no other purpose.

The next assembly kicked off in three weeks. A mere three weeks until his plans and schemes came to fruition.

Craaack.

The noise came from his left, the warriors within his sight line awake and aware, exuding a feral kind of hope as they observed the newcomers.

An unspoken question wafted through the air. *What happens next?*

They'd all suffered, their bones and muscles constantly aching with fatigue, their blood like sludge. At some point, every warrior had died, only to revive and start the process again.

Must fight my way free. Now! Nolalee and Vale had reinvigorated everyone's determination to escape.

For Bane, a five-inch gap separated flesh from frost. He'd often let the beast pour flames into his throat, so he could spit fire and melt the ice in front of his face. The action had done so much more, warm water drip, drip, dripping down to free parts of his body, too. Now, he could rock backward, ramming his shoulders into the ice, then push off his booted heels and ram the front of the ice.

He winced as his level of pain jacked up. Like his inner wounds, the gash in his shoulder still hadn't healed, the cut raw and angry, a symbol of his emotional state.

Did he stop, though? No. Rock back—rock forward. Back, forward. Ram, ram.

One of myriad cracks lengthened and widened, and he grinned, his heart thudding against his ribs. Closer than ever!

Nolalee flitted about, going from pillar to pillar before stopping in front of Zion—the one who'd supposedly impregnated her with a glance. She traced a heart on Zion's pillar, and every muscle in Bane's body knotted.

Why did she focus on the male? The enemy. If she bore an attraction to him…

Unacceptable! Bane required her cooperation *and* loyalty.

"We survived," she said. Survived what? "We're close to civilization, rescue a probability."

Rescue?

He'd known the day she was born, had felt it deep in his bones. He'd known the day she reached adulthood and they established a link, weakening his ties to Aveline.

Right now, he served both females. The moment he permanently aligned with Nolalee, pledging a blood oath to protect and obey her, his link to Aveline would dissolve completely. But Aveline would sense his loss. So, he could make no pledges until the bitch arrived to claim ownership of Terra.

Bane pushed his voice into Nolalee's head.

—*Return to me, princess.*—

A demand. To his shock, she obeyed—dragging her feet. She looked him over, whispering, "I know you're real. At least, I think you are. Maybe. But I don't know who or what you are, or why you keep talking inside my head. Just…tell me what's going on. I want to help."

A command. A royal command. As a hybrid princess, she was powerful, yes, but too weak to fully control a warrior in his prime. After the Blood Rite, however...

"Or don't tell me," she said, still whispering. "You're probably a delusion. Yeah, definitely a delusion."

Shock had left her addled. Noted. He—

Tingles erupted at the ends of his fingers, frozen nerve endings coming back to life. New, sharper pains shot up his arms, radiating through his torso and down his legs. Even his toes tingled.

Hope warmed his blood and thawed his insides, adrenaline coursing to his muscles.

Must get the princess to safety. As Bane continued to rock and ram his body backward and forward with more force, the width of the cracks increased, and his hope sharpened into anticipation. Rock. Ram.

Any warriors outside the females' sight lines fought their prisons, too. Those within their sight lines waited until the pair turned away, not wanting humans to know about the war, even now. They had no idea Bane communicated with Nolalee.

The first to escape would decide her fate.

"Are you thinking what I'm thinking?" Vale asked. "We'll have the celebration dinner of the year!"

The two discussed folded napkins, middle fingers, fish and vomit before vanishing around the corner, leaving the "lady-boner figurines" behind, seemingly forgotten. Nolalee's laugh drifted through the cavern, as sweet as a lullaby, and another growl rumbled in Bane's chest. Before she vanished, she cast a final glance in Bane's direction.

Soon enough, she'll lose that sweetness. Never forget. Ram, ram!

Crackkkkk.

Already knotted muscles drew tighter as Bane scanned one ice pillar after another. Same cracks, no change. Same cracks, no change. Same— Nope.

He returned his gaze to the combatant who'd won four All Wars in his lifetime—Knox. There *was* a change. Thicker lines bisected his ice.

Knox was a fierce competitor, ruthless, merciless, with no sense of compassion. If the bastard gained his freedom, Bane would be a major target, guaranteed. No telling what the male would do to Nolalee.

Ram, ram.

Crack.

This time, a fissure sprouted over the pillar belonging to Zion, a three-time champion just as determined to take out Bane.

Ram, ram, ram. Yes! New cracks spread. *So close to freedom.* The closest he'd ever come. Emboldened, he rolled back and lurched forward. Again. And again.

Suddenly, large wedges of ice tumbled from Knox's pillar, freeing his head and torso. As the male popped the bones in his neck and rotated his shoulders, breath misted in front of his face and rapture lit his features.

Envy and fear consumed Bane. *Hurry!* He fought harder, ignoring every prickle of agony. *RAM, RAM.*

The females must have heard the commotion. They returned in a rush, their shock and terror palpable.

Urgency owned Bane. *Get to Nolalee. Protect her, protect your vengeance.*

Knox pointed at the women and snapped, "You will stay put. Do not run."

"You're talking. You're talking, and you're alive," Vale babbled. "You're alive, and you're real."

Bane thought he picked up Nolalee's thoughts.

—Part of me knew they were real, but the other part of me was so sure I was wrong. Yes. I must be wrong, my delusion strong enough to affect Vale.—

A crazed gleam entered her starry eyes. Voice rising several octaves, she said, "He's not real. He's just…not." She clasped Vale's hand, as if desperate for a lifeline. "Right? Hypothermia causes hallucinations. *Right?*"

What had made her think she'd be better off without a real warrior at her side?

Once again, Bane projected his voice into her head. *—Run! The freeman is Knox, a dangerous killer. I will escape and find you.—*

She remained in place, her mouth floundering open and closed.

Fury and fear collided inside him. He tried again. *—Do you* want *to die, you foolish girl? Help me help you. Run!—*

Again, she remained in place and worked her mouth. Had fright stolen her wits?

How was this girl going to defeat Aveline?

Knox kicked away the final block of ice and stalked across the cavern, a dagger in each hand. The warrior's target: the Rod of Clima.

Erik the Widow Maker had left the weapon close yet beyond the assembly's boundary, ensuring it remained active, summoning a continual snowfall. Even still, the past few years, the frost had started to melt on its own. Either the temperature outside had risen, or the weapon's potency had dulled. Perhaps the females were responsible.

Either way, Erik was the only one able to activate and

deactivate the Rod, but everyone else could break it, removing it from the war.

"We need to leave." A pallid Vale tugged Nola toward the exit, insistent. "Now!"

Her words spurred Knox to change directions. He strode to the females and reached out. Bane bellowed with rage, going silent only when the bastard caressed the blonde's cheek, ignoring Nolalee.

A look of utter bliss softened Knox's overly harsh features. Vale's eyes widened, black spilling over hazel. Nolalee gaped, tremors threatening to knock her off her feet.

—*Move away from Knox.*— Again, Bane projected his voice into her head.

She jolted, but she did not obey. He ground his teeth, fury giving his next forward ram more steam.

Hanks of ice began to fall from *Zion's* prison, not his.

Urgency at an all time high, Bane settled the bulk of his weight on his heels and pushed up. Ram. Ram. *Crrrrrrack.* Finally, a huge chunk of ice toppled, freeing his upper half. Cool air kissed his face, a sensation as excruciating as it was euphoric. Oxygen filled his battered lungs as he inhaled; the sweet scent of honeysuckle stung his nostrils.

Hate honeysuckle! But, underneath the despised fragrance, he detected notes of lavender and jasmine, the luscious blend turning his blood to flame.

He punted the final barricade, his legs screaming in protest. As he took a step, then another and another, he marveled. He was walking. After being stationary for centuries, he had mobility.

A new man with an old purpose, he charged for Nolalee. She had paled, panic setting in, her starry gaze darting wildly.

When her gaze landed on Bane, she mouthed, "Help."

Yes! But, just before he reached her, other combatants escaped captivity and leaped into action. Chaos erupted in every direction. Bloodthirsty warriors moved between Bane and his princess. Emberelle, Petra, Ronan, Slade and Ranger.

Swords swung, and daggers plunged. A glowing whip lashed out. An arrow soared past. Blood sprayed, grunts and groans ringing out.

His fury skyrocketed to new heights. The combatants endangered the princess!

Bane considered grabbing Nolalee and portaling to his mountain lair. Simply carrying her away would be foolish. There were too many warriors, with too many weapons able to injure her in the process. Plus, a portal would remain open for an entire minute, allowing others to follow them through. And, considering how much time had passed, someone could have found the lair and set traps.

There was only one solution. He had to exit the cavern through the only door. To exit through the door, he had to fight. To decrease the odds of Nolalee getting injured during the fight, he had to first thin the herd.

Very well. Mission accepted.

He told her, —*Press yourself into the corner. The walls will guard your flank while I clear a path for us.*—

She stood there, rooted in place, her arms wrapped around her middle, gaze still darting. Searching for him?

—*Nolalee! You will obey me.*— He quickened his pace, ducking when he needed to duck, blocking when he needed to block, but always moving forward. An enemy lunged into his path. With a war cry, Bane grabbed him by the throat, snapped his spine and tossed his limp body aside, maintaining a clear view of Knox, who had just shoved Vale into a corner.

The pale-haired female shouted, "Nola!" Just Nola, not Nolalee? Very well.

Knox pushed Nola into the corner, and propped a big block of ice in front of them to fashion a barrier. Knox then used his supernatural ability to control shadows, causing sheets of darkness to rise from the ground like ghosts, and hide both females. He *protected* the females? Shocking.

Bane roared. He *needed* to see Nola, needed to assure himself she remained unharmed.

He picked up speed, barreling into anyone foolish enough to get in his way. Bodies fell. Just as he reached Nola's corner, breathing in her wonderful scent, the combatant Orion crashed into him, knocking him to the ground. As they rolled, Orion swung a pair of motorized axes.

Bane latched on to the male's wrist and jerked, the ax slicing through his elbow, the lower half of the arm detaching. With his free hand, Bane ripped out his trachea, silencing a scream of anguish. His go-to move.

Orion slumped over, warm blood spurting from the new hole in his neck.

The desire to kill proved strong, but Bane resisted temptation. In a situation like this, many warriors could, and would, die. If the All War ended tonight, before he'd had a chance to prepare Nola...

No! He would stick to the plan, and keep the war going for another three weeks.

He stood, just as Emberelle lunged at him. Using Orion's severed arm as a club, he sent her stumbling back, then rushed to Nola's corner...

Damn it! The ice and shadows remained undisturbed, but she was long gone, her scent faded. No sign of Vale, either. Where had they—

There! Thorn, the combatant who wielded a glowing whip, clasped Nola's ankle and dragged her toward the exit, unaware another warrior approached, gliding through the air thanks to a pair of winged boots—Ranger—a sword raised and ready, aimed at Nola's vulnerable throat.

"No!" Bane blazed across the cavern. *Come on, come on.* Panic hammered at him, his blood flash-freezing. He wasn't going to reach her in time.

Zion caught Ranger's sword midair, the blade shattering, no match for his metal glove, saving Nola's life. A new tide of relief flooded Bane, only to evaporate when Zion knocked out Ranger, gathered her close and bolted.

She fought him, a veritable wildcat, but she didn't win her freedom until Ronan challenged Zion, claiming his full attention.

But Nola didn't bolt, as Bane expected. She stood in place and spun, her eyes wide, her cheeks pale, shouting, "Vale?"

Keeping her within his sight line, he targeted any combatant foolish enough to approach her, snapping necks and ripping out spines. Did she notice? No. Annoyance scraped his chest raw. He—

Shouted a curse. The combatant named Petra had just twirled past him, stabbing the tip of her sword through his left foot. Excruciating pain exploded inside him, but he knew the worst was yet to come. Her sword possessed an insidious skill he abhorred. Whatever the blade touched, it could recreate, causing a tower to grow in its place. Since the tip had gone through muscle and bone, hitting ice, a tower of ice grew around his foot—*over* his foot—quickly forming a waist-high wall.

Pinned in place. Every bone from his toes to his ankle had been crushed into powder.

And Petra wasn't done. She returned, swinging the sword again—aiming for his throat. He ducked, the metal lodging in the wall of ice. *Ignore the searing agony.* He leaned his upper half over the ledge and punched her rib cage. Those ribs broke, as he'd hoped, the bone shards cutting into her heart. She clutched her chest and stumbled backward, slipped on a pool of blood and tripped over an unconscious body.

Do not deliver the deathblow. Walk away.

Nola, where was Nola? Bane scanned, finding her quickly. A warrior—Slade—shook a trident in front of her face and shouted, "Where is he?"

Who was "he"? Erik? Bane beat and kicked at the ice wall with all his strength. Stars winked through his vision, and fresh rivers of blood poured from his wounds. "Hurt her, and I'll make you regret it," he snarled. *Get to her. Must get to her.*

Slade paid him no heed. "Where is he?"

With a shriek, Vale raced over and leaped onto Slade's back, reaching around to hammer her fists into his eyes. But her punches had no effect.

Can't get to Nola until I get free. Think, think!

Bane watched as Knox slid across the distance, swung a sword up, up, and sliced through Slade's wrist. The hand *and* the trident plopped to the ground. No time to rejoice. End one battle, and another started. At least Nola remained safe—for the moment.

But all too soon, the world began to fade in and out. *Stay awake and aware. Fight! Get to her, damn you.*

"You're coming with me." As Knox dragged Vale away, she struggled against his hold, desperately trying to return to Nola.

Zion snatched up the princess, once again hefting her against his chest, then motoring forward, plowing into Knox and making a play for Vale. *That piece of shit thinks to abscond with both women?*

When Ronan inserted himself in the middle of the clash, Nola was able to wiggle free of Zion, and Vale was able to strike at Knox. Freed at last, the two females sprinted from the chamber.

Bane had seen no evidence of a wound, yet Nola limped, her face contorted with abject pain. *Must follow her!*

The cavern shook from foundation to roof. Any moment, the walls would come tumbling down. Pinned as he was, Bane would be crushed. If a stray piece of ice were to cleave his head from his body...

His vengeance would die with him.

Allow Aveline to live a long and happy life? No!

Battle paused as warriors fled. Bane bent down, stretched and twisted, grabbing hold of a discarded sword. No help for it. To save his life and reach Nola, he had to move from this spot. To move from this spot, he had to free his leg. To free his leg, he had to shatter the ice.

He struck the wall again and again, and realized he

was too weak to do any real damage. Very well. He would gain his freedom another way.

Deep breath in. Bane eyed his ankle. *Goodbye, foot*. As he inhaled, he lifted the sword. As he exhaled, he swung.

CHAPTER FOUR

Go ahead, strike out on your own!

CRADLED AGAINST SOME giant's chest, peering over his broad shoulder, Nola had a startling view of the cavern's collapse and Vale's abduction. The glow of northern lights illuminated both horrors. A different giant held her sister in a fireman's carry, whisking her away in the opposite direction.

In the cavern, the scary-looking brute holding Vale had introduced himself. *I am Knox of Iviland.* He possessed the coldest blue eyes Nola had ever seen. Her own captor—the guy she'd claimed had impregnated her with a glance—had the coldest *dark* eyes. But the truly terrifying thing? Neither man frightened her as much as her golden god.

Like an angel of death, he'd ripped off limbs, clawed out organs, chewed through throats and yanked out spines. And he'd done it all while blood-splattered and staring possessively at Nola, as if he owned her, body and soul.

Why had she ever decided to come to Russia? Seriously, a delusion would have had a much better outcome.

What had happened to GG, anyway? And why had he summoned her of all people?

"St-stop. Please," she told the dark-haired brute carrying her away. Her teeth chattered as she extended her arm, reaching for her sister. "I d-don't want to go with you."

He tightened his grip, bellowing, "Be quiet, girl. You'll give our position away."

Uh… "*You* just gave our position away."

In the distance, Vale hurled herself to the ground. She whimpered and scrambled to her feet. Chasing after Nola with a backpack in hand, she screamed at Nola's captor. "Stop! Please! You don't understand. She's sick. She needs medicine. Come get Knox. I'll help you kill him, if that's what you want. Honest! Or take me instead."

White-hot tears streamed down Nola's cheeks, only to freeze. *Stop crying. You're a grown woman, dang it.* Well, in her haste to exit the cavern, this grown woman had left the other backpack and all of her survival gear behind. Without goggles, a mask, a hat or gloves, the blood in her veins would soon thicken like a slushie.

Must act now!

Gathering what little energy she had, Nola beat her fists against her captor's face and chest. He evinced zero reaction, her punches not even a blip.

Hysteria seethed in the tangle of her thoughts. Where was he taking her? What did he plan to do to her—with her? "Please, let me go. Let me save my sister." If anything happened to Vale… *I would rather die.*

You just might.

Tone dry, he said, "Why would I let the mother of my twins go?"

Oh, crap. He'd heard her silly comment. "Will you *kill* the mother of your twins?"

"That depends, I suppose."

Terror seized her, paralyzing her muscles. She lost

the ability to move, which only worsened her terror. Her stomach began to churn, as if she'd swallowed razor blades. "I think I might vomit."

He picked up speed, saying, "Aim away from me." He had a deep voice and a heavy accent she couldn't place. "If we stop, a combatant will attack us."

Combatant?

Focus. Last year, Nola and Vale had taken a self-defense class. Now, a warning clanged inside her mind. *If someone attempts to take you to a secondary location, fight. Whatever pain you endure before transfer will pale in comparison to what you'll endure if you end up trapped and alone.*

"I'm coming for you, Nola," Vale called from the darkness. "Right behind...won't let anything—umph."

What just happened? Nothing good, that much Nola knew.

Blistering fury unlocked her limbs from paralysis. Instead of flailing wildly, she put her lessons to good use, poking her captor in the eye. As he grunted in pain, she slammed the heel of her palm into his nose. Cartilage snapped, and blood dribbled down his chin. He stutter-stepped, but dang it, he maintained his hold.

"I am Zion of Tavery." He raced around an ice-glazed tree. "Do not worry, little *dreki*. I will protect you."

Dreki? Another of her instructor's warnings clanged. *Never trust a stranger. Assume they speak Lies, the universal language of murderers and rapists.* "Wh-why would you *want* to protect me?" she asked, teeth chattering with more force.

"Before you arrived," he said, "I...saw you. In my dreams."

The way she'd dreamed of her golden god?

"Even if I hadn't, I'd want to protect you," he added. "Where I'm from, females are rare. A precious treasure. Harming one is a crime." He adjusted Nola against his chest, freeing one of his hands, wiped the blood from his face and pressed his fingers against the diamonds embedded in his shoulder.

What was he doing? "Wh-what did I do in your dreams?"

"That, I won't tell you."

Between one step and the next, they exited the wasteland and entered a sunlit jungle. As she scanned their new surroundings, warmth poured over her, as cozy as a fur blanket. Ripples flowed over the surface of a crystal clear pond. A patch of wildflowers perfumed the air with sugary sweetness, teasing her nostrils. Bees buzzed past, and birds sang. Fruit and nut trees swayed in a gentle breeze, and her mouth watered. Coconuts. Bananas. Pecans. *Gimme!*

"Where are we?" And how did she continue to go from one season to another in a matter of seconds?

"My home. While I'm on Terra, at least."

"Terra," she echoed.

Nod. "Every world and realm has multiple dimensions and planes, hidden pockets of land inaccessible by traditional means. I found and claimed this one centuries ago."

"Multiple dimensions? Planes? World *and* realm. There's a difference?" Had he used the word *centuries*?

After everything she'd witnessed, everything she'd experienced… *Keep an open mind.*

"Planes are stacked, one on top of the other, but they do not intersect," he said, setting her on her feet. "Dimensions exist within a world, and are accessible through some sort of doorway. Worlds are the planets as a whole, and realms are kingdoms within the world."

Her knees buckled, unable to hold her weight. Zion caught her before she hit the ground. He carried her to a bed of moss, where he gently laid her on her back.

Too vulnerable! She flattened her palms on his chest and pushed. When he refused to budge, she started punching. Her knuckles brushed the hilt of a dagger, and she froze. Her instructor's third tip? *If you find a weapon, use it.*

But…stab Zion? *Kill* him?

He gripped the hem of her shirt, as if he intended to rip the garment from her body, and Nola thought, *Yes. Kill him.* Though she trembled, she yanked the dagger free of its sheath and thrust the blade into his gut.

The ease with which the metal cut through flesh and muscle sickened her. *What have I done?*

Frowning, he plucked the weapon from his intestines. He wasn't wearing a shirt, so she had an unobstructed view as blood gushed from the wound.

She braced, expecting a swift and violent retaliation.

He merely sheathed the blade and said, "I only meant to check you for injuries, little *dreki*. Are you all right?"

Was "little *dreki*" some kind of an endearment or curse? And had he really accepted blame for her actions then asked about her well-being? "I'm sorry I hurt you. Well, not so much sorry as worried about your reaction."

"I'm fine. The wound is healing already."

Really? As she watched, wide-eyed, his torn flesh wove back together, his wound becoming invisible. But, but… "How is that possible?" Confusion welcomed a tide of dizziness, the world spinning faster and faster.

"How else? I'm not human," he said with a shrug.

"Now I must inspect my territory for traps. I'll return with food."

Leave her in an unfamiliar terrain? No! Bring her food? Yes! "Aren't you afraid *I'll* set traps?"

The corners of his mouth lifted in a patronizing half grin. "If someone like you manages to trap me, I deserve my fate."

Oh, that burned! "Someone like me?"

"Tiny. Fragile. Sickly." He offered the descriptors without hesitation, happy to help her discover her faults. And he didn't wait for her reply, either, just stalked off, disappearing in the foliage.

Stand up. Run! Search for Vale. Yes, yes. But even if she could walk, she had, like, a zero point nil chance of doing her sister any good. She was too weak and too slow. And what if she stumbled upon a "combatant?" Her chance of dying would jack up to 100 percent.

Must do something. Think! What did she know? Well, for starters, opioid withdrawal would knock her flat soon.

Nola had two pills in her pocket; she *always* had two pills in her pocket. A "just in case of an emergency" stash. If she took one now—half her usual four-hour dose—she would head off any major withdrawal symptoms for about six hours. Then, she could take the other pill, and buy herself another six hours. After that...

Okay, then. She set an internal timer in her mind. Twelve hours to form and enact a plan. *Ticktock.*

Nola lumbered to her hands and knees, the dizziness worsening. When she tried to stand, she toppled. Dang it! She slammed a fist into the dirt.

Calm down. Don't rage, act. Once again, she lumbered to her hands and knees. She crawled to the pond and popped a pill. Though she knew the dangers of drinking nonsanitized water, she sipped it from her hands. *Bottoms up.* If her digestive system revolted, her digestive system revolted.

Bonus: if she had raging diarrhea, Zion would be less inclined to touch her. Yay.

As the dizziness eased, she used a tree limb to clamber to her feet. Her legs wobbled, her knees threatening to buckle all over again, but she fought to gain her bearings.

An idea sparked, and she reeled. What if she convinced *Zion* to rescue Vale?

Could she trust him? So far, he'd exhibited pretty decent behavior. Nola hadn't been hurt. At the very least, he had answers to her questions. Who was Knox, and where had he taken Vale? Who were the others, the ones who'd been frozen alongside him? For that matter, how had they survived being frozen? Did everyone heal as fast as Zion? Could Nola get in on the action? Why had all the sexcakes tried to murder each other when they'd gained their freedom? And who was GG and why was she drawn to him?

As sunlight filtered through a leafy canopy, stroking and warming her further, a twig snapped, footsteps reverberating. Zion marched past a thick tangle of gnarled tree limbs, holding a small satchel.

Without a battle raging around them, she was able to catalog previously missed details. Four tattoos etched his muscular chest, each image set inside a circle. In one, birds. In another, flames. Another, clouds. In the last, a tree of life. The diamonds embedded in his broad shoulders were arranged in some sort of starburst pattern. *So sparkly!* He was six and a half feet, the same height as GG, and exceptionally handsome, with that thick cap of dark hair, those dark eyes and skin a lovely shade of brown.

While GG had simmered with rage and brutality, every move he made an invitation to the chopping block, Zion exuded calm and determination.

"I brought a snack," he said.

Twelve hours. For some reason, she heard "*ticktock*" in the back of her mind. "The other girl," she blurted out, diving into the deep end. "Vale. She's my sister, my best friend and business partner, and the only family I have left. A murderous warrior carted her away. He could be hurting her."

His features softened. "I tried to save her, too."

"You tried and failed, so you're just giving up? I have to find her, Zion. She's my reason for breathing." Truth. A few times over the past year, Nola had come close to giving up on life, the future too bleak to contemplate. What did she have to look forward to? More flares. More pain. More medication. But, for another day with Vale, she would endure *anything*. "Will you help me?"

"No." He sat across from her and placed the satchel between them. The material gaped open, revealing bananas, pecans and carrots. "From the moment Knox broke free, he did everything possible to protect her. I doubt he'll hurt her."

A barbed lump grew in her throat, even though he was right. Knox had focused on Vale the same way GG had focused on Nola.

Where was GG now? Was he all right? He hadn't spoken telepathically since she'd exited the cavern. Though he'd been savage and disdainful, she didn't want him hurt. Or worse! He was her freaking dream man, after all.

Zion cracked a bundle of pecans and peeled a banana, then offered both to her. She took a bite of the fruit and moaned with bliss. The sweetness! So much better than canned fish and chili. She all but shoveled the remaining banana into her mouth, then started on the nuts. Once she'd swallowed the last one, guilt set in. Here she was, enjoying a tasty snack. Meanwhile, she had no idea if her sister was in danger.

"*Doubt* isn't good enough," she finally said.

"Well, it'll have to work for the time being. I'm part of the hundred and third All War. An immortal combatant fighting to rule your world."

Immortal. All War. Rule the whole dang world. Forget having an open mind. Forget the wild things she'd seen. He was lying. He must be.

But...I kind of believe him. "What's an All War?"

"A fight to the death."

And? "Please expound."

He thought for a moment, sighed. "There are thirty-nine worlds in the All War Alliance. Correction. There *were* thirty-nine worlds before a viking froze us in the arctic. I'm unsure how many new ones were found over the centuries. Anyway. To prevent other-world armies from invading and destroying newly discovered territories, one representative from each world is sent to battle the other representatives—to the death."

The food she'd consumed turned into lead in her stomach. So, Zion believed himself to be an extra-terrestrial alien? Meaning, GG was an extraterrestrial alien. *No way, no how.* But...

Maybe? Nola doubted any other explanation would make sense, either. If Zion *had* told the truth, if the All War was real and a group of warriors truly hoped to win control of Earth *300* meets *Highlander* style, the future was bleak for all humans, not just her, and...and...

She couldn't deal with this right now. Hysteria teased the edges of her mind.

Wrapping her arms around her middle, she said, "Do you know where Knox took Vale?"

"To his base camp, no doubt. Unfortunately, I have never glimpsed it, so I cannot escort you there."

"I don't understand." What did seeing a camp have to do with anything?

Zion tapped the trio of crystal rings he wore. "These are Rifters. They open a portal anywhere I've preciously visited or seen in photographs."

Rifters. Portals. Everything he said painted a very un-mortal-y picture. "Escort me somewhere I can get survival gear, then. Maybe a pharmacy, too. Definitely a pharmacy. Then return me to the arctic."

He blinked rapidly. "You know you cannot find her, yes? You are too weak, and you lack the proper training and tools." Cruel words—true words—spoken in a gentle tone. "What is your sickness?"

"None of your business." She wasn't physically strong, but so what? She had a heart of steel! "Is your planet medically advanced? Can you cure certain diseases?"

"Advanced, yes. Cure, no." He slanted his head to the side. "How did you find the ice cave?"

"Went for a hike, got lost." Why even try to explain her connection to GG, and the instinct to reach him? Selective mutism would stop her, guaranteed. "How long were you frozen?"

"Thirteen hundred years."

Nola floundered. A statement so wild it had to be

truth? "Do you happen to know the name of the golden warrior?"

"I do." Zion's eyes brightened, as if he knew a secret she did not. "He is Bane of Adwaeweth."

Bane. *The bane of my existence.* Add-way-with.

"Adwaewethian warriors are dangerous shape-shifters with an aversion to light."

"Shape-shifters," she gasped out.

"Long ago, I heard your people refer to Bane's beast as a *dreki*. Or dragon," he clarified.

What? An even wilder statement. Yet, she could easily imagine Bane transforming *I Am Dragon* style. But... why had Zion referred to *Nola* as "little dragon"? Unless he knew Bane and Nola shared a mental connection.

So, *why* did Bane and Nola share a connection?

Stop focusing on noncritical details. Ticktock. Ticktock. It was time to gain Zion's cooperation, and make him an offer he couldn't refuse. "Help me find and save Vale," she announced, "and I will..." What? What could she do, and what did he want? "I know the modern world, you don't. I can help you win your war. So. What do you say?"

CHAPTER FIVE

Your fantasy man is back. Now what?

ZION ABANDONED HER. *Without* making any promises or explaining where he was going, what he'd be doing or when he'd return. All he said? "I have a war to win. Stay here, and you'll stay safe." Then, he used his Rifters to open a portal and vanished, leaving Nola gaping.

Ticktock. At least the opioid had kicked in, more easily digested thanks to the food. Warmth spilled over her body. She took an experimental step, then another…yes! Using a fallen tree branch as a cane, she trekked through the, uh, dimension, on the hunt for another person, shelter, a vehicle or an exit. What she found? A whole lot of jungle.

The trees were overgrown, the flowers oversize and the lichen plentiful. Birds chirped, frogs croaked and bees buzzed past, providing super fun background music. But, no matter what direction she traveled, she always ended up at the pond. Did the dimension loop?

All the while, the twelve-hour countdown ticked in her mind, every lost minute chiseling away at her calm. Desperate for a distraction, she reworked a mental list of must do's. ~~Convince Zion to find and save Vale~~. *Stop hoping Bane will send another telepathic message. Escape. Save Vale before withdrawal sets in. Go home.*

Forget the war and its "combatants." Forget my golden god's potential alien status.

She began to suspect—and fear—a portal was the only way in and out of the dimension. If she continued on her current path, searching for an exit, she would only waste more of her limited time and precious energy. Better to do something with a slight chance for success.

Maybe she should set some kind of trap for Zion? He'd dismissed the idea. She shouldn't. If *she* captured *him*, she could force him to take her to Vale. Or maybe Bane.

Like it or not, Nola shared a formidable connection with the guy. Ever since her eighteenth birthday, he'd starred in her favorite dreams. When he'd requested aid, she'd traveled halfway around the world to help. Now, he owed her. With little effort on his part, he could help her rescue Vale.

Excitement bloomed. Okay. New list. *Set trap for Zion, force him to open a portal. Find Bane. Convince Bane to save Vale before withdrawal sets in. Go home. Forget the war and its "combatants." Forget my golden god's potential alien status.*

Her tired brain could think up only one trap. The old "dig a hole, cover the top and watch 'em fall" trick.

Where was a good place to—there! The spot where they'd eaten. She crouched and got to work, digging with her hands and a rock. Wasn't long before fatigue and tremors set in, slowing her progress.

A fine sheen beaded on her skin, her heart a sledgehammer against her ribs. Only three hours had passed, but the opioid had already begun to wear off. Next would come the nuclear aches.

Dang it! *Ticktock, ticktock.* Yet she was no closer to achieving a single goal.

Deep breath in, out. Crap! Dizziness invaded. Shallow breath in, out. Better. In, out. Excellent. *Focus. No telling when Zion will return.*

As she continued to dig, tears of frustration welled, stinging her eyes. What wouldn't she sacrifice to obtain strength like Bane's?

When she wasn't in the middle of a lupus or fibro flare, she forced herself to walk five miles a day. Per her doctor's orders, she avoided foods with gluten, dairy and chocolate. Even though kale belonged in the garbage, she consumed it twice a week. At least! She drank a thousand vegetable smoothies packed with vitamins and minerals. And yet, her stupid body decided to betray her now, when her sister needed her most.

Her chin quivered. A lone tear scalded her cheek, and she hurried to wipe it away with the back of her hand. Give up? No! She had to push through. She *would*.

Leaning forward, Nola slammed the rock in the ground and scraped pile after pile of dirt toward her knees. Muscles burned from exertion. Another tear fell as one side of the hole collapsed, undoing all her hard work.

"Come on!" she snarled. Slam. Scrape. More tears. "I can do this. I can…" Her vision blurred. A sob bubbled up from deep, deep inside, unleashing a toxic flood of frustration, fear and everything else she'd buried while trapped in the mountains with Vale. All the panic. Hysteria. Uncertainty. And regret.

With her head bowed and her shoulders shaking, she allowed new sobs to overtake her. If she were stronger, if she'd fought harder, she could have saved Vale already. But she wasn't, and she hadn't. *Worthless. Help-*

less. Good for nothing. Insults foster parents and siblings had lobbed at her throughout the years.

Well, they were wrong, and she would prove it! *Trap Zion, and get to Bane. Just get to Bane.*

A wondrous sensation washed over her, as if she'd injected extra potent opioids. Aches and pains faded. Sweat dried, and her heartbeat slowed. Nola luxuriated. This was the way she was always supposed to feel, wasn't it? This had to be what "normal" people experienced on a daily basis.

She wanted to dance and sing, laugh and play...until the jungle vanished, walls of rock and crystal now surrounding her, different odors saturating the air. Old pennies, limestone, exotic spices and masculine musk.

Nola clutched her stomach. *Do not vomit.* What just happened? And why did four dead bodies occupy the far corner of the cavern? They were fresh kills, their blood only beginning to congeal.

Somehow, she'd traveled to another location in a blink, without the use of Rifters. How?

She was a baker and a writer, and these impossible things kept happening to her. No doubt a freak-out was imminent. But not here, and not now. Though terrified, Nola stood to surprisingly steady legs, gliding to her feet with a grace she'd never before displayed.

A low growl drew her gaze to the left. Bane!

Seriously. How is this possible?

He was awake, slumped over...and totally and completely naked. Blood and dirt smeared his bare skin while fury, pain and contempt blazed in those golden eyes. Mud clumped in his hair and crusted around the angry, oozing gash on his shoulder. Row after row of muscle cut his glorious chest, creating a bona fide eight-pack. *Am I drooling?* Like Zion, he had circular tat-toos on his torso. A tree of life, a cluster of stars and an ocean wave.

Her cheeks heated as she skipped her gaze over his groin. His *extra large* groin.

Oh, hello. No way, no how his penis could be *that* big. Right? She supposed she needed to take another peek, just to be sure.

Back up her gaze went. *Sweet goodness! Look at that thing. A Jumbotron galore, with—*

No! Bad Nola!

Shivers cascaded along her spine, her blood warm-ing as if…no way. As if she experienced sexual arousal without an upset stomach. Another impossibility, right?

She fanned her cheeks and returned her gaze to his thighs, his knees. His legs stretched out in front of him and—

"Oh, Bane." Her hand fluttered over her mouth. Only hours ago, he'd fought hulking warriors with unmatched skill and ferocity. Now, he was missing a foot. His leg ended in a bloody stump. "You poor baby," she croaked, sympathy welling. The anguish he must be suffering. If she gave him the last pill in her pocket… He might have a bad reaction. *Not human, remember?*

Right. The pill might kill him. Never mind. The fact that she'd even considered sharing her last precious pill proved how much he meant to her, despite everything that had happened.

"Let me guess," he grated, his voice as deep and husky as always. Despite his wounds, he eyed her up and down with slow, sexually charged precision, as if she were a virgin on an auction block and he planned to make the winning bid. "Zion told you my name."

Breathless, she replied, "He did." That look should frighten and intimidate her, yes? So why did Nola find him sexier now? "Why do I feel so good? How did I get here?"

"You don't know?"

"Do you?" *Ticktock.* "Never mind. There's only one topic that interests me. My sister, Vale. Knox has her. With your help, I can find her."

He pursed his lips, an action born of anger. Even still, he just seemed sad and vulnerable, a sensation she knew well. An ember of kinship flourished. "I can't even find a tourniquet right now," he said.

"I can! I'll take care of the tourniquet, and you'll take care of Vale. Deal?" She didn't wait for his response. She scanned the cave. Rock…dirt…crystal. Dead bodies. The guy in the middle wore a belt. *Gonna have to do.* She rushed over, saying, "Did you, uh, kill these guys?"

"Yes. Happily. They're part of my decorating style," he said, his tone dry.

Surely she would feel fearful now. Waiting…

Nope. She felt exhilarated. *Finally making progress!*

"Poor Bane. No one told you 'macabre chic' is out." Pretending the corpses had gotten what they'd deserved—heck, maybe they had—she strained and maneuvered until she freed the strip of leather, then dashed back to Bane. Spices and musk teased her nose, fogged her head and heated her blood another degree. Great! Now tremors racked her. Sighing, she crouched beside him and slid the belt under his thigh as gently as possible.

"What happened to you?" she asked.

He hissed in pain and snapped, "You happened."

"Me?" She looked left and right, hoping he'd used that harsh tone for someone else.

For some reason, he calmed when his gaze locked on her hair. He looked...enchanted. He reached out to sift a lock between his fingers. The jet-black strands complemented his golden skin tone.

"Pretty," he said, then scowled and released her with a huff. "You have work to do."

Oookay. Losing an appendage made him cranky. Noted. And dang it, had anyone told her she'd one day calmly and casually regard an immortal warrior's foot amputation, she would have laughed in their face.

To keep him distracted from the coming pain, she said, "How did I cause you to lose a foot?" As she spoke, she looped the belt and slid the leather to the middle of his calf, then cinched it as tight as possible.

He bellowed a curse with such fury, she ducked, expecting a punch.

The action only made him angrier. But he gentled his tone, saying, "I won't hurt you, Nola."

Deep breath in, out. "Good to know." *If* he'd told the truth.

A look of homicidal murder crossed over his face and he bellowed, "Has someone hurt you in the past?"

Great! He sounded rage-y again. "Let's, uh, focus on you and the foot. Okay?"

Between panting breaths, he told her, "I fought to protect you and got pinned for my efforts. To escape the collapsing cavern, I had to remove the foot. So I could track you. Only, Zion is very good at hiding. I quickly lost your trail."

"The foot," he'd said, not "my foot." The distinction mattered, and roused her sympathies. She knew he felt removed from his body, a phenomenon she'd often battled, as well. "Do you know where Knox is? He absconded with my sister."

"Sister?" His brow furrowed. "I didn't sense Adwaewethian blood in the other girl."

"But you sensed Adwaewethian blood in *me*?" Oh, crap. Was *she* an alien? An other-worldly lineage might explain some of her stranger idiosyncrasies.

A muscle jumped underneath his eye. "Yes, I did. And no, I don't know where Knox is. None of us do."

Double crap! She rocked back on her haunches, saying, "I've lived on Earth—Terra—my entire life. How can I be from your world?" They'd circle back to his inability to search for Knox and Vale after she'd warmed him up a bit—conversationally speaking.

"How else? There's an Adwaewethian breeder in your family tree."

How blithely he made an announcement that had the power to change the entire course of her life. If true, of course. "Is that why you spoke inside my head and demanded I find you?"

Snubbing the question, he reached out and cupped the back of her nape, his grip bruising. Shock and fury darkened his expression. "You're real. You're real, and you're here. You're here with me."

Things started softening inside her. "Yes, I'm real. And just so you know, if you break me, you buy me."

With a single yank, he forced her face closer to his, their mouths only a whisper apart. She gasped. He stared, hard, his gaze searching hers.

Up close, his eyes resembled liquid gold, molten and smoldering, his frame of long, black lashes the stuff of dreams. Literally! Nola had never thought to be within

touching distance of her golden god, and now she was…
reeling. "I'm real, and you are an honest to goodness
alien, like Zion. And me, apparently." *To believe, or
not to believe?*

He didn't seem to hear her. "Did Zion harm you?"

Did he care? "No. He was good to me."

"How good?" Bane's eyelids slitted, those gorgeous
amber irises hidden. "You like him."

"Kind of. And very much," she said.

He growled. Growled! Like a big, beautiful, *jealous*
animal.

A man like Bane, jealous because another man got
to spend more time with Nola? No way. She must be
misreading the situation. "I don't know him well, but
he doesn't look at me as if I'm the dirt on the bottom of
his shoes so…" Shrug.

"Dirt. Yes." Though his eyes closed and his head
lolled to the side, he didn't release her. He did jerk to attention a moment later and snarl, "Hate you."

She flinched, the admission hitting her like a fist.
What had she done to deserve such rancor?

Why give him the satisfaction of asking?

If he'd shown her a little kindness, she would have
given him her all—all of her caring, all of her aid. Now?
He'd be lucky to get half of either.

"Where did Zion take you?" he demanded.

She jutted her chin, saying, "Even if I knew, I
wouldn't tell you."

"Then you are a fool. He's using you to get to me."

"Right, because a man wouldn't want me for any
other reason?" she bit out.

He traced his tongue over straight white teeth. "Stay

with me, and I will protect you from him. From everyone."

"Trust the man who hates me? No, thanks. Besides, you can't even protect yourself, Stumpy." Guilt sparked. Never before had Nola used such a scathing tone with another living being, but come on! In just a few minutes, he'd shredded what little hard-won self-esteem she possessed. "Besides, why would you *want* to protect me?"

He looked away, his demeanor changing. From fierce to determined. "I don't have to like you to help you. We need each other."

This mighty golden god needed *her*? "I know why I need you—Vale. Why do you need me?"

"Tell me you will stay away from Zion," he insisted, snubbing another question.

Dang him! "If you won't help me save Vale, Zion will." Maybe. But she'd have to push. So why not push *Bane* instead?

Hoping to arouse his jealousy again, she said, "Zion is hot and *very* good with his hands." Probably. She leaned closer, pressing her breasts against his chest, and whispered straight into his ear. "I'm his dream girl." Literally!

Bane tightened his grip. "Dream…yes. You are a dream, and a nightmare, just like Adwaeweth. You are my salvation and my damnation, rolled into one beautiful package."

He thinks I'm beautiful?

Ugh! *That* was what she focused on? "How can I be your salvation *and* your damnation? Actually, how can I be either one?" she asked, and dang it, every time he exhaled, she inhaled, breathing in all that spice and musk. Her belly quivered, and heat pooled between her legs.

I'm experiencing arousal without an upset stomach.
How wonderous! But why here, why now? Why *him*?

Did he feel arousal, too? He must. As they stared at
each other, awareness charged the air.

Again, he pretended she hadn't asked a question and
chose to ask one of his own. "How did you reach me
without Rifters?"

"I honestly don't know. One second I was wondering
if you'd help me, the next I was here."

For some reason, her response infuriated him all over
again. "Already embracing our capabilities, I see. Typical
royal," he muttered with disgust.

Royal? Capabilities?

"Tell me to heal," he commanded. "Tell me to grow
a new foot as quickly as possible."

"You mean I should whisk you to a hospital, using a
supernatural ability I might or might not have and definitely don't know how to use? Sure thing. Why don't
you watch as I pull a rabbit out of my invisible hat, too?"

His golden brows drew together, a crease forming in
the middle. "Hospital…a medical facility. No. You will
aid me here."

"How? My phone is dead, and there's no way I can
carry you."

"Tell me to heal, Nola. Exactly as I requested."

Annoyed, she said, "You didn't make a request. You
made a demand."

He squeezed her nape until she whimpered, more with
surprise than pain. But even now, she wasn't afraid of
him. "Tell me. Now."

"This is protecting me?" she snapped.

Immediately, he loosened his hold. "Please," he
rasped.

Why not humor him? "Heal," she said. "Grow a new foot as quickly as possible." For the briefest glimpse of time, she felt warm, feverish, but the feeling ceased abruptly.

As soon as the last word left her mouth, he threw back his head and roared with agony, his entire body seizing. *Now* fear descended upon her. She wrenched away from him, chanting, "I'm sorry, I'm sorry." What had she done?

"Do not leave," he shouted. "Nola, don't you dare leave."

Too late. The cave—and Bane—vanished, the jungle reappeared. She jolted. Once again, she'd transported to a new location in a mere blink of time, with no idea how she'd done it.

Transported…or teleported?

"Zion," she called.

Birds took flight, but no response was forthcoming. So. No Bane, and no Zion. Great!

Nola scoured her mental files for any information she might have read about the ability, but her thoughts were as jumbled as a barrel of plastic monkeys. A symptom of withdrawal. The other symptoms returned with a vengeance, her heart racing, sweat beading on her skin. Aches and pains reignited, and she struggled to catch her breath.

Somehow, Bane had staved off her withdrawal. Now that they were apart…

Should she try to return to him, despite his temper tantrum?

No need to think about it. Yes, she should. *Ticktock.* She was no closer to saving Vale, but she *was* close to getting an agreement from him. But, no matter how hard she concentrated, she remained in place, frustrated and disappointed.

One fact cleared up, though. Bane *had* forever altered the course of her life. Only time would tell if those changes were for the best...or the worst.

CHAPTER SIX

When his ex is the queen of mean!

"NOLA!" BANE ROARED. He jolted upright, frigid limestone-scented air nipping at his exposed skin.

He reached out to Nola with his mind, wanting her close, but some kind of block prevented a connection. Why?

Panting, drenched in sweat, he took stock of his body. His clothes—gone. His shoulder—unhealed. His foot—regrown. Finally, something favorable had happened to him. But how had it happened so quickly?

His internal clock said one night had passed since he'd escaped the ice prison. A foot usually required two days to regenerate—if a queen gave an order. When a princess gave it, you had to tack on another couple of days. So what had sped up the process for Nola?

Breath misted in front of his face as he scouted his surroundings. A rocky cave. Not his lair. This cave contained no weapons or treasures. Here, glistening crystals spilled from the ceiling. Water drip-drip-dripped from rocky walls, splashing onto a pile of dead mortals. Old kills. Their blood had congealed and darkened.

The beast must have snagged the foursome from a nearby village and holed up…where? He racked his brain for an answer. Every thought but one sank to the bottom of mental quicksand as quickly as it formed. Did anyone wait nearby, hoping to ambush him?

He closed his eyes and listened intently. No voices, no footsteps, just a bluster of wind. He breathed deep and sorted through the different aromas. Limestone, decomposition and dirt. Honeysuckle and jasmine.

His body jerked, a bolt of lust slamming into him. Honeysuckle. How long had Nola been gone? Where was she? *Want her back!*

Back up. Lust—for *her*? Unacceptable! He would never bed a royal and disrespect Meredith's memory. He would never bed a royal, period. He'd learned his lesson with Aveline. Nola might be a sweet, tasty little treat— *and I might be hungry, starved*—but in three weeks, she would change. He would perform the Blood Rite, and she would rise as a true queen, cold, callous and pure evil.

Nola…evil…

He'd had centuries to wonder about her. Who she'd be, what she'd hope to accomplish. Not once had he entertained curiosity about her personality or appearance. Now, he found himself fixating on her thick mass of blue-black hair, or her luscious heart-shaped lips, or her starry eyes, sparkling with happiness one minute, darkening with hurt the next.

When he'd held her nape, he'd imagined wrapping the long length of her hair around his fist, and angling her face to his. He'd wanted to hear her breath hitch, wanted to watch as a passion-fever deepened the color in her cheeks and the pulse at the base of her neck raced.

His shaft shot as hard as steel. Not because of Nola. His body hungered for sex, that was all. He'd gone more than thirteen hundred years without a lover. A circumstance he could easily rectify, if he so desired. Which begged the question—did he so desire? The moment he thrust inside a woman, his precious wife would no longer be the last one he'd kissed or touched. Even the thought filled him with gnawing guilt.

Enough! War now, sex later. Think.

A stunningly vivid memory filled his mind. When Nola appeared in the cave, she'd evinced such unadulterated joy, she'd made his chest ache. Because he'd known he would never again feel the emotion.

Fast-forwarded to the moment she'd crouched beside him. Her starry eyes had widened, and he'd noticed signs of hardcore crying. Puffy, red-rimmed eyelids. Tear tracks on her dirt-smeared cheeks. Pink splotches on her skin. Dirt had caked her fingers.

Before coming to see him, someone had made her cry. Zion?

Bane's next breath proved fiery, heat seeming to forge daggers from air and slash at his lungs. Zion would pay.

Where the hell had Nola gone? Nowhere nearby, that much he knew. The presence of a royal calmed the beast. Here, now, the beast growled and pawed at his mind, expressing hatred and resentment more volatile than Bane's.

Must find Nola. With her, the beast would quiet.

As he racked his brain more forcefully, new memories escaped the mental quicksand. He remembered crawling from the ruins of the ice cavern, leaving a trail of blood in his wake…remembered deep fractures spreading across the ground, nearly swallowing him whole. When he'd rolled away, a combatant had stabbed him in the back. That was when the beast had overtaken him, flying him to a nearby village.

The fact that Bane had transformed at all meant Zion had whisked Nola somewhere beyond his range.

Tension stole through Bane. Before his imprisonment, he'd hunted Zion to no avail.

If I cannot find Nola, perhaps she'll find me. Like Aveline, she could teleport. She could also heal him with a command. His eyes widened. *That's right.* She'd commanded him to heal, and he had. He'd healed faster than ever before, almost as if her authority had more reach than Aveline's, a full-blooded queen. Impossible!

For beasts like Bane, a royal's word equaled law. His body would always obey her demands...unless something was powerful enough to supersede her will. Like Valor's sword. Until she became queen, she wouldn't be strong enough to heal his shoulder. Proof: she'd said, *Heal.* So, all of him should have healed. Yet, that one injury remained as deep and painful as ever.

The sword! If someone had stolen the weapon during Bane's years of captivity...

His hands curled into fists. He considered opening a portal to his lair to check on the sword and his goggles, only to discard the idea. Someone might be hiding nearby, waiting to catch a glimpse of his hideout.

He'd search the cavern. If empty, he would portal to his lair, then turn his sights to Nola.

Want her now! The lust resurged, overtaking him in a heated rush. *Not for her. For closure.*

With a curse, Bane leaped to his feet. His new ankle held steady. Good. He filched a pair of pants and boots from the largest of the beast's victims. Too small, and too tight. He must look ridiculous, but at least his range of motion wasn't limited, so he'd deal. The boots were too big for the corpse, but a perfect fit for Bane, as if tailor-made for him. A simple coincidence? Seemed unlikely, but stranger things had occurred.

He only made it a step before a familiar vibration rocked his hand. He scowled. His communication ring. Only one person had access to it. Aveline the Great and Terrible, who could not speak inside his head while they were worlds apart.

He ground his molars. Muted light burst from the ring's center, a holographic image of Aveline appearing.

Rage seared his chest, every muscle in his body knotting. The lust he'd experienced only moments ago? Gone. His body had *some* standards.

"You live," she said, her voice flat.

The Adwaewethian queen had changed little. Still golden from head to toe. Still deceptively fragile. Still evil as hell.

While the beast quieted, he didn't go silent. Proof that the link between queen and warrior had already weakened. *Do not grin.*

Modulate your tone. Proceed with caution. No matter what, he had to ensure Aveline remained ignorant of Nola's identity. "Where's your excitement?" he asked with a sneer. Or *not* modulate his tone, apparently. "Your warrior survived." *Not hers, never hers.*

"You'll see my excitement when you win the war," she retorted. "A lot has happened since you were frozen."

"Such as?"

"The All War Alliance allowed another group of warriors to venture to Terra. When *those* warriors vanished, a third war kicked off. But they vanished, too."

Rules forbade the High Council from interfering in a war. Of course, no clash had ever ended in a stalemate. "Who did you send?"

"Cayden and Mount. Cayden survived, Mount died."

Aggression scraped at his insides, the urge to strike something, anything, almost irresistible. Cayden was ruthlessness to the core, with opponents and lovers alike. At least she hadn't sent Micah, the most violent combatant on her payroll, the man who'd helped her murder Meredith.

"Were their orders the same as mine?" he asked.

"Yes, of course. Cayden thought he'd found Terra's current princess just before he disappeared."

Bane's nail beds burned, his claws lengthening, preparing to strike. The other Adwaewethian warrior would make Nola's death a priority—*if* he was found before the end of the All War.

The time for plotting had ended, and the time for action had arrived. He would execute his plan, winning a handful of weapons he desired, and ending the war at the assembly. Finally! Only three weeks to go. Twenty-one days. Anticipation *seethed* inside him.

After Nola's Blood Rite, she would yearn to slay every threat to her rulership. With an army of hybrids at her beck and call, she could—and would—succeed.

How many hybrids lived on Terra now, their beasts in perpetual hibernation?

Since three full-blooded beasts had roamed the planet on and off—Bane, Cayden and Mount—the High Council would never learn Aveline's crimes. In their minds, each warrior could have bedded and impregnated hundreds of women, thus explaining all the hybrids. No one knew Aveline used a mystical toxin to sterilize her warriors before sending them off to war. In exchange for victory, they received the antidote.

"There's something else you need to know," Aveline

said. "A little over twenty years ago, I sent Micah to Terra in secret, with orders to slay every royal he came across, as well as search for you and Cayden."

Bane saw red. *Calm. Steady.* If Micah lived, Bane would find and kill him. Another task to add to his ever-growing list. This one, he would enjoy. "You risked—"

"Quiet," Aveline bellowed. "You are a soldier, nothing more. We share a past, yes, but it means nothing here in the present. You do not get to chastise me, or question my decisions."

Furious, he popped his jaw, but he also obeyed, lest she suspect his connection to Nola.

The queen smiled with smug superiority. Tone as soft as silk, she said, "Tell me, my pet. Has the urge to kill me faded?"

There was no reason to lie, the answer probably stamped on his features. "Not. Even. A. Little."

"Excellent." Another slow smile. "Then get to work and win the war. Quickly! Your odds of success will shrink the moment the other combatants are found."

More combatants, more obstacles in need of elimination. "I will win. You have my word."

As her image faded from view, the beast roared and rammed against his skull with more force, loosening a single thought. *Get to Nola.* One day, she would become his enemy, his greatest foe, but that day was not today. Today, she was the answer to his problems, and he would protect her no matter the cost.

Incentivized, Bane sprinted down a long corridor. Rainbow fluorite glittered in the walls as bright rays of light filtered through a wide opening. Without his goggles, he was partially blinded. The moment he stepped outside, he would lose all sight. He didn't care. *Get to a private location, portal to the lair. Communicate with Nola.*

He increased his speed, faster, faster, the desire to speak with her, to see and touch her, to hear her voice, growing stronger. Nothing would stop him—

He slammed into an invisible wall and ricocheted backward, toppling over a rock.

Trapped in another prison? No! Nothing and no one would keep him from the Terran princess.

Snarls rumbled in his chest as he leaped to his feet. The first thing he noticed? The wall wasn't invisible. With his compromised vision, he'd missed the metal bars.

His snarls grew louder as he clawed and yanked. Damn it! They didn't budge.

His ears twitched, and he frowned. What was that sound? Squeaking hinges? Must be. To the right, a section of rock lifted, revealing a large black screen with an image of Erik the Widow Maker—he was smiling.

"Hello, Bane. You remember me, I'm sure. Bad news. You are currently imprisoned in my mountain, with no way out. I'd apologize, but I'm not sorry. Since your incarceration, I've learned about your All War. A thousand times, I've been tempted to kill you, but lucky for you I recognize the greater threat. The High Council and their Enforcers. They must be stopped. Together, we can neutralize them. Think about it, and we'll talk again soon." The screen went blank.

Deep breath in, out. Help Erik, the one who'd frozen him? Even though he agreed with the male, no, just no. The High Council and Enforcers were a threat, yes, but Aveline's defeat trumped everything.

Deciding to portal just beyond the bars, Bane brushed

his thumb over his Rifters. He waited one minute, two, but nothing happened. So. Erik had somehow managed to deactivate the rings. How?

Think later, escape now. Bane rotated, scanning… scanning. No other exit presented itself. No matter. He popped the bones in his hands and peered at a rocky wall with spiked crystal protrusions, the need to reach Nola clawing at him. *I'll make a new exit.*

CHAPTER SEVEN

One big (un)happy reunion

THE COUNTDOWN CLOCK had zeroed out, Nola's twelve-hour window nothing but a fond memory. This marked day two without a pill, her withdrawal symptoms worsening every minute. The truly awful part? She felt as if the clock had reset, and she hurled toward something else—or someone. When the time came, she would crash.

In the meantime, her pain was excruciating and all consuming, with no end in sight. She writhed, pouring sweat, desperate to soothe her aching joints. Her blood pressure skyrocketed, her heart thudding against her ribs. A thousand times, she projectile-vomited…among other things.

One minute she was frozen to her core; the next, she was overheated. Her body shook constantly. Bursting into tears had become a regular occurrence, the physical, mental and emotional toll too much.

She would do anything for a respite; even contact Bane through their mental connection. But, though she'd reached out again and again, the jerk had gone radio silent. She'd attempted to teleport back to his cave, too… then to a hospital, then to anywhere but here. No luck.

How was she supposed to replicate an accident, anyway? Last time, she'd thought of Bane and boom, she'd been whisked into his presence. To get home, she'd panicked and moved away from him. Two different methods of operation.

Unless she hadn't teleported to Bane originally? Maybe, after Zion's abduction, her mind had broken, and she'd hallucinated the visit with Bane. Maybe she finally had a legit reason to blame a freaking delusion.

Lacking the strength to stand, Nola remained near the pond. Her new forever home and her future coffin—two for the price of one. Yay. Zion visited upon occasion, but mostly stayed away, warring like a pro. No matter how much she pressed, he refused to tell her anything about anything.

Where was Vale? *How* was Vale? And what had happened to Bane, the man who hated her for no reason? Had he truly lost a foot? Had he…died from blood loss?

Nola swallowed a sob. Bane was the only person she knew with firsthand knowledge of Adwaewethians and dragon shape-shifters. Maybe truth, maybe lies. No, after everything that had happened, everything she'd witnessed, she believed. Her mind wasn't broken. She just didn't know how to feel about everything. Excited? Frightened? Hopeful? Full of dread?

Could *she* shape-shift? Had she come to this planet before or after her birth? Had her parents been otherworlders, too? She had no memory of them.

No, not true. Though she'd been a toddler when they'd died in a tragic car crash, sometimes she dreamed about the vehicle flipping over, heard the sound of screams and grinding metal, felt warm blood dripping all over her as she struggled to escape her car seat. Nola tensed, the echoes of memory flaying her heart.

Where are you, Bane? Silence.

Please, talk to me. Again, silence.

She closed her eyes, envisioning her golden god. Tall and muscular, intense and masculine. Aggressive and savage. Carnal. Mysterious and dominant. She waited, hoping, praying, but she didn't travel to him. Dang it!

Bane! she shouted. *Speak to me. Now!*

A sense of connection tingled soul-deep, and she thought, hoped, she had reached him this time. Then she heard —*What's wrong, princess?*—

That worked? Sweet validation! The shifter's voice had infiltrated her mind, a homecoming of sorts. Unless *this* was a—

Stop! *I'm not delusional.* Despite her fear of Bane, despite his abysmal treatment, she'd kinda sorta…missed him. He'd been part of her life for years. And, though his tone brimmed with contempt, she experienced a tsunami of relief. He lived!

But why did he hate her?

There had been a few times he hadn't looked at her with disdain. No, oh no. He'd looked at her with hunger. Remembering, she shivered.

—*Princess?*—

Right. *I'm sick…hurt so bad. In the cave, you made me feel better. Can you do it again?* Begging the guy who considered her garbage? Well, why not? Pain stripped her of pride.

—*Come to me, like before.*—

How? She'd tried everything she knew to do.

—*Instinct, perhaps? I am unsure. Unlike you, I don't have the ability to teleport.*—

Confirmation: she *had* teleported.

She told him, *Last time, I thought of you. For my*

return trip home, I thought about escaping you. Now I'm overthinking about you, but I'm not teleporting.

He made a sound of fury and frustration. —*Command me to come to you, then.*—

So, he couldn't come to her *without* a command?

Welcoming a combatant to Zion's dimension would be a full-on betrayal. But he'd abandoned her and withheld information. Or he'd…died, and wasn't ever coming back. Her stomach twisted, and she dry heaved.

The pain… She would rather die than endure another minute of this.

Before she started blubbering, or talked herself into standing down, she blurted out, *I command you to come to me right this instant.*

With her next inhalation, the scent of exotic spices and masculine musk filled her nose. Heat dribbled through her veins, her stomach calmed and the body aches faded. Tears of bliss cascaded down her cheeks. Then Bane appeared, right there in the heart of the jungle, and Nola gasped with surprise and delight. She'd done it. She'd actually teleported him. *How?*

"Bane," she whispered, peering at him with wonder. "You heard me and responded. How? I have to know! And why ignore me for so long?"

"I *couldn't* speak with you. You blocked me."

Really? "How?" she asked again.

"Don't know." He cataloged the terrain while gripping two daggers.

No doubt he'd taken in every detail.

Well, she cataloged *him.* Locks of pale hair stuck out in tangled spikes. Contempt glittered in his amber eyes, stronger than before. *No big deal. I don't care.* Dirt streaked his skin, and caked under his nails and around the edges of his shoulder wound. He was shirtless, of course, his only clothing a pair of ripped camo pants. On his feet, scuffed combat boots.

Wait. He wore boots. Plural.

"Your foot," she said, easing into an upright position. His foot had grown back, just as she'd commanded— *Heal. Grow a new foot as quickly as possible.*

The first order—heal—should have encompassed every injury, even the shoulder one. Still. He'd regrown a freaking foot and teleported! Because she'd given an order. The implications of this were mindboggling. Wonder enveloped her.

"Your shoulder," she said next.

"A mystical sword gave me a wound that cannot be mended."

"That sucks!"

"I will find a way."

So would she!

But first, she wondered if he would obey *all* of her commands, no matter what. Would others?

Nola squeezed her eyes shut and whispered, "Appear before me, Vale."

Moments passed in suspended anticipation. She pried open her eyelids and… Nope. No Vale.

Disappointment settled over her. Maybe the ability— or whatever it was—worked only with Bane.

"Since we were last together, the foot grew back and I clawed my way out of a mountain. I also saw your sister," Bane said, dragging his gaze over her. "As of three hours ago, she was alive and well."

"Thank God!" A thousand pounds of worry lifted. "And a thousand thanks to you for telling me."

"Don't thank me. Inform me. Where's Zion?" Even

before she responded, he made a show of sheathing his weapons. With his gaze locked on Nola, he dropped his chin to his sternum and crossed the distance like a total predator. Crouching in front of her, he smoothed a lock of hair behind her ear, uncharacteristically gentle. "Tell me, Nola."

"I don't know where he is," she admitted, stretching her arms overhead. As her spine arched, her breasts thrust forward. She let her head drop back, and a wealth of tension seeped from her muscles. A slow smile bloomed. So good!

Little growls rumbled from Bane. "Cease moving about. Wipe that rapturous look off your face."

Why would he... Unless he... Did Bane find her attractive? He must. He just didn't want to want her.

"I have a better idea," she purred. "I keep moving around however much I wish, and I wear whatever look I choose, and you deal with it. Now, if you'll excuse me, I'm parched. Bottoms up." She toasted him with Zion's canteen of water, then drained the contents.

Once her thirst had been satisfied, she dunked a rag in the pond and cleaned her face. She brushed her teeth and anchored her hair into a messy bun.

"Going to pretend I'm not here? Wonderful." Bane pinched her chin and tilted her face this way and that. Rage darkened his features, frightening in its intensity, yet his touch remained gentle. "You've lost weight. Has Zion starved you?"

"I told you. I've been sick," she said, and this time the admission embarrassed her. Bane was a warrior to his core, who admired strength in others. Therefore, he would never admire *her. I don't care. I don't.* Whether human or alien, all people were inherently flawed, *in-*

cluding Bane. Why should his opinion matter more than her own? "Strangely enough, I feel better—healthy— when you're around." And hungry. Where could she find chocolate? No, sour gummies. No, butterscotch.

He grated, "You draw strength from your warriors, just as we draw strength from you."

Wait, wait, wait. Hold up. "*My* warriors?"

A muscle jumped in his jaw. "I will explain every- thing, but only when you are safely tucked inside my lair. Here, we can be overheard. Trust me when I say Zion will desert you if ever he learns about your origins. Other combatants will want your head."

She shook her head. Zion already suspected some- thing was amiss, yet he'd still aided her. "You're wrong. I stabbed Zion, and he never retaliated."

Bane arched a brow, all *the little mortal gave the big, bad warrior a boo-boo? How adorable.* "A combatant saves a human for one reason, and one reason only. The human can be used to win the war."

Maybe, maybe not. "Is that why *you're* interested in me?" Either way, Bane and Zion would fight to the death when Zion returned, and she would be at fault.

Guilt torched her calm, leaving her shaking.

"In part," he replied. "But again, you'll get no expla- nations outside of the lair."

"Good thing we need to leave, then." And yeah, okay, she was serving Zion a big bowl of steaming crap pie, and he deserved better. He might not have been an A+ host—he hadn't spent a whole lot of time with her, or answered her questions, or aided Vale—but he'd hadn't been an F- host, either. He'd kept Nola safe. But Bane kept her pain-free, so there was no contest.

He brightened.

"But," she added, and the light faded. "Let me clue you in to a little not-so-secret secret. I'm going to stay with the man who helps me find and save Vale. Nothing matters more, not even my health."

"Your sister," he said, his voice laced with concern. Looking as though he'd aged twenty years, he scoured a hand down his face.

Her stomach bottomed out. "What's wrong? What happened?"

"Vale killed a combatant and joined the war."

Horror crept down her spine, plucking at her nerve endings. Vale…forced to fight others to the death… forced to fight Bane and Zion… "No!"

"I am sorry, Nola, but her fate is sealed."

Colder and shakier by the second, she shook her head.

"Now, combatants will come after you," he continued, "hoping to use you as bait against her."

"I don't care about me." She grabbed his hand and clung for dear life. "Vale is my everything, Bane. My reason to keep fighting, to keep living. We met in a foster home for troubled girls. She was the first person to love me. Please," she beseeched. "Promise me you won't harm her."

At "please," he flinched. "I can make no such promise," he groused. "Nor can Zion."

Not good enough. Maybe, if she *ordered* him to protect Vale, he would be forced to obey? There was only one way to find out, but the thought of making him do something—anything—against his will left her uneasy.

How many times had a foster parent forced her to eat foods she hated, or clean her plate when she was full to prevent waste? On the other hand, she needed to know what she could and couldn't do.

"Bane," she said, a slight tremor in her voice.

He sucked in a breath. "Do not issue a command, princess. I will hate you for it."

"I'm not responsible for your emotions. Besides, you already hate me. And I don't care!"

"You should. I'm willing to keep Vale safe until we are the final two."

Not good enough. But maybe good enough for now?

Before she could render a verdict, he straightened and pulled her to her feet. "Come. We're leaving."

Considering she'd vomited everything she'd eaten for two days straight, her legs proved surprisingly steady.

Rather than opening a portal, her golden god eyed her like the last slice of cake in a baker's display case and stalked a circle around her, unhurried. When her shoulder brushed his chest, a bolt of electricity shot through her. He must have felt it, too. He startled as he stopped directly in front of her.

Their gazes held, her senses heightening. Awareness of him magnified. His delectable heat engulfed her, bolstering his tantalizing scent, making her belly clench. The warmth of his exhalations fanned her face, teasing her skin, her lips.

Touch...

Desire rushed through her veins. Her nipples beaded, and she shivered. But the more aroused she became, the angrier he appeared.

He said nothing. She said nothing, speech beyond her skill set. The need for contact eclipsed the need to protect herself from yet another rejection. And he *would* reject her. That disdain...

Giving him a chance to rebuke her, Nola lifted her arms as slow as molasses. His shallow breaths quickened, but he remained silent. Finally, she flattened her hands over his pectorals, skin to white-hot skin. Muscles jumped, his heart racing beneath her palm.

"Such strength," she muttered, entranced.

"Such beauty." He wrapped his fingers around her wrists, holding her in place as if he couldn't bear to let her go?

A thousand desires bombarded her at once. *Kiss him. Pet every inch of him. Tear off his clothes. Shove him to the ground. Impale my body on his massive erection.*

Oh, no, no, no. Sleep with Bane, a (kind of) stranger and a killer? No! Yes! Maybe? If she could be with him without sickening...

What are you doing? Vale came first, sex deliberation second.

Panting, Nola stepped back and wrenched from Bane.

He stepped forward, keeping her close. A volcano of violence threatened to erupt in those golden eyes. "Have you slept with Zion, princess?"

She lifted her chin, refusing to cower, and forged ahead. "Why? Are you jealous?"

His nostrils flared. "I've never been jealous." He took another step closer, consuming her personal space. "I'll never *be* jealous. It's a childish emotion, for petulant people."

"I'll take that as a yes." Watching his expression for a hint of emotion, she said, "As for Zion, no. I haven't slept with him."

Some of Bane's tension faded.

Then she added, "Yet," and he scowled.

Do not grin. No one had ever been jealous over Nola before.

He dragged his fingertips down the length of her

sternum…around her navel. The thin cotton T-shirt offered little protection from all his blistering heat. "So fragile," he said as she shivered. "Easily breakable. You would do well to curry my favor."

Fragile. Breakable. "That never gets old," she grumbled. "Shouldn't *you* curry *my* favor? I speak, and you're forced to obey."

"And so the transformation begins," he muttered, then bared his teeth at her. Were his chompers sharper than they'd been last time she'd checked him out?

"What does that mean?" Transformation—into a queen? At least he hadn't denied her skill. Lightbulb! "Is that why you hate me? Because I have a strange ability to control you—an ability I don't even understand? Well, guess what? You're a total hypocrite! You condemn me while reveling in your own power over me."

He bowed up, gearing for a fight.

Why do I remain unafraid?

But he didn't strike at her. He switched topics, saying, "Your sickness. Tell me about it."

Her cheeks heated. "I suffer from three conditions. One causes overactive nerves. One causes inflammation. Both of those cause tremendous amounts of pain, so I take pills to help me function, but they are addictive. Without them, I get a million times sicker."

Pensive, he rubbed two fingers over his jaw. "If I acquire these pills, you'll feel better even when we're apart?"

"Yes. But you'll expect something in return, yes? Like, I have to agree to your final two deal with Vale?"

"Nola?" Zion called her name, his voice reverberating through the jungle.

Bane stiffened and reached for a dagger.

Crap! "You're right. Final two. Let's go," she rushed out. "Now, now, now."

He grinned slowly, his anticipation palpable. "We will go. *After* I deal with Zion. His war has come to an end."

"Just leave him be. He's a good guy."

"He is an obstacle to my vengeance. Obstacles get mowed down," he snapped softly, fiercely.

Ah! Finally, a clue about the mysterious Bane of Adwaeweth. "What vengeance?"

He scowled again. "He owns a wand, and I want it. I won't leave this place without it."

Had she ever encountered such malice? "You want it. So what? Wanting something doesn't mean you get to have it. You will take me from this dimension without argument."

A vein bulged in his forehead, the volcano in his eyes about to erupt. Still he snagged her by the waist with one hand, and opened a portal with the other.

Oh, sweet goodness, she *did* have authority over him. Laughter bubbled up.

Bane stalked through the portal, into an empty house with boarded-up windows. He released her and gave her a gentle push toward a shadowed corner, remaining at the portal and palming two daggers. A single overhead bulb provided light, glinting off the blades.

The moisture in her mouth dried. "Where are we?"

"We won't stay here. The portal will stay open for sixty seconds. I know Zion won't let you go easily. If he's fast enough, he'll—"

Zion dove through the portal, slamming into Bane. Nola gasped as the two men rolled over a concrete floor and savagely, brutally grappled for dominance.

When they made it to their feet, Zion threw a punch.

Bane ducked, the fist going through the wall, plaster raining down.

Staying low, Bane punted the back of Zion's knee. At the same time, he shoved Zion's *head* through the wall. More plaster.

Upon her next inhalation, Nola breathed in the particles and coughed.

The noise distracted Bane. He whipped around, his gaze concerned.

With a war cry, Zion punched his wounded shoulder—no, he punched *through* Bane's shoulder, a bloody fist coming out the other side. Nola gagged as blood sprayed.

Bane threw back his head and roared a beastly sound of agony.

Afraid for his life, she shouted, "Leave, Bane. Leave now, heal and stay away from the other dimension."

Again, he faced her. This time, he was snarling, evincing betrayal. A second later, he vanished.

The aches and pains returned in a rush, and she whimpered. Her stomach grew queasy. The sensation worsened until she hunched over and vomited bile.

Ugh. She should have gone with Bane. She'd *wanted* to go with Bane. But, by staying with Zion, she could keep him from giving chase, granting Bane time to heal.

"Bane obeyed you," Zion said, crouching at her side. "Why?"

"Don't know," she replied, and it was the absolute truth.

To her surprise, he let it drop. "Did he hurt you?"

Taking a page from Bane's playbook, she ignored the question and said, "Need my pills." Ragged moan. "Get my pills. Please, Zion."

Welcome to life with an addict.

He thought for a moment. "I know nothing about human medicine. You must tell me where to acquire the pills, and you must accompany me. Are you healthy enough to travel?"

"I'm not healthy enough to breathe." Despite an influx of pain, she labored to an upright position. The world spun, and the nausea worsened. "Carry me?" she asked, refusing to be embarrassed by her need for aid.

Zion gathered her in his arms and stood. What he didn't do? Open a portal. He remained rooted in place, rocking her back and forth, lost in thought. Then he nodded, as if he'd just come to a major decision.

"You know, little *dreki*. You once asked about my prophetic dream. Still wish to know what I saw you do?"

Ohhh. A bedtime story. "Yes, please."

He pursed his lips. "You clutched a dagger and stepped up to a combatant. Then you smiled—and shoved the dagger into his heart, killing him. A feat no one else could manage."

She *murdered* someone and *smiled* about it? "Who?" Zion had already given her two clues. *A feat no one else could manage*—like, say, taking down a dragon shapeshifter? And *his heart*—the victim was male.

"Who do you think?"

She gulped. The fact that he *wanted* her to make the kill…well, the victim had to be Bane, who would (probably) want her dead if ever he heard about Zion's dream.

Her dark side stirred, awakening. She whispered, *Strike first, die last.*

Apparently, Dark Nola was a real bitch who liked to hibernate, only coming out to play at the most inconvenient times. And she wasn't done talking.

He speaks the truth. You will kill Bane, and you will like it. His death is the key to obtaining everything you desire—health, happiness and incomparable strength.

Killing Bane would be the equivalent of going through a fast-cure drive through? Oh, the temptation.

In the end, she gave a violent shake of her head. As if she would ever listen to her dark side. Bane's death wasn't the key to anything. No one's was.

"Go to him, then, and see what happens," Zion said. "He'll die sooner rather than later. I'll be happy either way. But, if you stay with me, I will protect you from him and save your sister. The choice is yours."

CHAPTER EIGHT

Stalker shocker!

HE'D FOUND HER! It had only taken a day.

When Nola had dared dismiss Bane, he'd thought she hoped to save Zion from his wrath. Then he'd realized she feared for *Bane's* life—which was far worse. A sickly royal lacked confidence in his skill. The indignity! He would teach her better. Soon.

Bane had used their connection and her incredible scent to track her to a mountainous land known as America.

He fumed. Had he used the word *incredible* to describe honeysuckle? He'd meant *despicable*. Of course. Although, sometime during his centuries away, he'd begun to associate honeysuckle with home. How he missed Adwaeweth. He'd met Meredith there, trained with fellow soldiers and planned a future.

Anytime he'd envisioned the future, he'd never pictured a dark-haired royal who made him feel as if he were two men. The smart one who despised her, and the lusty one who wanted her desperately, madly, who felt like he inhaled sex every time she neared.

Again and again, Bane's lusty side replayed the moment Nola pressed her small, delicate hands against his chest, her skin as soft as silk. How her pupils had expanded, those starry irises more mesmerizing than a nebula. How she'd flushed, making him desperate to touch her, if only to feel the burn—he'd *wanted* to burn. How her feminine curves had molded to the hard planes of his body.

As soon as he had Nola in his possession once more, he would squire her away and pick another female to sate his body's needs. No more reluctance. Pain, yes. There would absolutely be pain. *Saying goodbye to Meredith...* But necessity beat sentimentality, so, there would be no reluctance. He had to vanquish any desire he harbored for the Terran princess.

Since Nola had already puzzled out the truth, she knew she held mystical sway over him. He couldn't force her to stay with him—as he'd proven. He required her cooperation.

Bane stalked down the sidewalk, determined. The beast unleashed an earsplitting roar, protesting the pursuit of the royal. *Remain calm. Do not transform.* He stuck to the shadows, multiple humans stopping to gape at him. Why? He'd washed the blood and dirt from his skin. He'd even stolen proper clothing—a black T-shirt and some kind of "camouflage" pants with multiple pockets. His daggers were hidden in his boots.

Get in my way, get mowed down.

Buildings knifed to the sky. Waning sunlight glinted off strange rolling boxes with humans seated inside. Bane's eyes burned and watered. He fastened his goggles in place, welcome darkness weaving through his sightline. Last night, he'd visited his lair, happy to discover his treasures untouched by time.

Bane turned a corner, losing Nola's innate fragrance. The beast unleashed another roar.

Quiet. Bane paused to sniff. An awful deluge of aromas clogged the air. Some type of oil, sweat, clashing perfumes, pine and—there. Honeysuckle, jasmine and lavender. His blood heated, and his guts tightened. His shaft swelled in an instant, throbbing painfully. For sex. Any partner would do.

Gritting his teeth, he crossed the street and turned another corner. Her sweet scent intensified. So close! Impatience frothed inside him, and he feared he would begin foaming at the mouth.

Remain on guard. Bane had scented six combatants in the area, Erik the Widow Maker, Knox and Vale among them. Like the others, Nola's sister had to die. But Bane wouldn't—couldn't—take a shot at Vale, or Nola would punish him.

Next time they were together, she could *order* him to die for Vale, and he would be forced to obey. She could demand he never seek revenge against Aveline.

Even after Bane had offered Vale a final two deal, Nola had chosen to remain with Zion. Because she didn't trust Bane. He started to stiffen, but fought it. *I am the only one she* should *trust.*

How did he convince her to switch allegiance? Answers were beyond him, his mind a chaotic mess, the beast continuing to protest his actions.

Bane slammed his fists into his temples and snaked around another corner. Finally! The beast quieted.

Nola was close.

His gaze darted. There she was, his princess, exiting a building across the street. He drew up short, his wits abandoning him, different parts of him experiencing different reactions. His mind—relief and a crazed need to yank her into his arms. His heart—an ache. His cock—the most intense throbbing of his life. *Harder than steel.*

Pale and shaky, she leaned against a brick wall. Above her hung a sign. Pharmacy.

His translator supplied a definition. *A place where medicines are sold.*

Fury chiseled through a layer of Bane's calm. The male courted her, procuring her medicine.

Could he truly begrudge Zion this victory? Nola had lost weight she couldn't afford to lose. Half-moon bruises marred the flesh beneath her eyes, her cheeks ashen. One hand clutched her stomach. The other rubbed her temple to ward off an ache.

But the pills harmed her as much as they helped her. So, yes. He could begrudge Zion. Nola needed Bane.

His chest puffed up with pride. He made her feel better. Him, and him alone. But, damn it, why was she sick? There had been many hybrid sovereigns over the years, yet none of them had ever battled disease.

In this condition, Nola wouldn't survive the Blood Rite, a rebirth in blood and flame. Although, he suspected she was, perhaps, maybe, possibly…stronger than she appeared. After all, she could teleport him, not just herself, a unique quality among royals, and one that required vast amounts of energy.

Bane took a step forward, intending to snatch Nola and run. Then he paused. How would he handle this?

Render her unconscious—gently!—so she couldn't order him to release her, then whisk her to his lair, where he would tape her mouth shut? When she awoke, he'd have to work as quickly as possible to win her over.

Could he win her over? He'd never courted a female,

not even Meredith. In Adwaeweth, females selected males, not the other way around.

No matter. He wouldn't allow the hand of his vengeance to fall for Zion, granting her loyalty to him, making things more difficult for Bane.

A telltale hum of electricity charged the air, signaling a combatant's nearness. Zion, no doubt.

Hurry! Once again, Bane jolted into motion. He crossed another street, and a rolling metal carriage—a metal horse of sorts, with many names; car, vehicle, sedan, truck and SVU—screeched to a halt, blaring a high-pitched horn.

He bared his teeth at the humans inside it, but kept motoring forward. Time wasn't his friend. Seconds, minutes, hours kept ticking away. Now, there were only two and a half weeks until the next assembly.

Zion came barreling out of the shop, his expression a dark mix of anger and concern. "I told you to remain at my side no matter what."

Bane darted into a tangle of shadows, only a short distance away. Still closing in fast…

"I didn't want to barf on the tile," Nola said.

"And you thought you spotted Vale," the male quipped.

"Maybe." She jutted her chin, just as she'd done with Bane. "It's not like I've failed to mention my priorities."

"You could have been harmed." Zion handed her a small white bottle. "Is this the medication you required?"

"Yes, thank you." The bottle rattled as she popped the top. "I don't want to know how you got a controlled substance without a prescription. I'm sure the answer will be blasted on the morning news." Trembling, she tossed two white pills into her mouth.

The warrior stiffened and scanned the surrounding area. "Come. I sense another combatant." He draped an arm around her waist, then led her down the sidewalk. "Let's find a safe house for you."

He'd clocked Bane's location before exiting the shop, hadn't he?

"You know," Nola said, panting, "if we were in an episode of *House Hunters*, this out of work author slash baker would have a budget of six million dollars."

"I have no idea what that means," Zion replied.

Neither did Bane, but he liked the amused gleam in her eyes.

He considered his next move. There were no rules against fighting in public, but a single skirmish would cause major problems. The more mortals who learned about the All War, the higher the likelihood other humans would become combatants.

Then I'll kill them, too. One way or another, Nola would be in Bane's possession before the sun set. He gave chase, reworking his plan along the way. A snatch and go was no longer possible. If he killed Zion, he could win and activate the magic wand—if he found it. Nola would have no one else to turn to; she'd have to choose Bane.

A dick move? Yes. Did he care? No. *I'll just disregard the prickle in my chest.*

When the couple disappeared around a corner, Bane increased his pace. He followed. Already halfway down the street, Zion lifted Nola to cradle her against his chest.

Growls reverberated in the back of Bane's throat, and they were *not* courtesy of the beast. *My princess. Mine!*

She glanced over the male's shoulder, clearly searching for something. Or someone.

Does she sense me?

Her gaze skittered over Bane, then zoomed back and widened.

Awareness seized him, heat sizzling under his skin, maddening him. Maddening the beast, too.

She shook her head and mouthed, "No."

Another layer of calm got chiseled away. No, don't let her get away? No, don't hesitate to murder Zion? No, he shouldn't resist her appeal any longer?

The muscles in Zion's upper back went rigid as he carried Nola around another corner. Oh, yes. The male definitely knew Bane nipped at his heels.

Very well. No need for secrecy.

As claws sprouted from his nail beds, Bane increased his speed. Approaching the corner…

The fine hairs on the back of his neck stood at attention. Zion would take precautions. He'd probably set Nola down. He might be manipulating energy in some way or another even now. His specialty, made possible by the diamond-like objects embedded in his skin. The type of energy didn't matter. Electrons, muons, taurine, quarks, gluons, time, space.

Somersaulting around the building, Bane shot out his legs—

Contact! His boots slammed into Zion's middle, the warrior stumbling backward.

Bane's momentum propelled him to his feet. He took stock. All around, Terrans had been halted midaction. If not for the mystical wards tattooed on Bane's nape, he would have been forced to halt, too.

Where was Nola? She had to be close. The beast had lapsed into silence. Where… There! She sat on the sidewalk, leaning against a building. Her head lolled forward, a pained moan slipping out.

Why hadn't she strengthened with Bane's nearness? Unless the block to keep him out of her head also affected her body?

His jaw hardened. "Give me the girl, and I'll let you live. Today, anyway."

"What do you want with her?" Zion fisted and unfisted his hands, his metal gloves glinting in what little light remained. He walked backward, putting a car between them.

Admit the truth to an enemy? Never. Bane sneered, saying, "What does any man want with any woman?"

He expected disgust from Zion, even rage, but it was suspicion that glowed in the male's dark eyes.

Even those who'd studied Adwaewethian culture had no idea the royals wielded absolute control over their warriors. Instinct prevented Adwaewethians from speaking about kingdom business with outsiders, ever, even when tortured.

Anyone who'd studied Bane specifically would know only that he'd won two All Wars, and he'd lost his wife right before the start of this one.

"What do *you* want with the mortal?" he demanded. What had the warrior dreamed about her?

Zion flashed a cruel smile. "You could get *what any man wants* from any woman here." He waved to indicate the bevy of frozen mortals. "And yet you follow this one. Perhaps you need her for something more, eh?"

Bane heard the implied threat. *You need her...so I will keep her just to spite you.*

"Instead of fighting, let's work together," Zion announced. "Erik the Widow Maker spent centuries planning for our escape. He has allied with a handful of combatants, Union among them. Union is on your trail, and Erik is on mine. They are determined to take out the strongest combatants, and they are always many steps ahead of us, their numbers increasing daily. At this rate, they'll win in a matter of weeks."

Union owned a belt that doubled his strength. Ability-wise, he could cast illusions. Nothing Bane couldn't handle. "My answer is no." He extended his hand and waved his fingers. "Come to me, Nola."

Her gaze met his, and for one suspended moment, they were the only two people on the planet, currents of awareness arcing between them. Then she shook her head and told him, "I'm staying with Zion. Please, trust me. This is for the best."

Another refusal. His fury exploded into rage. With a roar, he picked up the car parked between him and Zion and hurled it, further tearing the gash in his shoulder. *Worth it.* The vehicle crashed into a building across the street, busting a brick wall and shattering glass, granting Bane a straight shot to his target.

"I go with plan B, then." Zion launched across the distance, too, drew back his elbow and threw a punch.

Bane raised his arm to block. The metal glove shattered every bone in his hand, pain snatching the air from his lungs. An overflow of adrenaline kept him on his feet. With his uninjured hand, he clawed Zion's gut and confiscated one of his daggers. Blood and intestines poured from the wound.

Zion stumbled back once more, and Bane tossed the dagger, nailing him between the eyes. The other male dropped, and Bane raced over to stomp on his face.

He faced Nola. As he approached, she shook her head. "We can't stay together, Bane."

"We can. We will." Needing a hand free, just in case, he hefted her over his shoulder. Then, he launched down the street, her breasts bouncing against his back.

"You don't understand," she said, beating at his back.

"Make me understand, then." Behind him, footsteps sounded. Damn it! Zion had already healed and now gave chase. "Make me understand in a minute." He set Nola on down and turned. Shit! The bastard was closer than he'd realized.

They collided, Zion throwing a punch. His fist shattered Bane's sternum.

Breathing? Nothing but a pipe dream. In seconds, his level of pain reached new heights.

When the male threw another punch, Bane was ready. He ducked, then slammed his knee into Zion's testicles. A low blow, both literally and figuratively. No regrets.

Zion retaliated quickly, crouching to knock his ankles together. Bane hit the ground, rolled backward and popped up, slashing his claws over Zion's thigh. Leather pants and flesh tore, his opponent grunting.

Next, a ballet of movement ensued. Punching, ducking, kicking. They moved from the road to the sidewalk, crashing into frozen mortals and brick walls. With only one working hand and a single usable lung, Bane fought from a massive disadvantage. The smart thing to do? Retreat and heal. *Will die before I willingly abandon Nola.*

Zion's fist crashed into his temple. Stars winked through his vision, and he lost track of the world. Just for a second. Or so he thought. When he blinked, his opponent and his princess were halfway down the road.

Once again, Bane gave chase. He made it three steps when a loud honk rang out, a vehicle clipping his side. He took flight and smacked into the ground, new waves of pain racking his body.

By the time he made it to his feet, Zion and Nola were gone, the mortals no longer frozen. Other vehicles sped down the road.

The beast roared, and a blistering curse burst from Bane.

He had to change Nola's mind. Somehow. Nothing would stop Bane's quest for vengeance. *Nothing*.

CHAPTER NINE

Breaking up is hard to do

HAD NOLA MADE the right decision? The look Bane had given her...such betrayal.

With the golden god at her side, she could endure opioid withdrawal without actually going through opioid withdrawal. For her, Bane equaled pure, perfect strength. With Zion, she merely maintained the status quo, pounding back pills to survive. Addiction equaled weakness, and she was so danged tired of being weak. Especially now.

Aliens existed, and they warred for the right to rule Earth.

But staying with Bane meant endangering him. What if Zion's dream came true? Once, Nola would have laughed about the very idea. Her? Kill someone? Please! But if ever she lost control of her dark side...

Someone's gonna get cut.

"The magic pills must be working," Zion said, racing up, up a dark hill with Nola clutched against his chest. "You haven't vomited on me...again."

Her cheeks heated. Earlier this morning, she'd barfed on his shoes as he'd portaled her to the heart of Denver, Colorado. "Are you complaining? I'm sure I can rustle up more bile, if it'll brighten your day."

"No, thank you." With awe-inspiring stamina, Zion maintained a swift, steady pace, never huffing or puffing. He dodged towering trees, bits of cotton twirling on a soft breeze.

Looked like snow was falling. Reminded her of Russia. Russia reminded her of Bane. Beautiful Bane, who'd claimed he only wanted to screw her. Knowledgeable Bane, who had answers about her past, present and future. Injured Bane, who she'd abandoned yet again. Vulnerable Bane, the warrior she kinda sorta already... missed.

A crown of foliage blocked beams of moonlight. Frogs, locusts and crickets sang a midnight lullaby. *Croak. Buzz. Chirp.*

"I'm sure you have questions," Zion said.

Where to start? "You can freeze time, huh?" The people who'd milled around them had halted, not even seeming to breathe. Then, as Zion had carted her away, they'd started moving again, unaware minutes had passed.

"No. I manipulate energy, a far better skill." He looked left, right, then over his shoulder, on the lookout for a certain golden shadow. Then he used his free hand to open a portal. Just before he stepped through, he tensed and muttered, "Someone other than Bane invaded my dimension."

"How do you know?" Nothing looked out of place.

He motioned to a spot beyond a cluster of trees, and Nola cast her gaze over the lush, sunlit jungle—a hard breath clogged her throat. A severed leg dangled from a gnarled limb, blood dripping, pooling on the ground.

Her stomach performed a series of backflips. Had Bane

opened a portal for someone else, since he'd been unable
to visit the dimension himself, thanks to her command?

She wouldn't put anything past him. His savagery…
The man had disemboweled Zion and stabbed him between the eyes…and she'd been both horrified and excited by it, a shocking combination.

Maybe she had multiple personalities? Light Nola
and Dark Nola.

"This is Erik's doing," Zion snarled.

"How do you know?" she repeated.

"He's the one who placed cameras throughout the
ice mountains. He must have watched me enter or leave
the dimension. Without my knowledge." He sounded
incredulous.

The portal closed, wind whooshing, locks of hair
dancing against her cheek.

He trudged down the other side of the hill, saying,
"We will remain in this dimension, but leave Colorado."

"I can find us a place to stay." Somewhere she could
rest and recharge. Tomorrow, she would renew her hunt
for Vale.

"Where can we go that Bane won't find you?"

"I doubt he'll look for me again." His parting glare
had promised untold anguish.

"Oh, he'll look all right," Zion said, his voice infused
with satisfaction. He craved another battle, didn't he?

Her tired mind couldn't cobble together a clever response, so she pressed her index finger to his mouth,
saying, "Shh. It's quiet time now."

Only days ago, this guy had terrified her. Now she
had steel ovaries and shushed him?

Well, yeah. He was a good guy. He'd had plenty of
opportunities to harm her, but never had. As for Bane,

she didn't know if he was good or bad or both. She still didn't know what motivated him to chase after her.

At the bottom of the hill, Zion set her down. To help her stay upright, he anchored an arm around her waist. "I'm fighting two wars now," he said. "One to save myself, and one to save you."

"I'm not useless," she spat, defensive. "I'm contributing to your success."

"I never said you were useless."

Hadn't he, though? "Take me back to town, and I'll find a doctor to stitch your wounds—"

"I don't need a doctor," he interjected. "I've already healed."

Lucky! Had Bane healed? Where had he gone when they parted? Why hadn't he tried to speak in her mind? Had she inadvertently blocked him again, or did he hate her even more than before?

Gah! Why did she care? "Let's go shopping. We'll get new clothes, toiletries, a cell phone for you and a charger for me. And tampons!"

"Tampons?" His dark brows drew together. "Some type of weapon? My translator is showing me a bloody—"

New heat spread over her cheeks. "Just take me shopping. Please."

"Very well." He portaled them to a dark alley between two warehouse-type buildings.

There were no signs to indicate where they were. A full moon glowed alongside a million stars, the jewelry of the sky. The scent of rotting food, urine and waste tainted a warm breeze, and she screwed up her nose in disgust.

Zion pressed the diamonds before ushering her out

of an alley and into the warehouse on the right—a superstore. The shoppers were already frozen.

"I'll give you five minutes," Zion said. "No more."

"What about security cameras?"

"I've interrupted their feed." Strain created fine lines around his eyes and mouth.

Nola rushed down the aisles, tossing items into a cart. Later, she would tabulate the amount she owed, and mail the store a check. Oh! Pancake and maple syrup jelly beans. *Gimme!* Screw healthy living. She could have died today. Why not enjoy a treat now and then?

When she finished, Zion's dark eyes glinted with relief. He opened a portal to a small, two-bedroom house, with well-loved but chic furniture. A lace doily draped the coffee table and both side tables. The china cabinet displayed creepy porcelain dolls, while wall shelves held roadkill dressed in formal gowns—squirrels on the way to prom. Stained glass windows had the same flowery pattern as a faded rug with frayed edges.

"We will stay here tonight, and rest up," he said. "Tomorrow, I resume the war."

And Bane? What would he do? "Whose home is this?" she asked. "And where are we, exactly?"

"The house is ours. For now. There are no neighbors or tenants. As for our location, I think it's better for us both if you don't know." He headed for the front door, telling her, "Stay here. I must check the traps I placed around the perimeter."

Nola picked the master bedroom, the only room with a private bathroom, plugged her cell phone into an outlet and hid pills in the pockets of her new pants. Old habits might die hard, but they resurrected quite easily. She showered, brushed her teeth a thousand times, then changed into a T-shirt that read Official Hug Collector, sweatpants and house-shoes with fuzzy dogs.

The last dose of painkiller wore off, aches returning to torment her. She reclined on the bed, devoured the bag of jelly beans and sent Vale multiple texts, just in case.

Nola: Are you okay? Where are you? I'm so worried!

Nola: When Zion originally absconded with me, you tried to sacrifice your life for mine, and I will never ever forgive you!

Nola: I'm so sorry, V! You're forgiven, I promise. I'm just worried about you. I love you, and I miss you. If Knox hurts you, I will rip out his other-worldly heart. (You know he's an alien, right?)

With access to the internet, Nola did a search for "Addwaywith," "Adwaeweth," "dragon shape-shifters," "All War" and "alien sightings" but nothing helped.

Dang it! She wanted, needed more information about Bane. Knowledge was power.

A shirtless Zion stalked into the bedroom, his bronzed skin glistening with sweat. Why, why, why wasn't she attracted to him?

"You're safe," he said, easing onto the foot of the bed. "For the moment, anyway."

"But you're not?"

He shrugged. "I'm a combatant. Combatants aren't safe until the war ends."

Meaning, Vale wouldn't be safe. Nola rubbed her churning stomach. "I got a cell phone for you. Now we can communicate whenever we're apart." She taught him how to text, make calls and Google images of specific locations, so that he could portal to places he'd never visited.

Intrigue lit his eyes. "Amazing." For well over an hour, he played with the phone, asked questions about different websites, weapons and the "Terran military." She answered to the best of her ability, wishing she could help Bane this way, too. Maybe he'd finally view her in a better light.

Her cell rang, and she jerked. An unknown number flashed over the screen, and she twittered with excitement. Could be Vale, could be a solicitor. *Please be Vale, please be Vale.*

Zion frowned and looked around. "What's happening?"

"Someone's using their phone to call mine." She slid her finger over the screen and placed the device at her ear. "H-hello?"

"You're alive." Her sister's voice whispered over the line, equal parts joy and relief.

Tears of joy welled. Not wanting to worry Vale, she attempted an upbeat greeting. "Vale, you gorgeous ball-breaker, you're alive, too." A sob escaped, ruining her efforts. "I've been so worried."

"Nola," Zion said with a frown. He collected a teardrop as if it were a fragile butterfly's wing. "This call upsets you?"

"No, no. I'm happy." Her sister was alive and well.

"Where are you?" Vale asked, still whispering. "*How* are you? Is Zion treating you well?"

"He is. He told me it's better if I don't know where we are, and I agree. He's protecting me from a blond giant who hopes to abduct me, reasons unknown." "Hoped," not "hopes." Past tense. She wanted to say more so, so badly, wanted to admit everything. But, of course, the words died on her tongue. "I'm surviving minute by minute, some tougher than others."

Zion frowned again, his brow furrowed with the barest hint of irritation. No doubt he'd wished to glean more info about Bane. Well, too bad, so sad.

"Tell Zion to steal pills for you," Vale said. "I don't want you in pain."

"He did. Got me a whole bucketful, in fact. I've taken one or two." *Or four.* "I'm tempted to pop a couple more, but I'd rather get clean." The desire solidified. Yes! She would get clean. No more pills, period. No more bargaining with herself, as she'd done every other time she'd tried to quit. No more promises to herself, only to break them.

Countless times, she'd tried tapering her dosage to lessen the severity of her withdrawal, cutting another five milligrams every week, but she'd always failed, making bargains with herself. *If I take more now, I'll take less later.*

But she never took less, so the bargains never worked out in her favor.

"Enough about me," she said. "How are *you*?"

"No changing the subject, sis. You know you can't go cold turkey," Vale said. "The strain on your heart—"

"Someone comes," Zion interrupted.

Nola's heart leaped. Maybe Bane—

"Multiple someones," he added, and she withered. Bane was a lone wolf. "We must go, Nola."

In unison, she and Vale professed their love. Nola tried to say more, to reassure her sister that she wouldn't end up in the hospital like last time. And she had a thousand questions about Vale's time with Knox and her new status as a combatant, but Zion plucked the phone from her grip, ending the call.

Dismay tickled the back of her neck. "How do you know someone's here?"

"As long as a combatant isn't close to another combatant, we can sense the approach of others, the air suddenly electric." He replaced her house-shoes with tennis shoes, as if she were an invalid. "I planted devices throughout the house. They prevent anyone from portaling inside, and us from portaling out. I'll have to fight to get us out."

Her palms sweat. "Why don't you freeze our uninvited guests? Then we can sneak away."

"I would if I could. I must recharge."

So, Zion's ability to manipulate energy required some kind of internal battery. Good to know.

"I'll kill everyone, and then sneak you out. Better?"

"Uh…"

He picked her up, carried her to the walk-in closet and sealed her inside the small, darkened space, calling, "Do not exit until I return." His footsteps sounded, then faded.

Her heart raced faster, faster, and her stomach twisted. She rocked back on her heels. If he got hurt while she hid in the closet like a coward, she would hate herself forever.

If only Bane had agreed to the alliance. They could have guarded the other's back. Of course, if Zion's dream was a genuine prediction, an alliance would put Bane in more danger.

Or would it? Earlier, when she'd decided to stay with Zion in order to keep Bane safe, she'd been sick, exhausted, foggy and afraid of her dark side. Now, she had a clearer mind and wondered why she'd entertained so much fear. Dark Nola had never overtaken her before. Why should she believe Dark Nola would *ever* overtake her?

She shouldn't. She would continue to control herself, and that was that.

And why should she believe Zion over herself?

Again, she shouldn't. *I won't let myself harm Bane.* Not now, not ever. Which meant they could spend time together!

Not taking time to think this through, she closed her eyes and pictured her golden god. A method that had both worked and failed. Maybe, like Zion, she'd just needed to recharge. She—

—gasped, a tide of warmth flowing over her. For a moment, she felt weightless. Then, the closet vanished and cool air kissed her face as she scanned her new surroundings. A night-darkened forest. A stream of moonlight illuminated Bane, sending shivers down her spine.

He battled five…ten…sixteen men. Humans? Most held guns, grunting and groaning when Bane struck and their bones gave an audible *pop.*

With an animalistic roar, Bane hurled two large men across the distance. The pair slammed into different trees and slid to the ground, where they stayed, their heads hanging at odd angles. They were dead, and Bane had killed them viciously, without remorse.

The two sides of Nola warred about the proper reaction. Horror or excitement?

Bane lunged and grabbed another man by the throat. A man with two knives, doing his best to land a killing blow.

Nola looked away when Bane used his claws to

remove his opponent's hands. A howl of pain pierced the night, followed by a thud, the weapons and appendages plopping on the ground.

Do I leave, or do I stay?

Leave, definitely. Wasn't like she could help him. Oh! Unless she managed to portal Zion here, and convinced the two guys to work together. But Bane must have sensed her presence. Even as he disemboweled a soldier, he zoomed his gaze in her direction. Their eyes met, locked. Surprise shook him, and he stilled. A mistake. A soldier sank a blade into his chest.

Roaring, Bane batted the weapon away.

Horror shoved a protest out of Nola's mouth. "No!"

The remaining soldiers focused on her. Blood flash-froze in her veins. A tide of panic surged, threatening to drown her.

She backed up a step, then another and another, stopping only when she ran into a tree. Problem: the tree reeked of sweat. And it breathed. And moved.

Oh, crap. The tree was a man.

He hooked an arm around her neck and pressed a gun against her temple. "Behave, and you might walk away from this."

CHAPTER TEN

Will he live—or die—for you?

A HUMAN TERRORIZED Bane's future queen. The human would die screaming.

Sweat beaded on his brow, and panic gnawed on his mind, devouring his good sense. He kept thinking, *Can't lose her. Not her. Anyone but her.*

Anyone but her? Hardly! If necessary, he would find another royal.

He swallowed a harsh denial. He wanted *this* princess. To save time and energy.

Saving time and energy is the reason I feel so...crazed when she's nearby? Or faraway.

Nola's eyes widened with terror, her cheeks ghostly pale. The sight shredded what remained of his control.

Bane remembered the last time an armed man had stood behind a woman he wished to protect...remembered how Meredith had gasped for breath she couldn't catch, death unstoppable as it spread through her body.

He stalked, no, ran, charging after her. Adrenaline pumped through his veins at warp speed. Muscles doubled in size and bones hardened into steel. The pain in his shoulder dulled. His mind devolved further, his thoughts fragmenting but also sharpening. As sharp as daggers.

Save her. Kill—them—all.

Despite Nola's nearness, the beast roared with fury, making his rage a thousand times worse.

Closing in, faster and faster...

He was grateful Nola wasn't sobbing, begging or screaming hysterically. Actually, he was impressed. She had a weak body, yes, but such a keen mind and—

Monstrous wings popped from his back, and he hissed a curse. Quick glance. No feathers, just a membranous web edged by a bulbous substance, with a bony hook extending from every joint—the beast's wings.

He'd never partially transformed before. Never maintained consciousness while the beast fought on his behalf. And in the presence of a princess no less.

How it occurred, he didn't know. Why it occurred, he could only guess. Perhaps, as a hybrid, she could control the beast only half as well as a full-blooded queen. Perhaps the beast planned to protect her. Yes, the fiend hated Nola with the same vehemence as Bane, but no one—no one!—had the right to harm what belonged to them.

Bane grinned. Two warriors for the price of one.

Let's do this. He unleashed hell, using the wings' razor sharp tips to slick through the neck of every soldier he passed.

The scent of blood tainted the air. Songs of agony played in the background.

"Stay back!" Nola's captor shouted, tapping the barrel of the gun against her temple. His finger twitched on the trigger.

He was a human mercenary on Erik's payroll. His love of money would be his downfall.

Nola whimpered, the sound scraping at Bane's ears.

His cells became embers. His organs became kindling. An inferno raged inside him.

Careful. If he fully transformed, he could harm his princess irrevocably. She wouldn't know she could order the beast to stand down; or that, without a verbal or telepathic command, the beast could do anything he wanted, anytime, to anyone. *Calm. Steady.*

Gunfire exploded behind him, bullets piercing his wings. *Ignore the flare of pain.* They wanted him to slow; he picked up speed. *Must save Nola, whatever the cost.*

A golden beam of moonlight illuminated her and her captor—and the contingent of humans who loomed behind them in no discernible pattern.

"I told you to stay back! I'll shoot her, I swear I will." The mercenary holding Nola cocked his gun, making her jerk and gasp. "Stop!"

When Bane thought he'd reached the limits of the soldier's patience, he did it, he stopped and held up his hands in a gesture of innocence.

"I'm so sorry," Nola mouthed.

He balled his fists. Earlier, he'd come upon Erik, who'd been on the trail of Knox and Vale. Bane had thought to snatch Vale and use her to gain Nola's cooperation. Just before he made his move, Erik and two other combatants—Adonis and Rush—ambushed the couple, ultimately stealing away with her.

Hadn't taken long to realize the viking and his allies had no plans to harm the girl. Bane then turned his attention to Erik's army of humans. The perfect outlet for his rage. He'd planned to decimate the army—an obstacle to his prize—find Vale and whisk her to his lair, then contact Nola. Instead, Nola had teleported to him once again. Why?

If she'd already realized the error of her ways—never teleport without speaking to him first, or she might end up in the middle of a battlefield—he would consider the possibility of thinking about forgiving her—for the right price.

With her life in jeopardy, he retooled his tasks. *Kill her captor in the fastest and most violent way possible, grab Nola, find Vale and rift to my lair.*

"I've decided to walk away," Bane told the mortals. A lie. "I suggest you let me."

"What?" Nola squeaked. "You're abandoning me?"

Never. But he needed the males to think so. Needing a genuine reaction from her, he adopted his darkest, meanest sneer, and put genuine fury into his tone. "The way *you* abandoned *me*?"

She flinched, and his chest tightened. "I hurt you, and I'm sorry, but I did it to protect you," she said. "And yeah, okay, I was about to abandon you here, too, but only to protect you. Shouldn't I be praised for my sacrifice and selflessness? My utter brilliance?"

She'd decided to stay with Zion to protect Bane? He... didn't know what to think about that. He only knew the hottest flames of his fury gained new ground. She'd tried to shield him, and now some human thought to shoot her in the head?

A human who grinned, smug, thinking he'd cowed a beast. "You aren't walking anywhere."

Boom, boom, boom. Another round of bullets pierced his wings. His legs, too. Bane rolled over the ground again, grabbing two guns his victims had dropped. He aimed and hammered at the triggers, shooting one

missile after another. Grunts of shock and agony re-
sounded, men toppling.

While the other soldiers were distracted, Bane lurched
to his feet and sprinted into the cover of trees, pretending to retreat. In reality, he circled the army without
their knowledge, planning to come up behind Nola and
her captor. As he tore around trees, his ears picked up
different voices.

—*Where'd he go?*—
—*Follow him!*—
—*Go, go, go! I'll take care of the girl.*—

His control? Almost completely razed. One gun, out
of bullets. He dropped it and palmed a dagger. The other
gun had one bullet left. Excellent. He charged into the
masses, using the dagger to swiftly and quietly kill everyone in his path. Bodies toppled. Soon, no one stood
between him and the object of his rage.

The male sensed him and turned. Too late. Bane
reached him, batted the gun away from Nola and shoved
the dagger into his temple. No hesitation. The bastard
jolted and squeezed off a shot, the blast deafening.
Thankfully, both bullet and man hit the ground.

Bane aimed and fired off the final shot—in the male's
face. Brain tissue and blood sprayed.

Nola wrapped her arms around her middle and stared
down at the dead body. Tremors racked her.

He'd thought her terrified before. Here, now, she
looked broken, and the sight was doing strange things
to Bane's chest. It felt like someone had cracked open
his ribs and strapped a barbed wire around his heart.
Maybe she won't turn out like other queens, after all.

A few feet away, a gun cocked. Cursing, he threw
an arm around Nola, yanked her against him and spun.

A bullet tore through his back, in one side, out the other. The pain proved intense but manageable. Though he yearned to punish the shooter, he wouldn't risk Nola's life.

Lifting her into his arms, he raced into a thicket of trees. As he ran, satisfaction filled him. Finally! He had the princess in his possession. Once he evaded the army, he would open a rift to his lair. Soon, she would be safe and surrounded by his things...

One step closer to my goal. After he convinced Nola to work with him, he would return to Colorado, alone, and rescue Vale. All would be well.

Footsteps echoed behind him. Faster.

"Thank you," she whispered, embracing him. Tremors still racked her. "For everything."

The barbed wire tightened, and he winced. For centuries, he'd yearned to see Aveline ruled by terror. Since a royal was a royal, he should enjoy Nola's suffering, too. One day, one day soon, she would deserve this. But...

He experienced no enjoyment. He wanted to raze this world and present the remains at her feet, wanted to vow he would forever protect her from feeling this way again. *Ridiculous!*

Bane rushed around trees and boulders, leaped over gnarled roots. Sharp branches sliced at his upper body, deepest in his biceps.

Nola mewled, and he cursed. *Already failing at my task.* He'd let the branches slice her, too.

He waited for a volley of complaints...

Odd. Aveline had complained even before her change.

Pleasantly surprised, he readjusted Nola's position against him, pressing her face into the hollow of his neck. Her soft curves molded to his muscular frame, the simple action somehow battering through his defenses, leaving him bare.

He hardened, painfully so. *Neglected body, that's all.* Teeth gritted, he asked, "Better?" Would her nearness always affect him so strongly?

"Yes, thank you," she whispered, remaining lax. "Bane? Heal quickly."

Two words, yet he heard absolute and utter command in her voice. In an instant, pain consumed him, bullets popping out, flesh weaving back together, until only the shoulder wound remained, as raw and angry as ever.

All the while, Bane's thoughts swung from the highest of highs to the lowest of lows. Nola was concerned for his well-being. Concern often heralded caring. If she came to care for him, she would want to stay with him. Better, she would do as he wished. But it was clear she understood the worst of her talents, which created a major complication for him. He couldn't share too much about his past, his goals or his motivation, for fear she would order him to relinquish his vendetta and lose the war. He'd have to win her over another way.

"Why did you come to me, princess? Mere hours ago, you chose to stay with Zion."

She sighed, the warmth of her breath tickling the base of his neck. "We were ambushed. I thought if you and Zion worked together—"

"No. Not happening. Not now, not ever." Tension knotted his muscles. "Why do you continue to aid him?"

"Why do you hate me?" she countered.

He needed her aid, and didn't want to scare her off, but he couldn't blunt the truth. "In your quest to save Vale, you will ruin my life."

"Maybe, but you hated me *before* Vale joined the war."

A pause. Then, "Do you know what you are, Nola?"

"Yes." She flattened her dainty little hand against his pec and sank her nails into his skin. It was the touch of a lover...or a woman who expected a terrible emotional blow and needed a shield. "I'm a girl, a baker, a writer, a worried sister and an...other-worlder?"

He bit out, "You are so much more than an other-worlder."

"It's true, then." Her breath hitched. "I suspected it, so I shouldn't be freaking out on the inside. But I'm totally freaking out on the inside, Bane."

Why did he suddenly want to smile?

Sensing he'd lost the army at last, Bane pictured his lair, and stroked his thumb over the Rifters. Roughly a hundred yards ahead, a portal opened, layers of air separating, revealing inky blackness.

He rushed through the opening and spun, facing the forest in case anyone attempted to follow. Portals couldn't be closed manually, so he had to wait until this one shut on its own.

As soon as he and Nola were sealed inside the cave, his satisfaction returned. Long ago, he'd built this one-room shelter in the heart of a mountain, and refortified its walls with stone pillars. Now, limestone scented the cool, musty air.

"So dark," Nola cried.

Bane excelled in darkness. Nola should, too. The fact that she didn't... *Is she more human than Adwaewethian?*

Could a human survive the Blood Rite?

The barbed wire tightened again, a sharp, shooting pain striking his lungs, slaying his next breath. He placed Nola in front of a rocky wall and pressed against her shoulders, urging her to sit. He remained on his feet.

Deep in his throat, the beast ignited embers. When enough embers had formed, he angled his head and unleashed a stream of fire, flames licking the torches he'd anchored to the walls. Amber light chased away the darkness and bathed Nola, paying tribute to her delicate features.

Ignore her allure. Do not harden again. Do not—

Too late. He hardened again, overcome by ravenous hunger.

"You sprayed fire," she said, her eyes as wide as saucers. "You sprayed fire from your mouth."

"I did, yes." He crouched in front of her and spread his wings to block out the rest of the cavern. For this conversation, Bane intended to be her sole focus. "Do you. Know what. You are?"

She met his gaze. Her pupils were blown, her starry irises glazed and wild. The pulse at the base of her neck thumped in time to his as she wrung her fingers together.

"I'm an other-worlder," she said, breathless.

"You are. And you will never be able to tell anyone but other Adwaewethians. We are blessed with a natural-born instinct that prevents us from discussing our secrets with outsiders."

She nodded, eager. "I've experienced such an instinct."

Concentrate. Stop staring at her mouth. With the fuller upper lip, and heart-shaped slant in the center. "Centuries ago, my queen discovered your world, and sent a contingent of breeders to mate with the inhabitants.

It's a crime punishable by death for *every* Adwaewethian. Including you. But Aveline did it, anyway." He couldn't mask his rage, his hate or his bitterness, so he didn't even try. "She sent me here with two objectives. Win the All War, and destroy the evidence of her misdeeds."

Nola gave her lips a nervous swipe with her tongue. Damn it! He hadn't stopped staring. "Kill the breeders, or their children?" She gulped. "Or both?"

"Only a handful of the children. The ones who would grow to be queen of all hybrids."

Realization dawned on her features, right along with dismay. "D-did you kill babies, then?"

"No." He held her gaze, not daring to blink. "Before I found a single royal, I was frozen in the arctic. Centuries passed, more and more hybrids born, the line diluted. But I never gave up hope. I often sensed a royal's birth and death, but never a true connection. Until one fateful day. I felt her, and she felt me. I knew she would find me."

Her jaw dropped. She searched his gaze. "And did she? Find you, I mean?"

He framed her exquisite face with his big, calloused hands, the contrast between their skin tones mesmerizing. Gold against snow-white. "She did."

The muscles of her neck worked as she swallowed. "Through the link you both share?"

He nodded and the shine in her stunning brown eyes dimmed. Her hand flew to her mouth, and she shook her head.

"I need a fact cleared up," she said, her voice unsteady, but also filled with a strength he admired despite himself. "You were ordered to kill her?"

Again, he nodded.

Her gaze clashed with his. "Are you here to kill *me*?"

CHAPTER ELEVEN

Beat the heat with these tried and true tips!

NOLA'S MIND WAS a field of land mines. Every new thought caused an explosion, starting a chain reaction of emotion. Shock, fear and incredulity. Disbelief and uncertainty. Excitement, hope and happiness, even dread. Queen. Queen Nola. Queen Magnolia Lee. Orphaned as a baby. Sickly, unwanted by other families. Shuffled from one foster home to another, some good, some bad. Some *really* bad. The weird girl with strange impulses she couldn't discuss with anyone other than a golden god she'd just met but had known in her dreams for years. The grown woman unable to enjoy intimacy with a man without vomiting. The addict. Fledgling teleporter. Controller of dragons. Alien.

"I will *not* harm the Terran queen," Bane said. "I will protect her with my life, even though—yes—I hate the power she wields over me."

He'd avoided her question. Or had he? "That power. Are you bound to her—" *me?* "—forced to do whatever she commands?"

"Yes," he hissed.

"D-does this future queen have a name?" *Can't be me. But it might be me.*

Would he say her name?

"She does." He released her, then. No connection, no body heat. Numbing cold infiltrated her bones. Peering deep into her starry eyes, he finally said, "Her name is Nola Lee."

Gulp. "I can't be a queen. I can't rule anyone, much less an entire race of warriors and beasts. I can't even rule myself! My life is a mess." Except, the prospective job did kind of thrill her. Had she finally found her calling? Her passion?

Ruler of the freaking world, baby!

Too many flaws. Or maybe just the right amount?

Argh! The back and forth was beyond annoying.

"You're right. You are not a queen. Yet," Bane replied. "Until your…coronation, you hold the title of princess, your abilities limited."

What! If she could teleport with limited abilities, what would she be able to do with limit*less* abilities? The prospect alone made her shivery.

Bane shifted, adding, "I am your warrior, forced to obey your every command."

Her warrior. Hers, and hers alone. Bane, who killed with such ease. Who aroused her and frightened her for reasons she didn't yet understand. Who was currently looking at her as if he wanted to strip her naked and eat her for dinner…or bag and tag her, then hang her on the wall as a trophy. At last she comprehended his hot and cold treatment.

Too often lupus, fibro or opioids had acted as *her* master, forcing her to stay in bed when she'd rather be anywhere else, doing anything else.

"Once, you all but begged me to order you around. *Tell me to heal quickly and regrow my foot.* Dance monkey dance," she mocked. "Remember? I obeyed you, and you obeyed me, and look at the magnificent result." Deep breath in, out. "I didn't ask to be your queen, Bane. So why blame me for our situation?"

He narrowed his eyes. "I've served many royals. One day, you will change into the worst version of yourself. You will be cold. Determined. Deadly. You will exert your sovereignty over me, forcing me to do reprehensible deeds. Queens always do."

The hatred in his tone clanged like a death knell. He *really* hated Adwaewethian royals. But that wasn't the reason she withered inside. What he described...she'd *already* met the worst version of herself. Dark Nola.

Realization: *I'm not delusional... I'm transitioning.*

Fight or flight took over, fear welling and denial surging. This couldn't be happening.

No, she couldn't *let* it happen. She would stay and fight. Dark Nola wouldn't win. "Did you, perhaps, date a princess who became queen?" Beneath the hatred, she thought she'd heard torment. Why agonize about what he was saying unless he'd been in love?

"I did," he offered tightly.

"And she changed?" Nola persisted.

His gaze lowered, snagged on her lips and warmed. "She did."

Heart speeding up, she said, "As long as you leave Vale alone, I have no intention of harming you, or ordering you around. Besides, I'm nothing like your other queen."

He laughed without a shred of amusement, raising her hackles. "You think you're stronger than Aveline, that you can do what she did not and remain kind, caring? Sorry to be the one to hit you with truth, Nola, but all royals change. You will, too. You won't be able to help yourself."

Tired of being called weak, she lifted her chin. "Challenge accepted."

He peered at her for a long while, silent, and she peered right back. A mistake. Torchlight loved him, painting his rough, masculine features with raw, sensual strokes. His flaxen mane glowed like a halo.

"Not a challenge. A fact."

"I've been rejected my entire life, Bane. I've been found lacking in every way. I've had zero advantages. No money or special education. What I *have* had? So many absences from high school I nearly flunked out. Constant sickness and pain. Medical bills I'll never be able to pay off. Months spent in bed, dreaming of being someone, anyone else. Foster families who starved me, called me terrible names, or beat me. So yeah. Physically, your Aveline can take me down, no doubt about it. Yay for her. She can do the same thing as a gust of wind. But mentally? Emotionally? I'm unmatched." The more she spoke, the higher her tone and the louder her volume.

Why were some people born into blessing and others born into curse?

Bane's temper detonated, his breathing faster, his color brighter. "Who beat you?"

Why? So he could go and kill them? "Doesn't matter."

He gripped her forearms and shook her. "Tell me."

A little smug—okay, a lot smug—she grinned up at him. "Why don't you make me? Oh, that's right. Because you can't. In this, *you* are weak, my will stronger than yours."

He narrowed his eyes, huffing and puffing like a big, bad wolf. "You're right. In this, I'm the weaker of us. But

I understand the future, you do not. Do you want to know the first thing queens do after their coronation? Kill their loved ones to ensure no one can be used against them. I was spared because I was too valuable as a warrior and trainer. Years later, Aveline ordered me to stand down while she killed the woman I loved right in front of me."

His confession tore her to shreds, his grief like salt in her wounds. The pain he must carry inside him…more than any one person could bear. And oh, the loss he'd suffered. A loss she knew well.

Would she one day want to kill Vale?

No. No way.

As she and Bane stared at each other, something wonderful…terrible…happened. Defenses melted away, desire stirring inside her, hot and liquid, past pains fading away. Where they touched, she burned and ached.

"Bane," she rasped.

"Nola." He loosened his grip and traced his hands up and down her arms. Every upward glide gentled, and yet the aches intensified. With every downward glide, he lost a layer of calm. Now, only savage hunger remained.

"You hate me," she said, his incredible heat seeping through her clothing. "For what you believe I'll become."

"I do."

"But you…you want me, too?"

"I do," he repeated and this time, he sounded drugged. Up, down. Up, down. "I want it to stop. Why won't it stop?" Agonizingly slow, he trailed his fingers along her collar, then down, down to her breasts.

She gasped, arching into his wicked touch, shocking him, but delighting him, too. As he squeezed and kneaded her, she watched his face for any type of reaction. His pupils dilated. The sight sent shivers coursing through her. No hint of sickness.

How many times had she made it to second base with a guy, her mind rock solid but her body plagued by extreme nausea? Before each incident, she'd convinced herself things would be different. Alas. With Bane, her stomach remained calm while the rest of her revolted. Goose bumps spread over her chest and arms, sensitizing her skin. Her nipples beaded, pressing against her bra. Every time she inhaled, friction sparked. Mmm. Friction. Between her legs, the most delicious ache ignited, so unlike anything she'd experienced in the past. Glorious arousal, untainted by sickness.

What would happen if she yanked Bane closer and—
No! Don't go there. Not with him.

Using the pad of his thumbs, he traced circles around her nipples. "Tell me to walk away, princess."

Ahhhh. Please don't walk away. But, but…he had to leave before she humiliated herself and asked…begged… for more. "Be strong enough to walk away on your own, sweetness."

He flinched, then scowled, his arms falling to his side, leaving her bereft and far colder than before.

Drawing her knees up, creating a block between them, she asked, "What do queens do, exactly?" Back to the subject at hand.

"Whatever they desire." He fisted and unfisted his hands, breathing in slowly, exhaling heavily, some of his tension evaporating. "Most queens are cosseted from birth, hidden until their Blood Rite."

A new prickle of foreboding. "What's a Blood Rite?"

"A time when a potential queen kills an enemy and

wears his blood. A warrior breathes fire into her body. She burns to death and rises from the ashes."

Nola didn't know a whole lot about mythology, only tidbits she'd picked up from sci-fi–obsessed Vale, but Adwaewethians sounded more like phoenix than dragons. Burn to death, rise stronger. "Commit murder… paint myself in blood…let myself be burned to death? That's what you expect *me* to do?" He had to be kidding.

"Yes, yes and yes. You will rise different. Evil. Your humanity, gone."

He'd just described her dark side to a T. But she'd meant what she'd said. Mentally and emotionally she was strong. She would prevail against any twisted urges. "Why tell me these things? To scare me into refusing?"

"I tell you these things so you'll be prepared. I want you to take part in the Blood Rite. And you'll want it, too. An increase in power is irresistible."

More power would be amazing, yes. Beyond amazing. More power meant better protection for Vale, beating Nola's addiction and curing her diseases. More power meant…everything.

"There she is," he said. Malice dripped from his tone and glittered in his eyes. "The royal who understands that her abilities and dominion are life."

How could he read her so easily? "Has a queen ever *not* risen from the ashes?"

He gave a clipped nod. "Yes. Many."

Great! Wonderful! Understanding of abilities and dominion might be life, but working to gain understanding could spell her death. "What happens if I refuse?"

He flinched as if she'd punched him. "I'll find another princess. She'll seize the crown and take what's yours."

"Give me a moment to deal with my disappointment.

An-n-nd done. You can't miss what you'd never had."
Except—no, no, not another "except." *Too late*. Nola's
dark side frothed with fury at the thought of someone—
anyone—trying to take what belonged to her.

The weight of Bane's mighty gaze nearly drilled her
into the dirt. "You're not the only Adwaewethian hybrid
on this planet. The others—the males—play host to a hi-
bernating beast. As soon as you complete the Blood Rite,
those beasts will awaken. Though they despise you, they
will be bound to your will, will die to protect you. Now,
imagine it's another female who does the waking. Afterward, she and her new army will hunt you down and
slaughter you—as well as everyone you've ever loved."

Scare tactics, or truth? The truly terrifying thought?
It was probably both. "Will I gain a beast?"

"No. Only males are born with a beast, and they are
nontransferable. You will have something better. The
ability to heal yourself, and your men. The regenera-
tion of my foot was merely a foretaste of your healing
potential."

For a moment, she felt like dancing and singing
Disney princess style. No more withdrawal! No more
anguished nights and pain-filled days! No more weak-
nesses! Oh, the temptation. But there had to be a catch.
There was *always* a catch.

As Carrie used to say, *The devil doesn't show up with
a pitchfork. He shows up with a lie about your fondest
dream.*

No matter how desperately Nola wanted to heal, she
wouldn't kill someone to do it, not even an enemy. "I'm
confused about your tie to Aveline. She's your queen,
but not your queen, and you both do and do not have to
obey her orders?"

A muscle jumped underneath his eye. He gave a stiff nod. "The situation is…complicated."

"Don't worry, I can catch up and keep up. So, this royal who you both can and cannot disobey, she ordered you to murder all royals, including me?"

Another stiff nod.

"Well," she said, tossing up her arms. "How are you able to betray her and help me?"

He slanted his head to the side, features alight with surprised intrigue. What, he'd expected her to be dumb as a box of rocks?

Heck, maybe she was. His scent kept screwing with her concentration. And dang it, she kept getting lost in his amber eyes and the frame of long, black lashes. Her pulse points fluttered, the urge to touch him almost overwhelming.

Gah! She'd begun to straighten out her legs—her shield—unbidden. Begun to reach out… When she realized what she was doing, she tried to stop herself. Too late. She traced her fingertips along the golden stubble on his jaw. A white-hot bolt of electricity shot through her, pricking her nerve endings. For a moment, the princess and her warrior didn't move, or even breathe. Then he clasped her wrist in a bruising grip.

She expected him to push her away, if only to prove his strength. She *wished* he would push her away.

Breathing more heavily, he pressed her open palm against his cheek and leaned into her touch. "Anytime a princess lives to adulthood, a warrior's link to a queen is gradually weakened. The moment I sensed you, Aveline lost her vise-grip on me, allowing me to speak inside your head, and you inside mine. After your Blood Rite, I can bond to you, officially, severing all ties to Aveline."

Reeling. "Why would you pick me over her? She harmed your loved one, yes, but you don't even know me." *I'm not sure* I *know myself anymore.* "There's a phrase Earthlings—Terrans...whatever!—use. *Better the devil you know than the devil you don't.*"

"I know you are not a devil. Yet." He ran his tongue over his straight white teeth and released her hand. "Why did you choose Zion over me?"

Telling him would only freak him out and prove his theories about her supposed personality change. "I'll consider telling you, *if* you answer my question."

He bristled, grating, "Aveline can drain others to death with a simple touch. The woman she murdered? Meredith. She was...my wife. Nothing you do or say will ever hurt me worse."

Her chest swelled with sympathy. Poor Bane. He'd lost the woman he loved because of another woman's selfishness and greed, leaving a hole in his heart. A hole as unfixable as the wound in his shoulder, since Aveline helped fill it with hatred. Now, it festered, leaking poison.

If only Nola could reach inside his mind and soothe every agonizing memory. On the other hand, he wouldn't be the same man without them. His experiences had shaped him, and Nola liked the end result.

Her eyes widened. She did. She liked him. His intensity and his drive. His determination and strength. The man never gave up. When he got knocked down, he fought his way back up.

"I'm so sorry, Bane," she said.

"You didn't kill Meredith. Aveline did, and with your help, she will pay. *My* price is blood and pain," he said, his satisfaction almost tangible. He raised his chin. "In return for your aid, I will win the Terran All War in Aveline's name, since she's the one who sent me here, and I'm registered as her representative. But, as soon as we defeat her, you'll acquire all of her territories. You'll rule this planet and multiple others."

And forever battle other royals? Three cheers and three boos. The real kicker? He'd casually suggested cold-blooded murder again.

Nola might not be a queen—yet—but he already considered her morally bankrupt. Well, no matter. In time, she would prove her mettle.

Note to self: *get mettle.* "To win the All War, you'll have to kill Vale. I will *never* endanger my sister."

He searched her gaze. "Your loyalty is unexpected and impressive, but misplaced. Vale died the moment she joined the war. No matter the scenario, there's no way to save her. Best you come to terms with her loss."

Though Nola gave a violent shake of her head, he continued, saying, "To win, Vale must kill me. But, without me, you cannot defeat Aveline and her beasts. If another warrior wins the All War, Vale dies. If anyone other than an Adwaewethian wins, Aveline will send beasts to murder you and your loved ones."

No. No! "There has to be a way to keep her away from my planet while saving Vale. And you. And Zion. And Knox." He'd protected Vale at her most vulnerable, so, Nola would protect him, too. "In fact, I order you to win the war, and live, without killing Vale, Zion or Knox." There! Problem, meet solution.

He blinked rapidly, as if baffled, then shook his head. "You aren't formidable enough to enforce such an impossible command."

Trembling now, she glided a fingertip around his

one remaining gash. "Is that why you didn't heal completely?"

"Yes," he said, his jaw clenched.

"There's got to be a way to get everything we both want, and I *will* find it."

Again, he looked surprised. "Aren't you the one who told me people don't always get what they want?"

"I'm not most people."

"Are you saying you refuse to fight to liberate our people from Aveline's oppressive reign?"

Our people. "I don't... I can't..." Gah!

"You claim you have no desire to kill someone, yet your order to save Vale is a death sentence for me. You realize this, yes? You simply don't care?"

Gulp. Bane certainly had manipulation down to a fine art. An impressive and infuriating skill. Needing more time to think, she changed the subject. "Earlier, you asked why I chose Zion over you. I'll tell you—when I know I can trust you with the information." That should buy her, oh, an eternity.

With a growl, he retracted his wings. "Perhaps I can purchase the answer."

When the appendages vanished altogether, the arches no longer rising above his shoulders, a cave came into view. A spacious corridor brimming with gold, loose gemstones, jewelry and weapons. He prowled to the other side, watching as she stood.

His unwavering gaze singed her, teasing all the best places. She ached and trembled as she glided to the different piles of treasure, selecting her favorite trinkets. A diamond bracelet. A ruby choker. Sapphire earrings. An emerald tiara. Oh! There were blocks of gold and slivers of silver. And gauntlets. Oh! A bigger tiara with black diamonds.

Okay. Maybe it was the jewels. Maybe it was the man. Maybe it was a combination of the two. Whatever the reason, arousal thrummed inside her, cells fizzing.

"Where did you get these?" she asked, stroking her bounty.

Bane leaned against the wall, crossed his arms over his chest and observed her with a strange look on his face...and heat crackling in his golden eyes. Those golden eyes put the gems to shame. "I stole them from mortal tyrants before I was frozen, planning to use them to purchase weapons."

The huskiness of his voice sent fresh shivers careening down her spine.

With lazy, sensual movements, he closed the distance once more, as if he couldn't stay away. He stopped directly in front of her, bringing the scent of exotic spices with him.

"The jewels suit you." His gaze held hers as he traced a fingertip over the choker.

He looked tenser than before, but also more relaxed, the juxtaposition odd and impossible, but so Bane. Her hot and cold warrior. And dang him, the weight of his gaze trapped her in place. She couldn't move, didn't *want* to move. He was close, so close, but she longed to have him closer. Her breasts ached more desperately, and her belly quivered harder.

"Thank you," she said, fighting the urge to beg. *Kiss me.*

"You need to stop looking at me like that, Nola." He hissed the words. "You won't like what happens if I give you what you seem to want."

"Or *you* will like it too much?" she quipped. If he kissed her, would he hate her more? Blame her?

"If you taste half as good as you smell, I will absolutely like it too much."

The raw admission liquefied her bones. "Do Adwaewethians sicken when they are intimate?" she asked, stepping closer to smash her breasts into the rigid strength in his chest. She licked her lips, secretly thrilling when he clocked the action with his gaze. A gaze he flipped up, meeting hers.

New thrums of intrigue danced over his stunning features. "Do *you*?" He combed his fingers through her hair before cupping her nape, hard. The gleam in his eyes...a dark ferocity she'd never before encountered. "And don't tell me I must answer your question or you won't answer mine. I've learned my lesson."

"Fine. Yes, I sicken anytime I attempt intimacy."

He tightened his grip on her. "I was with Aveline before her Blood Rite. We were intimate countless times, and neither of us sickened."

"Oh. I see." The problem came from Nola. Aching, wretched Nola.

"But," he said, something hot and dark simmering in his voice...something possessive. "I might know why you alone sicken..."

Shivers. Heat. "Tell me."

"First," he said, "I must know if you'll sicken with me."

Her pulse jumped. "I suspect I...won't. I haven't so far. And I want... I want pleasure." The words rushed from her. "I'm so hungry for it, even you look good."

"Even me?" He sputtered a moment, incredulous, his muscles plumping right before her eyes. "I see I haven't given you an accurate impression of my skill. Time to change that."

Swooping down, he pressed his mouth against hers and kissed the breath from her lungs.

CHAPTER TWELVE

How to beat those first kiss jitters

NEVER, IN ALL his days, had Bane been this hard, or ached this intensely. After everything he'd suffered over the centuries, he *deserved* sexual release with the most beautiful female he'd ever beheld. The woman who maddened him beyond all reason.

Being so close to Nola…breathing in her honeysuckle and jasmine scent, *home*…touching the silken softness of her skin…watching her ruby lips part, and the pulse quicken at the base of her neck… He'd raced from reality to fantasy, starved for everything she had to give.

Now, he drowned in sensation, and she'd become his only source of oxygen. He kissed her like a man who couldn't live without his woman. At the moment, he *couldn't*.

In his arms, she was a live wire of passion, her responses unguarded. She trembled, kissing him back with utter abandon, their tongues thrusting together in a wild and carnal dance. Her little gasps pushed him closer to the razor's edge of sanity. Bane, *and* the beast.

The beast loved sex, *needed* it—*finally! please!*—but still hated royals with the heat of a thousand suns; he uttered protests and conflicting commands. Translation: *Stop. Don't stop. Stop, damn you. Never stop.*

Amid the chaos, Bane's desires should have cooled. But the inferno of need blazing through his veins only grew and strengthened, torching his control. As he devoured her mouth, he imagined this beautiful female draped in those jewels and nothing else.

I will strip her, palm her breasts and tongue her nipples. When I will thrust a finger deep inside her...then another and another...she'll be wet for me.

The moment Bane had realized Nola sickened during intimate moments, two equally compelling urges had hit him. To learn if he would be an exception, and to prove Nola was a means to an end to him. Then he would stop softening whenever he looked at her, stop aching whenever she revealed a tidbit about her past, stop craving what he shouldn't want more than his next breath. But as soon as their lips had met, he'd lost all sense; the reasons for initiating the kiss had ceased to matter.

The taste of this woman...

He required more. *As necessary as water.*

The kiss never paused as Bane stalked forward, forcing Nola to walk backward. When she bumped into the cave wall, he kicked her feet farther apart, fisted locks of her silken hair to angle her face and took her mouth deeper.

Need ruled him, and standing still ceased being an option. He ground his throbbing shaft between her legs, the intimate contact startling them both. She moaned, melting against him. His neglected body screamed for more, for everything.

"Bane, I... This..."

His name, spoken in her passion-drugged voice, only ratcheted up his need. "I know," he growled against her lips. A second later, the tempo of the kiss changed. From exploratory to nuclear, becoming a frenzied mating of tongues and teeth.

A woman possessed by primal desire, Nola kissed him back wildly, hungrily. As if she would die if she didn't experience complete satisfaction. The pleasure! She clawed at his flesh, rocked against his length, retreated, then rocked again. Every point of contact sizzled.

Oh, what luscious curves she possessed. Curves forever branded in his brain. Curves he needed to resist.

Resist. Yes. He must resist her—and this incredible arousal. And he would. Soon. As soon as his needs mattered more than his wants: penetration, coming inside her, branding her with his essence. Other males would scent him on her—the musk of a volatile predator—and be overcome with fear.

"More," she gasped, so he happily gave her more. "My breasts."

Rumbling growls left him as he cupped and kneaded those pert beauties, her distended nipples teasing his palms.

Again, she rolled her hips and rocked against his length, lost in the throes. Rolled, rocked. The friction…

Had any woman ever fit against him so perfectly?

His wants continued to escalate. *Want her desperate for me. Want to devour every inch of her luscious little body. Want to sink to my knees, unfasten her pants, shove her panties aside and suckle on the soaked bundle of nerves at the apex of her thighs*. Her cries of pleasure would echo through the cave. She would pull his hair, squeeze his head with her thighs and gyrate against his face, giving him every drop of feminine honey. She would demand a climax or five, and he would provide them. For once, a royal's whim would be his joy to fulfill.

Perhaps she would return the favor and devour his length…

The act was forbidden in Adwaeweth. Long ago, a queen before Bane's time decided no female should "debase" herself in such a way, and females must always top males.

He'd despised the law while Meredith had revered it. He'd never asked for head, and she'd never offered.

Now, the desire shamed him. As much as he hated Nola—*did* he hate her still?—he didn't wish to debase her. And as big as he was, as small and delicate as *she* was, he could harm her irreparably. After all, he wasn't just bigger than this woman; he was infinitely stronger, burning with lust after centuries on ice. When he came, he would be crazed, frenzied and beyond maddened.

But damn it, the desire remained, and not just for her lips around his shaft. He longed to assert his dominance, to pin her down as he'd never done to another and prove his mastery. To rule her, before she ruled him. To give as much as he took and experience true contentment after centuries of anguish.

Would he experience contentment? His lust for Nola was so strong—Correction: his lust for *sex* was so strong, he wasn't sure it could ever be quelled.

Nola responded uninhabitably to his every suck, nibble and touch, the most sensitive female he'd ever enjoyed. "You are…" Everything. Necessary. "Driving me insane."

"You share blame. You're driving me wild!" Between panting breaths, she said, "That feels so good. *You* feel so good."

Her voice had a throaty undertone, making it—her—seduction incarnate. His erection grew harder, wider, longer, threatening to bust through his fly. "You want me? *Need* me?"

"Yes! Please! I'm dying without you."

Mmm, such a delicious entreaty. As delicious as her candy-sweet skin. How could *anyone* be this delectable? How could he want her this much, despite his past, despite the beast's protests?

Wait. The beast no longer protested? *Why* had he gone silent?

Bane knew he needed to end the kiss and think. Something more than desire was at play here. But he couldn't do it in slow degrees; he didn't have the strength. He had to wrench his head up.

Nola groaned with disappointment, cupped his nape and yanked his face back to hers.

He couldn't not kiss her back. Once he started, he couldn't bring himself to stop, not again. He nipped the line of her jaw, ran her earlobe between his teeth and kissed his way down the elegant column of her neck. Delectable mewls escaped her, an irresistible siren's song.

Where her pulse raced, he sucked, hard, and she moaned in surrender.

Surrender...

What he hadn't known he wanted, needed. The tone of the kiss changed again. Faster, harder. Hotter, rougher. He lifted his head and claimed her mouth. Nola went wild, clawing at him. She hooked a leg around his waist and undulated against his length.

Sweat beaded on his brow, her desperation a match for his. The rich complexities of her innate fragrance deepened, an intoxicating drug he feared he would forever crave.

"Your shirt," he prompted.

With no hesitation, she ripped the material overhead, revealing a lacy black bra. Her flawless skin was a magnet for his tongue. As he bit the tendon that ran along her shoulder, goose bumps spread over her skin—skin like wildfire. He tracked those bumps with his mouth, grazing her collarbone with his teeth. Inside him, pressure built, a climax beckoning. He rubbed his erection between her legs, his thoughts jumbling.

Losing control…

"Bane." Moaning, she threw back her head, watching him with a heavy-lidded gaze. "I think I'm close." Her lips were wet and slightly swollen from his kisses. A flush pinkened her skin, her pulse racing ever faster. She had her nails embedded in his shoulders, holding her prey in place.

Her prey. Her pet.

Her slave.

Fool! She was a princess, a royal, a queen in the making, and this was a betrayal to Meredith. He would be with a woman, yes, but not this one.

With a growl, Bane released Nola and wrenched backward. One step. Two. Ten. He panted, every shallow breath as sharp as a dagger, his blood like fire.

He remembered the day Aveline summoned him to Hivetta to discuss the Terran All War. He'd hated withdrawing from his wife without finishing, but he'd done it—easily. Here, now, he could walk away from Nola to preserve his sanity just as easily. He could. He would.

"Kiss me, Bane. Pretty, pretty please." She leaned

against the rocky wall, breathtakingly carnal, and squeezed her pert, lace-clad breasts.

Seduction incarnate... He'd wanted her lost. Mission accomplished. Magnificently so. Need for her skyrocketed, consuming him. But he would walk away. Any moment now...

Any. Damn. Moment.

She slid her fingertips down the flat plane of her stomach and fingered the button on her pants.

Growling, he stepped forward. To stop her, probably. But probably not. She stepped forward, too, meeting him in the middle, all but launching her body against his, reinvigorating his shock and delight. She pressed her breasts into his chest—how he'd missed them. As she jumped up to wind her legs around his waist, he took her to the ground. Their lips crashed together once again, their tongues dueling. What he felt...

A mad rush of desire...rapture...*homecoming?*

"I want you on your back," he rasped, the admission scalding his throat.

"Yes! Please!"

Though he knew it was wrong, he rolled and pinned her with his weight. He waited for her regret, but she seemed to revel in his dominance, running her hands all over him.

Magnificent female. He kissed her until he'd stolen her breath, and she needed his to survive. When he fisted the hair at her nape, angling her face to deepen the kiss more than before, she rewarded him, sucking on his tongue. When he gripped her ass, forcing her hips to lift and her core to cradle his length, she whimpered in thanks, and Bane comprehended an undeniable truth. He was seconds away from stripping her bare and sinking inside her. Taking her virginity. Willingly bedding a royal.

What would happen afterward? Would she choose to return to Zion?

Bane swallowed a roar of denial. Nola could be the hand of his vengeance, or a scorned ex-lover, but she couldn't be both. Queens were notoriously selfish, greedy and possessive of their property, more so than beasts. He needed her focused. And unharmed.

Though his shaft throbbed, and Bane was desperate for release, her passion nearly burning him alive, he found the strength to sever contact a third time and shoot to the other side of the cave, putting distance between them. Along the way, he spotted a pair of gauntlets. Feminine, delicate. Exquisite. Reminded him of Nola. He shoved the pieces into his pocket. *Foolish.* Did he return the metal gloves, though? No.

"Bane?" She stood and stumbled in his direction. The way she looked at him, as if he epitomized her every secret desire, it did something to him. Made him want ridiculous things. A fresh start. A long-term relationship. Pleasure instead of revenge.

Obviously, arousal made men stupid.

Had Nola surprised him today? Yes. She'd resisted the urge to order her new pet to perform ridiculous tricks, faced his anger head-on, refusing to back down, and revealed a heartbreaking past. Her unshakable loyalty to Vale was admirable, and her uninhabited passion would haunt him for the rest of his miserable life. But he'd told her the truth—one day soon, she would cease being this amazing woman and become a living nightmare.

A living nightmare who held his fate in her dainty hands.

Although, after the things she'd suffered, hell, she might be the first and only queen to retain her humanity. He doubted it, but the mere possibility made him sweat. If Nola remained sweet and passionate…

He scrubbed a hand over his face. If he pitted her against Aveline…*like a flower petal trying to battle a thorn?*

No, no. She would change. No question.

"You kissed me, and I didn't sicken," she said, awed. "I'm—"

"The kiss was a mistake." He wiped his mouth with the back of his hand, hoping to rid himself of her luscious taste. *Needing to. Too good.*

She flinched, looking shell-shocked and wounded.

Something in his chest clenched.

The beast bellowed commands to finish what they'd started. Bane beat his fists against his temples. *Quiet!*

"There will be no more kissing," he grated. "No more touching." He couldn't risk it. His control had too many cracks. He shouldn't want her this much, anyway. And he damn sure shouldn't let himself grow to like her.

"But why?" A crease developed between her furrowed brows, and she frowned.

If he boiled his thoughts and concerns down to a single sentence…"I don't want this, don't want you, not like this."

Comprehension dawned, dulling the stars in her dark eyes. "Then you won't get me."

Pale and trembling, she swooped down to grab her shirt. After donning the garment, she wrapped her arms around her middle, an instinctive gesture meant to protect one's vital organs from harm. Guilt seared him.

"By the way. Thanks for nothing," she said. "I didn't get sick during our kiss, just afterward."

Ah. A defensive strike. He'd hurt her, and now she lashed out. His guilt heated anew. "You don't look sick. You look aroused."

She shrugged. *Shrugged!* The action of an uncaring queen who most assuredly did *not* consider Bane her exclusive property. "I don't like you, so I'm pretty disgusted with myself for making out with you. But I'll get over it, and find your replacement. Clearly, I'm over my kiss-and-puke affliction."

Rage propelled him a step closer. "You belong to me. Any male who dares to enjoy you will die by my hand." He would kill savagely, and without an ounce of mercy.

Her mouth floundered open and closed. "If I belong to you, you belong to me."

He belonged to vengeance. "Sorry, but you aren't my type." Truth. Cruel to be kind. "I've always preferred warrior women."

Though a shadow passed over her features, she smiled with cold calculation. "One day," she said, sweetly batting her lashes at him, "I'll make you eat those words. Until then, I see we've got ourselves into a troll-under-the-bridge situation here. Meaning, yes, you are the troll, and I want nothing to do with you. Now be a lamb and explain the kiss-sick thing. You were going to tell me earlier, but you got distracted by your insatiable desire for me, the wrong type."

Her easy dismissal irritated him. Before, she'd referred to herself as an emotional and mental juggernaut. Now, Bane had to agree. She'd wanted him, but he'd turned her down, so she'd moved on, as simple as that.

Struggling to maintain his composure, he tightened

and released his fists. "Once, there was a queen. Queen Jayne the Incandescent, more violent and savage than Aveline. Upon her death, she was stricken from our history books." He'd been a boy at the time, and she hadn't reigned long, but he'd never forgotten her charisma and confidence. She'd awed him.

"Though she hadn't yet met her mate, she'd sensed him, causing a bond to form. One that prevented her from being with anyone else. Him, too. They found each other, and their union became the strongest of any other queen and warrior."

The fact that Nola hadn't sickened with him…

Had she bonded to him?

She sputtered for a moment. "Are you saying some part of me wants you, and only you, and no one else will do? Like, ever?"

"Yes, but we both know I'm not your mate. There must be another explanation." Although… "You sensed me as soon as you reached adulthood."

"How do you know?"

"How else? I sensed you, as well."

"Oh." She looked away, assuring him he'd gotten this right. He—

A strange noise captured his attention. What *was* that? When Nola opened her mouth to say more, he held up an index finger, requesting silence. Astonishingly enough, she acquiesced.

His ears twitched. That noise…

Tick, tick, tick. A clock? No. *Tick, tick, tick.* A timer—on a bomb.

Horror slapped him, the sound suddenly all he could hear. *TICK, TICK, TICK.* While he would survive an explosion as long as he kept his heart and head, Nola would not.

Too weak, too fragile. No wonder he'd always hated those qualities. But he hated them more than ever. *Might lose Nola when I've only just found her.*

Reflexes on point, he opened a portal to an island he'd found on month three of the war, when tailing Zion.

The scent of coconut and salt wafted into the cave, exotic to someone like Bane. The sound of lapping waves, chirping birds and buzzing insects rang out. A quick scan. Glaring sunlight, crystal water, glistening sands. Behind the beach, an overgrown jungle. No one lurked nearby—that he would see.

Fast as lightning, Bane gathered his goggles, Valor's sword and the shards that made up Malaki's armor. Perhaps they could be used as spear tips. Faster, he swept Nola into his arms.

"What are we—" she began.

Keeping her close, Bane launched through the opening. Though he maintained his humanoid form, he experienced a partial transformation again, wings ripping past muscle and skin to spring from his back. A painful process, but highly effective. He wrapped the appendages around Nola to act as a shield and a cushion.

Tick, tick—boom!

The bomb detonated. A violent gust of fiery air blasted through the open portal, picked them up and tossed them across a great distance. They landed on the beach, flinging sand. Shrapnel pelted him, and debris rained over them both.

CHAPTER THIRTEEN

Decoding his inner dragon!

ONE MINUTE NOLA basked in sublime pleasure, the next she wallowed in anger and resentment as Bane accused her of unconsciously choosing him as a first lover and forever mate—and fear that he might be right. The next minute, she floundered as he picked her up and hurried through a portal, protecting her in the shelter of his wings as a bomb destroyed his home.

Nola landed first, impact jarring her lungs. Then two hundred and fifty pounds of beastly warrior slammed on top of her aroused, needy body. Stars sprinkled her line of sight, and her lungs emptied.

Bane grunted as flames licked over his back.

The portal closed, the flames vanishing. Keeping a tight grip on a bloodstained sword, he rolled to his side.

She blundered to an upright position, wincing as she looked him over. Gashes and blood everywhere. Soot-smeared skin and a broken wing, the lower half shredded. Injuries he'd gained by saving her life.

Heady warmth spread through her, only to cool as realization struck. They'd come close to dying. Just boom—gone forever.

To never again know his kiss or his touch. To never again hear his husky, sex-rich voice as they verbally sparred. To never ever see his smile. *What I wouldn't give to see his smile.* Would his golden eyes sparkle?

Stop mooning over him! He didn't matter. He *couldn't* matter. To Bane, Nola was merely a sword. An extension of his hatred.

"Thank you for getting me to safety," she said between panting breaths.

"Are you hurt?"

"Shockingly, I'm good." But he wasn't. While the sunlight merely heated her fair skin, it baked his. "You?"

"Good," he echoed, his voice strained. He stood, cursing all the while, and limped to a shadowed area protected by a massive black tarp. Once the shadows enveloped him, he breathed a sigh of relief.

To tell him to heal or not?

Not. Definitely. No more orders.

With her heart banging against her ribs and adrenaline burning through her veins, she studied their new location. Beyond the tarp—

"An island!" Crystal waves lapped at white sands, leaving a layer of sea foam behind. On one side, boulders and cliffs jutted. On the other, a lush jungle teemed with trees and foliage. The scent of salt, coconut and orchids saturated the overly warm air, making her feel as if she inhaled a vacation with every breath. The sound of rippling water and chirping birds soothed her frazzled nerves.

Wait. She frowned. What was *that*? A glint of… metal? Oh, wow. Yes, metal. From a section of a plane.

"Where are we?" she asked, glancing at Bane.

"Another dimension sometimes accessed by humans." He positioned his goggles, hiding his eyes—and emotions—behind their pitch-black lenses. "Zion has a talent for finding lost dimensions within any world. Long ago, I followed him here." As he spoke, crimson rivers poured from his gashes.

A bone from his ribs had cut through his skin and hung at an odd angle. She winced with sympathy, her stomach churning.

He looked himself over and said, "Tell me to heal quickly, Nola."

"Sorry, but no. You can't have it both ways, Bane. You can't hate me for being your boss, then demand I use my position to aid you. Don't worry. Girls love scars. You're welcome."

"Tell me to heal," he insisted.

Argh! "If I do, you have to vow you'll never again complain about my royalness."

A muscle pulsed beneath his eye. "Patch me up the old-fashioned way."

Stubborn fool! "Is there a first aid kit hidden somewhere?"

"There is. It's in a trunk buried under this tarp. Dig it out while I search for bombs and other traps. Someone found my lair. They might have found the island, too."

She wanted to respond, but a strange scene rose to the surface of her mind. A little movie she couldn't turn off.

In it, a couple drove a midsize sedan down an abandoned road, a toddler strapped to a car seat in back. The driver had close-cropped black hair, dark eyes and pale skin. The passenger had dark blond hair, brown eyes and tanned skin. Variations of gold. *Adwaewethian* gold.

So beautiful…so familiar. *My parents*, she computed with a gasp. A single photo had survived her chaotic childhood, and it featured a younger version of these two.

This was a memory, then? But Nola couldn't be more than a year old. So young. Too young to remember this.

As the couple argued in hushed tones, Nola picked up individual phrases. "A monster." "Must hide." "The others." And "How much."

Monster—had they seen a beast? Hide—baby Nola?

Suddenly, a tall, muscular man with pale hair and a circle tattoo similar to Bane's appeared in the street. Had he used some kind of invisible portal, or teleported? A sword hilt rose above each shoulder, leather sheaths crisscrossing over his torso. An Adwaewethian and a combatant, but how?

Nola's father jerked the wheel, and the vehicle swerved, barely missing the other-worlder. Tires squealed, and smoke billowed. The car flipped, once, twice, again and again, the sound of crunching metal assaulting her ears.

Finally, the flipping ceased. The car was upside down, seat belts holding everyone in place. Baby Nola didn't have a single scratch, yet a metal spike impaled her dad's neck. His head lay at an odd angle and his eyes stared at nothing.

Sobbing, struggling for freedom, her mother continually glanced at the shattered windshield. No, not the windshield, but the scuffed leather boots approaching the vehicle. Boots attached to the man who'd appeared in the road.

This couldn't be real. This couldn't have happened. This couldn't be the way they'd died.

The man crouched next to the passenger side, reached through the opening, and grabbed her screaming mother by the arm.

"No!" real-life Nola shouted. "Leave her alone. Don't you dare—"

"Nola?"

Bane's concerned voice yanked her from the dark mire of her thoughts. Panting, unable to catch her breath, she blinked into focus. The images in her head faded, revealing Bane. He crouched in front of her, his hands on her cheeks. While she'd gotten lost in a memory she couldn't have retained, he'd braved the sunlight to whisk her to the tarp.

Tears swam in her eyes. *Can't deal. Not yet.* Too much had happened today. Bane had saved her from a mercenary, kissed her without causing sickness, rejected her, insulted her and saved her again. And she hadn't processed any of it!

Now, she didn't want to. She erected blocks around her mind. Maybe they were real, maybe they were imagined, but either way she would puzzle out answers later. The next time she was alone, probably. Or never. Yeah, never was good. Her chest felt as if someone had replaced her organs with rocks. And dang it, she needed to stop leaning into Bane's touch, needed to stop seeking comfort from a man who considered her scum.

"What's wrong, princess?" He pressed two fingers against her throat, gauging the quickness of her pulse. "For several minutes, you became mist. You were here, but not here."

"Mist? Me?"

"A royal ability, I'm sure, unique to you."

So he didn't know what had happened to her, or if it would happen again.

Puzzle it out later, remember? "Forget the mist thing.

You've got to check the island and I've got to unearth a first aid kit."

Seeming to realize the intimacy of their pose, he released her and staggered to a stand. "Shout if you need me." He strode away, his limp actually improving.

He stuck to the shadows. Before disappearing in the jungle, he cast her a glance. Shivers raced down her spine and contradictory urges hit her, one after the other. She wanted him to rush back. She wanted him to stay gone and never return. She wanted everything. She wanted nothing.

Why am I so conflicted about this man? Nola recalled what he'd told her immediately following their kiss: *I prefer warrior women.*

Translation: *You, Nola Lee, do not even qualify as spank bank fodder.*

The hurt she'd experienced… While he'd found her lacking, she'd found him irresistible. When they'd kissed, she'd lost control. Sickness hadn't been a blip. For a moment, Bane had become her reason for breathing. But she would never be *his* reason for breathing. The honor would always belong to his beloved wife.

Jealous of a dead woman?

Seriously, one kiss and a little light groping, and Nola turned into a sex-starved fatal attraction wannabe?

The thought resurrected a good mad—at Bane. How dare he make her crave him like this!

With a huff, Nola went looking for the first aid kit. She found it partially buried beside a fallen trunk, complete with rags, bandages, different ointments and clean clothes. Also present, a set of daggers. Nola slung a dagger to her calf, hidden by her pants.

Struggling and straining, she rolled a large rock under

the tarp, so Bane would have a chair while she doctored—
and questioned—him. The stubborn man would chat with
her whether he wanted to or not.

When he returned at last, she drank him in. *Too gorgeous for his own good.* Her body came alive, heating,
tingling, *needing*; *he* had awakened a sexual beast inside
her. Maybe because he looked crazed with lust, his gaze
glued to her as he prowled closer, a predator intent on
running his prey to ground.

He'd taken a dip in the water. His hair was drenched,
blood and dirt washed away.

"No bombs or traps," he said, his voice a harsh lash.
A few of his injuries had already healed, his broken rib
among them. But fresh blood trickled from his shoulder.
"No sign of any recent visitors."

"Good. Now sit." She waved to the rock, then blinked
with surprise when he obeyed. *Must remember to phrase
my words as a suggestion, not an order.* "I'll patch you
up, and we'll get to know each other better. If you're to
think the worst of me, you should get to know me first,
so I'll start."

He gave a clipped nod, but remained silent. His crazed
edge had dulled, as if her nearness had soothed him.
Things were changing between them.

Where to begin? "Something specific you'd like to
know?"

"Tell me anything, everything." Tension emanated
from him. "I find I am…curious about you."

Oh, yes. Things were definitely changing. As Nola
used a rag to rinse the blood and dirt from Bane's
wounds, trying not to drool over his muscles, she said,
"I'm twenty-two. I bake the best donuts you've ever

tasted, I have a singing voice Vale calls Cats Being Murdered and the dance moves of an angel…on crack."

The barest hint of an almost-smile teased his lips, enchanting her.

Nola had wanted to see a real one so danged bad. A mistake. With only a small lip-quirk, he'd stolen her wits and reminded her body of all the pleasure she'd missed throughout her life…the pleasure she could have with him.

I prefer warrior women.

He had a type, and Nola would never qualify. Got it. Or, was his taste in females changing?

She trembled, but continued on, saying, "I only graduated high school because a kind foster mom homeschooled me when I was too sick to attend class." Her heart squeezed inside her chest. "All right. Tell me something about you."

"I was twenty-two over twenty-two centuries ago."

"Yes, we've already established that you're as old as Father Time and should be wearing diapers. What else you got?"

He thought for a minute. "In Adwaeweth, males are removed from their homes as young children to begin training for war. At sixteen, our beasts awaken and we train another ten years, learning to control it."

Such a sad life. He'd been raised for war, never asked how he envisioned his future. She sympathized. Lupus and fibro had negated her sense of choice, too. "Look at that. We have something in common. We both grew up without parents, our lives preplanned for us."

"I suspect your life might have been…tougher than mine."

What? Had Mr. Hate Weak and Fragile just acknowledged her trials and tribulations, maybe kinda sorta admitting there were different kinds of strength?

"Tell me about your wife." On her knees, with her body situated between his legs, she applied salve to the wounds on his torso, and the one in his shoulder. "How'd you meet her?"

He cast his gaze somewhere far, far away. "Every Adwaewethian belongs to one of five factions. The royals, the warriors, the breeders, the scholars and the laborers. Meredith and I were both warriors, part of the same military unit. For many years, we fought side by side. Later, we realized we loved each other."

"What caused the realization of love?" she asked.

Another slight quirk. "During training, a soldier knocked down Meredith and stomped on her ankle. She got up and continued to fight. He knocked her down again, but again, she rose. I couldn't look away. Such an indomitable spirit and unbending strength humbled me. When I offered aid, she punched me in the face."

His *words* punched Nola. And kicked. And stabbed. "She sounds fierce, like the heroine of a romance novel." Nola loved to read. Alpha males and sizzling sex, everything her own life had been missing.

Her eyes widened. "Had been." Past tense. She was kind of *living* a romance novel right now, with Bane playing the role of hero.

"If ever someone broke my ankle," she said, "the first thing I'd do is sob. And if you offered to help me, I'd probably hug you."

"I wouldn't be able to offer you aid, I'd be too busy murdering the one responsible."

Be still my beating heart.

He canted his head. Seemingly entranced, he reached

out and rubbed locks of her hair between his fingers. "Tell me more about you."

His curiosity emboldened her, and she decided to delve a little deeper, reveal a little more. Admit things that impacted the woman she'd become. "Most of my life, I've been found lacking in one way or another. Countless foster parents and siblings complained about my sicknesses, accusing me of faking. Teachers considered me a nuisance, and classmates made fun of me for everything from heritage to poverty." She ran her hands up and down his arms, seeking contact, comfort.

He stiffened, his muscles hard as rocks. "I'm sorry for the past you suffered, Nola." She thought he added, "And the strength I overlooked," but he'd turned down the volume, so she couldn't be sure.

"You're forgiven," she said, reeling.

"Have you ever been in love, princess?" He clasped her wrist and lifted one of her hands to his pec, then repeated the action with the other. His heart drummed against her palm, every beat sending a surge of heat through her body.

"No one has ever measured up to my dream man," she said in jest. Yet, the words hit too close to home, painting a bull's-eye on her soul.

"And who is your dream man?"

She mimed locking her lips and throwing away the key.

His eyes narrowed as he returned her hands to his chest. "Keep your hands where they are," he said, then released her to slip two bejeweled gauntlets from his pocket.

He secured the bottom end to her wrists, and secured

thin links of chains to her fingers. The tips were pointed, like claws.

Magnificent. She marveled over the sparkling jewels in the center, saying, "I don't understand. You're loaning me a pair of gauntlets because…?"

Their gazes met, the air between them simmering. Always simmering. He looked enthralled and utterly amazed. A trick of the light?

Voice gruff, he said, "I'm *giving* you a pair of gauntlets to thank you for patching me up."

But he'd saved the jewelry *before* she'd patched him. Before the explosion even. "I…you're welcome. I'll treasure these." Forever.

"Now. Tell me about him." There was a command hidden in his tone.

"My dream man?" she asked, and he gave a clipped nod. Tell him that *he* was the dream man? No, thanks. So, she decided to describe the man she hoped to end up with. "He's not a pretty boy who's never known pain. He's been through trials, so he has an appreciation for the trials of others. He's tall and handsome. Kind and gentle. All the usuals. But, most important, he absolutely, positively must have a massive…"

Brow arched in intrigue, Bane leaned closer to her and said, "Muscle mass? Kill list? Bank account?"

"A massive *cock*, of course."

As his own tongue seemed to strangle him, she fought a grin and failed. Nice to know she could shock the stoic brute *somehow.*

He stopped abruptly, his gaze on her mouth, his features stripped of any calm. "Your smile," he croaked.

She gulped, shivers trekking down her spine. "Yes? What about it?"

He licked his lips. "I want to *taste* it."

CHAPTER FOURTEEN

What his scars reveal

BANE BATTLED A raging hard-on. Again. But then, "raging hard-on" was a semipermanent condition whenever Nola neared. She had a smile so bright it could be a beacon in the darkest night, a heart more dazzling than any diamond and a past more tragic than his own.

He'd sorely misjudged this woman, and his abysmal treatment of her would forever haunt him. Guilt would forever eat at him…but neither doused his desires. No, unease settled in and did the honors.

All his life, he'd tended to his own wounds. He and Meredith had agreed: only the weak required such "pampering." Nola had fussed over him and…he'd liked it. Liked it enough to look forward to his next injury.

The sheer lunacy of the situation panicked him.

He wanted Nola too much. The *beast* wanted her too much. But she yearned for a kind and gentle man, something Bane could never be. Never mind that he'd once been that way with Meredith, and the lovers he'd enjoyed before meeting his wife.

Aveline's actions had changed and hardened him. And yet, Nola made him want to try. Especially when her angelic rosebud lips uttered the word *cock*.

Her eyelids seemed to weigh a hundred pounds, dipping low as she said, "You want to taste my smile? Too bad, so sad."

"A denial? If I shoved my hand into your panties, you'd be wet. Soaked."

A flush warmed her cheeks. "So what?"

"So. We should find out if I'm right." Before he realized he'd moved, he'd used one hand to urge Nola closer and the other to pin both of her arms behind her back. She remained on her knees, her breasts smashed into his chest. Just the way he liked. The feel of her against him, all softness and heat, the scent of her skin, all sweetness and wicked delight…he had no defenses.

With his free hand, he tenderly smoothed a lock of hair from her cheek. The inky color of the strands—so different from a typical Adwaewethian—mesmerized him.

Nola leaned into the caress, snagging his gaze. Her lips parted, freeing a moan.

The beast faded to the background as Nola permeated his senses, her vulnerability like a mating call. Except, the song had a resonant frequency strong enough to shatter glass—and any resistance he'd built. A ferocious need to bed her invaded his every thought.

"Your nose is burned." But not blistered. Perhaps Aveline had created her super-beasts at last, able to tolerate the sun.

He bent his head and sniffed the column of Nola's neck, and had to cut off a groan. The sun had scented her skin and hair, warmth pulsing from her body.

He grew harder. "You are not sensitive to sunlight."

"I'm not, no, though I do burn easily."

Oh, yes. Aveline had her super-beasts. Too bad she would lose them to the new queen. "That's an Adwaewethian trait."

"Good to know. But, uh, I believe we had other business matters to discuss?"

She seeks pleasure? Resist!

Damn it! She was temptation made flesh, forbidden fruit, and he'd never been so ravenous. "I want to slide my hand into your panties, but I won't," he said, praying he had the strength to follow through. What he wanted wasn't what either of them needed. Instead, they would stay focused and complete their tasks.

Kill Zion, win the wand. Train Nola in self-defense. Save Vale. Perform Nola's Blood Rite. Win the All War.

He thought he'd found a way to save the sister, but he needed her cooperation.

Disappointment flashed over Nola's features. Then she rallied, leaning into him, pressing her new claws into his pectorals.

Desire sharpened inside him. She placed her mouth over his ear and whispered, "Someone is all smolder and no action, huh?" When she pulled back, she nipped at his earlobe. Then she trekked her gaze down his abdomen and lingered on the erection strangling the fly of his pants. Another dark passion-flush spilled over her cheeks. "Or do you want to hear me beg?"

Resist her allure. Ignore the challenge of her words. Bane plucked her metal claws free of his skin— a travesty—stood and took a step back. "We mustn't do this."

The disappointment returned, the stars in her eyes dulling. "Who's the weakling now?" she taunted, and came to her feet.

Resist! Ignore! But damn her, she played with fire. "I don't want to be with someone I know. Someone I'll see again. I want someone I can use, who uses me in turn.

Easily had, easily forgotten. A relationship isn't for me. If I were to care for you and lose you…no. I won't suffer another loss. We will stay together as…temporary friends. You'll keep my beast as calm as possible, and I'll keep you healthy. No more."

Now the flush drained away. "Message received. No nookie hooky. Got it. So. Tell me about the All War. Please," she added, gathering the medical supplies and returning the bundle to the trunk he'd left here yesterday. "Do combatants spend their days hunting and killing each other?"

"Or setting traps. Once a month we attend an Assembly of Combatants."

"Mandatory, I assume."

"Yes. It forces hiders out of hiding and speeds up the war. Speaking of the assembly, the next one takes place in two and a half weeks." Time ticked away without pause or mercy, his self-imposed deadline closing in fast. The end of the war, the end of Aveline.

The end of his life.

Not ready to die. So much left to do…things I'm desperate to do with Nola.

His hands curled into fists. *Focus up.* Would her sister be ready for the assembly?

The muscles in her shoulders tangled with tension, and he knew she'd wondered the same thing. Without aid, Vale would most certainly be killed in one horrific way or another. A fact Bane could use to advance his agenda.

Terrible of him? Yes. Did he care? Not a bit.

"I have an idea," he said. "If Vale takes the Mark of Disgrace, she can exit the war without death."

"Mark of Disgrace?"

"A symbol will be carved on her forehead, telling the other combatants to leave her be. Usually, deserters are returned to their sovereign for punishment. She'll simply stay here."

Nola's shoulders rolled in. "I know her well. She'll refuse. She'll want to win the war to protect the world from invaders."

"Then you can order me to guard her at the assembly. At *every* assembly," he said, preparing to bargain. "However, as Aveline will soon learn, there's a difference between what a willing warrior will do to achieve a goal versus an enslaved one. One lets your sister get hurt, while adhering to the order to keep her alive. The other ensures she emerges unscathed. Guess which is which."

She licked her lips, and damn it to hell, he couldn't stop himself from clocking the action with his gaze. "What do you want in exchange for your cooperation?"

"I'll protect Vale from harm and death at every assembly except the last one. Unless and until we are the final two combatants, I won't strike at her, even if she strikes at me." The beast, however... "In return, you will agree to complete the Blood Rite whenever I deem it necessary."

NOLA'S MOUTH FLOUNDERED open and closed, choked sounds leaving her. Should she accept right away, lest he change his mind? Should she refuse and try to hold out for something better? *Was* there something better? Should she slap him for being so stubborn, sexy and infuriating all at once?

The third option had the most appeal.

He'd gone from looking at her as if he planned to devour her at his earliest convenience, to claiming he wouldn't be kissing her ever again, to caressing her like she was the most precious person in his life. One moment, he'd incited the sweetest, wettest ache between her legs, the next he'd roused frustration, hurt and anger.

The anger didn't last long. The man had resisted her attempt at seduction for legit reasons, and she couldn't fault him for it. He wasn't looking for a relationship; she was. He'd suffered enough loss in his lifetime; Nola had, as well, and she'd once shared his outlook. Now, she disagreed. Shutting down to prevent pain never actually prevented pain. It just made you miserable before the pain hit.

Nola had even given up on romance...not knowing a man was on ice, waiting for her. Had she not crawled out of her sickbed and gotten on that plane, they might not have ever met.

Life happened, whether you gave it your all or only a half effort. Though she and Vale had planned for every eventuality during their vacation, they'd gotten lost and almost died. Nola was ready to live!

"Well, princess?" Bane unveiled a glorious, sardonic smile. He knew he had her by the lady balls. "If nothing else, the bargain buys you time to figure out a better plan."

Finally! A full-fledged smile! It made her weak in the freaking knees.

Concentrate. If Vale somehow won the All War, Aveline might come to Earth to execute her. What would happen to the hybrids if their beasts never awoke? Did they know they differed from other humans? Did they feel like something was wrong with them? Were they sick, like her?

"Fine. I'll agree to your terms, if Vale does, too,"

she said, a familiar crackle of energy pricking her. She frowned and whispered, "Do you feel that?"

Literal flames crackled in his golden eyes. He jumped to his feet and unsheathed his sword, the tendons in his neck pulling taut from strain. That strain flowed down, down his arms, ending in his fists. His nails blackened, then lengthened into claws longer and sharper than her own. His muscles expanded, no doubt deluged with adrenaline.

Lines of molten gold forked through his skin—no, not liquid gold, but actual *lava*. Had to be. Heat flowed from him, his body like a furnace. Plus, she'd witnessed him blowing fire out of his mouth, an image branded into her mind.

Nola marveled at him. A real-life superhero.

Before her trip to Russia, she would have cowered before a man like this. Such fury! Here, now, the beastly warrior enthralled her. *He is mine to command.*

No, no, no. Stupid dark side! *I'm no one's master. He's mine to admire.*

"A combatant has just arrived on the island." He scanned the beach. "Stay here, and stay hidden. I'll deal with the threat."

Her blood did that flash freeze thing. What if Zion had come here looking for her, thinking to save her? "Did every combatant attend the same 'how to put the little woman in her place' seminar? Never mind." Words left her in a rush. "I agree to your terms. With one— two exceptions. You must agree we can revisit our negotiation at any time, and for now, you can't kill Zion or Knox until the end, either."

Slowly, with lethal precision, Bane turned to face her. Those flamed-filled eyes promised pain and death, his body vibrating with aggression. "You make me want to kill Zion *faster*."

All doubts fled. He *was* jealous. Smiling, she twisted a lock of hair and rocked from side to side. He might not want to like her, or care for her, but he already did.

"What?" he demanded, staring daggers at her. Then splashing sounds registered, and his attention whipped toward the water. Snarls left him. "Our visitor is Union. He casts illusions, so you cannot trust anything you see. He wears a belt that doubles his strength, allowing him to break multiple bones in your body with a single punch. You aren't to approach him." Giving her a little push toward the jungle, he said, "In this, there is no reason good enough to disobey me."

Nola dug in her heels, saying, "If he casts illusions, how will *you* know what's real and what isn't?"

He tapped the goggles perched atop his head. "With these, I can see through anything. Now go. Hide. And Nola? If I transform into the beast, you are to teleport from this island. I will find you, I swear it."

Had she been strong like his wife, he might have asked her to fight at his side. They could have protected each other! But Nola wasn't that kind of warrior woman, and she'd never rushed headlong into anything, especially danger.

These guys were trained to kill. Heck, they *lived* to kill. Her skills revolved around a three-week self-defense course. She would be a hindrance, maybe even a distraction, endangering Bane further. On the other hand, if she hid, he would think her weak again.

Did it matter? Trying to fight a trained assassin would be the epitome of stupid. *Know when to hold 'em, know when to fold 'em. Live to fight another day.*

"Please be careful, Bane. If anyone hurts you, I'd prefer it be me." Nola refused to glance in his direction; she didn't want to know what emotion shone in his expression. She didn't want to listen to his response, either.

She sprinted to a thick bed of foliage as fast as her feet would carry her, and crouched behind a cluster of gnarled limbs, and palmed the dagger sheathed at her ankle. Every time a tremor swept through her, the leaves and branches surrounding her clapped.

Less than an hour ago, Bane had gashes all over his body. He'd lost multiple pints of blood. If he got hurt...

The moisture in her mouth dried. Why hadn't she insisted he heal? Why had she used his injuries to make a point?

Thoughts fled as a man—Union—emerged from the water and stalked up the shore, where he shook out his bright red mane. He was shirtless, water droplets sluicing down pale, marble-ish skin. His muscle mass... duuuude. He resembled a bodybuilder who'd been bitten by a radioactive steroid. The guy *bulged*. He wore leather pants and combat boots. A thick metal chain wrapped around his waist. The belt of double strength? Spiked leather cuffs circled his wrists, and swords rose over his shoulders.

The man had come ready for war.

Bane stepped to the edge of the tarp and moved his goggles over his eyes. How much would his sensitivity to light weaken him?

"You made a mistake, coming here," he called.

The other man noticed him and grinned. He spread his arms, all *come and get me*. "You should surrender and let me take your head. The more you fight me, the more I'll hurt you." He wiggled his fingers as he spoke.

Graceful motions. *Odd* motions. Then, cat-size scorpions crawled from the sand, each one focused on Bane.

Nola swallowed a screech of terror. *Just an illusion, just an illusion. Right?*

Must be. Her golden god yawned, as if bored. "I hope you enjoyed your day, Union, for it was your last."

CHAPTER FIFTEEN

How to be his badass babe

UNLEASHING AN EARSPLITTING war cry, Bane charged across the beach. Along the way, he unsheathed his sword. Thanks to his goggles, he knew Union had created an illusion of murderous insect-rodents. Creepy, but harmless. Still. Focus mattered. He tried to banish Nola from his mind, an impossible task.

Kill Union, return to Nola. Protect her, whatever the cost.

Whatever the cost, yes. A frenzied need to stand between the world and his woman—no, no, his princess—consumed him. Fury surged with new force, spilling out, sweat beading over his skin. If anything happened to the current "bane" of his existence, he would not rest until everyone paid.

Only minutes ago, he'd confessed the truth to Nola: he wanted a release without a relationship. But he'd lied to her, too. Every time they conversed, he grew to like and admire her a little more, and crave her a *lot* more. Part of him already…cared about her.

Can't lose her. Not today. Rip out Union's heart, and all will be well.

Having researched the combatants, Bane knew this

particular male enjoyed bruising and breaking the fairer sex. A crime Bane could not abide.

Nola, in this bastard's crosshairs. My future queen in danger...

More adrenaline fortified his muscles with strength. At the same time, beams of sunlight scorched him, allowing the strength to drain away. Though he could breathe fire and walk through literal flames, he would forever melt in daylight, those harsh sunrays causing some kind of chemical reaction deep inside him. No matter. He'd trained for this.

Union charged across the beach as well, and they met in the middle, crashing together. In unison, they swung their swords. *Clang. Whoosh. Clang.* Metal hit metal with crushing might, vibrations rushing up his arms, cracking bone; those cracks turned his bones into tuning forks, unearthing more and more fury. The wound in Bane's shoulder opened up and lengthened, flesh and muscle tearing.

Roars echoed inside his head, loud and long. The beast wanted blood, wanted to drink every drop and feast on Union's remains. *Soon...*

Never! But the farther away from Nola he got, the more he had to struggle to maintain control. If he unleashed the beast, the belt would be destroyed.

Must have that belt! After he won the war, Nola would be able to activate any weapons he retained. She could wear the belt and double her strength the day she met Aveline.

Clang, whoosh, clang. Bane lunged, swung, slashed and blocked, then blocked again, intermittent grunts, groans and growls peppering the silence. Never before had he fought Union one-on-one. Now he could say with utmost certainty that the belt did its job. Every time their swords clanged, a multitude of damage occurred in Bane's body. Muscles tore and bones cracked worse.

All the while, those insect-rodent illusions inched closer. He wondered if he'd been foolish to dismiss the critters. What if they could cause genuine harm?

Not much was known about Union's ability, his people relatively new to the alliance.

Amid a whirlwind of violence, Bane alternated between swinging his sword and swiping with his claws. During a swipe, Union blocked and twisted his blade to sheer off three of his fingertips, severing an artery in the process. Streams of crimson spurted in a continuous rush, propelling the beast to new levels of malice.

Pain is simply weakness leaving my body. Pain is simply—

Screw it. Pain is a bitch.

Considering he had yet to fully heal from the explosion, he should have grabbed Nola and run, leaving Union in their dust. But he'd decided to win the belt now, not later. By waiting, he risked losing it to another. And yes, there was a chance he'd also hoped to show Nola his battle skill and incomparable strength, proving he could protect her better than Zion. Or *any* male.

Breaths heaving, Bane herded Union toward a cluster of trees. Shadows spilled over him, offering a measure of relief. Still the insect-rodents followed, drawing ever closer.

Union dodged the next blow and pivoted, his gaze darting over the island. "I sense a female. A tasty one, at that. The one who visited us in the ice prison." Dark intrigue radiated from him, mingling with darker anticipation. "Once I finish with you…"

Do not react. In battle, emotion makes you stupid. "Now you will die badly," Bane said, his voice so rough the words scoured his ears. He lunged, extending his sword.

Union expected the action and blocked, only to pause and gape when wings burst from Bane's back.

With a powerful flap, his entire body lifted off the ground. He kicked out a leg, nailing the underside of Union's chin. On contact, the blade attached to the toe of his boot ejected, cutting through skin, muscle and tongue.

Crimson rivers trickled from the corners of Union's mouth. Eyes wide, he stumbled back. Like Bane, like every combatant, he'd trained to fight no matter the extent of an injury, so he didn't run. He even blocked Bane's next strike.

The insects-rodents—insectents—reached Bane at last, crawling up his legs. *Biting* his legs. Mild pain, wicked aftershocks.

He cursed as his vision clouded. Damn it! The illusion *did* incite true harm, tormenting him. Weakness invaded his limbs, and he wobbled on his feet.

If they harmed him this severely, what would they do to Nola?

Union laughed. As Bane flicked and flung the insectents off his body, the bastard plunged a blade into his shoulder wound. Searing agony. Black dots in his vision. The beast roared louder, scattering his thoughts. All but one. *Don't transform, don't you dare transform.*

Another thought aligned. Nola hadn't teleported away. Her scent hadn't faded. Why had he ever encouraged her to stay put unless things got bad? Things always got bad.

"Go!" he shouted to her, even knowing he would transform the moment she obeyed. "Now!"

Damn it! He heard no telltale sounds to signal her departure. No whoosh of air, no rustle of clothing. Fury graduated into rage, slashing through his calm veneer.

Like any good soldier, Union used Bane's distraction to his advantage, planting a foot on his thigh, stepping up and wrapping a leg around his neck. Intending to rip off his head? Big mistake. Huge.

Even as the male whaled on his face, Bane made no move to defend himself. Retaining a tight grip on Union's legs, Bane purposely fell back and rolled, flipping over his opponent. The male expected the action and lashed out with lightning speed, stabbing him in the side—a countermove *Bane* anticipated.

He endured the newest flare of pain and blood loss with a cold grin, just to execute his next strike. As he unfolded to his feet, he slashed his sword up, up, raking the tip from Union's groin to his sternum. The shallow slice didn't nick an organ or bone; it delivered a paper-thin cut across his flesh, as hoped.

Bane's grin widened. The wound would *never* heal. And, with every action the warrior made, the cut would deepen. *Welcome to hell.*

Union bellowed and jumped up, blood trickling from the cut. He must have lost the ability to power his illusion; the insectents vanished.

To force the male into motion, Bane swung his sword wildly. Union dove across the sand and—

No, no, not Union but his illusion. The real Union had rendered himself invisible—to anyone but Bane and his goggles—and now raced toward the ocean, hoping to swim away.

He thinks to escape me? To fight again another day? To threaten Nola another day?

As Bane's control disintegrated, the beast roared and clawed, more determined than ever to break free. Soon, he would succeed.

Bane tossed his sword and goggles aside. Just in time. The transformation had already begun...

NOLA WATCHED THE brutal battle while undergoing a fight of her own. Her opponent? Fear.

She feared for Bane's life as much as his future. *Whether he admitted it or not, he cared for her...yet, she had a huge secret—Dark Nola.*

The instant he learned about Dark Nola, he would go back to hating Nola, certain she would morph into a cold-blooded monster. He would consider her a too-risky investment.

To him, I'm a bad bet.

Her stomach flip-flopped as Bane transformed. Bones elongated, and green scales grew over his flesh. His teeth...

Oh, sweet mercy. He'd turned into a nightmarish Godzilla-type being with wings, and her mind threatened to shut down. Aliens, she could believe. Supernatural abilities, too. But this...

Knowing he could transform was one thing. Actually witnessing it was another thing entirely.

She'd seen his wings before, of course, but never the full monty, and she didn't know whether to be awed or horrified by them.

Smoke curled from its—his—nostrils. He turned away from Union, who stood in place, daring him to attack, and centered his attention on the water. Why put his back to an enemy? So foolish!

The beast sprayed a stream of fire over the ocean's surface. A man's screams pierced the salt-and-blood-scented air. Nola frowned. The beast lunged, snatching—

The real Union.

The Union standing on the beach was an illusion, just like those giant scorpions. Real-Union thrashed around, trying to escape the beast's jaws of death. After shaking the male with enough force to snap his neck, the beast dropped its bounty and flinched, in obvious pain. Did he share Bane's injuries, or have ones of his own? Or both?

Union crawled away, exerting so much energy a vein popped up in his forehead. Despite the beast's gargantuan size, he proved shockingly fast. In a blink, he mauled Union's torso, ripping out his rib cage.

As she peeked through the foliage that shielded her from the fighters, a horrified gasp escaped. The slightest noise. And yet the monster whipped his head around, his large black eyes zeroing in where she crouched. Fathomless, deep, endless, *terrifying* eyes, with no hint of Bane's passion, only his fury. Blood splattered the creature's face, and viscera hung from its razor-sharp teeth.

Holding her gaze, he blew another stream of fire, setting Union ablaze. A scream brewed in the back of her throat. Union was dead, utterly eviscerated. *I'm clearly next on the menu.*

Teleport. Teleport now!

The creature turned his whole body in her direction, preparing to attack. She reared back, tripping over a tree root. Heart galloping, she toppled to her butt. Frantic, Nola scrambled up and ran. Fast. Faster. A cowardly move? Probably. But no sane person would stick around to challenge that...that thing.

She wracked her brain for a place to go. Back to Zion? No way. Someone had already found their hideout. Try to teleport to Vale?

Heck no. If the beast were to follow her...

What about going home?

Home! Yes! As she ran, she pictured the small, two-bedroom house she and Vale rented in Strawberry Valley, Oklahoma, the tornado and flood capital of the world. She adored the house's shabby chic furnishings, even though said furnishings were way shabbier than chic. They'd spent all their extra money on bills, Vale's business degree, and the trip to Russia, so interior design had taken a back seat.

Seconds passed. Nola remained on the island. Crap! Her stupid panic must have stifled her stupid ability.

The beast gave chase, the entire island shaking. Trees crashed behind her. Bile churned in her stomach, panic threatening to give way to hysteria.

Quickening her pace, she dared a glance over her shoulder. So close. *Too* close, murder gleaming in the endless abyss of his eyes.

By the time she faced forward again, the beast was almost upon her, the steam from his nostrils charring her shirt and blistering her skin. As she whimpered, he slammed his snout into the middle of her back, lifting her off her feet, sending her body flying through the air.

A tree trunk stopped her flight, its bark like razors, flaying off a layer of flesh as she slid to the ground.

Pain reverberated along her nerve endings, her world going black. Blink, blink, blink. When sight returned, she realized the beast loomed over her. He lowered his face to hers, and pressed one massive foot against her thigh, pinning her in place. His claws sliced her pants, her skin and embedded in her muscle. Hot blood trickled from the puncture wounds, pooling in the dirt.

A new lump grew in her throat, this one barbed, ensuring only a mewl emerged.

Huffing and puffing, the beast stared at her with malice and aggression, a look she'd gotten used to seeing from Bane. But, with the fiend's nose a mere inch from hers, his breath was like fire, blistering her chin. Gristle splattered his face and dripped from his teeth— teeth he displayed in all their horrifying glory when he peeled back his lips. On his shoulder, between a cluster of scales, was a bleeding gash the same size as Bane's.

Do not make any sudden moves.

With every fiber of her being, she wanted to command him to back off, leave, something! Would the beast be forced to follow her orders, like Bane? Maybe. Probably. Her golden god certainly believed it. But deep down, Nola suspected she would do more harm than good. *If* she survived this encounter, of course. *I will, I must.* By ordering the beast around, she would be no better than the queens he despised.

So, all Nola said? "N-nice dragon. My name is Nola Lee, and I come in peace." Ugh. How cliché. She tried again. "I'm in the market for friends, and I'd love to get to know you apart from Bane. What do you think?"

Steam curled from his nostrils, and she gulped.

"Do you go by the name Bane as well, or do you have your own?" she asked, determined. "Are you an extension of him, or a separate being entirely?"

His eyelids closed for a moment. One set of eyelids,

anyway. Another set blink-blinked, and the end result
was freaky. But the creature never made a peep.

Since he hadn't burned or chomped on her yet, she
figured she'd chosen the right track. So she tried again,
saying, "I could call you Bane Junior, Junior for short.
Or Puff. Oh! I know. What do you think of Drogo?" Of
all the movies and TV shows she'd watched with Vale,
one character had intrigued her more than any other—
Khal Drogo from *Game of Thrones*.

How fitting, considering Drogo's love interest was
known as the Mother of Dragons…and at the end of
the series, she'd gone off the deep end, becoming the
Mad Queen.

Preach.

Not that Nola wanted to be the beast's girlfriend or
anything. *Bane's* girlfriend, however…

*Maybe I could, I don't know, help his heart heal, the
way I helped his body heal?*

"H-how do you feel about being petted?" Doing
her best not to startle him, she slowly reached up. The
closer she got, the more her hand trembled. Finally, she
achieved contact.

He jerked, but he didn't punish her or move away.

Nola rewarded him, stroking his snout. Marveling.
His black-and-green scales were as smooth as glass, as
hard as steel and as hot as the sun.

"Drogo," she whispered. "I don't mean to complain,
okay, but you're hurting my leg." To be honest, the pain
caused by his claws and crushing weight didn't compare to the agony she'd endured again and again during flares and opioid withdrawals. "If you want me to
stay here with you, I'll stay here. You can free my leg.

Okay?" she said, always stroking, hopefully easing the fiend. "Give me a chance to prove I won't run. Please."

When his gaze slid to her leg, she knew he'd understood her words. If she succeeded in winning Drogo over, well, what *couldn't* she do? Save Vale? Surely! Save Adwaewethian hybrids? Of course! Ensure Bane's vengeance? Without a doubt.

"Earlier, you winced. What's hurting you?" she whispered, searching his gaze. "Maybe I can help you the way I help Bane, and order you to heal."

He snarled. Rather than easing off her leg, he applied more pressure, watching as she panted, squirmed and wheezed. Once again, the world began to blacken.

Okay. Friendship was out, and an order to heal would be met with certain death. Got it.

Just as she'd instinctively known he'd hate her if she issued an order, she knew he'd never respect her if she begged for mercy. Too weak, too fragile? Never again!

"Well," she squeaked. "If this is the end for me, I have one last thing to say. Congrats! You are officially as bad as the queens you're forced to serve. They hurt others, and so do you."

Before she passed out, he did it. He plucked his claws from her thigh and stepped back. The pressure eased, but the pain amplified as blood flooded back into her limb.

To her shock, his expression seemed to project, *Go, before I change my mind and eat your head like a cake ball on a stick.*

"Thank you," she breathed. Though she'd failed to teleport only minutes ago, she closed her eyes and pictured her home in Strawberry Valley. An-n-nd yes! Without a tidal wave of panic—and perhaps a stronger link to Drogo?—her ability had worked.

She experienced extreme weightlessness. Cool night air turned warm and musty, and excitement bloomed. When she opened her eyes, she stood in her living room, dripping blood on the carpet.

CHAPTER SIXTEEN

Relationship blues got you down?

GETTING AWAY FROM Bane proved easier than getting *to* Bane. Maybe because she didn't have hours of vomiting in her rearview? Nola scanned the living room she hadn't seen for a month.

Home sweet home.

All was as she'd left it. The same shabby chic furnishings remained: a floral print couch, a coffee table with peeling white paint, papered walls that displayed different kinds of birds and a rug with frayed edges. Christmas lights hung from the ceiling year-round. Framed photos of Vale and Nola making funny faces covered the side tables, intermixed with vases of dried flowers and a lamp shaped like a pair of rain boots.

Nola and her sis had created a beautiful, quirky environment with limited funds, and she was proud of everything they'd accomplished. One day, she hoped to buy designer drapes and—

"Nooo!" Without Bane's presence, withdrawal symptoms thundered to new life. Instant aches and pains, flop sweat and shakes so violent she probably looked like she was having a seizure. On top of everything else, she got to deal with the beast's parting gift.

Eyes watering, stomach roiling, she stumbled into

her bedroom…her private bathroom. Every movement a special kind of agony, she liberated the first aid kit from the medicine cabinet. Through sheer force of will, she found the strength to peel off her ripped, bloody clothes, drape a towel over the toilet lid and plop down. The sight of her leg…

Like ground hamburger meat. Bile surged, and she gagged. Since she was a royal, her word law to Adwaewethians…since *she* was part Adwaewethian… "I command you to heal," she told her leg.

One minute, two. Nothing happened.

Dang it! As she cleaned and bandaged each puncture, darkness infiltrated and battered her mind, threatening to pull her into a sweet oblivion. She needed a date with 9-1-1 and stitches.

Problem #1: no money to pay the bill. Problem #2: she was a drug addict, the use of prolonged opioids in her file; emergency doctors would most definitely assume she had injured herself for more pills. They had in the past. Problem #3: paramedics would ask questions she couldn't answer.

How was she supposed to explain a dragon/phoenix shape-shifter? Claim a wild animal attacked her? Authorities might go hunting. What if they killed an innocent creature? Just the thought upped her stress level. What's more, her "natural-born instinct" would erase any words about Bane. Not that she wanted to tell strangers about him.

My warrior, my secret.

What if someone had reported her and Vale missing? People would want proof Vale still lived. And what if Erik monitored nearby medical facilities? He'd track her down to use her against Vale, Bane and Zion. Three for the price of one.

So badly she yearned to return to Bane. Craved his arms around her, holding her close. Desired his breath fanning over her skin, and his scent filling her nose. Longed to tease and please him, and be teased and pleased in return.

Nola doubted she had the strength to teleport again. And what if he was still in beast form?

Her heartbeat sped up. Just before he'd transformed, he'd commanded her to run, wanting to save her from harm. She'd failed to comply, remaining nearby in case he needed her, and now she suffered the consequences. Her fault, not his.

Besides, despite the awful condition of her thigh, she didn't regret meeting Drogo. Better to know what you were up against than to forever wonder. At least she hadn't peed herself during the introduction. *Gold star for me.*

Once the punctures were clean and sealed with butterfly bandages, she removed and stored the jewelry she'd taken from Bane's cave, and tied a plastic bag around her thigh. Then, she showered off the blood and grime.

Her pain hit jacked up, and she hurried to come up with a decent plan. *Rest, if you can. Weather out the worst of the withdrawal. Figure out your next move.*

She exited the stall and removed the bag. Exhausted, she brushed her teeth and changed into a T-shirt that read Careful, I Bite, a pair of short shorts and fluffy bunny slippers.

Clutching a bucket like a life raft, she limped to bed and eased under the covers. *I've come full circle.* The trip to Russia had begun and ended in this room. Here, she and Vale had lain beside each other and planned every detail. They'd talked, laughed and dreamed, unaware of the trials awaiting them.

Tears gathered and fell, wetting the sheets. Unfortunately, sleep *did* prove impossible, her pain simply too great. A fever ravaged her insides, using her organs as kindling. She alternated between sweating and shaking, a wildfire and an ice storm tormenting her at alternating intervals. A moan slipped from her compressed lips. Her heart pounded faster and far too hard, then fluttered and squeezed. Her chest constricted, flattening her lungs.

In an attempt to distract herself, she charged her phone and checked her email. Lots of messages from her bosses, asking where she was. She replied, apologizing for the lack of communication and asking for more time off. The bakery owner and the magazine editor responded in minutes—to fire her. Her landlord had also reached out to inform her that rent was late, and she had one week to pay or he'd kick her out.

He'd sent the message three days ago. So, she had four days left. Unless he'd meant one business week, in which case the time got cut in half.

Lose her house? She gazed around the bedroom, and tried to see it as Bane might. The walls were pale pink and covered with framed photos of Vale and Carrie. *Pang.* Makeup littered the surface of the vanity, and romance novels dominated her nightstand. Wispy white lace draped the bed's four posters.

Too frilly and feminine for Bane's tastes?

Tragic and sexy Bane, who she wanted more each day. Before, she'd considered doing something to help mend his broken heart. Now she wasn't sure she could guard her own in the process.

Footsteps thudded, shaking the entire house. Wishing she'd held on to her dagger as she'd run from Drogo, or that she'd thought to keep a kitchen knife in her nightstand, Nola tensed. Had Erik found her? What about Bane and his beast? Zion? Vale? Should she try to teleport or hide?

Less than an hour ago, she'd faced a dragon and survived. Why run now? Why be afraid of a person, other-worlder or even death?

"Nola?" An armed Zion entered the bedroom, his stride long and strong. Spotting her curled up in bed, he sheathed his daggers and exhaled with relief.

"I'm happy to see you," she said, and she meant it. Yet, part of her wished Bane had been the one to walk through the door. "So glad you survived the attack."

"How did you escape the closet without disengaging the door lock?" he asked, getting right down to business.

"I'm happy to see you, too, Nola," she said, doing her best impersonation of him. At some point, she'd kicked off the covers, providing him with a direct line to the crimson stains on her bandage.

He went motionless, fury exploding in his eyes. "Who hurt you?"

No way she'd allow him to retaliate against Bane. So what could she—should she—tell him? *Think!* But her muddled, sluggish brain refused to work.

Why not tell the truth? "I can't explain. Literally, I can't. Something always stops me. But I'll be fine," she said, then hurried to change the subject. "How did you find me?"

He slitted his lids, a silent promise to return to the original subject—soon. "I found the cabin in the mountains, the one you and your sister inhabited after you got lost. I ransacked the interior and unearthed a small, hard paper with your picture and an address."

Ah. Her driver's license. She and Vale had left their IDs on the kitchen counter alongside a note, requesting aid.

Zion eased beside her, leery. "I come bearing news. While we were parted, Erik abducted your sister. But, with Knox's help, she mounted a successful escape."

Nola's heart plummeted, then soared. "That's wonderful—"

"In the process, hundreds of humans were killed, and Terran enforcers took Vale captive."

"—and terrible." So many people slaughtered, victims of a war they knew nothing about. Had law enforcement treated Vale like a perpetrator or a victim? "Is—is she locked up?"

"Yes, but she won't be harmed. She'll be freed. Soon. When she killed Celeste, she somehow absorbed the combatant's ability to enchant the people around her."

Really? "Do all combatants absorb the abilities of their victims?"

"No. She's the only one. Everyone else is granted access to the defeated soldier's weapon, no more, no less."

So why was Vale different? And how could Nola help her? "Who ambushed our safe house?"

"Erik and his men," Zion said. "They are following you and are currently stationed outside this house. Or they were. I dispatched them."

And she hadn't had a clue!

"Erik has realized you are special to the Adwaewethian," he added. "He plans to use you against Bane. And me, since I've expressed interest in your care. At the next Assembly of Combatants, I must convince him—

and everyone else—that you are dead. Your sister included. Her reaction to the news must be genuine."

"No way." She shook her head. "I won't hurt her, even to save myself a bit of trouble."

"A bit?" he asked, brow lifted. "How do you suggest we proceed, then?"

She thought for a moment, an idea crystallizing. "Do you have the cell phone I gave you?"

"I do. I plugged in your address, just as you taught me, and found shockingly detailed photos of your house, allowing me to portal here."

"Let's give the cell to Vale. I'll send a text message to it, telling her not to believe anything you say. That way, she'll reason out the truth after her initial reaction to your death bomb."

Before he agreed, she started typing a message, the number already programmed into her address book. Sorry our convo got cut short. Do whatever you must to survive, & don't worry about me, ok? I'm good as pie & gonna stay that way. Lady Carrie's girls forever! Oh, & don't believe Z. I repeat. Do NOT."

Lady Carrie's, the name of the gourmet donut shop they would—or would not—be opening. Proof of her identity.

Send.

Deciding to use her "fragility" to her advantage—a girl had to use the weapons in her arsenal, right?—Nola batted her lashes at Zion, saying, "Please do this for me. You're so big and strong, and I'll owe you one."

He pursed his lips but nodded. "I will do this, and yes, you will owe me. As payment, you will help me recruit Bane to stop Erik. The viking preserved the base camps he knew about, and planted bombs and other traps. When we escaped the ice prison, he watched as we portaled away. He and his people had placed cameras throughout the mountains. That's how he found my dimension."

Unease prickled the back of her neck, her stomach performing a series of flips. "He could be watching and listening right now."

"I have visited your house every few hours since our separation and already searched the rooms," he said. "There's no evidence of tampering."

Okay. All right.

"Now," he said, his tone hardening. He drew in a deep breath, held it, then exhaled slowly. "I've been tolerant of your secrets. Lenient, even. But I must take measures to protect myself, and my realm. I'm sorry, Nola, but men who trust others are the first to die."

Foreboding joined the unease, sweeping through her. "What are you getting at?"

He unsheathed one of his daggers. "I need the truth about your connection to Bane, and there's only one way to get it. I'm sorry," he repeated, "but this will hurt."

Must get to Nola.

Nearing frantic desperation, Bane secured his goggles around his neck, strapped Valor's sword to his back and anchored a piece of Union's belt around each of his biceps. The beast had sheared the link in half, turning one weapon into two. To his shock, both worked! Strength hummed inside his bones and flowed into his muscles. More strength than he'd ever wielded.

Must get to Nola. Must protect her.
Must not hurt her.

The beast protested, only to go quiet, as if uncertain about the best way to proceed. That was a first.

The lair had been destroyed. The sunny island had been the last place anyone should have thought to look for him. So how had Union learned his location?

All Bane knew for sure? If one combatant had found him, others would, too. And soon. But he had nowhere else to go. Where was Nola? How terribly had he harmed her? How much did she hate him?

When Bane had transformed, something shocking had happened. He'd remained aware as the beast overtook him. Another first. Maybe because he'd fought harder than ever before, determined to save his princess.

He'd learned the shoulder wound bothered the beast, too, a vulnerability they could ill afford.

A more shocking development? Nola's unwavering bravery.

She'd faced the beast, unflinching. And, though she'd been racked by pain, she'd issued no orders. Instead, she'd petted the fiend's snout and offered friendship.

The beast—now named Drogo, apparently—hadn't made up his mind about her. He was confused, and annoyed about it.

Bane had severely underestimated this precious female, with her kind heart and plucky determination. Her quiet strength blew his mind. She had something he envied: an ability to remain calm while the world crumbled around her—or when a dragon contemplated the many ways to end her life.

Scowling, Bane paced underneath the tarp, thoughts of Nola tolling on. If Drogo hadn't decided to let her go, she would have died. She would have died *badly*, and Bane would have been unable to save her.

Can't lose her. Not her.

He stutter-stepped. *I care about the woman who controls my future?* He...might.

Damn it! From now on, he had to remain on emotional guard.

Since the transformation had torn his clothes to shreds, Bane stalked to the trunk and liberated a pair of leathers and combat boots. As soon as he'd tucked his shaft behind his fly, he reached out to Nola.

Where are you, dove? Dove? The endearment left him without permission, and yet it fit her: small, delicate and graceful. *The beast is caged. You have nothing to fear from me, I swear it.*

An extended pause. Then—*I'm home.*—

Her breathy voice filled his head, igniting powerful, seething lust. He told himself, *Must remain on guard.*

Then, he pushed his voice into her head once again, saying, *I won't harm you again, you have my word. Tell me to come to you. Please.* Would she do it? *Let me teach you how to fight, how to lead your soldiers and how to help me defeat Aveline. You can yell at me for what Drogo did.* Then, Bane would talk her from her pique. Or kiss her from it.

No! No more kissing Nola. No more touching her, either.

Again, her voice drifted through his mind.—*Zion is here. He's doing something to me. Something I don't like, though I don't know what it is.*—

A growl rumbled in Bane's chest. Zion was doing something to Nola, so Zion would pay. *Let me see through your eyes. Let me see what he's doing to you.*

—*How?*—

The explanation rushed from him, a sense of urgency all but setting his feet on fire. *To communicate telepathi-*

cally, a queen and her warrior must be linked. You have the ability to deepen our connection.

When he felt a pinprick inside his brain, he said, *Yes, dove. Just like that.*

Suddenly, the world around him blackened. He blinked, another world appearing. He saw a small bedroom, with lots of pink and lace, and worn furniture unworthy of a queen.

This was working! Satisfaction punched him.

Look at Zion, he commanded.

She obeyed, craning her head to the side. Zion sat on the bed, too close for Bane's liking. The male had a bloody diamond pinched between his fingers—a diamond he'd ripped from his torso, judging by the bleeding hole left behind. He pressed the gemstone against Nola's forehead, and Bane knew. The combatant hoped to capture her thoughts with energy manipulation.

With a snarl, Bane grazed his thumb over the Rifters to open a portal. Having seen the room, he could now travel there anytime he wished.

At the other end of the tarp, two layers of air peeled back, revealing a live glimpse at the bedroom. The scent of honeysuckle and jasmine wafted to his nostrils, tainted by the metallic tang of blood.

Fury exploded through him, his muscles tensing. Ready to do murder, Bane marched forward...

CHAPTER SEVENTEEN

Does he want more, or are you fooling yourself?

ONE SECOND NOLA conversed with Bane, the next she heard a wealth of noises. Shattering glass. Pained grunts. A whistle of metal, a heavy thud and a loud crash. Animalistic rage electrified the air. What had—

Realization: Zion had stopped whatever he'd been doing to her mind, and now engaged in combat. With Bane, who'd gone quiet?

Oh, yes. Definitely with Bane. His scent cocooned and calmed her. He'd rushed to her defense, her safety a priority to him, just as he'd claimed, and she lo—liked him for it.

Such a fool. He hadn't saved Nola; he'd saved the Terran royal who would deliver his vengeance. Would he ever want her *more* than vengeance?

By the time the world came back into focus, her aches and pains had faded. *Bane, my sickness and cure.* Her bedroom lay in shambles, furniture overturned, hunks of plaster and glass scattered everywhere. Blood stained the tattered comforter.

Window curtains were wadded on the floor, streams of sunlight infiltrating the room. Wow. The night had passed. Zion occupied the light, while Bane remained in the shadows. They were inches apart, panting and bloodier than the blanket, in the midst of an epic staredown.

Pulling her gaze from Bane proved impossible, the sight of him soul-searing. And concerning. The permagash in his shoulder had worsened, spreading over his collarbone. If he and Zion fought again…

Who was she kidding? They would fight again, guaranteed. Bane projected fiery rage, his intensity making her heart flutter, while Zion displayed icy determination. Soon, they would erupt. This time, they wouldn't stop until someone ended up dead.

"Enough," she called, vaulting to her feet. Miracle of miracles, her legs held steady, the puncture wounds healed. Not even scabs remained. Zion's doing, or her own? Always before, her cuts and bruises had undergone repair at a normal rate.

Am I becoming immortal, my body preparing for the Blood Rite? How am I supposed to feel about that?

Figure it out later.

Nerves jacked, heart galloping a mile a minute, Nola moved between the warriors, arms outstretched to push the two rabid predators apart.

"Enough," she repeated, glancing from one male to the other. "Back off. And don't even think about arguing with me." Every time she refocused on Bane, another layer of his fiery exterior burned away. Soon, only raw sensuality would remain.

Her thoughts momentarily blanked. What else had she meant to say? Oh, yeah. "You *owe* me, both of you. Bane, remember when you insulted me, tearing my self-esteem to shreds and injured my leg? Zion, remember when you tried to invade my mind?"

Bane winced ever so slightly, and Zion raised his chin, unrepentant.

"She's mine, and I never share." With a speed too fast for the human eyes to track, Bane clasped her wrist, yanked and spun her behind him, putting her chest against his back. He snagged a strong, muscular arm around her, holding her in place.

Those astonishing words…that unshakable assertion… warm shivers trekked down her spine. What a difference in him! His heart had already begun to heal. This was… this… *I might have this thing in the bag.*

Zion lifted his hands, palms up, and stepped back, his frosty fury reduced to a slight irritation. "I'm not sorry I took measures to ensure my safety, Nola. But I *am* sorry I betrayed your trust to do it."

"Apology *not* accepted," she told him, detaching from Bane and moving to his side. "What secrets did you unearth from my mind?" Had Zion learned about her alien heritage, or her connection to the Adwaewethian?

"None. You have some kind of block," Zion said.

Truly? Neat! Bane had once said the same.

When she met his gaze, she got snared. Couldn't look away, the rest of the world forgotten. Sizzling awareness crackled between them. Her belly quivered, the clawing need she'd lived with since finding him in the cave demanding its due.

"Princess?" Bane asked, his voice strained and huskier than usual. Did he feel it, too?

Focus. Deep breath in, out. Crap! His scent had intensified and now infused her cells. She could *feel* him inside her.

"My offer stands," Zion told Bane. "Let's work together to slay Erik and his acolytes."

Bane looked between her and Zion, his eyes slitting. "Do you know who always loses the All War? Combatants foolish enough to trust the competition."

"Do it anyway," Nola said, forming a steeple with her hands. "Please." What would convince someone like Bane? "We can take out more competitors, win more weapons and accomplish what we want to accomplish. If you hadn't noticed, we're kind of losing right now." Wait. What if Zion planned to trick Bane?

No, no, no. Zion had secrets, sure, but at heart, he was a good man.

Bane stared at her, anger mounting. But he said, "I will do it. I will agree to a temporary truce." He cast his attention to Zion, adding, "But you will do no harm to Nola. You will not try to read her thoughts. You will not touch her. You do, and I'll end the truce with your heart in my palm."

Again, he'd staked a claim on her. Again, warm shivers trekked down her spine. Her blood transformed into champagne, her head fogging, pleasure making her giddy.

Zion growled, all *I'm so fierce, I only ever do what I want.* But like Bane, he snapped, "Very well. We have ourselves a temporary truce." He slid his gaze to Nola. "I'll do as promised and pass the cell phone to Vale. I'll even attempt to recruit her and Knox to our cause— again."

"Thank you," she said.

"I have no doubt Knox will try to kill me again."

"You'll both be fine, I'm sure of it." Desperate to see her sister, she said, "I'll go with you and—"

"You will not," Bane roared at the same time Zion

said, "I cannot convince other combatants you are dead
if you are seen alive. You must stay with Bane."

"Ah. A fake death. Wise." Bane inclined his head, his
version of a nod. "I will hide her before another combatant finds us. Be careful when you portal in. Or not.
I will be setting traps."

Exasperated, she bit out, "Do I get a say about any
of this?"

"No," they replied in unison.

Rather than lather-up about their caveman tactics, she
grinned, smug. "Look at you two. Already working together. Am I a good bromance matchmaker, or what?"

Bane rolled his eyes, yet his enlarged pupils suggested her courage had surprised—and delighted—him.
She preened.

Zion blew her a kiss, then told Bane, "Show me how
good you are at hiding and setting those traps, and I'll
show you how good I am at tracking and avoiding trouble." The words were half brag, half threat.

"You're on," Bane said.

Zion smiled and traced a thumb over his Rifters, a
portal opening in her bedroom. Judging by the mountainous background with wisps of cotton floating on a
warm breeze, the portal led back to Colorado.

The wind gusted into her room, strong enough to rattle the pieces of shattered glass on her floor.

He walked through and spun to face them. Thought-
ful, he peered from Nola to Bane until the portal closed.

Alone with Bane. His wicked scent filled her nose,
and his heat seared her skin. His staggering intensity lit
her up inside. Would he kiss her? Would she let him?

He prowled closer to her, the unhurried action languidly sensual. His magnificent eyes gleamed with hun-

ger. "What the beast did to you…" He lifted his chin and squared his shoulders. "I'm sorry, dove."

Dove. This might be the third time he'd used the endearment, and she wasn't sure what it was supposed to mean. "You were aware in beast form?"

"I was." He massaged the back of his neck. "He hates you, but he is also unwillingly intrigued by you. You could have issued a command. He wanted you to. When you didn't, you surprised and confused him."

Had she surprised and confused Bane, too? Maybe even…impressed him? She wanted to ask, but didn't. *I prefer warrior women.* Okay, so, no need to ask. One small act wouldn't prove her mettle. Although, there was a chance it would help her sneak past his defenses.

"I might be a princess," she said, "but I'm not a queen. I've never hurt Drogo, or you, and I'm tired of being punished for the crimes of other royals. If you attack me again, I'll do whatever is necessary to save myself, just as you would do anything to save yourself."

He continued his advance, prowling closer, forcing her to walk backward…until she smacked into the wall. He flattened his hands next to her temple, caging her in. With his towering height and wide shoulders, he all but engulfed her. She gulped and trembled, but not with fear.

"Why didn't you do whatever was necessary on the island? Rather than commanding Drogo to stand down, you petted him."

She plucked at the collar of his shirt, saying, "I didn't want to override your—his—free will, as other queens have done."

A moment passed, then another, the silence almost unbearable. His features were shell-shocked again. He quietly asked, "What am I going to do with you, Nola Lee?"

"Trust me?" *Fall in love with me?* "I'm never giving in to my—to a dark side like the other royals." She traced her hands up, up and cupped the sides of his exquisite face. A lover's hold. His beard stubble tickled her skin, flurries of desire dancing through her.

"I won't change," he said, his voice gruff. "I've been through too much, my will like iron."

When he wrapped his deliciously calloused fingers around her wrists, she expected a gentle push to separate their bodies. Instead, he tugged her closer, crisscrossing her arms at his nape. Her breasts smashed against his rock-hard chest, her nipples puckering.

"Where are we headed?" she asked.

He flicked his tongue over an incisor. "Erik has targeted Zion and me for elimination. We must stay on the move."

Planned to pretend his shaft wasn't hardening between her legs? Okay. "I'll pack a bag, just as soon as you let me go."

LET NOLA GO when he wanted to hold on forever? No! But Bane did it, anyway. He released her wrists, severing contact, and stepped back. Keeping her safe remained priority one, and her honeysuckle-jasmine scent agitated the beast. Everything else agitated Bane. Her heat. Her softness. Those starry eyes. Those rosebud lips. That breathy voice. That shocking carnality.

He wanted Nola. His gaze strayed to the bed. He wanted Nola *now*. He burned with desire, his cells like embers, passion-smoke filling him, his skin pulling taut, ready to burst apart at the seams. His heart raced, and shaft throbbed.

Thinking clearly had become an unattainable dream. The very reason he'd agreed to an alliance with Zion. Surely! Not because he'd wanted Nola protected at all costs, no matter the danger to himself, and two warriors were better than one. And certainly not because Bane was desperate for a friend, someone who would have his back, if only for a little while. Making friends and trusting others would only get him in trouble.

"Take me to the bathroom," he said.

She licked her lips, wrenching a growl from deep inside him, then turned to lead the way. A first aid kit waited on the sink, already open. Bloody rags rested at the bottom of a trash bin. Nola's blood, due to injuries Drogo had caused.

Bane pressed his tongue to the roof of his mouth. "Go ahead and pack your bag while I clean up."

Rocking from foot to foot, silent, she watched him, lost in thought. Finally, she nodded and padded from the bathroom, leaving him alone. He shut the door. After he cleaned and bandaged his shoulder—the wound worsened by Zion's hammering punches—he gripped the edge of the sink and stared at his reflection in the mirror. Golden hair mussed and streaked with blood. Eyes stark but also glittering with…excitement? No, absolutely not. Probably annoyance. Golden stubble decorated his jaw. Cuts and bruises littered his chest.

"Get yourself together," he quietly demanded. But damn it! Nola made him want things he shouldn't want. A family. A future. Things he couldn't afford.

Must purge this burning desire. Can't lose someone else. Just…can't.

Head high, shoulders back, he exited the bathroom.

"Almost done," she said, puttering around the bedroom, gathering the things she wished to take.

Curiosity drew him into the hall, where pictures of Nola and Vale covered the walls. One photo captured his attention more than any other. A close-up of Nola's face. The sun shone brightly behind her, creating a halo over her blue-black locks. Her eyes sparkled, and roses painted her cheeks. She radiated pure joy. The kind of joy he'd known when Meredith lived. The kind of joy he'd never thought to experience again.

His chest clenched. *Don't do what you're thinking about doing. Do not—* Bane plucked the picture from the wall, tossed the frame to the floor and tucked the folded image into his pocket. *Okay, you did it.*

Embarrassed for himself but still brimming with curiosity about the woman with a "will of iron," he checked out the rest of the house. Small, but well maintained, with countless feminine touches. Lace here, pink there. On the coffee table were enamel pots overflowing with dried flowers. On the kitchen counter, he found a stack of *Oklahoma Love Match* magazines. No two issues were the same, yet Nola's name occupied a tiny spot of each cover.

How to Go From Enemies to Lovers.

The Five Must Haves For Any Single Woman Looking For Love.

So You Slept Together. Now What?

Nola had once mentioned being a baker and an author. Had she written those articles?

Don't you dare. He glanced over his shoulder. No sign of her. As quietly as possible, he ripped out the article about going from enemies to lovers, folded the paper in half and stuffed it into his pocket, alongside the photo. What had his princess said about the ways of seduction? Perhaps, if he knew, he could better guard his heart against her allure. Because, he'd done a shit job of guarding his desires; they raged out of control.

Why resist her sexually? He lacked the will. In that regard, she'd broken him, her weapon of choice an indomitable spirit nothing and no one could destroy.

I want her, and I will have her.

Relief accompanied the decision. Finally, he would have the one he craved.

His ears twitched, the quiet pitter-patter of her footsteps registering. He tried not to watch as she entered the living room, a vision of loveliness in a pink tank top, jeans and tennis shoes, her dark hair flowing to her waist in glossy waves. But watch he did, his body aflame. *Must have her* soon.

"Where are we going?" she asked, stopping directly in front of him to drop a bag at his feet. "Because I have an idea."

Her nearness…affected him. Blood like fire, guts twisting. He tapped his temple and pushed his next words into her mind. *Erik might have cameras hidden here.*

She licked her lips and nodded in understanding. —*I think we should go to Roswell, New Mexico. About seventy years ago, something crashed there. A lot of people believe it was an alien spaceship. Now the government guards the area but…what if there are weapons they haven't found? Weapons only other aliens can activate? If we acquire them, we'll have a major advantage over Erik.*—

Interesting. Few other-worlds used spaceships. In fact, Bane could think of only one. Forêt. Had the ruler of Forêt broken the rules like Aveline, and sent warriors here?

Bane searched his mental files. In the Terran All War, Halo was the combatant from Forêt, and he'd brought a pair of detachable metal wings. A masterpiece of technology. While Halo engaged in combat, the wings guarded his flank.

He told Nola, *Roswell it is, then. Do you have photos of the area?*

—*I don't want to portal there. I want to drive in a car.*—

Why?

—*Out on the open road, we'll remain on the move. No one will be able to pinpoint our location.*—

He peered down at her, only then realizing he'd been combing his fingers through her hair. Now, he fisted the strands, angling her face the way he liked to better tilt her mouth toward his. But he didn't let himself kiss her. *Is there nothing you cannot do, little dove? So far you've freed men from ice, outwitted a beast and led multiple warriors around by the balls. Now you are outsmarting a viking. Yes, we will drive.*

CHAPTER EIGHTEEN

The #1 essential for every road trip!

NOLA AND BANE loaded up in her rust bucket of a car and drove into the city, where she pawned the jewelry she'd liberated from his cave. Everything but the gauntlets. *Mine. I'll never share!* She'd meant what she'd said. She would treasure them, now and always. In fact, they were coming with her on their trip.

Needful of a few other things, she took her golden god to a one-stop shop for hunters. Though a never-ending sense of urgency stabbed her, she decided to act as if this was a normal day, and she and Bane were normal people on their first date. Why not have fun? They were fighting for their lives, yes, but dying without experiencing true joy struck her as wrong.

On the way into the store, she moved ahead of Bane to reach the automatic doors first. In honor of her decision to enjoy their time together, she pretended to open those doors with magic, waving her hand and saying, "Hocus-pocus."

He gaped at her, amazed. "What strange power is this?"

She erupted into a fit of laughter. Dark lust eclipsed the amazement in his eyes, and she quieted.

"Your laugh," he said, his voice soft but rough. Fierce. "Drives. Me. Insane."

Oh la la. He's hard again.

As she shopped, Bane remained at her side, silent and stoic, tensing when anyone neared. People stared at him, some admiring, most afraid.

Someone snapped a picture of him. To post online, most likely, and she could imagine the caption. *Hot buttered buns. #DoMeBaby.*

Okay, she had better hurry this shopping trip along. If Erik monitored social media, he'd learn Bane's location. Quickening her pace, she threw different items into the basket. Backpacks, XL shirts, another first aid kit, camo pants, camping supplies, snacks, knives, even a handgun and a case of bullets.

When she came to an aisle overflowing with Halloween costumes, she paused. The holiday kicked off in just a few days. And talk about the perfect camouflage! For a single night, they could go anywhere and do anything, and no one would suspect their identities. She grabbed three costumes and headed to check out.

Spotting one of her ex-dates—James—she stopped cold. He stood in line, placing his items on the cashier's conveyor belt. Dang it! What were the odds? Why was he here? Why now?

Earlier this year, she'd let one of her coworkers at the magazine set her up with a cousin. They went to dinner and a movie, her hopes high. He'd held her hand, and she'd felt no sickness. So, when he'd walked her to her door and bent down to kiss her, she hadn't resisted... and ended up vomiting in a flower bed mid-tongue-swab. After that, she'd been too embarrassed to answer his calls and text.

"Nola," James said when he noticed her. He smiled and leaned in, planning to hug her.

Bane stepped between them, telling James, "You will not touch the girl."

The golden god towered over the human.

Color draining from James's cheeks, he reared back, hands up. "Sorry. My bad."

"You did nothing wrong," Nola assured him, flicking Bane a *behave* glance. "Nice seeing you again, James." Wanting everyone to walk away rather than crawl, she moved to another line.

Bane followed at a much slower pace, his aggression spiking. If he lost control of his temper, he would transform into Drogo. People would post pictures and videos all over the internet, and combatants wouldn't be the only ones hot on their trail.

To keep her warrior calm, she stroked his spine, petting him the same way she'd petted his beast. But she did no good, his muscles knotting with tension.

"Your jealousy is cute and all," she said with a teasing tone, "but I promise I'm not planning to fall on his penis…anytime soon."

He pursed his lips. "Tell me about him."

"There's nothing to tell. We only went on one date."

"I should have killed him," Bane hissed.

"Shh." In a soft but fierce voice, she said, "You can't go around threating innocents. Or killing innocents!"

"*Actually*, I can. You prefer that I don't." He pushed the cart, and they moved up the line. "Is he the type of man you usually find attractive?"

Once upon a time, yes. But, if she were being honest, she'd admit things had changed. She craved intensity and heat. Fire. God help her! "Why do you care?" Would he cop to the truth?

He worked his jaw. Rather than answering her question, he changed the subject again. "You once mentioned you write. Do you write what is true, or what is false?"

Uh, why did he want to discuss her job? "I write whatever my boss tells me. Or I did. He fired me. Anyway. I wrote things people hope are fact but could be fiction. I'm unsure."

Bane went still. "A man burned you?"

Sigh. "I meant, my boss told me I couldn't work for him anymore."

He relaxed the slightest bit. "Do you write what *you* believe to be true?"

Cheeks heated, she admitted, "I've never tested my theories."

"But you want to?"

After she'd given up on love? No. But here, now? "Yes." *So badly.* "Why?"

He said no more. *She* said no more, the tension too great.

They paid for their supplies, loaded them into her two-door piece of crap and settled in their seats, with Nola at the wheel. Despite the hour, the sun remained hidden behind thick gray clouds, a storm brewing. A cold breeze contained an electrical charge, and brought the scent of coming rain. Blackbirds flocked to poles and perched on the wires. Beyond them, flatlands stretched for miles, as far as her gaze could see.

They had a ten-hour drive ahead of them. Enough time to plan and scheme their way into Roswell?

After forcing Bane to buckle up, Nola merged onto the highway. "You're being quiet. I don't like it."

"Just thinking," he replied.

Uh-oh. His gruff tone had returned.

He had their purchases piled around him, filling the packs with clothes, camping gear and her gauntlets. As distracted as he appeared, she got the feeling he remained aware of absolutely everything around him, and even clocked her actions.

When he offered nothing more about his thoughts, she prompted, "Thinking about what?"

He offered a shrug, then opened the first aid kit to bandage his shoulder.

Argh! Frustrating man! She sighed. Waiting for something—the story of her life.

Several hours later, after trying and failing to converse with Bane, she spotted a sign and decided to tease him. "Look, Bane!" She faked a squeal. "A phallological museum. They display fake penises. Let's go. Can we? Please, please, please. Only a man with a very small penis would say no."

He opened his mouth, then closed it without saying a word, and she tried not to smile.

"No comment?" she asked.

"This is your brand of vengeance, isn't it? Well, excellent job. It's devious and effective. I must remember to remain on guard, lest my ego receive another flaying."

She tapped her nose and pointed to his chest. "Ding, ding, ding. Stop ignoring me, and I won't drive you into a ditch."

"I've never ignored you, Nola. From the beginning, I've wanted you. Every day—every hour—every minute, I've fought hard to keep my hands off your lush little body. I'm fighting for control even now."

She sucked in a breath. *Do not pull the car to the side*

of the road. Do not climb into his lap. "You know I want you, too," she said, her voice like gravel.

"I knew you were attracted to me, not that you wanted me…so desperately."

"What! Me? Desperate?"

He leaned back in his seat, all satisfied male. "This time, I teased you."

She would have given him the finger, but he'd only think she considered herself his number one fan.

"What made you agree to date him?" he asked. "What did he do to win you?"

"James?" she asked, stalling. Deep breath in, out. If she had to spill the deets in order to move on, she would spill. "He's my coworker's cousin. He came to see her one day. Neither of us knew she'd invite him simply to introduce us. We talked, laughed and he asked if I wanted to grab something to eat. I said yes."

"And?"

"And what?"

"What else did he do?"

"Nothing," she said, her brow furrowing.

"But you are a royal. You are beautiful, smart, courageous and witty. You are a prize. Did he not give you gifts, courting you properly?"

His praise echoed inside her head, the sweetness intoxicating. Before she could respond, a portal opened up in the road, only a few feet away, revealing a shadowy forest. Horror punched her. Too late to swerve!

Horror must have punched Bane, too. He shouted her name. She screamed his as the car shot through the portal—

And slammed into a bank of trees.

Metal crunched and glass shattered, gnarled limbs

forcing their way into the vehicle. Impact threw her forward, the seat belt preventing her from being ejected. An airbag deployed, stopping her face from banging into the steering wheel.

Though adrenaline surged through her, dulling the effects of whiplash and pain—for now—one side of her face blistered, as if she'd rested her cheek on a hot plate. Chemical burns from the airbag's detonation, no doubt. A loud ringing sound clanged in her ears, and her vision blurred.

"Nola!" Bane's voice sounded far away, but ragged concern clanged loud and clear.

She opened her mouth to let him know she had survived, for now, but blood spilled down her throat, choking her. Darkness invaded, mucking up her thoughts…

Blink. Suddenly, she was seated in the back seat of a sedan, healthy, whole and in her right mind. Her parents were up front, talking in hushed tones. Beside her was a car seat holding toddler Nola. Was she reliving the other crash *again*? Dang it, no! She needed to return to Bane. What if he was hurt?

"She's a monster," her father whispered. "We must hide *from* her, not *with* her."

She who? Not baby Nola. No way, no how…right?

"She played in fire without burning," her mom replied, glancing back at Nola with a worried expression. "That doesn't make her a monster."

Wait. They *were* talking about her, weren't they? *Monster*… Her stomach sank.

Her father gripped the wheel so tightly, color bled from his knuckles. Voice shaky, he whispered, "She loves drawing blood from others. She loves *playing* in blood. She's evil, honey, and you know it."

Don't cry. Don't you dare.

"She's my baby," her mother said.

Protective, despite Nola's faults. *There goes another piece of my heart.*

Just as before, a tall, muscled man stood in the middle of the road, and Nola's dad swerved to miss him. The next thing she knew, she had a severe case of vertigo as the car flipped.

Those scuffed leather boots approached the crumpled vehicle…their owner bent down, his golden skin coming into view first, followed by his golden hair and his golden eyes.

As her mother pleaded for mercy and begged for Nola's life, he cast his gaze through the car, exuding satisfaction when he spotted the toddler.

Real Nola bristled, remembering the way he'd reached inside and yanked out her mother.

Her mother met baby Nola's gaze briefly, then focused fully on the man. "There is no baby in the car. You do not hear her. You do not see her."

That hadn't happened last time. Of course, she'd only seen the highlights then. But other little details had changed as well. Had Nola affected the past, and the timing of events?

"Save yourself, Momma," Nola begged. To the man, she snarled, "Don't you dare touch her!"

He gave no indication that he'd heard her as he rubbed his finger over one of his man rings. A bright light suddenly glinted off the pieces of broken glass in the road.

As Nola cried out, she missed bits of a conversation the man was having with…someone.

She forced herself to quiet, to listen.

"Is she the one?" he asked someone Nola couldn't see.

"Yes," a woman hissed. Unfamiliar voice.

Nola frowned. No one stood next to the Adwaewethian, or near the car, yet the woman's volume suggested she stood nearby.

"Remove her heart *and* her head, then kill the child," the woman commanded, almost gleeful now.

"There is no child," he responded.

Nola gasped. He'd obeyed her mother. Her mother had been a royal, too, able to command beasts. She might not have known, but instincts had led her on this day. If only she'd told the man to walk away.

Fighting tears, Nola dove into the front of the vehicle. The warrior reached *through* Nola to grab her mother by the neck, and yanked her onto the street, pulling her through the shattered windowpane.

With a screech, Nola scrambled out the same way. "Let her go!"

"Calm down, little dove." Bane's deep baritone penetrated her awareness. "Please, calm down. Thrashing about isn't good for your injuries."

Injuries? She felt fine…kind of. As she blinked, the past waned and her golden god came into view. He was running through the forest, maneuvering around trees, clutching her close to his chest. Two packs were anchored to his shoulders, even the injured one, and they thumped his back with every step.

Oh…crap. She'd been punching and clawing at him instead of the assassin, and his face bore the brunt of her handiwork. He had a black eye, a bloody nose and a split lip.

Though she stilled, her heart continued to race. A lance of pain shot through her. A herald of what was to come. An instant later, excruciating pains racked her body. "Wh-what happened?"

"We crashed. Once I got you out of the vehicle, your body turned to mist, like it did on the island."

When would the violence end? "Are you hurt?"

"I'm fine, but I need you to remain motionless," he said, still running, running. "There's a piece of metal embedded next to your heart."

What! She reached up. When she wrapped her fingers around a small metal pipe, a whimper escaped.

"I will get you to safety, and you will heal," he rushed out, desperation and concern tinging his ragged voice. "Do you understand? You will heal. Say it."

"I will heal," she whispered, the words slurred. Would she, though? *Colder by the second.* Shudders rocked her against him, aggravating the muscles around the pipe. "Where are we?"

"Don't know. But I know where we'll be."

"Are we being chased?" The road portal…she didn't remember seeing anyone standing within it, or near it, but *someone* had opened it.

"We are. Ronan and Petra are combatants working together. Perhaps dating. Ronan has a glowing sword able to temporarily blind his opponents, and Petra has a sword able to create instant walls out of any material it touches. Metal. Ice. Bone."

She remembered both of those weapons from the cavern battle, especially Petra's. The beautiful female had swung at Bane and a wall of ice had grown from the floor.

Her dark side whispered, *I want the couple dead, killed by my hand. I want to rip out their hearts and feast. I want to take their weapons and slay the man who murdered my parents. I want to hold their hearts in my hands and rejoice as the organ performs its last beat.*

Nola...agreed. Her limbs even vibrated with excitement. *Gimme.*

Just then, she understood Bane's desire for vengeance in a way she hadn't before.

"Bane," she purred. The attempt on his life was another sin to lay at the couple's door. A sin her dark side used as fuel, gaining new ground inside her mind... and her heart?

"Yes, dove?"

"Be a dear and kill them both, but save their hearts for me." *I could use a snack.*

CHAPTER NINETEEN

What to do when he's the king of cling

THE BEAST RAMMED at Bane's skull, anxious to escape, as he sped through a dense, moonlit forest. Tree limbs slapped his face and arms. Sweat dampened his skin, and he labored for every breath, the internal damage caused by the car wreck inundating him with pain. With one hand, he clutched Nola close. With the other, he continually sliced his palm on a dagger blade and flung blood over foliage to create a noticeable trail for their pursuers to follow. He had a plan.

His most violent instincts demanded he stop and fight. *Will make Ronan and Petra pay!* Alas. The well-being of his princess mattered more.

Did Nola realize she'd asked him to kill the couple and save their hearts? Did royal instinct demand she eat the organs to absorb the strength of her enemies? Every queen experienced the urge at some point.

He'd convinced himself Nola would be different, that her iron will might save her from such morbid desires, that she wouldn't grow to crave the act, as Aveline and the other royals had done. Now...

He gnashed his teeth. If he performed the Blood Rite, he would lose sweet, giving and passionate Nola.

Can't lose her. Not her.

Damn it! The woman was more dangerous than he'd ever realized. She'd done what no one else could: she'd snuck past his defenses, past internal barbed wire and into the maximum security prison known as his heart.

Did he love her? No. He didn't. He didn't! He wouldn't, couldn't, shouldn't. Love without strength was misery. But he did care for her.

Can't lose her, he thought again. *Can't relinquish my vengeance, either.* Even the thought made him feel like he'd ripped out his rib cage and exposed his organs. As much as Bane hungered for Nola—frantically, frenziedly—he could not allow Aveline to live. She would only torture and torment his brethren. Would not allow her to enjoy life while her victims rotted in their graves.

Get Nola to safety. Figure out your next move.

The princess moaned and mumbled, "Hurts." How much blood had she lost? The yellowish pallor of her skin and the blue tinge of her lips suggested a lot.

He bit out, "I know, dove," and placed a hasty kiss on her brow. "If you can, rest. I'll make you better once I've dispatched our pursuers." If his plan failed…

Don't let it fail.

What if she became mist again?

Why turn to mist in the first place? Had to be a unique supernatural ability all her own. But what was its purpose?

When he felt he was the perfect distance from their hunter—timing mattered—he opened a portal to a lavender field overseas…also a base camp that belonged to Ranger, a savage warrior able to spew fire from his fingertips.

If Ranger had returned to the camp, he could dispatch

Ronan and Petra. At the very least, Ranger could keep the couple occupied while Bane tended to Nola.

Hoping to convince Ronan and Petra that he'd gone through it, he flung blood onto the lavender stalks. *Has to work, has to work.* Then, he hid nearby. He placed Nola on the ground as gently as possible, careful not to jostle the metal that protruded from her shoulder, and palmed two daggers. She was wide-awake, her features pinched, her skin more pallid than before, little wheezes leaving her with every labored exhalation.

Voice low but rough, he said, "Be as quiet as you can, dove." The portal would remain open for sixty—fifty—seconds.

Impatience gnawed on his nerves as he waited for Ronan and Petra to show. Forty...thirty.

Twenty.

Nola didn't reply or move an inch. Fear and impatience sharpened into all-consuming panic. "Just a little longer, dove," he whispered, feeling like he'd just swallowed a mouthful of rusty nails. "Hold on for me."

Fifteen. Fourteen. Thirteen.

The beast continued ramming into his skull, agitated beyond measure, and Bane didn't know if his companion wanted to murder Ronan and Petra extra bad, or strike at Nola while he had the chance. Or both.

She's off-limits, now and always.

Ten. Nine.

At last, the couple entered his line of sight. They followed the trail of blood, as hoped.

Seven. Six.

Would they make it through in time?

Yes! With only two seconds to spare, the fools darted through the portal. The doorway closed.

Knowing they could return at any moment, Bane shut down all emotion and straddled Nola's waist. A sliver of moonlight bathed her precious face, allowing him to watch her expression as he wrapped a hand around the pipe. With the other hand, he wadded up a brand-new T-shirt.

Her irises glazed with anguish. "I—I know what you're planning, and I d-don't want you to do it."

Even in the face of excruciating pain, she refused to make a demand. No wonder he cared for this amazing woman. She was a rare and wondrous unicorn. *And I'm about to make her bleed.*

"I'm so sorry, dove, but you cannot begin to heal until the pipe is removed."

"Please, just take me to a hospital. They'll knock me out and—"

With a fierce yank, he removed the pipe and pressed the wadded-up shirt against the gaping wound left behind. As she bowed her back and screamed into the night, birds took flight. At least the material absorbed spurts of arterial blood.

Shakes plagued Bane, his chest clenching. "I'm sorry, dove, but I must do more."

"What do you mean—no," she cried when the answer crystalized. "Please, no. I'm begging you. Won't this start the Blood Rite?"

Clench, clench. "I'll be careful."

"Bane—"

"I'm sorry, but I must cauterize your wound or you will bleed out. *I'm* begging *you.* When the pain hits, do not fight the urge to pass out."

She went quiet, tears pouring down her cheeks.

Hating himself, Bane used his free hand to rip off

her ruined top. His stomach rebelled at the sight of her crimson-streaked pale skin.

He was responsible for this. She'd placed her life in his hands, and he'd failed to protect her. *She* should hate *him*, too. By the time he finished patching her up, she just might.

I'd rather she live hating me, than die thanking me. "I'm sorry," he repeated. Out of options, he tilted his head, letting the beast spit fire into his throat.

"Please." She planted her feet on the ground and tried to scoot her entire body away from Bane, but as weak as she was, she only moved an inch, and it clearly agonized her. "Don't—"

Hardening his heart, he leaned down and blew into her wound. Crackling embers poured from his mouth, spilling over torn muscle and flesh. One of her bra straps got charred. She bowed her back again and unleashed another scream. A real glass-shatterer.

Her voice broke. She moaned and sagged against the ground. Even now, she remained awake, all quiet strength and courageous heart.

He readjusted the backpacks and opened a portal to the road they'd previously exited, then gathered Nola close. A storm brewed, the air damp. Thunder boomed in the distance, lightning splitting the black sky.

With a reedy tone, she asked, "How did the combatants pinpoint our location?"

"I don't know, but I will find out after I've secured another conveyance."

He flagged down a vehicle and forcibly removed the owner. Utilizing the skills he'd picked up by watching Nola, he drove. Poorly, yes, but well enough to ditch their current location.

He cast her a glance, relieved to see her injuries had begun to heal supernaturally. Perfect timing. The sky opened up and hammered the land with punishing rain.

He drove a good distance, chattering nonstop to distract his princess from her pain. "I bet you're curious about Adwaeweth. The entire kingdom is made up of six worlds. I won two of them in an All War. On five of those worlds, citizens live under a mystical dome. The sixth one is pitch-black and doesn't need one. Within each world, there are multiple territories ruled by princesses subject to Aveline. My mother was a breeder, and she chose my father as her mate. They had three boys, including me, and a girl. But, within a twenty-year span, my father offended Aveline, and Aveline...she ate his heart. My mother refused to choose another mate, so Aveline ate *her* heart a mere two months later. Both of my brothers were killed in an All War, and my sister died in childbirth, along with her baby. Fast-forward another hundred years, and I refused to fight in a third All War, so Aveline killed Meredith."

Meredith had been his bright light.

"So much tragedy," Nola muttered from the back seat.

"Tragedy after tragedy, loss after loss." *Not sure how many more I can withstand.*

"No wonder you prefer warrior women." She struggled to an upright position.

"Easy," he said, worry overshadowing his relief. "What did you mean?"

Shoulders rolling in, tone sad, she said, "You've admitted you cannot survive another loss. So, now you choose the people most likely to survive any future hardships."

Her observation...made sense. The fact that she saw

him…that she'd begun to figure him out… "Look at all *you* have survived. What you *will* survive."

A vivid flash of lightning momentarily lit up the entire vehicle, spotlighting her. He examined her through the rearview mirror. Pain etched every inch of her beautiful face, but also wonder.

Wonder? *So out of place.* What had caused the emotion?

When the storm lightened, he abandoned the car. Human enforcers might already be on the hunt for it. He carried Nola to a nearby RV park. At some point, she fell asleep, the hard patter of rain creating the perfect lullaby.

He worked a T-shirt from a backpack to drape over her face and chest. Then, using the money Nola had gotten by selling the jewels, he purchased an older RV. He must have overpaid, because the owner spotted the stack of cash and squealed.

After laying Nola in bed, he removed her shoes and pants, but left her undergarments in place. Too keyed up to rest, he searched the RV—a home on wheels. Small, but functional. There was a floral-print couch and a large black screen. The tiny kitchen had a stove and sink, counter, and a foldable table and chairs. In back, the world's smallest bathroom and the only bedroom.

Nola remained curled up under the covers, silken hair spread over a pillow. Raindrops had collected in her lashes. Or were those droplets…tears? *Clench.* Thankfully, her wounds had fully closed. Some of the char had even faded from her flesh. She would make a total recovery. So why was he shaking, his defenses crumbling? Why couldn't he get over how close he'd come to losing her?

No more waiting, he decided. He wanted her, wanted everything she had to give, so he would fight for her with every weapon in his arsenal. If he could win her away from Vale in the process…even better.

Bane trudged to the couch and emptied his pockets. He traced his fingertip over the photograph of young Nola, his chest constricting once more. Harder. She radiated such joy. Joy he would touch…possess, if only for a little while.

As he read the article she'd written, a half smile made an appearance. Nola's top three tips for going from enemies to lovers? 1) Focus on the positive, but don't shy away from discussing about the negative. 2) Exchange insults for praise. 3) End every argument with a kiss.

Thank you for the advice, little dove. I'll be heeding every word.

Bane was done resisting his desires.

NOLA STRETCHED HER arms overhead, arched her back, straightened her legs and blinked open her eyes. A slight pain in her shoulder made her wince…and unleashed a wealth of memories. The crash. Bane playing the part of Nurse Ratched. Carrying her through the rain. Driving. The RV park.

Heart pounding, she jolted upright and took stock. A bedroom, with a bed and two nightstands, but nothing else. There was a single window, flashes of lightning filtering through a crack in the curtains. The storm hadn't eased, the air electric.

"Bane?" The bedroom door was open, letting her slide her gaze over the rest of the mobile home. There wasn't a lot of space, but what was there was clean. No sign of her warrior.

She looked herself over next. She wore the black bra with a broken strap, matching panties and dried blood. Her wound had closed, even the scab gone, thanks to Bane's ministrations and supernaturally fast healing.

Had he enjoyed his future queen's pain? He certainly hadn't hesitated to yank out that pole, or spit fire into her wound. But…

I'm so sorry, dove. Anguish had saturated his voice. No, he hadn't enjoyed her suffering. The realization hugged her heart. But…if that little bit of his fire had hurt—oh, had it hurt—how much worse would the Blood Rite feel?

Nola tottered from the bed. Her knees shook, but didn't buckle. She dug in a pack, grabbed an energy bar and ate. Fuel equaled energy. She checked her phone, hoping to see a message from Vale or Zion. Bane, too, even though she hadn't yet taught him the technological ropes.

Booo. Not a single correspondence.

She gathered toiletries and clean clothes, showered, brushed her teeth and dressed in a tank top and a pair of shorts. Still no sign of Bane. Was he out chasing Ronan and Petra?

Kill them both, but save their hearts for me.

Another memory surfaced, and Nola sucked in a breath. Had she truly uttered those words to Bane, planning— hoping—to eat the organs?

Reeling, she plopped onto the edge of the bed. Did Adwaewethian queens often eat other people's hearts?

Queen of Hearts, yo.

Well, Nola would just have to use her iron will to ensure she never gave in to the urge. Because yuck. *If I put my mind to something, I will accomplish it.*

Hinges whined as the door to the mobile home swung open.

Anticipation propelled her to her feet, her heart a pounding fist in her chest.

Bane stepped inside, and the RV suddenly felt a thousand times smaller, the walls seeming to close in. He spotted her and stopped abruptly; the heart-fist started punching her ribs.

Locks of wet hair were plastered to his forehead and cheeks. He wore a T-shirt and leathers, both garments soaked through and clinging to his muscular body. The scent of rain blended with his innate fragrance of male musk and exotic spices. *Will never get enough.* A leather strap bisected his chest, anchoring his sword to his back, the hilt rising above his broad shoulder.

Lightning flashed behind him, gifting him with a temporary halo. Flutters erupted in her belly. The way he moved…as fluid as water, as graceful as a jungle cat, every inch of him pulsing with the hunger of a nocturnal predator. His eyes *blazed* with desire. And he was hard. Perhaps throbbing.

She shivered and hugged her middle.

Tone rough around the edges, he asked, "You are well?"

"Thanks to you, I am." She shifted from one foot to the other. "What about you? Where have you been?" Gross! Whiny, nagging girlfriend, anyone?

Wait. She remembered an article she'd written. The research she'd done. When you were in a relationship, it was 100 percent okay to want to know where your person was, and there was nothing whiny or naggy about it.

"I've been overseeing our defenses." He slid his dark

and hotly sexual gaze over her slowly, languidly. "Were you worried about me?"

Did she detect delight in his expression?

Arousal fizzed in her veins, the rest of the world vanishing. A series of stronger shivers traipsed down her spine. How could she want him this much? How could she want *anyone* this much?

As he took a step forward, the door slapped closed behind him, sealing them inside the RV. Alone. He took another step. He fisted and unfisted his hands, saying, "I like your mind—when it decides to obey my every command."

Husky, teasing tone this time. At least, she thought he'd tried to make his voice playful. He'd mostly sounded ravenous.

Thunder boomed, shaking the entire mobile home. Her pulse points hammered. "Thanks, I guess?"

"I like your body *always*," he continued. He took another step closer, removed and discarded his shirt, revealing a feast of muscle and sinew. "But I dislike that you are wearing so many clothes." Step. "I dislike that you are standing so far away." Step. "I dislike that your legs aren't wrapped around me." The final step.

Every new word had been gruffer than the last. A sign of his growing arousal?

Finally, he stood directly in front of her, a tower of masculine beauty. As he reached out, her heart nearly burst from her chest. What did he plan to do? What did she *want* him to do?

Easy—I want him to do everything.

His knuckles brushed her navel, her belly fluttering. When he began toying with her zipper, breath hitched in her lungs.

"Now," he said. "Tell me what you dislike about me. And hurry. As soon as you're done, we can end our argument properly—with a kiss."

CHAPTER TWENTY

How many orgasms should you expect?

AROUSAL CONSUMED NOLA, shocking her once-ignored hormones. Her breathing quickened and shallowed, welcoming a bout of light-headedness. Whatever had wrought this change in Bane…

I like!

While her mind wasn't sure what was going on, her body said, *I do. I know. He wants me madly! Almost as much as I want him.* Passion, primitive and wild, doused his gaze. His warmth and scent acted as kindling. Goose bumps spread over her limbs, sensitizing her skin.

One intimate touch, and she might go off like a rocket.

"I dislike… I…" To tell him what she "disliked" about him, she had to think straight. *He ruined my brain.*

New flashes of lightning lit the vehicle with a soft amber glow. A bandage covered the wound on his shoulder and metal links circled his biceps. Water droplets sluiced down his washboard abs. A golden goodie trail pointed down, where his erection strained the fabric. *Like a road map to perfection.*

He looked like a painting come to sizzling life.

"You dislike nothing about me?" he asked, one of his pecs jumping. "You think I'm perfect, just the way I am?"

"No, of course not." Was this how Adwaewethians flirted? "You have numerous flaws. Countless!"

"Wrong. I have one flaw, and it's a total lack of flaws."

She sputtered for a moment, only to burst out laughing.

He tensed, peering at her as though he could read every secret lurking behind her eyes. Aggression thrummed from him.

Her amusement died with a strangled breath.

Searching her gaze, he slowly dipped his head until his lips hovered over hers. "Allow me to tell you more of my dislikes."

"O-okay."

"I dislike that you aren't on that bed, accepting my cock as I feed you every throbbing inch."

Heat. More shivers. The most wonderful aches. She experienced all of that and more.

Sex with Bane, the male she craved more than water to drink. There were complications, and there would be consequences. Right now, she didn't care, her need too great.

"Yes," she whispered. She'd waited a lifetime for this moment, this man, and nothing would stop her from enjoying it.

"Argument over then," he snarled, desire frothing in his eyes. "Now we kiss and make up." With one hand on her nape and one on her waist, Bane yanked her against the hard line of his body and pressed his mouth against hers.

Argument? Her thoughts dulled, and she melted against him, opening her mouth eagerly, meeting the thrust of his tongue with a suck and a nip. He tasted like rain and arousal, and she couldn't get enough, a terrible, wonderful madness consuming her.

His tantalizing groan lit a fire deep in her belly, a fever swiftly spreading. How many nights had she lain in bed, enveloped by darkness, starved for a man's touch?

Bane soothed her hunger…and made it worse.

With a tug on her hair, he deepened the kiss. Harder, faster, every unfulfilled longing she'd ever harbored surging through her at once, demanding satisfaction now, now, now. Her heart pounded, and her breasts readied for him, tips distending. Between her legs, she ached worse.

He lifted his head and pressed his forehead to hers. Panting, he said, "I want to see you."

The fire in his eyes…she grew drunk just looking at him. Voice like silk, she replied, "And I want to show myself to you."

Needing no more encouragement, he yanked her shirt overhead and tossed it aside. His pupils flared as her hair tumbled into place. Then he turned his intensity to her bra, giving it the same treatment as the shirt. Snatch. Drop.

Cool air brushed her heating flesh, drawing more goose bumps to the surface. When her nipples puckered, he gritted out a curse.

The fire intensified. Feminine power wafted through her, leaving her drunker. She rolled back her shoulders to lift her breasts.

He unleashed another growl. "Perfect little beauties." Reverent, he cupped and kneaded them, ghosting his thumbs over their peaks.

"Bane!"

When he set back into their kiss, a frenzy overtook

them both. Maybe because her bare breasts pressed against his chest, heated skin rubbing against heated skin. Every breath drew her nipples up, then down, then back up, sparking the most amazing friction. Ecstasy and agony bombarded her, and she couldn't form a complete thought, only fragments.

Want. Need. More. Please. Yes, yes, yes. "Bane!"

He wrenched his mouth from hers, dragging a ragged moan out of her. He was panting, anguish cooling the fire in his eyes. "Shouldn't be this good. With anyone. Ever."

Thinking about abandoning her? *Let's see if I can change his mind.* She rose to her tiptoes, fisted his hair and bared her teeth. "I need to come," she told him softly. "Make me come. That isn't a demand but a desperate request."

"I will. Yes." With a snarl, he twirled her around and tore the button off her shorts, the two sides of the zipper gaping open. He shoved his hand into her panties.

She arched her spine, reaching up and back to comb her fingernails through his silken hair. Once, twice, he ground his erection into her backside while tracing his middle finger through her wetness. Teasing her clitoris. Kneading her breast. Teasing, kneading.

His hands were a brand, scorching her body and soul. As ecstasy drowned Nola in increasingly intense waves, his warm breath fanned her neck, mimicking a caress. She felt this incredible man in her cells, her marrow.

He nipped her earlobe, pinched her nipple and whispered, "You respond to me like no one else, as if you are a conduit for my pleasure. I give, and you take, then give right back to me. You give *more*."

Beautiful words. Heady. The big, bad beast was putty

in the virgin's hands, the knowledge life-changing. But...
"Less talking, more touching." Beyond conversation, she
gripped his wrist and lifted her hips, trying to wedge
his middle finger inside her.

His dark chuckle fanned her ears, sending shivers to
all her favorite parts. "Does my dove need to be filled?"
he asked, circling her clitoris with mounting pressure.

"Yes!" Circling, but never quite touching. Plaintive
cries left her. When she turned her head to nip his jaw, he
swooped down and kissed her again. Every stroke of his
tongue demanded total surrender—surrender she gave.

At last, he pressed his finger against the heart of her
need.

"Bane!" Rapture. Bliss.

Satisfaction.

Nola screamed, burning up, inside and out, stars
winking behind her lids. "It's good. So good. Never
want it to stop..." Sublime pleasure crashed over her,
rousing total euphoria. Her mind went on vacation, and
her body soared in the clouds.

"This is only the beginning," he rasped. As her inner
walls clenched, he plunged a thick finger inside her tight-
ness, and her climax sharpened.

Another scream barreled free.

"You are hot enough to scorch, and tight enough to
madden me forever." He thrust in another finger, stretching her, working them in and out, in, out. "I'm going to
love fucking you."

His crude language turned her on, need for him, for
this, roaring back to startling life. She mewled.

"Any sickness, dove?" He sounded so calm.

"None. But I might die if you stop."

"That's good, because *I* would rather die than stop."

He slipped those fingers out of her...in...out, then whirled her around to face him.

Breathtaking male. A bead of sweat ran down his temples, lines of strain tightening the skin around his eyes. She slid her palms up the muscular ridges on his abdomen, delighting when his nostrils flared. His breaths were shallow and ragged, as if he had to push the air through some kind of obstacle course. His irises were molten gold, with flames crackling throughout.

"I will..." He ripped off her shorts and panties, then removed and dropped the links that were wrapped around his biceps. He clasped her waist. "Addict your body to mine."

"Consider it mission accomplished."

"Yes, but let's be doubly sure." He tossed her on the bed. As she bounced up and down, he kicked off his boots, unfastened his pants and shoved the garment to the floor. Metal clinked. No telling how many weapons he had hidden.

Released from confinement, his shaft bobbed, a massive rod with a damp slit. He gripped the base and stroked once, twice, the rhythmic motion hypnotizing her.

When she purred, giddy, he clasped her ankles and jerked, sliding her to the edge of the bed. For a long, silent moment, he peered at the heart of her desire. He licked his lips. "The things I want to do to you. The things I want *you* to do to *me*. And we will do it. All of it. Even the things forbidden in Adwaeweth."

"Yes," she croaked. "I want to do *everything* with you. With us, nothing is forbidden."

He blinked with astonishment, before a look of

breathtaking wonder descended over his features. His chest puffed with pride—in her! "You undo me, dove."

I think I kind of...do.

He dropped to his knees and hissed in a breath. "Luscious. Pretty."

The ravenous gleam in his eyes… A promise of wicked delights.

Suddenly, Nola felt like Little Red Riding Hood, with a big, bad wolf between her legs.

With trembling hands, Bane pushed Nola's knees farther apart. Farther still. *The new center of my world.* Guilt surfaced. If he did this, if he took Nola, Meredith would no longer be the last woman he'd bedded. Yet…

I cannot walk away.

Her mouthwatering honeysuckle and jasmine scent obliterated any lingering doubts. The pain in his shoulder—what pain? His desire for Nola eclipsed everything else. He wanted this woman more than he'd ever wanted anyone or anything. Even the beast wanted her. Sexually, at least. Bane suspected she'd…beguiled the fiend.

He'd never felt so connected to Drogo, as if they were one being rather than two, drawing from each other equally, creating balance. A development he didn't understand, but wouldn't question. Not yet. Satisfaction beckoned. Pressure built.

The body she possessed…willowy and soft. Intoxicating. *Made for this. Made for me.* Her vulnerability made his shaft throb harder. Everything about her made his shaft throb harder.

Drawing circles on her inner thigh, he rasped, "Do you crave me, dove? Do you require another kiss?"

"Yes!" Eyelids hooded, lips parted, a passion-fever

spread over her skin. "Kiss me, slide inside me. Do one, do both. Just do *something*. Please!"

Once again, she filled him with wonderment. "My princess's need is so great she can hardly contain it."

I love my life.

Bane leaned down, but didn't kiss her. As she quivered, fisting the sheets and writhing against the mattress, he nuzzled his beard stubble against her thigh, on the same spot his fingers had drawn those circles.

He hissed. She groaned.

Will take what's mine! Bane dipped his head, licked her wetness and nearly roared at the rightness. Pure, sweet honeyed perfection. *Delectable royal.*

Bane set in with a vengeance Licking. Sucking. Nipping. She cried out and rolled her hips, chasing his tongue, driving him wild. Never, in all his days, would he get enough of this woman.

Between wanton forays with his mouth, he told her, "Never deny me this. I want it every day."

She uttered an incoherent reply, music to his ears. He sucked on her clitoris and sank a finger inside her hot, wet sheath.

"Yes!" she shouted, fisting hanks of his hair to hold him in place. "Bane! It's yours, always yours."

As a reward, he sank in another finger. He worked the two like scissors, spreading them again and again, stretching and preparing her.

When she came, screaming his name, he tongued her channel once, twice, mimicking sex. She screamed his name.

Desperate for a release of his own, he kissed his way up, up, tracing his tongue around her navel, before moving up, up again. One after the other, he laved her nipples.

She scoured his back with her nails. A first for him, because no lover had ever lain beneath him. The fact that he was on top, pinning her to the bed, her body a cradle for his...*better than I ever dreamed.*

"You ready for me, dove?"

"So ready!"

He reached between their bodies and positioned the tip of his erection at her entrance. He'd never wanted anyone so badly. *Control unraveling...* "I want to take you like this."

Between heavy breaths, she said, "Bare?" She nibbled on her bottom lip. "What about a condom? Birth control? Disease?"

"No disease, I swear it." He almost couldn't get the words out, his need too great. "I cannot get you pregnant."

"Ever? Never mind. Tell me after. I need you inside me. Just like this." She jerked his face to hers and kissed him, teeth clinking, tongues tangling. "Hurry! Please. Now."

Now. Yes. Mind ravaged by torturous arousal, he began to ease inside her. At first, she welcomed him eagerly, slick and hot. But the deeper he slid, the more resistance he met. *Too tight.*

He circled his hips. Again. And again. He worked his shaft in deeper each time. Sweat poured from him. Frenzied need urged him to thrust in fast, sure and to the hilt. Muscles tensed as he resisted. Oxygen singed his throat with every inhalation.

He kept his gaze on her face, mindful of her reactions. When he hit the evidence of her virginity, she flinched, and he forced himself to still, surely the most difficult thing he'd ever done.

"Pain?" he croaked.

"Yes, but I don't care." She breathed the words against his lips, urgent. "Been waiting for you so long...don't make me wait any longer."

Waiting...for him... Him and him alone.

The urge to plunge deep nigh overwhelmed him. *Do not harm this precious female.* Bane drew back his hips, preparing to thrust. He paused, teasing her clitoris forcing her to chase his finger, to rock her hips.

Moans left her in a continuous stream.

She's ready for me.

Heaving breaths, Bane surged forward, sinking his cock deep, deep inside her.

Nola screamed, coming, squeezing his shaft, nearly wringing his pleasure from him. His mind momentarily blanked, overcome by sublime bliss. *Do not come.* When he came, this would end. *Fight the need!*

Again he thought, *Never get enough.*

Giving her time to adjust to his invasion, he inhaled, exhaled. "I'm so sorry I hurt you. Tell me you're well."

"That was amazing." She wiggled her hips before nodding. "I'm almost ready for more." Wiggle, wiggle. Loud moan.

"Tell me when you *are* ready. Then and only then will I move." Or die. Whichever came first.

After wrapping her legs around him—another new delight—she gave her hips another wiggle, this one less tentative. Louder moan. Urgent. She flattened her hands on his pecs—*hot as brands, searing my skin.* He growled softly.

"Okay, yes. Move. Move!" she pleaded.

He did, hard. Harder than he'd intended, pulling out, then slamming in. The bed shook, the headboard slapping against the wall. And she must have loved it. Moaning louder and louder, she undulated with more and more vigor. Then she wrapped her arms around him, too, cleaving to him. He quickened his pace, hammering in and out of her. In and out. The *entire vehicle* shook.

She thrashed atop the bed and scoured his skin with her nails, all the while growing wetter and hotter. In that moment, she was everything he'd ever wanted, everything he'd ever needed, and a thousand things he hadn't known he could have. Pressure, so much pressure. Strain. The urge to possess and be possessed.

Then his communication ring vibrated.

Bane uttered a dark curse. *Aveline requests a video-conference now?* The bitch must have sensed his pleasure and decided to ruin it. Damn her! He had strict orders to answer her call, as long as he wasn't engaged in battle. He needed to stop and deal with her.

Come on, come on. Stop!

He'd had the strength to walk away from Meredith; he should have the strength to walk away from Nola, too.

He fought with every fiber of his being. A vein pulsed in his forehead. Muscles went rigid. But… Nola gasped his name and gripped his ass, and he thrust harder. Need to come, to make her come, overpowered him. Resist? Impossible.

Guilt lived and died in a single heartbeat, killed by Nola's uninhibited response to him. *More.* In, out. Slamming. Driving into her. Pulling out. In, out.

When he felt his testicles drawing up, he pressed his thumb against her clitoris. Like a magic button. She erupted a second time, shouting with wild abandon, her inner walls clenching on his length.

Too much, too much. He threw back his head, bowed his back and unleashed a savage roar. The beast joined him.

This is euphoria. His last coherent thought as shudders rocked him, and he saw stars. The rapture...

When the stars faded, he collapsed atop Nola. Huffed for breath. Heart still racing.

As she sighed with contentment, a strange sensation sparked, baffling Bane. He thought he might be... content.

Nola had blown his ever-loving mind. She hadn't let him top—she'd insisted on it. One had not dominated the other. They'd shared command, and he'd loved it. *Another memory seared into my brain.* One he would forever cherish.

How could he give this woman up, ever?

He *couldn't*.

Can't lose her. Won't. Not to circumstance, and certainly not to death.

He'd planned to end his own life after Aveline's defeat, but the idea had lost its appeal. Leave Nola without a guard? No! Never again experience this bliss? Hell, no.

He could stay on Terra—and be subject to her will, if ever she decided to enforce it. And what if she changed, becoming like every other queen, as he'd once feared? The heart-eating thing...must have been a fluke, he decided.

Besides, she's worth the risk.

With the thought, realization dawned and panic hit. *I think I'm falling in love with her.*

CHAPTER TWENTY-ONE

Turn your afterglow into a party for two!

OUTSIDE, THE STORM continued to rage. Nola fought to calm her labored breaths as Bane regarded her with a thunderstruck expression and rolled to his side. What thoughts tumbled through that head of his? What would he do next? Get up and leave without saying a word, or draw her closer for a snuggle?

She waited, dazed by everything that had happened, expecting option A but hoping for B. Her first experience had been better than she'd ever envisioned. Blissful. One avalanche of pleasure after another. A communion of bodies and souls, crazy hot and…perfect. But she'd never felt more vulnerable.

Waiting…

She had a thousand questions for him. Namely, had sex been so earth-shattering every time, with every one he'd ever been with? How soon until they could do it again? Next time, *she* wanted to kiss, stroke and suck on *him*. Did he feel as if his defenses had crumbled, and he was nothing but an open wound, too? He must be! The thunderstruck expression hadn't dulled.

Still waiting…

Bane didn't pull her close, but he didn't get up, either. Between panting breaths, his voice hollow, he said, "I need to contact Aveline. She tried to reach me while we were otherwise occupied."

She pasted on a small smile to hide her disappointment. "Do what you must," she said, and oh, wow, her screams had scratched up her voice. She could work a sex hotline and make thousands!

He underwent a metamorphosis right before her eyes, tensing, as if a heavy weight had settled over him. Next, he draped an arm over his eyes to shut out the rest of the world—to shut out *Nola. Then* he projected a staggering amount of guilt and regret.

Great! Just when the sun had begun to dawn on her life, chasing away the darkness, he'd summoned an eclipse.

The heat drained from her body, leaving her inundated by teeth-chattering cold. Somehow, she also felt scalded. Only minutes ago, she'd been resplendent. A woman worshipped by her man. Now, she was trapped in a miasma of confusion and contradiction. Powerful yet helpless. Certain yet clueless. Capable of doing anything and nothing, her heart both full and empty. Hopeful for the future, but terrified about what was to come.

Did everyone feel like a roller coaster of emotion after sex, or only the aliens?

Why couldn't she and Bane be a couple in a romance novel, her magic vagina curing his wounds, his every problem?

Had she made *any* progress with him? Had his heart mended even a minute amount?

Trembles growing more noticeable, Nola folded the covers over her legs…torso…breasts. A type of armor, she supposed. Protection from her own vulnerabilities.

As she scoured her brain for a topic of conversation,

or maybe a plan of action, Bane shifted and winced, and she noticed the specks of blood on his bandage.

"Your wound," she said, breathless. "It's opened up again."

"I grow more aware of it by the minute." He fisted his hands and lowered his arm. Whatever had been on his mind, he'd obviously made a monumental decision, his expression determined. "Nola…dove…we must talk."

Her hopes plummeted. "Look, if you're worried I'll get clingy, stop. I'm no longer a virgin. I bet I can be with someone else." *I don't want to be with anyone else.*

"No!" The denial burst from him. He clasped her arm and maneuvered her on top of him, flat on her stomach. Not missing a beat, he flipped their positions, pinning her down. Looming over her, he stated softly but firmly, "You will be with me and no one else. I will kill anyone who touches you, then kill their families and wipe their names from history!"

He didn't give her a chance to respond. He rose, the entire mattress shaking, and padded to the bathroom. The door remained open, the sound of running water drifting to the bed.

Alone, she hugged a pillow and smiled, his jealousy like a soothing balm. He might dump her, might even give her the "it's not you, it's me" speech, but he'd unwittingly shown his cards. He was as confused as Nola, just as hopelessly attracted to her, maybe even falling for the future queen.

Future queen. Queen Nola. Queen Nola Lee. Once, the title had struck her as wrong. After all, she'd never felt as if she had a genuine purpose or great passion. She should have known "feeling" wasn't the be all and end all. Feelings changed. They were often unreliable, and sometimes lied. Everyone had a purpose, what they were created to do. A reason they were born—a reason greater than themselves.

Nola was born to rule beasts with kindness, understanding and love.

Instinct shouted, *Yes!*

So far, she'd failed to aid her people in any way. She hadn't even given them another thought. Hadn't fought for the privilege to rule, secretly afraid she'd fail. But she *should* try. As many times as necessary. Through her failures, she would gain the strength she needed to succeed.

Only a split second later, her excitement popped like a balloon. Until Bane performed the Blood Rite, she *couldn't* rule. Should she force the issue, or wait for him to decide it was the right time?

Bane shut off the water and returned to the bed, pausing at her side. In the darkness, she had trouble making out the minutia of his features, but she felt…something. Terror? No, that couldn't be right.

A flash of lightning highlighted him for a moment, revealing haunted eyes glazed with—yep, terror. But what did he fear?

"May I?" he asked, lifting a wet rag.

He wanted to clean up the deposit he'd made in the Bank of Nola. An extremely intimate act. She licked her lips and said, "I…guess?"

He peeled off the covers and sat next to her, gently stroking the cloth between her legs. Tone soft, he asked, "Did I hurt you?"

Her cheeks heated. "During sex? Only for a moment. Afterward? A bit longer. I know you want to talk about ending us before we've really had a chance to start."

He closed his eyes, as if praying for strength. When he refocused, he tossed the rag and snuggled up to her, snaking an arm around her middle to tug her against him. His body heat engulfed her, and she almost—almost!—melted. *Feels too good.*

What if she got used to sleeping with him and he decided to go through with the dumping?

"Five minutes ago," she said, pushing at his chest to no avail, "you were ready to give me the stinky boot. Now you're cuddling me. What gives?"

"We took the edge off. We shouldn't need each other again." He rested his chin on her crown and trapped her legs between his own, letting her bottom cradle his erection.

"Why are you pushing me away, Bane?"

"For my sanity, I must."

"Let me go, then. Walk away."

A terse pause. Gloriously gentle, he brushed the hair from her brow. "I'm strong enough to slay an entire army, but too weak to resist the urge to hold you."

The guttural admission played havoc with her emotions, sending her on another roller coaster ride. What if he followed through and refused to bed her again?

Want to hold on to him and never let go, want to run away as fast as possible. Have already fallen for him. Will never fall for him, my heart guarded by hellhounds.

"Tell me your plan to defeat Aveline," she said to mask her upset.

He trailed his hand from her thigh to her throat and gripped her lightly. Not in a threatening manner, but a highly sexual one courtesy of an extremely dominant male. "I plan to spend the next two weeks winning the weapons that will help us fight Aveline."

"Such as?"

"Zion has a magic wand. Knox carries a healing sword, but *someone* insists I let the two live," he grumbled.

"She sounds smart." She wiggled her bottom against his erection, muttering, "Besides, we already have a magic wand slash healing sword."

He bent his head to run the lobe of her ear between his teeth. "Did my dove just make a penis joke?"

"Actually, I just uttered a statement of fact," she replied with a shiver.

His husky chuckle tickled her scalp.

Bane...chuckling... Nola maneuvered to her other side, facing him, but his smile had already dimmed. Dang it!

Picking up the conversation where he'd left off, he said, "After that, we will convince Vale, Zion and Knox to exit the war. Then, at the end of the two weeks, I will attend an Assembly of Combatants and win the All War. The High Council will then send armies of Enforcers to dethrone your world's leaders. That's when I'll perform your Blood Rite. As we wait for Aveline's arrival, I'll train you. With your help, she will die. Finally, you'll rule Terra." He petted her hair and lapsed into silence.

Nola suspected he'd gotten lost in his thoughts, several minutes passing in quiet peace. Fatigue hammered at her, and she closed her heavy lids, about to drift off...

"Tell me what happens when you turn to mist," he said, and she nearly jumped out of her skin.

Too tired to mentally debate the risks and rewards of sharing such personal information, she explained what she'd relived. How real it had been, how she hadn't felt truly there, sitting beside her toddler self. How her parents had worried about hiding from a she-monster. How an Adwaewethian warrior had stood in the road, causing a horrific accident before murdering her mother.

"The fact that your body turns to mist… I wonder if you actually go back," Bane said, all but humming with excitement. "If you have an opportunity to change the past."

"You mean time travel?" No way. Just no way. Impossible. Except, nothing was impossible, was it? She was a hybrid alien, who was in bed with a full-blooded alien able to breathe fire and transform into a literal beast. What if she *could* go back and save her parents?

"I told you each queen has a unique ability," he said, his excitement already more pronounced. "This could be yours. An ability against Aveline!"

Why would he want Nola to return to the past—

The answer slugged her with stunning force, leaving her gasping. His wife, Meredith. He wanted Nola to save the other woman.

She isn't the other woman. I am.

Nola choked down a cry of distress, crumbling inside. One moment Bane hadn't been able to get enough of her, the next he'd hoped to use her to get back the woman he truly loved.

Why am I so disposable?

Bane jerked upright, dragging her with him, then framed her cheeks with his hands. "You can try to return to the crash on purpose. Will you? We must know what, exactly, you can do." Hope shone in his eyes, brighter than the sun.

The tears gathered once again. *Do not cry. Don't you dare. Nod instead. Good, that's good.*

He smiled at her, the expression she'd dreamed of seeing, and it was as magnificent as she'd suspected. An exquisite display of undiluted happiness—with a dimple.

"Thank you, Nola." He pulled her close and kissed her lips.

A swift peck, no tongue, and she felt like she'd been vivisected. Did he know how terribly he was hurting her right now? Would he care if he did?

Unable to bear looking at him any longer, she closed her lids, drew a deep breath in and slowly released it. Though it pained her, she forced her mind to revisit the accident. Driving along the road...the hushed conversation between her parents...

When the bed bounced, she gasped, her eyelids popping open. Not the bed, she realized, but the car. She'd actually done it on purpose!

In the vision, or whatever it was, she sat next to little Nola's car seat. The baby wiggled her arms and legs. There was no sign of Bane, not even a hint of his scent. A much-needed reprieve. She would use the time she spent in the past to gain control of her emotions in the present.

Had she actually time-traveled, though? What if she could only see the past, not change it?

Aveline killed with a touch, and Nola had the ability to...remember. How special.

She reached out, her fingers ghosting through the child. How could she become solid?

Again, the man appeared in the road. Nola braced. The car flipped, and finally settled upside down. He walked over and crouched, just as before, and had his conversation with the unseen woman. When he pulled her panic-stricken mother from the car, Nola didn't panic. Not this time. She crawled from the wreckage, slipping through the mutilated door like a phantom—

just in time to watch as the warrior sheathed his daggers, picked up a metal pipe and rammed it through her mother's throat.

Just like that, her mother went quiet, her body lax.

Wheezing with horror, Nola pressed a hand her mouth. Her knees trembled, threatening to buckle.

Heartbeat.

Heartbeat.

Heartbeat.

Tears sprang again, momentarily blurring her vision. Her chest—raw. Her stomach—twisted. The cruelty of this man's deeds…the savagery… He'd had no compassion, no mercy or care. He'd ended a life as violently as possible.

And he wasn't done.

He grabbed her mother by the hair and tossed her back into the car.

Nola's tears spilled over, stinging her cheeks. *Can't let him get away with this.*

He lifted his hand, revealing a plethora of rings. A triangle of light glowed from one, the image of a flaxen-haired beauty in the center.

"It is done, my queen," he said, his tone bored.

Nola's muscles turned to stone. Queen?

The woman smirked, beyond superior. "You shall be handsomely rewarded, Micah. That, I promise you."

Micah. Finally, Nola had a name. *He will pay.*

With a low, intimate tone, he said, "Will you invite me back to your bed, sweet Aveline?"

Nola sucked in a breath. Aveline. This flaxen-haired beauty was Aveline, Bane's queen and Meredith's murderer. The one responsible for Nola's heritage and subsequent pain. The one who'd sent Bane into her life.

Rage hit her, and hit hard, her dark side utterly taking over. *I will slaughter the queen and her soldier. And every member of their families!*

"We will discuss it upon your return."

"Very well," he said. "Is she the one?"

"Yes," Aveline hissed, clearly giddy. "Remove her heart *and* her head, then kill the child."

"There is no child," he said.

With a snarl, Nola edged closer. Closer. *Careful. Do not draw their attention.*

Too late. Aveline looked her way. The queen's jaw dropped. *She sees me?*

Step, step, running now. Finally, Nola slammed into Micah—

No, she slammed *inside* Micah and stayed put.

She'd possessed his body? Did she have control? Could she force him to clasp a dagger and stab himself to death? Maybe, maybe not, but she was expelled before she found out.

Scowling, he wheeled around, his gaze darting wildly. "What just happened?" he demanded. He'd sensed her presence, hadn't he?

Eager, all but foaming at the mouth, Nola tried to jump back inside him…and ended up flat on her back, her world going dark.

She heard Aveline say, "There was a girl. A royal with long black hair, dark eyes and pale skin. Go. Find her before she finds you. Kill her."

"Who is she?" Micah asked.

"*Who* isn't as important as *when*."

She knows I time-traveled?

"Nola!"

Bane's voice. She blinked open her eyes to spy a

panting, sweating Bane above her. She was panting and sweating, too, her heartbeat erratic.

Her brow furrowed with confusion. They were on the floor of the RV, as naked as jaybirds. "I—I don't understand."

"As mist, you threw yourself against a wall. You should have gone through it, but you bounced back, as if tethered to the room. When you tried to take another run at it, I stepped in front of you. You didn't bounce back, but you *did* injure me, despite your intangibility." Cuts marred his face, blood dripping. "Were you able to prevent the accident?"

The awfulness of everything she'd witnessed returned in a rush, shattering her heart into a million pieces too small to ever be put back together.

There was so much to unpack. Later. Right now, the figurative blade Bane had sunk into her chest twisted. Pain flared, and a ragged moan escaped. How much could one girl endure before she waved the white flag?

"There's a warrior. Micah," she said, and Bane stiffened. "He's coming for me." *His mistake. When he finds me, he dies.*

She didn't dismiss the murderous thought. No, she let it hang out and settle in, getting comfortable. *Yes. I'll kill him the same way he killed my mother.*

"I'll protect you from Micah," Bane said, teeth clenched.

"I don't… I don't want your help." The man who'd asked his lover to save his dead wife didn't get to play knight in shining armor. *Vengeance is mine!* She pushed and pushed, more and more frantic. "Get off me. Now!"

Finally he eased back. Brows drawn tight with concern, he said, "Dove, please tell me what's wrong. Did something happen?"

Share her deepest hurts with her one-night stand? No, thanks.

Fresh tears welled and fell, his image blurring. Voice as broken as her heart, she said, "Don't call me dove. Don't call me anything! Just…get away from me. Please, just get away."

When he eased back a little more, she rolled to her side, curled into a ball and sobbed.

CHAPTER TWENTY-TWO

The secret to lowering his guard down!

WHAT HAD HAPPENED to Nola?

Bane picked her up as gently as possible. Her tears rained over his chest, stinging like acid, and she shuddered with increasing intensity. Though her weight barely registered, the gash in his shoulder tore, growing longer, wider. He didn't care.

Nola's good humor had survived a trek through the arctic, abduction—twice!—separation from her sister, bomb blasts and Bane's poor treatment. Until now, nothing had broken her.

What had she seen? He could guess the reason Micah had been there—Aveline had snuck him onto Terra to kill any and all royals.

Rage boiled in Bane's veins, a shout of fury rushing up his throat; he gritted his teeth, muffling the sound. The bitch had only ever left destruction in her wake.

In two weeks, the war will end, and Aveline's downfall will begin.

Fourteen days. Both a blink and an eternity.

In three easy strides, he carried Nola to the bed and eased her upon the mattress. Pitching her body to the side, she poured her misery into a pillow.

As a boy, he'd witnessed his mother and little sister

crying. During the course of his relationship with Meredith, she'd cried only once, when Aveline beat her to a pulp for daring to "speak out of turn." Before that fateful day, a woman's tears hadn't bothered him; he'd known he could fix the problem, whatever it was. This gutted him. How could he repair a past he couldn't visit, and an ability he didn't understand?

During moments of emotional upheaval, Meredith had requested his absence, always. With Nola, he didn't ask for permission. He simply settled atop the mattress, propped his back on the ruined headboard and shifted her against his chest. To his surprise, she didn't resist.

As he stroked her silken hair and cooed nonsense in her ear, she calmed. However, the opposite proved true for Bane. He continued to recall the devastating pain he'd seen in her eyes. What had she seen?

Although, if he were honest, he'd admit she'd experienced pain *before* traveling to the past. He replayed the last hour in his head. After her climaxes, she'd been happy. Glowing. They'd spoken of her ability to time-travel and—

Comprehension.

That. That was when this awful pain had first made an appearance. Because, after parting with her virginity, her lover asked her to save his wife. Now, regret ambushed him.

Upon Nola's return, the pain *had* increased. So, something she'd discovered had totally and completely upended her world.

Never should have asked her to go back. He should have left the past—Meredith—alone. Drogo had protested her actions and her absence. Loudly. The *beast* wanted Nola, though he still wasn't sure he liked her.

Bane was tired of dragging around so much baggage. Clawing guilt because he'd failed to save her. A constant, seething well of remorse. Never-ending sorrow. If Nola did save Meredith, it would all would vanish. *Poof!* He could make up for his mistakes.

The other part of him felt clawing guilt as well, but not for the same reason. He would love Meredith for all time, but he didn't…crave her the way he once had. Surrounded by Nola's sweet scent, he knew the cravings would never come back. His body wanted her, only her.

Cursed if I save my wife, cursed if I don't.

No, no. If Meredith walked into the room, he would be overjoyed.

To see a long-lost friend.

Damn it! A jagged pang ripped through him. He had no idea when it had occurred, but a part of him had already said goodbye to Meredith. The desire to be with Nola *consumed* him.

Without consciously registering a command to move, Bane tightened his hold. She'd turned him into a conduit for pleasure. The more his civilized veneer had stripped away, the more she'd loved it. She'd even pleaded for more.

Had the woman beguiled him, or the newness of it all?

No need to ponder. Absolutely the woman. She cracked penis jokes and looked at him as if she'd die without his touch. She laughed with abandon, and cared about his well-being as a man, not just a warrior. Her quiet strength constantly astounded him. She made him want a future.

He'd underestimated her—and so would Aveline.

Heaving a sigh, Nola sagged against him.

"I'm sorry, do—Nola. I shouldn't have asked you to go back."

She flouted his apology, saying, "I…I'm ready to tell you what I saw." Her voice was little more than a croak.

Aching for her and all she'd suffered, Bane kissed her temple. "Tell me everything. Every detail. Let me share your fury and pain."

A lone tear splashed onto his sternum. "A warrior named Micah stepped into the center of the road, and my dad swerved to miss him. The vehicle flipped." Shuddering breath. Then, a transformation occurred. Her tremors tapered off, and her tears dried. Tension seeped from her, chased away by emotional frost.

Nola had just shut down. Something he'd done countless times himself. A defense mechanism he used to help himself win those All Wars. The fact that Nola was doing the same, her torment so great she couldn't afford to feel *anything*…he had to combat the urge to turn the rain-drizzled RV into scrap metal—with his claws.

Voice devoid of emotion, she recited the rest as if reading from a book. "My dad died on impact, but my mother survived. Micah approached the car. He wore rings like yours. One of them produced a beam of light, and Aveline appeared in the center of it." There at the end, sorrow ignored her emotion-embargo and slipped free. "Before that, he yanked my mom out of the vehicle and stabbed her in the…the…throat. After it, Aveline ordered him to behead her."

Bane jerked. What had Aveline said to him before? Oh, yes. *A little over twenty years ago, I sent Micah to Terra in secret, with orders to slay every royal he came across, as well as search for you and Cayden.*

"I'm so sorry, dove." *Another failure to lay at my feet.*

He kept messing up with her, kept hurting her, and it had to stop. She deserved so much better.

He rocked her back and forth, back and forth, offering comfort, but seeking it, too.

Sniffle, sniffle. "*I'm* sorry. Bane, I doubt I can save Meredith. I'm mist here *and* there. I tried to possess Micah's body, so I could make him kill himself, but he expelled me like that." She snapped her fingers.

Thoughts whirled. "With practice, I bet you *can* control his actions and change the past."

"Yes, but how does that help you? I'm not sure how I travel to my own past. How am I supposed to travel to yours?"

Easy. "We are linked. We speak telepathically, and see through each other's eyes. Therefore, it stands to reason you can see my memories, too." But the same question remained—did he let go of the past or move forward? Would he crave his wife again if she were here in the flesh? "If you were to travel back to the day Aveline murdered Meredith, possess Aveline and save Meredith, the queen won't send Micah to Terra. Your parents won't crash."

Her lips curled, but the smile got upstaged by another sob. "I'll never go into foster care, never meet Vale or Carrie. I won't be me."

"But you suffered in foster care, did you not?"

"I did. And I can't justify what some of the parents and siblings did to me and to Vale. But I wouldn't be the person I am today without those trials. I wouldn't be as strong—and don't you dare tell me I'm weak."

"Trust me, dove, I've already learned my lesson."

She huffed, but continued. "As much as I needed Vale,

she needed me. If changing the past means screwing her over, I won't do it. Not now, not ever."

If Bane hadn't agreed to fight in the Terran All War, he never would have met Nola. Never would have enjoyed her brand of fun. Never would have learned her taste or feel the hot, wet clasp of her feminine walls. Those memories were meant to be savored, not erased.

Without him, another Adwaewethian would be sent to Terra. That representative wouldn't hesitate to murder Nola, as ordered. He stiffened. She was right; changing the past meant destroying her future.

Or making it better? What good had Bane really done for her? He pressed his tongue to the roof of his mouth. Another warrior might prize her from the start.

"What if she betrays you, choosing Knox?"

"So many books and movies portray female friends as secretly catty and malicious to each other, but that isn't real life. I know Vale. I love her. She loves me. I would rather die than hurt her, and she would rather die than hurt me." Stiffening, she added, "While I won't go mucking around in my past, I will muck around in yours. I mean, I won you over. I'll do the same with whoever is sent in your place."

Nola, with another full-blooded Adwaewethian? *Heads will roll!*

"I'll do it," she added. "I'll travel back to the day your wife died."

His chest clenched harder than ever before. So hard he was certain a rib cracked. "Why would you agree to that?" *Letting me go without a fight.*

The knowledge angered him. And damn it, the knowledge hurt like hell. Even though he was to blame!

Silence. Crackling with tension.

"Did you and your wife want to have children?" she asked softly.

Clench, clench. "We did. What about you? Do you want children?"

"I never let myself ponder the notion, too afraid I'd pass on my diseases."

He heard sadness and despair, and rested two knuckles under her chin to tilt her head backward. A flash of lightning illuminated her lovely face, revealing tear-damp lashes and splotchy pink cheeks. But her eyes...

They broke him. Her pupils were blown, her irises an abyss of pain, both old and new. He wanted to slay her dragons, and offer their heads as gifts.

"Before any All War," he said, "the queen issues a command—no children—and my body automatically obeys. That way, mother and child cannot be used against me. Upon my victory and return, she negates the order."

"That's sad. And awful. And horrifying! I'm sorry." She swiped her watery eyes with the back of her wrist, his chest clenching all over again. "Will you try to make her reverse the order before she dies?"

He shook his head. "When you are queen, *you* can reverse it."

"But not before?"

"Not before," he confirmed.

She thought for a moment. "Let me rest and recharge, then I'll try to navigate your memories."

He needed more time to get his thoughts straight. "First, I must train you to fight." Problem: if he trained her the way he'd been trained—the best way, in his estimation—he would have to break her bones again and again, so that she would learn to push through the agony. A roar of denial brewed in the back of his throat. "For now, get the rest you need. I won't let anything bad happen to you."

She closed her eyes, mumbling, "You stop my withdrawal and temper the effects of the diseases, but only when you're close. I wonder if the next warrior will do the same." Heavy sigh, muscles relaxing. Drifting away…breaths evening out.

The words *destroyed* him. He felt as though Zion had punched into his chest and squeezed his heart. *Emotions are fickle, remember?*

Never meet Nola Lee? Bane gave a violent shake of his head.

Confused by the conflicting deluge of emotions pouring through him, he continued stroking her hair. Though he wanted to hold her and never let go, he forced their conversation from his mind, a man on a mission. He extracted himself from the tangle of their limbs and stood.

After tucking the covers around her and smoothing a lock of hair from her damp cheek, his heart nothing but a hollowed-out cinder block, he stalked to the vehicle's designated living room.

Time to respond to Aveline's call.

Dread skittered through him, and the beast growled a protest. He couldn't lie to her, but he didn't wish to admit the truth, either. He'd have to be smart about this and guard his words.

Bane pressed his thumb against his communication ring. Light spilled from it, and Aveline appeared. The bitch had ordered her men to slay parents and children, yet she looked angelic, a white gown molding to her curves.

She glared at him, snapping, "You ignored me.

Something you are only permitted to do if you are caught up in a battle. Yet I've heard no reports of a combatant's death."

The beast sharpened his claws and rammed against his skull.

Bane struggled to maintain a neutral expression. "Not all battles require bloodshed." Truth. "What do you want, Aveline?"

"Micah contacted me. He was being held prisoner by a viking named Erik the Widow Maker."

Bane cursed, but only in his thoughts. "How did Micah escape?"

"About an hour ago, a memory of a hybrid princess seemed to download straight into his mind. He bellowed curses about her, vowing to murder her, and Erik decided to let him go."

Apprehension blended with foreboding, choking Bane. Micah had "remembered" what Nola had done when she'd traveled back in time. Aveline, too.

"Less than an hour ago, I awoke with the same memory," she went on. "The princess is a memory manipulator, an ability once wielded by Jayne, the worst queen in our history." Fear laced her tone. "I doubt you remember her. Jayne used her memories to change the past and the future."

Do not smile. Don't you dare. "Jayne," he said, pretending to search his mind for information about her.

Aveline's mother had killed Jayne while she was sleeping and stolen the throne. Then Aveline had murdered *her own mother* to do the same.

"Are you trying to say a hybrid princess is Jayne's reincarnation?" He would have laughed if he hadn't been busy shuddering. Rumors had forever abounded, of course, stating the strongest queens found a way to be reborn and reclaim their thrones, but Bane had never encountered one.

Was Nola a reincarnation? She had two things in common with Jayne. At least! The sickening before intimacy, and the ability.

"Either that, or the princess and former queen share a relative," Aveline said, "though I believed we had sussed out and killed everyone in Jayne's bloodline."

No way Nola had lived a past life. He would have sensed it. She would have remembered it. No doubt Aveline's second supposition was true. One of the breeders had come from Jayne's lineage.

"Right now, the girl's ability is weak," Aveline persisted. "All she can do is spirit walk. If she isn't stopped, she'll learn how to kill anyone she desires, at any time, and we won't know until it's too late."

How had Jayne— The answer arose from deep in his memories. Before traveling back, she'd had to make a blood sacrifice.

He sucked in a breath. The implications of this...

If *Nola* made a human sacrifice, she could travel back in solid form, rather than splitting spirit from body, leaving the two intangible. To save someone, another had to perish. Blood for blood, life for life. But she wasn't a cold-blooded murderess, and he could not—would not—ask her to be.

Therefore, she would not be going back to save Meredith.

Decision made. A tsunami of relief flooded him, guilt nipping at its heels.

They would forge ahead, as originally planned.

Bane had much to think about and much to do. Namely, keep Micah away from Nola.

Ready to end the call and whisk her to safety, he told Aveline, "I'm in danger." Truth. He was *always* in danger. "I must go."

As she sputtered a protest, he pressed his thumb against the ring. The light died.

With no time to waste, Bane rushed outside to unhook the RV, just as the previous owner had instructed him. Then he plopped into the driver's seat, programmed the GPS, also as taught, then buckled in and keyed the engine. Minutes later they were on the road, heading to Roswell, New Mexico, no longer stationary targets for Micah.

NOLA AWOKE ALONE. No, not true. She had her memories. Bane, making sweet love to her. Bane, all but begging her to save his wife. Bane, holding her while she sobbed about her murdered parents.

He was a wonderful man, with a tragic past, a big heart and a smoking body—literally! But...

Our romantic relationship is over. She wouldn't sleep with a man who would move heaven, Earth and Adwaeweth to resurrect his dead wife. *Lucky, lucky Meredith.* His warrior woman. The female able to fight at his side. How could Nola compete?

I wanted to mend his heart, and in the process, I broke my own. Grief scalded her.

She drew in a big shuddering breath and fixed her thoughts on the RV. Dappled sunlight slipped through a crack in the curtains, revealing a ransacked bedroom. Four perfect claw marks marred the headboard. Clothes were scattered over the floor and splattered with blood.

The urge to curl into a ball and throw the best pity party in town struck her. Instead of attending, Nola forced herself to stand to shaky legs and prowl about. A plethora of weapons covered the kitchen table. Guns, knives, a crossbow. Bane must have gathered more while she slept. No doubt he was seeing to their defenses even now.

Worried for him, she stalked to the bathroom to brush her teeth, shower and dress in a pink T-shirt and skinny jeans. "This was a new day," she told her reflection. She wasn't in the midst of a painful flare and she wasn't battling withdrawal. Like Bane, she had goals. When Bane trained her, she wanted to learn the dirtiest, most sinister moves he knew. *I will be like a virus. I'll sneak up on her, rip through her body and leave destruction in my wake. She'll never know what hit her.*

Before, Nola hadn't looked forward to Aveline's murder. Now?

Die badly, bitch.

Nola returned to the living room, rested a knee on the couch and leaned forward to peer out the slats in the window. She frowned. Blinked. Shook her head. She'd fallen asleep in an RV park, but she'd woken up in a dirt-filled flatland. Where were they, and why had Bane brought them here?

She took a photo with her cell phone, just in case Zion's tracking skills didn't elicit the desired results.

Hinges wailed as the door swung open. A hoodie-wearing Bane stomped into the RV. He wore the goggles and a leather jacket, too, but removed and tossed both on the couch. The leathers he kept on.

Ready, set, go. Her heart took off in a mad sprint.

Their gazes met, and he went motionless, tension

thrumming from him. "Your sadness remains," he said, a statement, not a question.

"Yes," she whispered. Why lie?

The last time he'd entered the RV like this, they'd had sex. Now, her body expected it. Demanded it. *Addicted...* Now that she knew the bliss of being filled, she felt empty without him.

Her nipples beaded and pressed against her bra, the little hookers doing their best to draw his notice. Her belly quivered, and her knees weakened, liquid heat pooling between her legs.

A plain white T-shirt molded to his muscular physique, and those black leather pants hugged his thighs. His fair hair was askew, the golden stubble on his beard thicker than before.

"Tsk, tsk," he said. "You are leering."

"Oh. I'm sorry. I'll stop."

"Don't you dare!" His tension grew as he looked her up and down. His shaft hardened, pressing against his fly.

The sight made her mouth water.

"Are you sore?" he asked.

Good job, hookers! No. Bad job. Bad! A flush spread over her cheeks. "A bit."

He scrubbed a hand over his mouth, as if he needed to wipe away drool. "There's much we need to discuss, but right now I have a better use for our mouths." He stepped toward her.

She licked her lips and walked backward. "We can't be together. Not again."

"Can't?" Like a bullet, he shot across the RV to loom in front of her. "Explain."

So commanding. So intense. Just the way she liked him. "You aren't over your wife. When she comes back, and she will, probably, I'll be a third wheel. No, thanks." *Say nothing more.* "I hope you know you're a fool! Whether you like it or not, I'm super good for you. You need fun the way most people need air, and I'm your dealer."

Okay, so she'd said something more.

"Meredith isn't coming back." He reached out to hook a lock of hair behind her ear, as casual as if he'd announced they were having salmon for breakfast.

"I don't understand."

"I'm happy to explain...after."

Shivers coursed through her, his scent teasing her nose. His body heat pulsed over her skin.

Had he meant after sex? "I won't be a fill-in for Meredith," she said, jutting her chin. "I won't be Miss Right Now, only to be cast aside when she comes back."

"You are no one's fill-in." Too fast to track, Bane cupped her butt and yanked her against him. His heart thudded in time with hers, a shocking revelation. She made him nervous and needy. "The reason I don't want you going back doesn't matter. Do you want me?" he asked.

"Yes," she whispered. "But—"

He leaned down, at the same time lifting her to her tiptoes. Their mouths smashed together, their tongues frantically tangling. Another lift, and she wrapped her legs around his waist, using him as an anchor.

He lowered her to the couch, the length of his erection pressed against her aching core. A hoarse groan left him while she moaned a prayer of thanks. How she'd missed his weight.

Maybe she'd been too quick to decide they shouldn't sleep together again. Maybe, if she fought hard enough, she could win him…forever? She could have *this* forever.

Forever…with Bane…

I want it, she realized. *More than anything!*

But a royal versus a beloved wife? Even though he'd claimed Meredith wouldn't be coming back, the odds weren't in Nola's favor. But, if she wanted him, shouldn't she fight for him, no matter the outcome?

He deepened the kiss, thrusting his tongue with more force in a mad dash to reach the finish line. The rest of the world began to fade…until the entire RV shook, dishes rattling. A panting Bane jerked his head up, ending their kiss.

A terrible scraping sound rang out, and she cringed. "What *is* that? An earthquake?"

He leaped to his feet, strapped on multiple weapons and wound two links of chain around her waist. "Do you know how to shoot a gun?"

Trepidation slithered down her spine, plucking at her nerve endings. "I do, yes." As part of her and Vale's self-defense training, they'd taken a course on gun safety and handling.

"Good. Because Aveline contacted me and confirmed her kill order to Micah. He's here, and he's hunting for you."

Smiling, she purred, "Let him come." Dark Nola had a surprise for him.

Bane did a double take. "I think he's here, and I think he's in beast form." He placed a semiautomatic in her hand, then lifted a battery operated…nail gun? "Stay here while I—"

Suddenly the roof of the RV ripped from the vehicle and was thrown aside, cool air and dirt whipping all around them as a great and terrible beast was revealed.

CHAPTER TWENTY-THREE

Personality makeover!

Bane hissed as sunlight bathed him, his eyes watering and blurring, his body shaking. *Must stop Micah. Must protect Nola, no matter the cost.*

Only seconds ago, Bane had luxuriated in primal arousal, needing his woman more than breath. He needed her...always.

I'm keeping her. Never letting her go.

Drogo prowled through his mind, enraged at the sight of the other predator.

Micah would die in blood and pain. But first, Bane had to transform. To defeat a beast, he must become a beast. Only another beast's teeth and claws could slice through those inch-thick, steel-hard scales. *Not yet. Hold...* He wouldn't risk harming Nola or his weapons.

"Stay away," Nola shouted at Micah, relish in her tone. It was clear she wanted to hurt him, that she craved vengeance...like a true queen. Bane wasn't sure what to think, or how to feel, his every thought upside down and inside out.

The beast hovered above them, watching, no doubt trying to make sense out of what he was seeing: a comrade in arms guarding an enemy.

"You cannot stop him with your commands. You

merely slow him," Bane said, shoving her behind him. "Your orders contradict Aveline's. As a queen who's killed hundreds, thousands, she's far stronger than you. As a warrior dedicated to her cause, Micah isn't like me. He'll have no desire to align with you, so you'll have no real sway with him."

Micah's beast had a longer-than-normal snout, and an extra row of teeth, his scales red rather than green. Black claws tipped both his front and back paws.

As the bastard tilted back his head, preparing to spew fire, Bane computed facets of the other male's plan. The fire would do no damage to Bane. But Nola...

Wings burst from Bane's back. In a storm of fury, he grabbed a bag of weapons and Nola, and flew up, up, out of the decimated RV. They landed several feet away—and got kicked back into the air when the entire conveyance erupted in flames.

When they landed again, Bane palmed the first weapon he could get his free hand on—a machine that shot small, sharp pieces of metal known as "nails." He hammered at the trigger, aiming for the beast's mouth to discourage another fiery stream.

The bastard darted through the sky, zigzagging to avoid further injury, but Bane never stopped firing. The beast had nowhere to run. Or fly. Bane had chosen this spot for its lack of cover. No cover, no hiding places.

Despite a hot flood of adrenaline, Bane's shoulder radiated pain through every inch of his body. Still, he kept hammering at the trigger. "Teleport. Now! I must transform." Even as he fought it, he felt the urge to change migrating to his bones, his body preparing. *Would rather die than hurt Nola.* "You're in danger."

"So? I've been in danger since the moment we met.

I can help you," she insisted, then screeched as Micah spewed a twenty-foot circle of fire around them. Sweat trickled from her brow. "His fire won't kill me, right?"

Sweat trickled from Bane's brow, too. Over every inch of him, pouring in rivulets as tendrils of smoke thickened the air, shielding his sensitive eyes and skin from the harsh rays of sunlight. "His flames will begin your Blood Rite, weakening you so he can more easily kill you. Once it starts, it can't be stopped. Go. Please." He opened a portal through the flames.

As he led her through it, emerging on the other side, she gasped out, "Slowing him down is better than nothing."

The smile she'd displayed moments ago flashed through his mind. Cold, merciless and mighty. *Magnificent.* She'd impressed the hell out of him. Now, she refused to run, displaying zero fears, exactly what he'd thought he'd wanted from the sickly girl he'd first met, and he feared for her life.

Swooping down with preternatural speed, Micah unleashed another stream of fire. Shit! Nowhere to go. Bane enfolded Nola in his wings, the flames dancing over him.

If she wouldn't go on her own, he'd have to portal her. But where would he send her, without stumbling upon Erik's bombs? Or Micah following?

Mind racing, Bane crafted a new plan. Portal *Micah.* Micah would portal right back, yes, but by then, Nola would be hidden away. Yes!

Bane rubbed the Rifters, opening a portal to shark-infested waters. His favorite combatant dumping spot. The other male hadn't noticed—yet.

"Do not release my hand. Understand?" Bane said as

he linked his fingers with Nola's. He didn't wait for her reply, just led her into a sprint back to the RV, around it, through it. The beast chased them.

Ten seconds...thirty...fifty. Now! Bane ushered the beast in the direction of the portal. Of course, Micah noticed it then and stopped midair. Too late. During their trek, Bane had gotten his hands on a crossbow and shot off a round of arrows, nailing the beast in the eye, sending him wheeling back. He vanished in the portal—water splashing.

Whoosh. The portal closed.

Any moment, the bastard would return. Bane had to send Nola somewhere he'd never been, a place he'd only seen in a photo. Like...the photo of young Nola, with her bright smile.

"What's the plan?" Nola asked.

"This." With no time to spare, he opened a portal to the playground and prodded her inside.

A snarling, soaking wet Micah hurried through a portal of his own, spotted the other portal and tried to zoom through it.

Bane shot into the air and blocked with a swing of his sword—a sword he then tossed into the portal, followed by his goggles and the chains. "Keep them safe," he shouted at Nola.

She had landed on a plot of grass and now leaped up, her furious gaze locked on Bane. "Don't you dare take this away from me!" One step, two, she rushed forward.

The sight of her, so determined, so fierce, nearly felled him. "I'll be your hand of vengeance, princess."

"Bane!" The portal closed before she reached it, her rage-darkened face the last thing he saw.

Send Micah to his grave, go to Nola.

Bloodlust boiled in his veins. Fueled by adrenaline, his fury mounting, Bane stopped fighting his transformation. He dropped the nail gun and charged toward his enemy. Drogo overtook him along the way, emerging with a world-rocking roar.

Let the battle begin.

IT TOOK A moment for Nola to gain her bearings. Bane had dropped her in Oklahoma, on the outskirts of a park she and Vale used to frequent as young girls. Sunlight and trees surrounded the area, a cold breeze chilling her bones. Kids laughed as they climbed monkey bars. Parents, babysitters and guardians perched on benches, watching over their charges, almost everyone wearing some sort of costume.

Why—oh, right. Days had passed, and Halloween had arrived. Thankfully, no one paid her any heed.

Nola gathered the items Bane had flung at her and hid in the shadows of a bank of trees. Though aches and pains flared up, and her stomach grew queasy, she secured the metal links to her arms, fit the goggles around her neck and anchored the sword to her back. Time was her greatest enemy right now. If she began to vomit, she wouldn't have the strength to teleport.

She wished she'd already undergone the Blood Rite. Wished she possessed the ability to heal all of Bane, not just part of him. Wished she could defeat Micah.

Yeah, Bane had been smart to send her away. In her previous frame of mind, she would have challenged the POS and lost. But. She could fight Micah in other ways. Unlike Bane, she *could* use Aveline's orders against Micah.

Frantic to return, Nola closed her eyes and concentrated on their mental link…yes! She picked up emotional fragments. Frothing rage. Sizzling hatred. Incomparable pain. Jagged frustration. All-consuming concern. An-n-nd suddenly, she could see through Bane's eyes. A smoke-doused sky, neon red eyes and the glint of scales.

Urgency vibrated in Nola's bones, and she whipped out her cell phone. She typed a rushed message to Zion, attached the photo of the desert and asked for help. Zion could prove his tracking skills another day.

The foundation at her feet vanished. For a moment, she floated, weightless. Then, a new foundation appeared.

She'd done it! The smoke filled her nose, and she coughed, her eyes burning and watering. Rapid blinking cleared her line of sight—

Horror devoured her, a living nightmare unfolding.

Only a few minutes had passed, yet everything had changed.

Streams of fire had charred sections of land, tendrils of smoke curling up, up and away. Bane was in beast form, the two creatures tearing at each other with teeth and claws. Vicious predators at war.

Micah clawed the gash in Drogo's shoulder. With an agonized bellow, Drogo reared back. Both of his wings were mutilated, the left hanging at an odd angle. The sight sickened her. He was a beast, yes, but he was *her* beast.

Heart galloping, she shouted, "Micah!" The two beasts swung around, pinning her with the weight of their neon red gazes. She kept her gaze on Micah. *Remember, your orders cannot contradict Aveline's.* Very well. "You will ignore Bane's beast completely.

No matter what he does, you will only try to kill *me*, the princess."

Both beasts sprinted in her direction, the injured Drogo a little slower. To her shock and delight, Micah obeyed her, focusing solely on Nola.

Red alert! Incoming dragon with murder on his mind... She stood her ground, chin up, shoulders squared, her stomach churning with more dread. Closing in... The closer they came, the more she smelled soot and ash. The better she saw murder in their eyes.

Had she made a terrible mistake?

For this to work, Drogo had to want Micah dead more than he wanted to end a princess's reign. Almost within striking range... If he still wanted to end her reign?

Micah tilted his head back, preparing to roast her alive. If the Blood Rite kicked off, the Blood Rite kicked off. She had to believe Bane would find a way to destroy Micah and finish the job, ensuring her survival. But, just before Micah could expel a single ember, Drogo clamped his tail in his jaws of death and used his entire body to fling the beast across the sky, *away* from her.

Yes! Her plan was working! Drogo was free to attack at his leisure, without any resistance.

He dropped down, landing several feet in front of her, his every action stiff and lumbered, without a shred of grace. The look he gave her...ferocious, anguished. Her heart stuttered, then skipped a beat.

Micah regained his footing and pawed at the ground, spraying hunks of dirt behind him raging bull-style. Then, he charged at her once more.

Drogo charged *him*, the two colliding halfway. Again, to her utter delight Micah paid Drogo no heed, even when Drogo...

Oh, good gracious. Drogo—utterly—unleashed. Blood sprayed, and bones snapped. Hanks of muscle plopped to the ground. An eyeball rolled away from the body. As he bit off Micah's hands—yes, these dragons had scaled hands—he used his razor sharp tail to slash the male's vulnerable underbelly.

Despite his growing list of injuries, Micah did his best to fight his way to her. But, no matter the damage Drogo sustained, he always blocked, safeguarding her.

Another swipe of Drogo's claws maimed Micah's remaining eye, blinding him. The beast swiped his stumps at his bleeding face, and her dark side thrilled, adoring the view.

The male who killed my parents suffers. As he should.

Nola began to wonder if she had more in common with Dark Nola than she'd ever realized; she wondered if they maybe…balanced each other? If Dark Nola was a type of beast she had to learn to control, the same way Bane had learned to control Drogo.

With an animalistic roar, Drogo restrained the other beast, pinning him on the ground and slamming a fist through Micah's chest cavity to remove his beating heart.

Just like that, the battle ended.

Upon death, Aveline's soldier returned to his humanoid shape, scales falling away, bones shrinking.

Once the metamorphosis completed, a naked man covered in blood remained.

Nola swallowed a rush of bile.

Drogo stumbled back and fell, and this time he didn't rise. Dismayed and worried, she rushed over, skidding halfway. As she gently maneuvered his head in her lap, he issued a low growl, but he didn't bite her so…win!

"Be at ease, beasty-boy." He was in pain, and she hated that.

What had Carrie used to say? *If you want a different outcome, you've got to do something different.* Rather than resisting Dark Nola, she drew from her confidence.

Ta-da! The answer—the "something different"—came to her in a flash. She needed to issue a command. That hadn't changed. But if she changed his outlook…

Petting his snout, she said, "In a moment, I'm going to heal you. But, as you know, I've got to issue a command to do so."

His whole body jerked. He huffed a shallow breath, then another, his large dark eyes wild and deluged with fury.

"I need you to listen, okay? I am your queen. Or I will be," she continued as gently as possible. Petting, always petting. "I guess that makes me your pre-queen. So get ready, because you won't like what comes next. A pre-queen doesn't make herself less powerful because others are afraid of what she might order them to do. No. A warrior rises up and does his duty. So, I'm asking you to show yourself strong, so I can do the same. Do not nurse a bruised ego or throw a dragtrum—that's a 'dragon tantrum' to the layperson. Rather than lashing out at every royal, get to know us as individuals. Let me prove myself worthy of your scorn or respect."

He huffed another breath, this one deeper, but he didn't attempt to flee. He might not like her tone or her words, but he *was* listening.

"You earned these wounds saving me. It would be my honor to help you heal. My way of saying thanks."

Again, he didn't flee.

Deep breath in, out. *Here goes*. "I command you to heal quickly and painlessly."

Big, swiping shudders shook him, missing scales growing back. His wings straightened and realigned. Torn flesh wove back together. Even the shoulder wound healed somewhat, shrinking in both length and width, assuming its original size. *Sweet!* But also—*dang!*

"There," she said. "Isn't that better?"

Smoke curled from his nostrils, yet he projected little malice. What amazing progress for them both! She even felt her bond to Bane and Drogo amplifying.

When two layers of air peeled back a few yards off, she tensed. A new threat? Or Zion? As Nola jumped to her feet and unsheathed Bane's sword, Drogo hopped to an upright position and roared at volume "earsplitting."

Tall, dark and stalwart, Zion stepped through the portal. Warm relief cascaded over her, only to chill when he spotted her and the beast. The color drained from his cheeks. "Move away from the beast, Nola, and I will—"

Drogo leaped between them and roared with more aggression, dotting Zion's upper half with spittle.

"No!" She raced between the two, extending her arms. "Please, don't hurt each other. We're allies, remember? We guard each other's back—not stab!"

Zion glanced between her and the beast, his eyes widening. He didn't make a move against Drogo, and Drogo didn't make a move against him. The beast *did* enfold her with an arm, flatten his claws against her belly, gentle so gentle, and tug her against him. A possessive action that shouted, *She's mine, and I would rather kill you than share*.

Dude. I tamed a beast who usually despises royals.

Me. Pleasure blended with more feminine power, rushing straight to her head. *Delicious.*

"You came," she said to Zion. "Thank you."

He kept his gaze glued to Drogo, the bigger threat. "There's a tracker in Bane's boots. Erik had planted them on a corpse, in a cave, where he once trapped you. That's how combatants have located Bane at every turn." He switched his attention to Nola. "You'll be pleased to know I passed the phone to Vale."

Oh, thank goodness! Now, when Zion and Bane informed everyone about Nola's "death," Vale would ultimately conclude Nola lived.

"More combatants are on their way," Zion finished. "I would have been here sooner, but I had to stop others from arriving first."

Nola told Bane, "You should throw the boots into a portal that leads to a seriously dangerous place." Any combatants chasing Bane deserved what they got.

Through their bond, he told her, —*Go with Z. I must dispose of the body, so that your people do not launch an investigation or learn aliens walk among them.*—

I don't want to leave you, she replied. Wait. Bane's voice had whispered through her mind, not Drogo's. Bane had remained at the helm, despite the transformation? She grew in might, and so did he. Because they were connected, the queen and her chosen warrior.

Drogo-Bane nuzzled the back of her neck. —*Do it anyway. When I finish, I'll come to you. Be ready, for I plan to finish what we started.*—

CHAPTER TWENTY-FOUR

How to kick a third wheel to the curb

BANE RETURNED TO humanoid form and spit out a mouthful of blood. Drogo snarled in the back of his mind the entire time. But…he and the beast seemed to be…one. One being. One conscious mind, with one objective—Nola's protection through Micah's obliteration.

With a cloud of smoke collecting overhead, protecting his skin from the too-harsh sun, Bane hacked the male's body into small pieces. "May your screams of pain echo into eternity."

He opened a portal above those shark-infested waters—a location he'd flown over before and after his imprisonment—and tossed the pieces inside. His boots received the same treatment.

A feeding frenzy erupted, water splashing, the scent of salt heavy in the air.

He ransacked his backpack, dressed in clean clothes and considered sticking around to ambush any combatants foolish enough to chase him.

More time away from Nola? Not happening.

When his little beauty had faced off with Micah, Bane had nearly dropped to his knees to worship at her feet. Warrior woman? Better. Warrior *princess*. Stronger than he'd ever realized. Braver, too, with courage to spare. Witty, fun and brilliant. Formidable. Loyal. Honest.

And right.

Once she'd told a very harsh truth. Only a hypocrite would admire strength in himself, but disdain those who were stronger...and only a hypocrite would despise her for having authority over him while making use of that authority anytime he required help.

When he considered how terribly he'd treated her, how he'd once thought her no better than Aveline... Bane dropped to his knees and threw back his head, roaring to the skies until his lungs emptied and his voice broke.

He'd been a fool, blinded by his prejudices. Her abilities, the very abilities he'd hated her for wielding, would help keep her alive in the endless years ahead. He could have her—he could *keep* her, death unable to easily steal her away.

Bane could have everything he'd ever wanted. A loving woman at his side. A family to love and cherish. *Forever.*

Dazed, he leaned back. A family. With Nola. *Want that so much.*

What did she want?

Frantic with need, Bane jumped to his feet. He used their link to peer through her eyes. He saw...a cloud of steam?

Hard as steel, he opened a portal and stepped into a spacious bathroom, with chrome fixtures and black-and-white tiles, Nola's dirty clothes piled on the floor. Inside the shower stall, water poured from an overhead spout, mist fogging up the glass door. The scent of honeysuckle and jasmine threatened to fray what remained of his control.

"How are you feeling, dove?"

"Bane?" She smoothed a hand over the door, wiping away a layer of mist. Relief pulsated from her. "I wasn't as sick this time. I'm getting better."

Or the link between them had strengthened, allowing her to take more from him at greater distances? "Where are we? Where's Zion?" He trusted the other man, in part, otherwise, he never would have placed Nola's life in the other warrior's hands.

"We're in Los Angeles," she said. "A fancy penthouse suite in an even fancier hotel. Isn't it glorious? Oh, and Zion mentioned he has some sort of present for you."

You are the only present I desire. "Don't care about Zion. Want company?" he asked, even as he yanked his shirt overhead.

"You're not angry with me?" she asked, hesitant.

He tried to hide his flinch. *She expects me to return to my default setting and punish her for issuing commands.* "I'm grateful to you. You patched us up. Am I happy you teleported back, putting yourself in danger? No. My life is expendable. Yours is not."

Her eyes widened. "Your life is *not* expendable, and if I ever hear you speak such a disgusting lie again, I'll do damage!"

The way she defends my honor. His chest bowed with pride. He knelt on one knee and lowered his head, saying, "Many times in many ways I did you wrong. From this moment forward, I will do what's right. You might be a princess, but you are my queen. I trust you, Nola, and your command is my privilege."

"I... You... What?" Just before mist returned to the door, shielding her face—a travesty he could not bear—she gaped at him, openmouthed. "Okay. You are

absolutely, positively invited to attend my shower. Fair
warning, I expect you to put out."

Put out…a fire? His translator supplied her meaning
a moment later. Get laid. Nookie. Horizontal mambo.
Sex. Ahhhh. His lusty royal desired him still, and he felt
the urge to bang his fists against his chest. "I'll put out
for you, dove, but you'll owe me."

She snorted. "Hey! You're getting our roles switched.
In this relationship, you're the hot piece of beefcake, and
I'm the funny, smart, gorgeous one." Her eyes widened.
"Uh-oh. I just used the *R* word. Are you about to freak?
Or maybe you kinda sorta…like the idea?"

"I love the idea."

His words earned a reward. A bright and happy smile
he longed to view every day for the rest of eternity. "I'm
yours, and you're mine? I get to keep you?"

"You say *get to*… I say *must*." He shrugged. "I won't
be letting you go." He stripped the rest of the way, kicking off his leathers, and entered the stall. Heat and steam
enveloped him. "I hope you're ready, dove. I'm about to
put you through an assembly line of orgasms."

Nola stood on the other side of the water, leaning
against the wall, naked, flushed and damp, exquisite
beyond measure, watching him watch her.

"If I get an assembly line of your orgasms, you get
the show of a lifetime." She cupped her breasts, then slid
one hand down the flat plane of her stomach.

As her fingers teased the tuft of inky hair between
her legs, he swallowed a groan. When a droplet of water
dripped from her nipple, the groan escaped, anyway.

Voice raw, dark seduction, she said, "I've never gotten
dirty while getting clean. This should be fun."

The barest hint of a grin appeared. "Did you miss me?"

"More than I've ever missed anything." He stalked under the hot spray of water and pulled her against him. "Does it please you to know I hurried to reach you?"

"Mmm." She traced her hands up his chest. "It does, yes. But it surprises me, too."

Rock hard and throbbing, he fit his nose in the hollow of her neck and breathed deeply. *Like inhaling sex.* "I don't like that you put yourself in danger," he said, combing his fingers through her wet hair. "But I'm pleased with the outcome. Your bravery is commendable."

She beamed at him. "Well, I've come to like Drogo. I'd totally swipe right for him. And you! Two for the price of one."

According to his translator, "swipe right" meant she found both Bane and beast sexually attractive. He smiled, nipped her earlobe and whispered, "That pleases me *more*."

Playful, she teased, "All I ask is that you don't fall in love with me. Got too much on my plate to deal with an immortal stalker."

The words were spoken in jest, and yet, that smile…

Comprehension. I'm halfway in love with her already.

Dazed, Bane washed every inch of her. Her curves maddened him. The throbbing in his shaft worsened, but he made no move to assuage it. He owed this woman so much. He didn't want to take this time; he wanted to give.

Breathing through the frenzied heat of desire, he shampooed and conditioned her hair, vacillating between ecstasy and agony.

As she washed him in turn, he clung to his fragile control. Then her slippery fingers stroked his length…

Perhaps he'd take a little.

With a growl, he pressed her against the wall and slammed his mouth to hers, thrusting his tongue against hers.

She kissed him back, rubbing and clawing, holding nothing back. "You make me feel so good," she breathed against his lips.

"You make me better." He spun her, putting her back to his chest, his erection resting in the cleft of her ass. Kneading her breasts, he turned his head to receive another kiss.

She ground her backside against his shaft. An invitation. He glided one hand down, down, to cup her mound. As she mewled, the tone of the kiss changed. *Control fraying.* He slid a finger deep into her hot, slick core. Her inner walls squeezed him, then stretched to accommodate a second finger.

"I will do anything you command," he breathed into her ear, "but you will do anything I ask. Won't you, dove?"

"Let's find out." She arched her back and threaded her fingers in his hair. "Ask me for something. Anything."

"Not this time. Tonight, I give you whatever you desire." He thrust his fingers in and out, in and out. "So hot. So tight. So wet."

Panting, she glanced at him over her shoulder, her bottom lip pouting. "What I desire is *your* fantasy."

"You are my fantasy." Earlobe—nipped. Mouth—licked and sucked. "Do *you* have a fantasy you'd like me to fulfill?" To punctuate his words, he scissored the fingers inside her.

Her head fell back, and she moaned. "So good!" But she whirled around, radiant, and rested her palms on his pecs. With a gentle push, she urged him to walk backward.

His knees hit the bench, and he sat. The wicked gleam in her starry eyes set his cells on fire.

"If you won't tell me your fantasy," she said, peering at his length, "I guess I'll have to enact mine." She licked her lips.

Breathe. Her fantasy...did she long to suck him, as he'd always craved? *Manage your hopes. She desires something else. Surely!*

Wicked intent gleamed in her eyes as she knelt between his legs and pressed his knees apart.

She did. She intended to do it. *Her fantasy is mine.*

Bane reeled. Tenderness swept through him, eroding whatever shields he'd managed to build around his heart. A heart now exposed to the world.

Protective instincts told him to stand, to run, to portal away and never return. If he continued on this path, he would experience gut-wrenching anguish, turning his past into a vacation and his future into misery. But...

Fear would not decide for him.

He couldn't live without this woman. He *wouldn't.*

Bane wasn't halfway in love with her. He was totally, completely, madly, passionately, fully in love. He wanted everything.

And he would not stop until he had it.

NOLA HOVERED ON at the brink of madness. Once again, something had changed for Bane. Since his arrival, he'd peered at her with awe, touched her as if she were a priceless treasure and whispered the sweetest somethings in her ears.

The thought of sucking on his shaft, of drinking him

down, excited her to the extreme. An action she'd sometimes wondered about in the dark of night. "I've never
done this," she said, her body fixed between his strong,
strapping thighs. "If I mess up…deal. I'll get better with
practice."

His eyes crinkled at the edges. Fighting a grin? "I've
never had this," he admitted. "But I want it from you."

Not even Meredith had gotten to enjoy this experience
with him? A sense of possessiveness unfurled, winding
through every inch of her. "You've waited long enough,
baby. And so have I."

Leaning down, Nola started at his knee and kissed
along his thigh, slowly closing in on the object of her
desire. Through the shield of her lashes, she watched
his face. His features tightened; he looked like a man
on the edge, the tendons on either side of his neck bulging, the veins in his biceps distended. Wet, his hair appeared darker than usual. He had yet to shave, a layer
of golden stubble dusting his jaw.

His gaze remained glued to her face, as if he couldn't
force himself to glance away. He shook. Well, well.
Sweet little Nola Lee had made this incredibly powerful male tremble, and the knowledge went straight to
her head. *Like a drug.*

"Ready?" she purred.

Had he tensed? "Beyond," he rasped.

Trembling with excitement, she licked the crown of
his shaft, tasting a hint of salt. His body jerked, a ragged
groan leaving him. The taste…that groan…*perfection.*
Her lids turned heavy, her thoughts dimming. *More.*

"Nola," he croaked, his fingers in her hair. "Don't
stop. Please, don't stop."

Now he begs me. Precious alien. "Never stop." She

sucked on the head for a bit, drawing ragged growls. Then she opened wide and devoured as much of his length as possible. The tip hit the back of her throat, and he jerked once again, white-knuckling the sides of the bench, as if he was afraid he would get too rough with her.

Nola *wanted* rough.

She gobbled him up, a little clumsily at first, but he reveled in everything she did, hoarse sounds spilling from him. Sounds that grew louder as she quickened her pace, working her mouth up and down, up and down.

"This is… Never knew… Need…every day…" The harshness of his voice only made her hunger worse.

Nola wanted him out of his mind with arousal. *As I am.* Her core ached, and her blood simmered. Did she detect his heartbeat along their bond, racing and pounding?

When she cupped his testicles—they'd drawn up so tight—he released his hoarsest growl yet.

"More," he pleaded.

Up, down. Faster.

"Ah, dove, you make me… I need to come. If you don't want—"

She sucked harder. *Mine!* She'd earned every drop, and she would settle for nothing less.

As she tugged on his balls, he threw back his head and bellowed his satisfaction, hot jets of pleasure lashing her throat. She swallowed, and oh, yes, yes, yes. *Better than a cocktail of drugs.* Instant high, her arousal soaring off the charts.

Nola relinquished his shaft with an audible *pop*. "Bane," she said, his name a supplication. The act had been everything she'd hoped and more. Better. Lips tingling, she rocked back on her haunches. Tremors plagued her. Need overwhelmed her.

Expression infinitely tender, he gently stroked two fingers along her jawline. "You couldn't be more precious, dove. Thank you."

"Bane," she repeated. What she wished to say, she didn't know how to articulate. She'd never wanted, needed, desire, craved anyone or anything the way she wanted, needed, desired, craved Bane. "Please."

His shaft hardened right before her eyes. Stroking himself, he said, "You require your man."

She nodded, yes, yes, and he slipped his hands under her arms, forcing her to stand. He lowered his grip to her hips and spun her, then stood and placed her palms against the tiles.

"You will have me. All of me," he said, and kicked her legs apart. "Do not move from this position."

Cool air kissed her most intimate place, tremors rocking her sensitized body. "Wh-what will you do?"

"Anything I wish." He squeezed her breasts, pinched her nipples and traced his hands down her sides before teasing her clitoris. "You've never been so wet. You loved sucking me off, didn't you?"

"I did." Why play coy? "I'm ready for more."

Bane settled his shaft at her opening. "You are the forge, and I am the sword. I make you stronger, you make me better. Together, we can accomplish anything."

Everything inside her softened for this man. "Oh, Bane."

He placed a tender kiss at the corner of her eye, on her cheek. Then...

He plunged inside of her.

The combination of his tender and ferocious ministrations shoved her over the edge. Another climax hit so fast and hard, she could only throw back her head and scream.

Pleasure. Bliss. Rapture. He filled her up, stretching her. He *owned* her...just as she owned him?

But the jerk ceased moving. Why had he ceased moving? "Bane! I'm not done. Want more!"

"I'll *never* be done." He pulled out, almost all the way, and she whimpered. Then he stirred his hips and plunged once again. And again. And again. Yes! Yes! Harder. Faster. He was merciless, ruthless—perfect. She arched her back, meeting his every inward thrust. "As your climax rages, your inner walls squeeze my cock. You are killing me with pleasure..."

"Please!"

He rammed into her with bruising force, and she loved it, needed it. Ram, ram. Harder, faster. Faster still. Skin slapped together. She moaned and groaned and panted every labored breath, her heart thundering, desire like lightning. She knew his heart thundered, too, their reactions synced.

One man, one woman, two halves of a whole. A fanciful thought, yes, but also reality. This...he...made life worth living.

He threaded his fingers through her hair and angled her head to bare neck. Dipping down, he bit the cord of her neck, sending shock waves coursing through her—

"Bane!" Another explosive climax ripped through her, her body singing.

With a final, rampaging thrust, he followed her over the edge, roaring, coming in hot lashes.

Nola's mind momentarily blanked. By the time the lights flickered on, she and Bane were both panting, his chest resting against her back. Her muscles were lax, her limbs boneless. Any minute, she would collapse, sinking into a coma of satisfaction.

He kissed her temple, then returned to the bench, dragging her with him. As she curled into a ball on his lap, she tried not to worry about his reaction to their lovemaking.

And that was what they'd done, right? Made love.

If he tensed up and went all guilty again...

"I have endless questions for you," he said, kissing her temple. "I'd like to know you better and eagerly await every detail about your life."

Truly? She ran her hands up his chest. Soft skin, hard muscles. Not sinking her nails into his skin, holding him in place lest he decide to bolt, required every ounce of her willpower. She was sated and quivering, genuinely content for the first time in...ever. Such a wild, wonderous feeling! Of course, with her luck, it wouldn't last.

A buzz of foreboding drew her notice, and she nearly yelled in frustration. Not here, not now.

Too bad, so sad.

Thoughts came, and they carried pitchforks and torches. At some point, Bane would recall Nola had the ability to retrieve his wife from the past and grant him the life he'd always dreamed of having. Would resentment flare like a disease? Would he default to contempt?

Why not remind him and get the process started and over with?

"You hate queens," she said, kicking things off.

"Do I?" With a teasing tone, he replied, "I don't find you so objectionable right now."

"Oh la la. I'm not objectionable." She rolled her eyes, saying, "Stop, before your praise goes to my head."

He nipped her earlobe. "I see the orgasms failed to improve your mood."

She lifted her head, shocked to find him completely at ease, with no hint of stress. The teasing light had even migrated to his eyes, brightening his golden irises. "Have you forgotten what I can do? Who I can save?"

"I have everything I desire."

"But—"

The jerk began to tickle her. Nola laughed hysterically while trying to beg for mercy. But the more she laughed, the more his expression veered into wonder, until she never wanted it to end.

"Tell me your favorite anything, and why," he said. "Only then will the torment stop."

Has to end before I pee myself! "Okay, okay." This playful side of her ultraserious warrior was doing strange, fluttery things to her insides. "My favorite things. Let's see. Color—gold."

"Like me."

"Like jewelry."

He pouted, and she laughed.

"Season," she said, picking up where she left off. "Winter. When I was bedbound and it snowed, Vale's school would close, and she'd get to stay with me, watching movies. Food—donuts. Delicious! In fact, Vale and I once planned to open a donut shop together. What about you? What are your favorites?"

"Wait. You planned to sell sweet treats?"

"Yep."

His lips quirked, making all the fluttering worse. "Anytime you wish to sell donuts, I'm willing to buy. Kisses are my currency."

"You heard the part about liking jewelry, right? I only accept precious gems and gold."

The grin widened. "Orgasms are more valuable, and I have an endless supply to give."

"Then Nola's Tricks For Treats Shop is open for business."

A laugh burst from him, and she almost swooned like a Victorian maiden.

"I owe you my favorites," he said. "Color? Blue. Season? Dark and stormy, no matter the time of year. We have no alternating seasons in Adwaeweth. The dome controls the weather. Food? You." He nipped at her chin. "Because...delicious."

She smiled. She *melted*. When this guy decided to show a girl romance, he freaking showed a girl romance. "Someone is crushing on me hard, huh?"

"My apologies." He lifted and resettled her, letting her wrap her legs around his waist. "Better?"

Amused and delighted, she laughed. He'd tickled and teased the troubles right out of her. "Crushing on someone is a figure of speech. It means you're into me. Digging my vibe. Gaga for Nola-puffs."

"Can you blame me? The brilliant wit...bright smile...seductive heat...and addictive scent. This exquisite face...pert breasts...mmm, the honeyed portal to paradise." Every place he mentioned, he touched, making her moan. "I never stood a chance. No one does. It's not even fair."

Those compliments...messing with my head. A swell of affection crashed over her. "Like you aren't packing a ton of heat yourself, bad boy. That incredible intensity...killer grin...dry wit. This gorgeous face... those soft lips...these hard muscles...your mouthwatering musk, your devastating smile and mating call of a laugh. Your incomparable touch." Following his example, she touched the body parts she mentioned. "This jumbotron of an erection."

His jaw slackened. He gulped. "Tell me your favorite memory."

"Right this second." Brushing the tip of her nose against his, she said, "And you?"

"Right this second," he echoed with a nod. "I have a feeling this day will be branded in my memory and resurrected, each and every time I climax solo."

She offered him the sauciest grin she could manage. "I'm your spank bank fodder? Aw. I'm honored." *This man is as good as mine. Nola Lee had herself a genuine boyfriend!* "Okay, I don't mean to ruin our afterglow or anything, but I'm too curious. What happened with Micah after I left?" This change in him…

"I simply realized you were never the unworthy one. I was. I didn't—don't—deserve you, but I want and need you." He cupped her cheeks, meeting her gaze with all the intensity she'd praised. "You are—"

A light tap, tap sounded at the door. "Judging by the moans and groans I heard, I'm guessing Bane has returned," Zion called. "Now that you've got your reunion out of the way, come out and see the gift *I* have for you."

CHAPTER TWENTY-FIVE

The romantic getaway is over. Now what?

DAMN ZION'S POOR TIMING.

Heart like a freight train, riding his ribs like rails, Bane untangled from Nola and stood. Though he'd experienced complete satisfaction mere moments ago, his nerves were raw and exposed, the rest of him knocked off-kilter. He wanted her back in his arms. She was the center of the storm. His calm. But she was also the storm itself.

To resist primal temptation, he had to draw from a reservoir of strength he'd reserved for emergencies. Didn't help that the beast wanted her back in his arms, too, and battered his skull in protest. Never had the fiend reacted this way to another. Hungry for a specific female, possessive of her and vulnerable *to* her. Totally out of control. Wild and fearful.

If anything were to happen to her…

Nothing will happen. I will protect her life with my own.

She stood and rested her head against his shoulder, as if she couldn't bear to part from him. *Pang.* When he held her like this, he couldn't regret the hardships that had brought them together.

To experience this time with her, he would gladly suffer *anything*.

"I hoped to cuddle you right this time," he said, bending to kiss her nape. At the site of contact, goose bumps broke out.

"Okay," she said. "What happened to my stoic grumble bear?"

Grumble bear? "He met you." He cupped her beautiful face and brushed the tip of his nose against hers, then pressed a tender kiss to her puffy, well-loved lips. "I'm keeping you, Nola. Do you understand what that means?"

Her eyes widened. "I think I do. Maybe." Water droplets clung to her lashes, and a flush stained her cheeks. "I mean, you're looking at me like I'm your next meal, and you currently don't want me going back for Meredith."

"Currently?" *She thinks I will change my mind?*

Heat descended over his spine, quickly spreading to his limbs. "I will *never* want you going back." *Forgive me, Meredith.*

When his wife needed him most, Bane had failed her. He wished she had lived, but even if she'd materialized right here, right now, he suspected things would be different between them.

The admission gutted him. The years apart had changed him. He wasn't the man Meredith had loved, and she wasn't the woman he…needed.

He could be a prisoner of his past no longer. He'd made mistakes, yes, and had earned punishments, but an eternal sentence wasn't necessary.

The time had come to pardon himself. To let go and say goodbye to his wife at long last. Only then could he truly embrace a future with Nola. And he *yearned* for a future with her. Before she entered his life, he'd had nothing but a heart brimming with hate.

Knowing Zion waited outside the door, but unwilling to part with his queen, Bane said, "I have a confession. Several, in fact. After we deal with Zion, I will eat my dessert. But we won't deal with Zion until I've told you that you've already changed the past. When you revisited the memory of your parents' death, Aveline noticed you. She compared you to Jayne, a former queen able to manipulate memories and change the past. In order to do so, however, she had to perform a human sacrifice. I think you must do the same, because I believe you come from Jayne's line."

Nola blanched. "Are you saying I can time-travel in corporal form if I *murder* someone?"

He held her gaze and nodded.

She sputtered for a bit before grating, "Who? Why? How?"

"Who—anyone. Why—blood is life, life is power. How—any way you wish."

She stumbled back. "Now I *really* don't understand. A single measly murder, and you can have your wife back. Like, I can think of a ton of people who deserve to serve as a sacrifice."

Measly murder? "When I said I wanted you, *only* you, I meant it."

Confusion drew a crease between her brows. "But why?"

Had he insulted her so many times, in so many ways, his compliments hadn't registered? The guilt… "Dove, you are the most beautiful female I've ever beheld. The strongest, the bravest. The sweetest, and the wittiest. I could pluck you from a crowd of millions."

Eyes wide again, pupils expanding, she stared up at him. Steam enveloped her in a dreamy haze, and Bane edged closer.

"But," he added, "Meredith wouldn't want a murder committed in cold-blood to bring her back. She believed in battle, honor and consequences."

"Who said anything about cold-blooded? I could do it during the heat of battle, just the way she prefers. Heck, I could even use Aveline when she shows up."

The whole time she spoke, he shook his head with savage determination and yes, growing fury. He'd made a decision, and he wouldn't reverse it. Why did Nola continue to insist on this?

Ready to be rid of me?

Could he blame her if so? No. But he grappled with his temper, anyway.

Before he left this bathroom, he would cement their relationship.

Rap, rap, rap. "My gift has a time limit," Zion called. "Trust me when I say you don't want to miss it." A harder rap. A crack appeared in the door, the wood no match for his metal glove. "I don't hear you scrambling in there. Perhaps I didn't make myself clear. Time. Limit."

Very well. Bane's personal desires could wait. "We'll talk later, yes?"

"Yes," she whispered, a little choked up.

After shutting off the water, he toweled her off, then dried himself—without kissing all his favorite parts. A true travesty.

Bane donned a black T-shirt and camouflage pants

with pockets, watching as Nola hooked a lacy bra in place and shimmied into a pair of matching panties.

Later, I'll rip those panties off with my teeth.

She covered the undergarments with jeans and a pink T-shirt that read Pre-millionaire. The grace of her movements turned the simple act of dressing into a dance of seduction, and he remained rapt.

Nola plopped onto the toilet lid to tie her tennis shoes. Again and again she opened her mouth as if she had something to say, only to change her mind.

"Things will be better now," he told her gently. "Whatever happens, we will get through it." He crouched in front of her to finish tying, his shoulders keeping her knees apart. "Together."

She nodded, but kept her gaze downcast, inciting a sense of urgency in him.

"Nola? What's wrong?"

"I just… I feel like a yo-yo. Up and down. Happy one second, certain something terrible is about to happen the next."

Clench. "I won't let anything bad happen to you."

"I don't mean me," she croaked.

"Me?" Bane thumped his chest, just to be sure. At her nod, the clenching worsened. "I have something to live for. I'll let *no one* get the better of me." He brought her wrist to his mouth, kissed her hammering pulse, then stood, drawing her to her feet.

With a final kiss to her brow, he ushered his beautiful female into the bedroom. A brief glance, and he memorized his surroundings, a habit every combatant developed to aid their survival. A large bed topped by a fluffy comforter. Two nightstands, a desk, a television and three lamps, everything black, white or silver and shiny.

Dagger in hand, Bane entered the hallway, where Zion waited. He didn't glance at Nola, proving he understood Bane's cooperation was conditional. Leer at the girl, and their alliance ended. "Let's see this gift."

A trick?

"This way." Zion wore lightweight cotton pajama pants and a grin. Though he displayed no visible injuries, splatters of blood wet his skin and clothing.

Bane and Nola followed, cutting through the living room. Once again, he memorized his surroundings with only a glance. Two couches, two chairs. A piano in a windowed corner, adjacent to a wet bar.

Next came the kitchen. Large table, seven chairs. Bane pursed his lips. Had Zion taken the eighth?

They entered a different bedroom, half the size of the other and similarly furnished. Except for a small detail—Zion had taken the chair, placed a plastic tarp underneath it…and chained a human to it. Interesting development.

One of the victim's eyes was swollen shut, the other rimmed red from tears and glazed with fear. Blood caked his mouth and chin, choking noises leaving him.

Zion had removed his tongue.

Nola burrowed into Bane's side, her body racked by tremors. "Who is this? Why have you done this, Zion?"

The human spotted her and silently pleaded for help.

A growl rumbled from Bane, drawing the male's gaze back to him, and the fear magnified. "Do not look at her. Do not ever look at her."

"The next assembly is less than two weeks from now,"

Zion said, patting the human's head. "This male leads a human army employed by Erik. He and his men plan to attend the meeting from afar and pick us off from the mountaintops. They must be neutralized."

"So why haven't you killed him?" Nola asked, shedding some of her unease.

Bane ran a hand up and down her side, accidentally brushing the underside of her breast. Shit! Touching her had been a mistake, but letting her go had become an impossibility. "I can guess. The wand," he said. "Only Zion can wield it."

She frowned. "The magic wand? You weren't joking about that?"

"No joke." Zion tapped the diamonds embedded in his skin, in a specific order, then held out his hand. A thin wooden stick appeared in the center.

Bane's mind buzzed. Could the weapon heal his shoulder or not?

"You might want to turn away for this," Zion told Nola.

"I'm fine," she said, but she inched closer to Bane, seeking comfort.

His chest puffed with pride. *She's falling for me.* "Do it," he said to the other male. "Nola can handle anything."

Now *her* chest puffed with pride, and he almost smiled.

Zion moved behind the shaking captive, placed the wand's tip against a groove between skull and spine—and shoved. The wood plunged through the man's brain.

Nola squeezed her eyes shut as the victim grunted, jerked and sagged, his head lolling forward. His eyes remained open, a bright light shining from them. Brighter. Images formed.

"We're watching a movie—through a dead man's eyes?" Nola gasped out.

"Everything is energy," Zion said, "even our thoughts. The wand can extract and project them, allowing us to view whatever part of his life we choose."

In the light, a movie version of Erik paced in a warehouse filled with hundreds of soldiers who were riveted by his every move. A warehouse Bane and Zion could now portal into, but shouldn't. Considering they were dealing with the viking, there had to be countless traps. Poisonous sprays and gases, most likely, with an electrified floor. That was Bane's preferred set of traps, anyway. No doubt there were specific traps for specific warriors. Like brighter lights for Bane, perhaps?

"Your job is simple," Erik said. "A week before the meeting, one hundred of our best snipers will travel to the arctic. I have a cabin there, with an underground bunker beneath. The shooters will remain hidden until the assembly kicks off. Then, they'll hunker in the mountaintops and shoot anyone who challenges me. Bullets won't kill them, but that's all right. Blind them, slow them, whatever you can, and my allies will take care of the rest."

"That is what I wanted you to see." Zion yanked out the wand, blood dripping on the floor. "Thoughts? Questions?"

"I never knew about the bunker," Nola muttered. "Would have come in handy!"

"If we portal nearby and sneak into the warehouse," Bane suggested, "you can freeze everyone in place, and I can kill them, ensuring they never make it to the assembly."

New tremors rocked her, but still his woman offered support. "We should raid the warehouse *tonight*. It's Halloween, so we can cart around every weapon in our arsenal without causing panic. Onlookers won't give us a second glance. And, because I wanted to see you and Zion dressed up as Dothraki warriors, I picked up your costumes when I went shopping with Zion, so you're both ready to roll."

"Dothraki?" Zion said, crouching to clean the weapon on the tarp.

"Only the fiercest warriors ever." She placed her hand on Bane's pectoral, her skin white-hot, and the muscle jumped. "You'll be Khal Drogo, the Dothraki leader."

Drogo, the name she'd given his beast. "Agreed," he said. For her? Anything.

"I will also be this Khal Drogo," Zion announced. "We are coleaders."

"Sure." Nola glanced between the two. "But let's maybe dispose of the body before we go?"

His pride gained new ground. How quickly she adapted to problems. "Allow me." Bane opened a portal to his favorite shark-infested waters and dumped the body.

"Before anyone tells the little woman to stay behind," Nola said, "I should probably inform you both that I'm going, and that's final. My mission? Ensuring the other Drogo doesn't burn down the entire world. Like you guys, I'll be wearing a costume." Not giving him a chance to protest, she raced from the room.

Willingly put her precious life in jeopardy? Never. But he couldn't leave her here and not sink into madness. Worry for her would distract him.

"Can you use the wand to heal my shoulder?" he asked Zion.

"Of course." Zion didn't hesitate to jam the stick into Bane's shoulder.

He hissed, pained, but remained in place. Head back, hands fisted, enduring. Hoping. Any blood left by the human would not affect him.

When Zion jerked the weapon free, Bane looked down…

Nothing had changed. He spewed a stream of curses.

Zion glanced at the wood, then the wound, and frowned. "That should have worked."

Would he be forced to deal with the gash forevermore? With the danger to Nola heating up, weakness of any kind could no longer be tolerated. "Forget the shoulder. Once we've raided the warehouse and dispatched the army, I'll turn my sights to Gunnar of Trodaire."

"Gunnar is dead." Once again, Zion crouched to clean the wand. "Killed by Knox."

He pinched the bridge of his nose. "I'll pick another weapon, then." But which one? Emberelle's time-traveling wrist cuffs still topped the list. But, like Nola, he now feared mucking around in the past.

A strange noise caught his attention, his ears twitching. Was Nola…singing? Bane had never before heard her sing, but he remembered she'd claimed Vale liked to refer to her voice as Cats Being Murdered. An accurate description.

Bane pressed a hand over his mouth to silence a laugh. Warmth spread through his chest. *This must be joy.*

Fingers snapped in front of his face, and he blinked. Zion stood before him.

He scowled. He'd gotten lost in his musings in the

presence of a combatant. Yes, he trusted Zion—to an extent—but they were two men with the same goal. Survival. As things currently stood, only one of them could win.

"When you scanned his brain before, did you see outside the warehouse?" Bane asked.

"I did. For a split second."

"A split second is long enough." He scoured a hand over his weary features. "We will portal nearby, then."

Zion nodded in agreement.

"Be ready. We'll leave in one hour." With that, Bane stalked off to join Nola. He meant to chat with her, but when he walked into the bedroom and saw she'd stripped down to those lacy undergarments, those plans changed.

He shut the door and turned the lock with an ominous click. Zion could wait.

"Don't you dare try to talk me out of accompanying my guys," she said. Her back was to him, her ass on magnificent display.

"Guy. Singular," he all but snapped.

She pivoted, facing him, spied his straining erection and fanned her cheeks. "Well, well. My golden god isn't here to argue. He's here to seduce me into staying put."

"No. He's here to seduce you, period," he said. And then he did.

NOLA COULD NOT get over how sexy Bane looked in his Game of Thrones costume. He'd let her braid several locks of hair, and smear black streaks on his face and shoulders. He'd donned arm and wrist bands, draped a thick leather belt around his middle, and pulled a loin cloth over his leathers. Finally, he topped off the outfit with tall brown boots. The sword rested against his back, and daggers hung at his sides.

As she'd suspected, no one glanced twice at his weapons. They did, however, give his body multiple once-overs and wipe away drool.

She wished she'd chosen the Mother of Dragons costume for herself. Alas. As an inside joke, she'd gone with a sexy alien, coloring her skin green and shimmying into an ultratiny silver dress. On her head was a band with two bulb antenna rising from the sides.

Zion looked good, too, of course, but he couldn't compare to Bane.

Now, they walked the streets of New Orleans, on their way to the warehouse. Night had fallen, crowds illuminated by an array of streetlamps as people celebrated the holiday. So far, she'd spotted a handmaid, Black Panther, Deadpool, Thor and several versions of Aquaman. There were also nurses, sexy cats, cavewomen, cops, Playboy Bunnies, unicorns and a seductive skeleton. No one seemed to mind the freezing temperature. Colored lights flashed here and there. Laughter rang out, booze passed around. In the air, different perfumes clashed with the smell of fried foods and car exhaust.

"I know we're out here to do murder and all," she said to Bane, "but I've set my phaser to fun."

A drunken man in a wedding dress stumbled past them. Bane pulled her closer to his side. Anyone who'd looked twice at her soon came face-to-face with a hulking golden god ready to spew fire.

"When we retire for the evening," he said, "my phaser will show you all the fun you desire. I've *always* wanted to bed a green other-worlder."

She chuckled, the most decadent shivers traipsing

down her spine. He'd been saying the sweetest, most romantic things to her. And, after they'd done another mattress mambo in the hotel, he'd cuddled her, as promised.

A sense of contentment kept trying to sweep her away, but she continued to resist, afraid she'd only set herself up for heartbreak. Before she could even think about a forever with Bane, she had to tell him about Dark Nola. How would he react? Would he grow to hate her again, as she feared?

"Always…meaning the past two hours?" she asked, wiggling her eyebrows.

"No laughing, dove." The grip on her hip became bruising, and she loved it, loved when his intensity came out to play. "You know it annihilates my control."

Oh, yes. She knew. "Maybe I like what happens when you lack control."

He paused to lower his head, about to kiss her…

"You have a choice, Bane," Zion said from her other side. "Continue to let yourself be distracted, endangering you and your woman in public, while I invade the warehouse alone or help me as planned. You can't do both."

Feeling feisty, Nola flipped him off. "You two go in together and guard each other's back. And you had better return to me or there will be dire consequences. Understood?"

She loved that the two warriors were kinda sorta friends now. She had a sinking suspicion neither man had enjoyed many friendships in his long, long life, never knowing who to trust. But. Unless they found a way to stop the war or Zion took the Mark of Disgrace, their friendship wouldn't, couldn't last.

Ignore the sense of foreboding. It hadn't fled, had only grown stronger. *Ignore your churning stomach.*

Zion cast Bane a quick glance. Voice laced with amusement, he said, "Shouldn't you get your woman in line?"

"Hardly," Bane quipped. "The man who gets his woman in line is the man who sleeps alone."

Nola rewarded him with a spontaneous kiss on his neck, where his pulse raced. "I'm so proud of you. You've learned so fast."

His fingers clenched on her hip bone as he gave her a strange look—a soft look, setting her aflutter.

When an obviously drunk man plowed into her, she gasped, startled. If not for Bane's stalwart hold, she would have pinwheeled to her butt.

"Are you all right?" he demanded.

"Yes, I'm fine."

"Good." The next thing she knew, he was barreling after the drunk man.

To issue an order, or not issue an order? "No, Bane. No. Please come back," she called, opting to go with *not.* Would he heed her request or plow ahead anyway?

Plow ahead. He grabbed the offender by the scruff and hauled him to the other side of the street, away from her. Thank goodness! Killing Micah had been self-defense *and* revenge. Killing Erik, who kept endangering Vale, Bane and Zion, would be straight up self-defense. This would have been cold-blooded murder.

Zion used the opportunity to quietly say, "You are so at ease with Bane, and yet my prophetic dream has not changed. One day, you will kill him."

"No way." Shaking her head with enough force to rattle her brain, she replied, "I won't. Your dream must be symbolic of something else."

A frown. A cant of his head. "How can you be so sure of this?"

"I just am." Her feelings for Bane ran too deep.

He returned to her side, his eyes narrowing as he glanced between her and Zion. Sensed the new tension, did he? Either way, he made no comment. He couldn't. They'd reached their destination. A seemingly abandoned warehouse.

The lights were off, and no one loitered about. Bars covered the windows, broken glass scattered over the ground.

They moved into the shadows, next to a Dumpster. Zion pointed to the warehouse, saying, "Cameras are there, there and there. Doors are there and there. Windows there, there, there and there."

Bane leveled a hard stare at Nola and fisted two hanks of her hair. A possessive hold. "You will stay here? You swear it?"

"I will. I swear." If she insisted on going in, he wouldn't be able to stop her. But he would be distracted, worried about keeping her safe, and her gruff warrior would be in more danger. "You swear you'll come back to me?"

"I will. I swear," he said, echoing her. "You have your gun?"

"I do." The "phaser" anchored to her belt was actually a semiautomatic spray-painted silver.

He kissed her, another brief press of his lips against hers, then turned on his heel. "Let's do this, Zion."

"I'll come back, too. Not that you cared enough to make me swear it," Zion said with a roll of his eyes.

"Great," she replied. "Maybe bring me a souvenir."

Bane snorted, a silly sound yet it made her heart soar.

As the two stalked toward the building, cloaked in the shadows and barely discernible, she lost her "everything's gonna be all right" vibe. Fear choked her.

What if something happened to her guys?

Yes, they'd trained for war. Yes, they knew how to fight, how to survive a worst-case scenario. Yes, this needed to be done, or Erik's army would make a play against them at the assembly. A play against Vale and Knox, too. But there were hundreds of soldiers in there, who'd trained just as staunchly.

I'm starting to hate Erik. If he hadn't targeted her friends, Nola would have pursued him as an ally. He was a fellow Earthling, after all. Born and raised here. But he'd continued to strike at them and had earned a top spot on her elimination list.

Different sounds assaulted her ears. The *pop, pop* of gunfire, ebbing and flowing in waves. Screams erupted. Curses, too. Then grinding metal. Anyone nearby would consider the warehouse a haunted house. But she knew better.

The battle had begun.

I won't vomit, I won't, I won't, I won't.

A squeaky sound caught her attention. It came from *inside* the Dumpster. She tensed, blood heating, bones icing.

Should she shout for Bane?

Better not distract him. For all she knew, a rat had caused the noise.

When the lid swung open, she pressed a hand over her mouth to silence a squeal. Breath misted in front of her face.

Not a rat, and not a real trash receptacle—an escape hatch? A man in a black T-shirt and jeans climbed out, stepping into a ray of moonlight. Blood smeared his face and hands. He looked from the warehouse to the nearest street, most likely deciding whether to run or go back to help his friends.

Palms dampening, she stumbled back and reached for her gun. The movement caught his notice, and he palmed and aimed a semiautomatic. While her hand shook, his remained steady.

Where was Dark Nola when she needed her?

Was this it? The end? Denial screamed inside her head. There was so much more she'd wanted to do. With Bane. With Vale. With her freaking people. She had beasts to awaken!

Finally, Dark Nola stepped up to the plate and seized her tongue. "Put the gun away—before I make you eat it."

He bared his teeth. "I know you. You're with them. The ones trying to overtake our planet." That said, he pulled the trigger.

Nola braced, expecting pain. Bane appeared out of nowhere, the bullet nailing him in the chest. As his body jerked, she screamed into the cold night.

Took a bullet for me. Would die for me.

As she reeled—a common occurrence in his presence—he clawed the shooter's neck. Gut. Groin.

So brutal. So savage. The man collapsed. Blood pooled around him...and she loved the sight. *So pretty.*

Her mouth actually watered.

"You think to hurt *my* woman?" Bane spit on the corpse.

So fierce. So mine.

Zion appeared next and assessed the situation with

a visual sweep. "Good work." He opened a portal and tossed the body inside, saying, "Partners."

Her adrenaline crashed, and her teeth chattered. "We can go now?"

"We can." Bane gathered her close.

An alarm screeched to life.

"We relocated their weapons," he said. "Now, we only have a thousand more things to do."

CHAPTER TWENTY-SIX

How to survive the big day

FOR THE NEXT two weeks, Nola played house with her gorgeous barbarian protectors.

Every morning, they switched hotels and often states. Sometimes they even switched countries. They preferred extended-stay locations with kitchens.

While being on the move had already lost its appeal, Nola enjoyed cooking for her men. Whatever she made, they devoured. Especially casseroles. The rest of the day, Bane and Zion would hunt combatants, strategize and set traps.

Erik would make trouble. He and his allies had a hankering for roasted beast.

In the evening, Bane and Zion would train Nola tag-team style, teaching her how to fight with her fists, swords, daggers, guns and any innocent object that happened to be close at hand. Like pens, pillows and cups.

All went smoothly, until Zion accidentally elbowed her in the chin, causing her to bite her own tongue. Blood had trickled from her mouth, and Bane had nearly shattered glass with his roar, almost transforming into Drogo right then and there.

Calming him had involved kisses, stripping, sex and

hours of snuggle time. The man who'd taken a bullet for her had a major jones for cuddling.

Their relationship continued to evolve, Bane smiling and laughing more, despite the ticking countdown clock, and it always sent her heart soaring higher. Every day, he became a little more protective, a lot fiercer and a megaton more passionate. She loved sleeping in the security of his arms, and he delighted in whispering sweeter everythings in her ear.

Your strength amazes me.

Your courage humbles me.

Your beauty maddens me.

Now, fear aggravated her nerves. Today, the clock zeroed out, a new one beginning. In less than three hours, the Assembly of Combatants would begin. *Tick, tick, tick.* Bane had already begun to prepare.

"No one took the Mark of Disgrace," she said, pacing in front of him. Not even Vale.

Just her name elicited a pang of homesickness. Nola missed her sister so danged much. What she wouldn't give to hug her. To cry with her. To talk and laugh with her. To discuss everything that had happened and the hardships of dating an All War combatant. To cook her favorite meal, the way Nola had been cooking for Bane and Zion.

"You can't end the war after the meeting," she finished.

"I know," he replied, and to her amazement, he didn't sound the tiniest bit upset. He sat at the desk, sharpening a sword—a weapon she was forbidden to touch. It was responsible for his shoulder wound. He glided some kind of rock over the edge of the blade. Up and down.

"You won't perform the Blood Rite until the war ends, which means your vengeance must wait."

"I know," he repeated, still not upset.

Dang him. Why the heck wasn't he stressing? Something she couldn't stop doing! As their romance had blossomed, so had her sense of foreboding. Never, in all her life, had she gotten to keep something she lo—cared about. She'd lost her parents, Carrie and even Vale, at least for a little while. Why would Bane be any different? One day, she would lose him, too.

"Tell me again what you'll be doing while I'm away," he said. Up and down. Up and down.

"Besides worry?" For their last few hours together— *he'll come back, he'll come back*—they'd locked themselves in the master bedroom of their newest penthouse suite. A gorgeous room with windowed walls and a massive bed.

"You shouldn't worry for your man." Up and down. Sloooowly. Rhythmically. "I'll be strong for us."

Us. One word, two letters, infinite shivers. Pacing, pacing, she said, "I'll stay where you put me, talk to no one, trust no one and do nothing."

"Very good."

He would be portaling her into a different hotel room, in a different state. The combatants would be too busy to attack her and anyone Erik had hired wouldn't know where to look or how to reach her. "Your turn," she said. "Remind me about what *you'll* be doing."

"Besides survive?" Up, down.

"Obviously." Their futures depended on the outcome of this stupid assembly.

"I will protect Vale and work with Zion to win a weapon. Preferably a ring owned by Colt."

Nola had listened in every time Bane and Zion had discussed the war or tweaked their master plan. Most recently, they'd decided to target a warrior named Colt.

Apparently, Colt owned a ring able to break into hundreds of tiny bots that could burrow under other people's skin, allowing him to track and/or kill them with ease.

If Bane controlled the ring, he would be unstoppable! Bonus: he could use the bots to shred Aveline's internal organs.

"Why hasn't Colt already pegged you guys with a bot?" she wondered aloud.

"He hides from the war, never engages in battle."

"So why was he chosen as a representative?"

"Perhaps he's the bravest among his kind? Sovereigns rarely share their reasons."

Or Colt had a secret ability no one knew about? Her stomach twisted into knots. "I hate this!"

On her next pass by the desk, Bane set his tools aside, pushed the weapons back, then looped an arm around her to haul her closer. He lifted her onto the desk, trapping her knees on either side of him.

She wore a shirt and panties, nothing else. Correction: *soaked* panties. Her nipples puckered as her core heated and ached.

He'd trained her body to react to his slightest touch.

"Will you miss me?" He traced his fingers up her bare thighs, gripped her hips and drew lazy circles on her belly with the pads of his thumbs.

Miss him? Only with every fiber of my being. "There's a slight chance I…might."

A smile teased his mouth—*another one to add to my collection*—softening the rugged plains of his face.

"*I* will miss *you* *v*ery much," he said, his eyelids going heavy. "And you don't have to worry about my well-being, dove, not even a little. Knowing you're waiting for me, your body hungry for mine, I'll let nothing prevent me from returning to you."

And there's another sweet everything. When he said things like that, she fell a little harder. If this kept up, care would soon deepen into love. *Are you sure it hasn't already?*

Wait. The truth behind his words registered. "You're going to wind me up before you hit the road, aren't you?"

He moved his gaze up, lingering on her feminine core, then her breasts, before meeting her eyes. A wicked gleam lit those golden depths as he toyed with the elastic band on her panties. "I'm going to wind you up so desperately you'll be ravenous for weeks to come."

FINALLY. THE ASSEMBLY OF COMBATANTS had arrived.

Bane and Zion decided to arrive separately, with Bane going first. Leaving Nola had proved more difficult than ever, the urge to return to her unrelenting. The woman had bewitched and transfixed him, and he had no regrets.

However, beneath affection and arousal was an endless pit of fear. He'd once swore he would never need another person, ever. But he needed Nola like a thirsty man needed water. She made his world better. If anything happened to her...

His claws lengthened. Without her presence, the beast became frenzied, prowling and growling with more vigor.

Hurry, hurry. Get this over with. Bane had portaled near the remains of the prison. What used to be the remains, anyway. Someone had cleared the area. Probably the Enforcer, Seven.

Frigid winds blustered, shards of frost pricking his cheeks. In the middle of an ice valley, invisible walls of energy formed a wide circle. Already a handful of combatants waited inside it. In a hooded black robe, face obscured by shadows, Seven stood off to the side. Like a grim reaper of legend, he carried a scythe.

Enforcers were forbidden from interacting with combatants outside the assemblies and ceremonies like the Mark of Disgrace—Enforcers weren't allowed to interact with anyone, period. They were tools used by the High Council, never allowed to live lives of their own. Or have names. They were given number designations, one through ten, and there were hundreds of thousands of each number. The higher the number, the more vicious the individual.

Head high, Bane approached. As he stepped past those energy walls, tingles ran the length of his body, and his goggles ceased working. *Nothing* with a mystical component worked until the meeting's conclusion.

"Look at the little beasty-boy," Ronan called. "Word is a Terran female has removed his balls."

"Who said he came to Terra *with* balls?" Petra retorted.

They taunted with words rather than lashing out, fighting forbidden immediately before or during an assembly. The only time a combatant didn't have to worry about being ambushed or tricked.

The pair had caused the RV crash, putting Nola's life in jeopardy. One day, they would pay. Unfortunately, he wouldn't let himself kill them tonight. Circumstances hadn't changed. Until he decided to end the war, he had to make sure plenty of combatants survived each battle.

As the other combatants issued taunts of their own, Bane tuned them out, letting his thoughts drift back to Nola. No better time to reflect.

For two weeks, they'd lived together. When he'd dared to sleep, he'd gotten to hold her. He'd made love to her in a thousand different ways, cuddled her and talked for hours. She'd cooked meals that had made his taste buds weep with joy.

If Nola was his reason to live, Aveline was his reason to rage. The queen had called him repeatedly. Afraid she would order him to harm Nola, he hadn't responded. But…

He thought he sensed the queen nearby. Which had to be a mistake. Surely! No way Aveline would risk the wrath of the High Council or Bane's disqualification by coming to Terra before a winner was declared.

No way? Please. She'd do it in a heartbeat. Anything to feed her need for more power. He pressed his tongue to the roof of his mouth. If she *had* come to Terra, he would have to perform Nola's Blood Rite right away, regardless of the war. He couldn't allow Aveline to awaken the Terran beasts. They would hunt and kill Nola, and he wouldn't be able to stop them.

As new taunts rang out, Bane cleared his mind of any debris. More combatants had arrived. In ten minutes, roll call would begin. They were missing Zion, Knox, Vale, Colt and Carrick, a prince who owned a dagger able to turn blood into lava.

Scratch that. Carrick arrived next.

Where were Knox and Vale? Bane knew how badly Nola desired information about her sister, and he couldn't wait to be her hero. If something had happened to the couple—

Bane expelled a relieved breath as Knox entered the circle, Vale only a few feet behind him. The two didn't touch, or glance at each other, but they didn't move away, either.

Physically, Vale hadn't changed. She had the same black-and-white hair, slender build and tough yet ethereal beauty as before. But she carried herself far differently, confidence wafting from her. She'd even altered the way she walked, adopting a sensual, challenge-issuing swagger.

In one of their late-night cuddle sessions, Nola told him how Vale had helped her during every illness, ensuring she ate, helping her get to the bathroom and giving her a reason to go on. Now, Bane felt beholden to the other woman.

"I didn't realize this was bring-your-whore-to-work day," Carrick called.

Knox bristled, but said nothing, silently fuming.

Vale spread her arms and said, "What makes you think we're sleeping together? And news flash. Whore isn't exactly an insult to my way of thinking. You just implied I like sex and money. Guess what? I do. Oh, and good news. This whore is trolling for customers. Tonight is the grand opening of Vale's Little House of Slays, and you're all invited. I give good beheadings, free of charge."

Bane almost smiled. In many ways, Vale reminded him of Nola. Spirited, witty and unwilling to let anyone gain the upper hand.

The trash talk amped up, but Bane lost track. Colt had just strode into the circle, his head down.

Anticipation battered the dam of Bane's control, unleashing a tide of impatience.

Finally, Zion arrived, and Bane gave him the barest nod. The male had been a surprisingly good ally, keeping his end of their bargain. In every recent battle, they'd guarded each other's back, often bleeding for each other. Bane even liked him.

Another frosty wind kicked up, whistling in spurts. Carrick said, "You're the one who ran off with the other human, isn't that right, Zion? Didn't you get the memo? You were supposed to bring her here for our enjoyment."

Bane dropped his chin to his sternum, his narrowed gaze fixing on the lava maker. *He'll pay for that.*

Zion crossed his arms over his chest, preparing to deliver his bomb. "Sorry I couldn't oblige. As soon as I was done with her...I killed her."

Shockwaves crashed over the others. Though Vale had received a text telling her not to believe anything Zion said, she paled, emanating horror. Tears filled her eyes and splashed down her cheeks.

For a moment, Bane wondered how he would have reacted if the news were true. Losing Nola...

He beat his fists into his skull, ripped at his hair and fell to his knees. Throwing back his head, he roared to the sky. The sun had disappeared behind the mountains, bright lights beginning to glow in the sky.

A debate rang out, some warriors believing Zion, some doubting him. Seven paid no heed to anyone, gliding to the center of the circle to lodge his scythe in the ice.

The assembly had officially begun.

In fifteen minutes, Seven would finish with roll call, and a bloodbath would erupt.

Erik glided forward, the Rod in hand. Frost glinted in his beard. Though he'd once spoken ancient Norse, he used Nola's language today. "This is your chance, your only chance, to join my cause. While you were trapped, I used my freedom to my advantage. The measures I've taken to ensure victory are vast. I've done things you can't imagine. Things you can't protect yourself against."

"And yet, we remain alive," someone said, and chuckles abounded.

Bane believed the bastard planned to gain the trust of as many combatants as possible, and kill them when they least expected it. The viking had no king to command him, no reason to stop the war; but he had every reason to win it.

With a humorless smile, Erik added, "If you want to live here the rest of your days, if you hate your realm for forcing you to fight and threatening your loved ones, you will cease killing and ensure a winner is never declared. If you want to win the war so your realm can enslave mine, I will come for you, and I will defeat you."

A debate rang out, Bane uninterested in listening.

In the end, two others joined Erik's team. Bold, who wielded a hammer able to break every bone in someone's body with a single strike, and Ryder, who'd had a strange ability to stand in one location, then create a second version of himself to send out to fight on his behalf.

That made four allies in total—that Bane knew about. Adonis and Rush, the other two.

Bane remained on his knees, head bowed, mouth zipped, biding his time. Five minutes until roll call ended...

More insults were brandied about.

Four... He clenched and unclenched his fists, his

shoulder throbbing more than ever. He'd been careful to avoid further injury the past few days.

Three... He eyed his target—Colt—and palmed the daggers he'd brought. He'd left Valor's sword hidden with Nola. *Win the ring, better protect your queen.*

Two... His ears picked up a light shuffle of footsteps. Many footsteps. Frowning, he lifted his head and cast his gaze up—and saw red. Men dressed in black crouched along the mountaintops. Damn this! Erik had rallied a new army.

One minute left...

Silence erupted, aggression charging the air. Bane counted down the seconds. Fifty-nine, fifty-eight. He rolled his head, his shoulders, preparing his muscles for action, then shifted into a crouch. He would have to avoid gunshots from above...while helping Zion, Vale and Knox do the same...while avoiding strikes from his competitors.

He caught Zion's gaze and motioned to the soldiers.

Zion caught sight of them and scowled.

They shared a moment of communication: *Erik dies today.*

Focus. No battle had ever been so important. No matter what, Bane could not let himself transform into Drogo. Two weapons would be destroyed.

Five. Warriors got into position.

Four.

Three.

Two.

Seven banged his scythe into the ice a second time. The invisible walls of energy came crashing down with a *whoosh*.

For one suspended moment, no one moved.

Then all hell erupted. War cries pierced the night, blending with the clang of steel as warriors threw themselves into an all-out brawl.

Bane ducked, dodged when necessary and mauled anyone in his way, making a beeline for Colt. Colt first, Erik second. Someone's blood spurted, spraying his face. *Scorching* his face. His vison blurred.

Go, go! Stop and die. His vision cleared in time to see a glowing whip lash out, snagging his wrist. Bane fought the instant flood of agony, using the whip against Thorn, its wielder, yanking the male closer. One slash of his claws, and Thorn dropped, screaming.

Quick glance at Vale. Doing well. Zion? Edging closer to Colt. Knox? Fighting to return to Vale.

Moving on… Petra whirled in Bane's direction, sword raised. Recalling the car wreck that almost ended Nola's life, he threw an elbow, nailing her in the jaw. Ronan rushed over to safeguard his partner, but he had Carrick on his heels.

Carrick engaged Ronan before the other warrior reached Bane. The two were distracted. Bane grinned— and cleaved Carrick's arm from its socket with a quick scratch-and-bash. As the smug prince fell, black blood spraying from his wound, Bane turned his sights to Ronan, but the male had already engaged with another.

Moving on once again. Colt, where was Colt? Blood, viscera and severed limbs littered his path. Grunts and groans provided a macabre soundtrack.

A distinctive scream rose above the others—Vale's. Without hesitation, Bane switched directions; Knox wouldn't make it back to the girl in time.

The things I do for my woman.

CHAPTER TWENTY-SEVEN

Tips and tricks to wreck your life

NOLA WRITHED ON an unfamiliar hotel bed, inundated by unspeakable pain, too hot, too cold, sobbing and shuddering. She'd pretty much vomited out all of her internal organs. Her heart beat too hard and too fast, her joints had swelled and every bone in her body throbbed.

Had her link to Bane weakened somehow? Or had something terrible happened to him?

No, no, no. Not Bane. He was too strong, too cunning. But, but...*why am I so sick?*

Fear invaded, spreading like flesh-eating bacteria. She covered her mouth, hoping to ward off the next round of dry heaves.

And what if Bane had shifted? Drogo wouldn't hesitate to harm Vale, Zion and Knox.

Now terror invaded, skittering down her spine.

Should have accompanied the guys to the arctic. She could have hidden near the meeting site, and calmed Bane at the first sign of a transition.

Nola Lee, dragon tamer. Oh, the irony. She could stop a bloodthirsty beast with a word, but she couldn't walk into the bathroom to pee, her body simply too weak. In fact, if Bane didn't return within the next hour or so, she'd probably wet the bed.

Humiliation prickled beneath her skin.

She'd tried to mist and travel back in time to revisit a favorite memory, anything to distract her from the pain, but the weakness affected her abilities just as much as her physical form. All she'd managed to do? Time travel the old-fashioned way—aka remembering.

Desperate, she did a little more remembering, closing her eyes to relive the time she'd sat on a porch swing with Carrie and Vale, sipping sweet tea.

That day, Carrie had said:

Do you think a twenty-dollar bill is worth any less if it's dirty and wrinkled? No way in heck! You might be a little rough around the edges, but you are still priceless.

She'd gone on to add:

In boiling water, the potato softens, the egg hardens, but the mighty coffee bean changes the water. Don't let difficult times weaken or harden you, girls. Get up and change the situation.

Happy to. But how?

Nola recalled the time she'd been too sick to attend prom, and too poor to afford a dress, so Vale had thrown a party at Carrie's house.

She replayed the last time she and Bane had made love. He'd been on top, pinning her down. A "vanilla" position for so many, but a forbidden delight for them.

"Hey, hey, little dove." Bane's voice caressed her ears. The side of the bed dipped. "I'm here now, and I'm not leaving you again."

He'd returned!

"You're here." Tears welled, blurring his visage. His heat and scent enveloped her, offering comfort. Aches and pains faded, and she threw her arms around him. "You survived!"

"So did Vale and Zion. A bullet nailed Knox in the spine, temporarily paralyzing him, but he'll pull through." Bane tucked her close, using his body to buffer her from the rest of the world. "You probably sickened because I was trapped inside the circle with walls of energy that disabled my mystical abilities."

"I—I don't care about my c-condition." A sob burst from her. "I've been so w-worried about you and them and, and, and..."

Bane petted her hair, saying, "If you'd like to see what happened, I can use our link to show you."

Would she like?

"You can see your man's strength."

Okay, yes. She'd like. "Please and thank you. But first I *reeeally* have to pee." She attempted to stand... nope. Still a nonstarter. Despite the reprieve from pain, she was too weak. Cheeks burning, she whispered, "I need your help."

Like a knight in invisible armor, he carried her to the toilet, and held her up with one hand while pulling down her shorts and panties with the other. He even helped her sit down gently.

"This is mortifying," she groused. She kept her gaze to the floor, too embarrassed to face him.

"Consider it a favor. One day, I'll be injured, and you'll have to carry *me* to the bathroom."

As if. "Sorry, babe, but if that day comes, I'll put you in a diaper."

He chuckled, the most beautiful sound she'd ever heard.

With the back of a shaky hand, she wiped her eyes. Vision clearing, she slowly lifted her gaze. The moment she saw his condition, she grimaced. Poor, darling Bane. He had serious cuts and gashes all over his body. "Heal quickly and painlessly, Bane. And, maybe turn around, please?"

He caressed her cheek before presenting her with his back. "Do you think a bodily function will make me think less of you?"

"No. It's just, you didn't sign on to be my caretaker." She shuffled her feet. *Come on!* But her overly full bladder was shy, refusing to cooperate.

"Actually, I signed on to be your everything."

Shock slackened her jaw. Bane of Adwaeweth had *not* just uttered the most romantic thing ever. "You've made it clear how much you admire strength and warrior women in particular. Look at me. No!" she rushed to add when he began to spin. "Don't actually look at me. I just meant I'm not your usual type of, uh, warrior. Yes, you and Zion have trained me well, and I've gotten pretty good at landing blows. Yes, I'm amazing in a thousand different ways. But I'm just…me."

He squared his shoulders and straightened his spine. "In a multitude of ways, you've proven the state of someone's body has nothing to do with their level of strength. No matter how many times you've been felled, you've climbed to your feet, ready to go again. *That* is the hallmark of a *great* warrior."

Any leftover defenses finally crumbled, tenderness engulfing her.

I'm in love with this man.

The knowledge sang within her, accompanied by a deluge of excitement and a tsunami of dread. She did. She loved him. She'd given her heart to Bane, all of it, every piece, nothing held back. She loved him and his intensity. His wit, and his ferocity. Loved his touch, and his pretty words. His strength. His stubbornness, however...

Nah, she loved that, too. His stubborn side had brought him to Nola, giving him centuries of purpose after the murder of his wife.

How did Bane feel about her? She knew he desired her body. Protected her at all costs. Talked about keeping her forever and always. And he'd even accepted her royal status. But...

Would his emotions ever run deeper?

One day soon, she would ask.

With his praise echoing in her ears, she overcame her bladder shyness, and oh, wow, had anything ever felt so wonderful?

Once she'd finished, Bane clasped her elbow to help her stand. "Shower or straight to bed?" he asked.

"Shower, please and thank you."

He kissed her brow and removed their clothing. In the stall, hot water rained and steam wafted through the air, creating a dreamy safe haven.

For good measure, Nola brushed her teeth twice. She didn't speak again, but neither did he.

Nola knew why *she* remained quiet—she'd never felt so vulnerable or exposed. Did Bane feel the same?

After they toweled off, he carried her to the bed. Bare, she settled under the covers. He double-checked the locks on the windows and resealed the curtains so no one peeked inside. His every action highlighted his body's muscular build and stunning grace. By the time he finished, she was panting.

He stalked back to the bed, their gazes locked. Awareness blazed between them. They were alone and naked...

Light from the lamp spilled over him. He was hard as a rock.

Her breath caught. With a flick of his fingers, he turned off the lamp. Darkness descended over the room.

Sliding into bed, he drew her close, one arm under her nape, one on her belly. She curled into him, needful.

"Bane," she said, and chewed on her bottom lip. Was her voice slurred, thanks to the potency of her desire?

His breath hitched, a telling reaction as wonderfully maddening as blistering heat. "You crave your man?"

"Yes!"

"More than you wish to see what happened at the assembly?"

"More than *anything*."

He kissed her, softer and gentler than ever before. Dirtier, too.

"Your weight… I want it," she pleaded. "Give it to me."

"With pleasure." He rolled her over and pinned her arms overhead, shackling her wrists to the mattress with a single hand. He kneaded her breasts, his touch softer and gentler, too, almost reverent. No, not almost. Definitely. He *worshipped* her, every caress conveying a message to her cells: *you are adored.*

He might actually...love me back. The possibility hit her like an injection of morphine.

Writhing in sublime pleasure, she kissed, lapped and caressed him right back, their hearts beating in perfect sync. But the hornier she got, the more she wondered what it would be like on top. One of the only positions they'd never tried.

"Want to try something," she said between panting breaths. She gave him a little push, but he didn't budge.

He lifted his head, savage desire crackling in his irises, lines of strain branching around his mouth. "You want to be on top." A statement, not a question.

She chewed on her bottom lip some more and nodded. "I want to try everything with you."

For a long while, he held her gaze, silent. Just when she began to squirm, he rubbed the tip of his nose against the tip of hers. "In Adwaeweth, the female is always on top."

"Oh." Disappointment surged. "So you have no interest in doing it with me?"

In lieu of an answer, he rolled to his back, allowing her to rise over him and straddle his waist. He rested his hands on her knees, groaning when she cupped her breasts.

"I might be topping, but you're in charge," she said. "You tell me what to do, and I'll do it. To you...to myself. With us, nothing is off-limits."

He tensed beneath her, his grip crushing. "Never diminish your strength to soothe my ego, dove. We are equals, yes?"

"Yes. But I'm not diminishing my strength, or soothing your ego. I'm experimenting, learning what I like."

He grinned slow and sure. "Well, then. I'm happy to help."

White-hot arousal *devoured* Bane. He had a gorgeous female perched on top of him, his to command.

Life did not get any better.

Drogo purred his approval, ready to be inside her again. *Not yet, not yet.* He dragged her up his torso, so that her drenched core hovered over his mouth.

"Let's get you ready. Scream for me, love," he instructed…just before he thrust his tongue into her sweet feminine sheath, drinking down her sweet honey.

She did scream. "Bane!" Clutching the headboard, she brazenly rode his face, head thrown back, chest bowed, the long length of her jet-black hair tickling his navel. Their scents mingled, creating an intoxicating musk, wrapping his head in a sensual fog.

This woman… She drove him wild, kept him on edge, tormented and delighted him with equal measure. Yet, he felt as if he'd finally found a home. His priorities and goals had changed. A future with Nola mattered more than his vengeance.

He licked and sucked until she babbled incoherently. Another scream burst from her as he brought her to a swift climax. Her taste sweetened, and his control shattered. *Beyond repair.*

Tremors plagued her as she fought to catch her breath. "That…that was…*incredible.*"

"That was only the beginning." He slid her down, down until she straddled his waist once again. Mindless bursts of pleasure battered him. "Take me inside. Need you. Need you now."

"Yes." Shifting her weight to her knees, she rose up.

He angled the tip of his erection at her soaked entrance. Contact. As she slid down, he thrust up, entering her in one mighty heave, filling her up.

Nola, lost in the throes, released another scream and climaxed once again.

Bane hissed air between his teeth, sweat trickling down his face. The pleasure…too much but not enough. Why had he ever resisted this position with her?

He had easy access to all his favorite parts. He could even reach around to grip her ass…or strum her clitoris until she bellowed his name. He could watch her beautiful face as pleasure besieged her. With his supernatural senses, he could gauge the pulse at the base of her neck; when he did something she liked, it quickened.

Didn't take him long to learn she liked fast, hard and rough. His preference, also. She liked when he sucked on her skin or squeezed a little too tightly, leaving a mark. A *claiming* mark. *He* liked knowing she would feel him later, every time she moved, and remember everything he'd done to her.

Nola whipped her hips, and his thoughts dulled. The pleasure…

"I'm going to come so hard, baby. I'm so close…" Nola licked her way into his mouth, and he opened up, unable to resist. Never wanting to. When she whipped her hips again, her puckered nipples rubbed his own, and he grunted. "I waited for you today. Don't make me wait any longer. Please, Bane."

Baby. How he loved the endearment, a type of claim. "No more waiting. Come hard for your man."

Holding his gaze, she whipped her hips again. And again. The pleasure intensified, pressure building. They stared at each other, lost, never wanting to be found.

He took her hands in his, linking their fingers, and lifted his arms overhead, stretching her atop him. The rest of the world faded from his existence. Her warm breaths stroked his skin. Breaths that came faster and faster, increasing in tempo to keep pace with his thrusts.

"Bane…baby…" Her nails embedded in his skin as she threw back her head and screamed. Her inner walls milked his length, demanding his surrender, and he gave it.

Every. Last. Drop. He came in a rush, praise spilling from his lips.

She collapsed atop him, panting faster, shaking harder, her cheek resting on his uninjured shoulder. He released her hands and lay back, then maneuvered them both to their sides.

They cuddled for a long while, silent, letting their bodies calm. Although, he wasn't certain his body would ever calm again. Everything he felt for Nola amplified—attraction, tenderness and affection. She fit him in every way. Even her delicate appearance. It was her armor. No one suspected a warrior lurked beneath.

A warrior who'd stripped away his defenses. *I'm falling in love with her.*

No, no. He couldn't love her. Not until she'd survived the Blood Rite and Aveline was dead. If he let himself love her, and she died, he would not survive her loss.

You think you'll survive anyway? Fool!

Desperate for a distraction, he said, "Ready to view the battle through our link?"

She traced a heart over his, well, heart. *Clench.* "I am," she said.

"Fair warning. It's bloody."

"The very reason I need to see it. I want to witness what you and the others go through at these assemblies."

BANE PLACED HIS hands on Nola's temples, and closed his eyes. When he exhaled, she inhaled, and vice versa. Tingles grazed her mind, their link heating. Gradually, images appeared and brightened. In an icy valley between two mountains, over twenty warriors, both male and female, stood in a circle, Bane among them. A legit grim reaper loomed off to the side, dressed in a black robe and clasping a scythe. Where was—

There! Vale. A beautiful warrioress with a cocky smile. No, a *warrior*, period, and Nola whimpered with relief. The last time they were together, Vale had been starved, freezing and frightened. Now, her sister wore black leather, appeared fit and healthy, and ready for anything—anything but an announcement about Nola's death. Vale crumbled, and the sight broke Nola's heart.

Minutes later, some kind of starting bell sounded. The warriors leaped into action, attacking each other. As Bane had warned, there was blood, and a lot of it. There was violence and pain. To her awe and amazement, Vale held her own against every opponent. Anytime she needed help, Bane rushed to the rescue. Not that she or Knox realized it.

Moving with the controlled grace of a jungle cat, Bane took out anyone who locked their sights on the couple, even when he had to injure Knox to remove him from the line of fire. Even when his own life was endangered, with different warriors making a play for his head and an army hidden on the mountaintops, firing long-range rifles. As bullets ripped through Bane and Zion, Nola's stomach churned.

"Erik rallied another army," she said, appalled.

"Yes," Bane replied, his teeth gritted.

In the memory, Bane plowed into a man who was sneaking up on Zion. The two fell, the wound in Bane's shoulder deepening. Blood loss slowed his reflexes and erased his control.

A glowing whip wrapped around his wrist and yanked him backward. He shuddered, looking like he was trapped in a grand mal seizure. The whip had an electrical charge.

Nola had to remind herself Bane had survived, and he was with her now. But oh, if she could dive into the memory and kill the one with the whip, she would do it with a smile. The pain her beasty-boy must have experienced as he'd fought his way free.

When that wreck-causing witch Petra challenged Bane and Vale, things got dicey. Knox sprinted over to help her sister, but Petra slammed her sword into the ground. An ice tower grew, blocking his progress. Unfortunately, the tower served double duty, hiding Ronan, who shadowed Knox's every move, waiting for the perfect time to strike. Bane saw him, though.

Merely pushing Knox out of the way would do no good; the guy was far too strong. So, Bane did the only thing he could. He slashed Knox with his claws. The wound sent the warrior crashing to the ground, Ronan's sword swinging over his head.

Vale raced around the tower, saw what Bane had done and assumed the worst. Unleashing a battle cry, she stabbed him in the gut. And he let her. Because the alternative was hurting her.

Nola groaned, a hand fluttering to her mouth. "Oh, Bane. I'm so sorry."

"There was some kind of poison on her blade. I went motionless for several seconds, unable to move."

Yes, she watched as Knox lifted a sword of his own, intending to remove the motionless Bane's head. But Zion saved the day, knocking Bane out of harm's way.

"Colt escapes," past Zion said, vaulting to his feet. He, too, bore countless injuries.

Colt wasn't the only one escaping. Two warriors

dragged an unconscious Erik, who left a trail of blood in their wake. Someone had amputated one of his feet.

"I got the foot," real life Bane said. "Would have gotten more if a male—Pike—hadn't focused on your sister."

"Thank you," she repeated. She owed him a debt she might not ever be able to repay.

No, not true. She *could* repay. With Aveline's heart.

And she would.

Past Bane's paralysis proved temporary, as he'd assured. He lumbered to a stand. "Go. Take him out, and win the bots." He ducked, a blade narrowly missing him. Without missing a beat, he stabbed his attacker with a quick jab, jab to the throat. "I verge on turning. I must get to Nola."

The images faded, real-life Bane lowering his hands and rolling to his back.

"I hate that you have to go through that every month." She shuddered and snuggled closer, resting her cheek in the hollow of his neck, tracing her fingers around the scab left by Vale's sword.

He kissed her brow. "I wish I'd made more progress. Wish I'd won more, done more. We're running out of time. I…sense her, Nola. I sense Aveline. I suspect she's done the unthinkable and come to Terra, but pray I'm wrong."

Panic and urgency collided, tangling in her muscles. "We can't wait, then. We *must* perform the Blood Rite."

"No." He shook his head, adamant. "No."

"What if she wakes the hybrids?"

"She can create blocks, like yours. She won't awaken the beasts until and unless she wants to. And she won't want to until the end of the war."

"We can't wait," Nola repeated, sitting up. "Let's do the Blood Rite today. Now."

"No," he grated. Torment etched every line of his face. "You've been sick. I need your body at its strongest."

"Tomorrow, then."

He looked agonized. "Twice in my life, I've lost everything. As a younger male, I loved Aveline. We courted. I thought we would wed. Then she underwent the Blood Rite and became the monster who murdered the woman I *did* marry."

"Do you still think I'll change?" she asked. Croaked, really. "Do you still think *I'll* become a monster?"

"Not even a little. But you are all I have, all I want, and I refuse—*refuse!*—to lose you, too. I told you I was keeping you, Nola Lee, and I meant it."

Beautiful words, lovely sentiment. But, if Nola didn't defeat Aveline, she and Bane would become a modern day Romeo and Juliet. *Doomed.*

CHAPTER TWENTY-EIGHT

How to love him and leave him

As Nola drifted to sleep, Bane clutched her close.

—*Bane!*— Aveline's voice boomed, making him jerk with shock and fury. —*Stop whatever you are doing and come to me.*—

Familiar words. This could not be happening.

—*Now!*—

He hissed a foul curse. The only way to communicate with him, sans the ring...

She'd come to Terra, as he'd feared, bringing a thousand consequences with her. Or she'd strengthened exponentially. Either way, his fury murdered his shock. His hopes for a better tomorrow imploded one by one.

No. No! She'd spoiled centuries of his life. Enough was enough. She would not take Nola from him, too.

Using his bond with Nola, he crafted an internal block, just as his princess had so often done. Must have worked, because he ceased hearing Aveline's voice.

What should they do about her? If the murderess *had* come to Earth...

Nola was right. He needed to perform the Blood Rite. A prospect he found as exciting and dreadful as his lo— like for her.

He would begin hunting Aveline. He would find her,

and he would secretly spy on her. Somehow, he needed to test her power over him.

Since he had cut off her communication, he knew her hold over him had weakened considerably.

Enough to let me strike her down?

He could pick a time and place and summon *her*, testing the waters. When the time came, he could make his move. Nola wouldn't have to be involved.

The thought calmed him. All would be well.

He put his nose in her hair and breathed her in, then drifted off, content…

NOLA AWOKE A short time later, her mind in turmoil.

She knew how desperately Bane wanted to be the one who killed the queen, but instinct told her only a royal could kill another royal. She and Aveline *would* fight.

She had to prepare for war. Bottom line: Bane's fate rested in the hands of the winner.

Her dread amplified. What if she performed the Blood Rite on *herself*?

Nola considered what little she knew about the ceremony. 1) Must wear the blood of an enemy. 2) Must burn to ash. 3) Might rise again.

Enemy…enemy…who qualified, other than Aveline? *Uh, try lupus and fibromyalgia.*

Wait. Could she use her own blood without, you know, killing herself? Her heart began to pump with more force. Lupus and fibromyalgia had been her worst enemies for years. And burning to ash would be agonizing, but it wouldn't be difficult to do. Rising again… yeah, that one came with serious snags. Would it occur automatically, or did something specific have to happen first?

Did it matter? Once she initiated the Blood Rite, no one could stop it. In fact, Bane would be forced to finish it. If she started it, then alerted him, he'd have to finish it or watch her die.

Already thinking like a cold, callous queen.

The sad thing? For the first time, she couldn't distinguish Dark Nola from Original Nola. They were morphing into one person.

I can figure this out. With no conscious knowledge of Adwaeweth, she'd linked with Bane, teleported and misted into memories. *I can do* anything.

Nola's stomach gurgled, shattering the veil of silence.

After I eat. Before this, she'd been too sick to hold down water.

Careful not to wake Bane, she disentangled their limbs, surely one of the most difficult things she'd ever done—*so warm!*—and climbed out of the bed.

She dressed in a long T-shirt, clean panties and sweatpants. But she didn't head for the door; like an addict, she returned to the bed for another hit of her morphine.

The sight of Bane left her gobsmacked. His golden hair was tousled, his features soft, his tension gone. He was almost…boyish.

If her stomach hadn't gurgled again, she would have crawled back into bed, just to be close to her love. Instead, she tiptoed to the kitchen…and found Zion seated at the table, sipping a glass of whiskey. A single-bulb lamp hung above, bathing him in golden beams. He wore a black shirt and leathers, his hair damp from a recent shower. On his hand was a ring she'd never before seen—Colt's ring. It was metal, with a rounded silver top the size of a quarter.

"I'm surprised you can walk," he said, his tone dry.

Heat infused in her cheeks. "You jealous of my sex-capades?" When a muscle jumped underneath his eye, she laughed and said, "I'll take that as a yes."

He waved her words away, downed his whiskey and poured another shot. "I've been waiting here, hoping you'd emerge alone. We must talk."

Her foreboding returned and redoubled, her empty stomach filling with acid. Needing a moment, she stalked to the minibar, selected a candy bar and bag of peanuts, then poured a cup of water before plopping into the seat across from him. "All right. Hit me," she said, and popped a handful of nuts into her mouth.

"Hit you?" He blanched. "I will do no such thing."

Gah! The language barrier was still a serious nuisance. "I meant, tell me what you need to tell me."

He sighed. "My dream—" he downed the newest shot "—it will come true..." Poured. Downed. "Very, very soon. In a matter of weeks. Maybe days."

"Wrong." She shook her head. "Your dream prediction is a dud this time."

"My dreams are *never* wrong, sweet *dreki*." He gave up pouring shots and drank straight from the bottle. "I have never lied to you, and I won't start now. You *will* murder him."

She continued shaking her head, adamant. "I won't hurt him, ever."

Gaze bleak, he said, "At first, I needed more time with him, time to defeat Erik. Now, I've come to like and admire Bane. He's a fierce competitor, very strong, and he's good for you. As good for you as you are for him. I..." He scoured a hand down his face. "You know I refuse to fight females, yes?"

"I do."

His expression acquired a bitter cast. "I've won three All Wars, a feat few understand, since I've never killed a female. No one knows I dreamed of the ones who *would* fight and kill the females. I just had to put the killer in their paths."

Light bulb moment. Or rather, new logs tossed on the fires of her rage moment. "That's why you rescued me. So you could use me as a weapon against Bane." *Breathe, just breathe.*

While she'd been busy falling in love with Bane, Zion had been busy overseeing his eventual murder.

The bastard offered another nod. "In my dreams, you pick up a dagger. The blade catches fire, and you stab the Adwaewethian in the chest. He falls, and he does not move."

Her brow wrinkled. "Bane is impervious to fire."

"On the outside, yes."

Her hopes soared, then crashed. But what about his internal organs?

If not for Dark Nola, she would have brushed away Zion's concerns. But she and her dark side were one now, and it was getting harder to resist the littlest temptations.

She shuddered. "Bane isn't a man who lets someone come along and stab him all willy-nilly. He defends himself, always." Violently.

Unless she ordered him to remain motionless. Then he *couldn't* defend himself.

She'd entertained the thought before, but this time, she couldn't dismiss it. Because deep down, Dark Nola, Original Nola, *instinct* agreed.

I will do it. I will command Bane to remain motionless and stab him with a fiery blade.

For the sake of my reign, I will kill.

Blood whooshed out of her head and roared in her ears. Could she really take a chance with Bane's life?

Her shoulders rolled in. "I'll leave and I'll stay far away from him." Bane wouldn't willingly let her go. His promise echoed—*I'm keeping you.* He'd meant it…at the time. Once he found out about the knifing, he might change his mind.

Might? Ha! Although, he *had* reacted to her confession about Dark Nola in the sweetest, kindest way possible.

At the time, Dark Nola hadn't been a life-or-death situation.

Everything had changed.

"I'll take you to your sister and Knox," Zion said. "You'll be safest with them."

"Yes. Okay." Bad news: she would sicken again. Good news: the link with Bane would be blocked as soon as she did. He wouldn't be able to look through her eyes, or talk to her. Or visit her. Or touch her.

Don't you dare cry. You are a royal. Act like one! Rise above for the greater good!

"You don't have to worry. I'll work with Bane until the final battle. I'll protect your sister." Zion stood, the barest hint of pain flashing over his features.

"Are you injured?" she asked, concerned.

"Knox stabbed me, and I have yet to heal. Bastard must have poisoned his blade." He traced his thumb over Colt's ring, saying, "I tagged your sister with a bot. I can find her anywhere, anytime."

Then her time with Bane was over. Why put off the inevitable? "Just…give me a minute." Nola combated those stupid tears as she tiptoed into the living room area, hunting for a piece of paper and a pen. She'd stick with highlights.

As she scribbled a goodbye note, she almost broke down about a thousand times. Several teardrops escaped, wetting the paper. Once again, life had changed in a blink, and not for the better.

Though she longed to return to the bedroom and be with Bane one last time, she returned to Zion. One look at the love of her life, and she might not have the strength to leave.

"Ready?" her friend asked.

He *was* her friend, wasn't he?

Rustling sounds spilled from the master bedroom. Bane was waking. Crap! She whisper-yelled, "Let's go, let's go."

Zion opened a rift into an unfamiliar bedroom, with a brass bed, colorful quilt and crystal chandelier. On the wooden floor, a pretty pink rug.

A tall, trim woman with black-and-white hair stood in a windowed alcove, studying the lavender field below.

Vale! Nola's heart tripped inside her chest.

Zion stepped deeper into the room, and Nola followed, throwing a final glance over her shoulder, wondering if she would receive a final look at Bane. No such luck. The second the rift closed, aches and pangs erupted.

"Hello, Vale." Zion's voice echoed through the room.

Vale dropped a cell phone and swung around, palming a sword. Then she paused. "Zion? What are you doing here?"

"He's with me." Nola gathered the strength to step out of the big brute's shadow.

Vale's eyes widened as they filled with hope. "Nola? You're here? You're really here?"

Even as her pains intensified and her limbs grew weak…weaker…she offered a wobbly smile—just before darkness swallowed her whole.

NOLA BLINKED OPEN her eyes and took stock. She lay on an unfamiliar couch, in an unfamiliar living room, with country chic furnishings. Vale sat beside her, color high and healthy, beautiful in every way, and smelling like the best dessert in any bakery. No sign of Zion. No doubt he was searching the house for traps.

"There you are," Vale said with a wide, toothy grin. She reached over to squeeze Nola's hand. "I've missed you so much."

"I've missed you, too." She twined their fingers and held on tight, afraid to let go. "Knox has been good to you?"

"Very good. He's… Nola, he's my person." A dreamy expression dawned. "Every day, he risks his life to protect mine. He worships me."

"Oh, Vale. I'm so happy for you." And maybe a little envious. *I want a future with my Bane!* Had he found the note?

Vale added, "We're going to find a way to stop the war and be together."

Could the war be stopped? "Have you reconsidered taking the Mark of Disgrace? I hear it's—"

"No way." Vale shook her head. "I can't allow an alien race to rule our world. If the war can't be stopped, I'll win it."

And kill Bane and Zion? Nola almost shouted a denial. "What about Knox?"

"He'll take the mark. Or we'll find another way to save him," she said, then changed the subject. "Has Zion been good to *you*?"

"He has. And so has Bane." Her selective mutism allowed her to admit Bane had kidnapped her a few times, but no more. So frustrating! She'd never needed her sister's advice more, and she hated not being able to share some of the best things to ever happen to her. Bane. Royalty! Sex. Health. Bumbling into an upright position, she said, "What are you guys doing here?"

"There are bombs in the lavender field. Knox is out leaving a trail of breadcrumbs for Erik to follow."

Nice. *May he die screaming.*

"All is presently well," Zion said, striding into the room and easing onto the couch next to Nola. He cocked his head to the side and frowned. "I believe Knox will arrive in three...two..."

Knox busted through the door, a giant brute vibrating with malice. Dried blood streaked his bronzed skin, the sight almost obscene.

Zion lurched to his feet, aimed a semiautomatic at his chest and grinned. "Glad you could join us, Knox. We have much to discuss."

Betrayal marred Knox's features. He glared at Vale before facing off with the other male. They shouted insults at each other, fraying Nola's already battered nerves.

Vale leaped up and stepped between them. "Guys. Please," she said, extending her arms. "Talk first, kill later. If we're all alive, we've got options."

Ready to make a difference, Nola forced herself to trudge to her feet. She clasped Zion's wrist, saying, "If you hurt my sister's boyfriend, I will be supremely displeased."

"For once, I'm willing to risk it." Zion kept his attention on Knox. "Whatever you cut me with left a wound on my leg that hasn't healed. I am not amused." Despite his words, he lowered his gun and nudged Nola with his shoulder. "Sit, mortal, and don't get up again."

Mortal? Why act so formal?

In a quieter tone, he added, "If you ever approach an angry combatant again, or get in the middle of an impending fight, I will… I'll…"

Ah. That was why. He was tee-icked! Nola arched a brow and replied, "What, there's no threat bad enough?"

"There is. I'll tell Bane."

Ouch. Low blow. "He might not care." She blew him a kiss with her middle finger, then resettled on the couch.

Vale and Knox openly argued about whether or not to trust Zion.

"Stand down and trust me," Vale said. "I won't risk your life, or my sister's, or our shot at victory. And yes, I realize how contradictory I sound, considering we're trapped in a murder-everyone situation, but I expect us all to survive this."

Nola opened her mouth to admit she knew about Vale's plight as a combatant, but a lie left her unbidden. "Hold up. You're a soldier in their war? How can that be?" Uh, what the what?

Dark Nola didn't want to admit what she knew? Or, would an admission somehow invite questions about Bane?

"I'll explain later," Vale said, then refocused on Knox. "Please, trust me. I want to be with you. A family, not just surviving, but thriving."

A family. Vale and Knox. Nola, a friendly outside observer. Suddenly her insides felt like they'd been dropped in an ant hill. *First I lost Bane. Now I'm losing Vale.*

The petty thoughts shamed her.

Knox flinched. But only seconds later, he softened, his anger completely evaporating, revealing an endless well of pain.

Nola didn't have to wonder why. She recognized the gleam in his eyes: shattered dreams. He'd just made some kind of realization about his relationship with Vale, and it wasn't good.

Tone gentle, Knox ended the disagreement with four sentences. "My truce with you stands, Valerina of Earth. Now and always. But I won't be fighting at your side. Today, we part ways, and I take out combatants from the shadows, where I belong."

Vale drew into herself, clearly crumbling inside. Nola's heart broke. Knox was leaving her sister the way Nola had left Bane. He must think he would harm her if he stayed. Did he love her?

Knox looked to Zion and said, "I will ensure Vale reaches the final two. As long as you're guarding her, I won't target you. If you try to stop me, or hurt her in any way, I will make your death a cautionary tale, and even Seven will shudder with revulsion."

Oh, yes. He loved her, and he thought he would harm her if he stayed. He'd decided to put Vale's well-being over his own happiness, and Nola adored him for it.

"Agreed," Zion said with a nod, and she wondered if he'd had a dream about Knox, too.

Knox wasted no time. He walked away, never looking back, leaving the strong, once untouchable Vale near tears. She peered at the exit, her eyes wide and wounded.

Was that how Bane had looked after reading Nola's note? She gulped, guilt slicing her good intentions to ribbons. "I'm sorry, Vale," she said, aching for her beloved sister. "Beyond sorry."

—*Nola!*—

Bane's frantic voice exploded in her head, and she nearly jumped out of her skin. In her note, she'd commanded him not to contact her. Lesson learned. Orders had to be spoken.

Inhale, exhale. She trembled, waiting, afraid she would hear him again—just as afraid she wouldn't. Hope and dread went to war. But he didn't speak up again, and dread won.

You know it's for the best.

Vale donned a brave face and waved a dismissive hand. "Nothing to be sorry about. Good riddance, right?"

Zion eyed the door Knox had vacated, pensive. "Had I not seen it with my own eyes…that man loves you."

Unequivocally. Knox had looked at Vale the way Bane looked at Nola. Well, *used to* look at Nola. How would he look at her now?

An-n-nd the dread gained new ground.

Tone emotionless, Vale said, "I don't agree. But even if you were right, it wouldn't matter. Sometimes love isn't enough. And really, we don't have time for sentiment." No emotion, and yet her pain was palpable. "Anyway. Enough chatter about Knox. Did you happen to tag any other players with a bot?"

"There wasn't opportunity." Zion helped Nola stand. "If Knox created a footpath to the cottage, other competitors will arrive soon. He'll probably stay out there to pick them off, but I won't take a chance soldiers get past him and harm Nola. We must stash her somewhere safe."

"Where can I go?" she asked. "Your base camp is compromised." With Erik around, all base camps, safe houses and dimensions were unsafe.

"There's a tunnel beneath the house. Come on." Vale marched into the kitchen, Nola and Zion following.

In the pantry, her sister kicked away a dirt-stained rug to reveal a secret hatch. So cool! Every house needed an escape hatch.

Zion descended the ladder first, wincing whenever he put weight on his leg. Nola went next, her body screaming in protest, and Vale claimed the rear. Darkness enveloped them—until the tips of her sister's fingers caught fire, without burning her.

"Oh. My. Gosh," Nola said. "You do realize you are the coolest person I know, right? How is this even possible?"

"One day soon we're going to sit down and have a nice long chat." Vale kissed her cheek and strode over to pick up a lantern.

Zion reached out to take the handle—

Boom!

The ground shook, toppling each of them. Because her sister stood directly underneath the hatch, she got hit with the worst of the blaze, an inferno licking over her. Embers burned holes in her clothes, but didn't harm her skin. Lumber, concrete and pieces of kitchen appliances crashed over her. As she bellowed, agonized, Zion limped over, manhandled the blocks out of the way and helped her stand.

"What happened?" Nola said between coughing fits. Smoke stung her nostrils and tickled her throat.

"Bomb blast," Vale replied, her eyes wells of fear and concern. "Are you okay?"

Another bomb, courtesy of Erik, no doubt. More proof that life could change in an instant. As if she'd needed any reminders. "I—I'm fine." Kind of. She didn't have the strength to stand. "You?"

"Fine," Vale said, sounding anything but.

"This is Erik's doing, I know it," Zion spat.

"We shouldn't wait for his next trick," Vale said. "Let's go."

"Guys," Nola began, but Zion understood.

Her swept her into his strong arms and sprinted for the exit. "Once we're aboveground," he told Vale as he kept pace at her side, "you'll stay with Nola, and I'll confront Erik."

"Strategy isn't your thing, is it, hot stuff?" A sword bounced on Vale's back. "Nola will stay in the tunnel. You and I will head out together and fight side by side, guarding each other's six."

I love being discussed as if I'm not present. But the truly sad thing? They were right. She had power over her beasts and warriors, but no others. If she tried to fight combatants, she'd die badly.

Vale wasn't done. "I must be the one to kill combatants. I absorb their abilities and memories, learning their plans and hiding places."

How and why did Vale absorb abilities but other combatants did not?

"Memories? Truly?" His brow knit with confusion, but he nodded. "Very well. You will make the kills."

What had changed his mind? If Vale made the kills, Zion wouldn't be able to activate the weapons. Plus, Vale would grow stronger. A *lot* stronger. Not that Nola was complaining. She wanted her sister invincible. But she wanted her guys well, too.

When they reached the exit, Zion set her on her feet and said, "For all the times I've saved you, you owe me, Nola, and I expect you to stay put."

"Don't worry. I'll heed your desires. For now." Because she didn't have the strength to do otherwise. *Must recharge and figure out my next move.* There had to be something she could do, *anything* besides sitting idly by while her loved ones risked their lives.

"You're going to be all right." Vale hugged her. "I love you. Never forget."

"I'm not worried about me." Only everyone else. "Just…you had better return. Alive, in case I wasn't clear."

Vale smiled, but no humor glowed in her eyes. "I'll return alive. I'm a superhero. Intangy Girl, trademark pending. I pity our opponents."

They climbed up the ladder, emerging in daylight to face their foes, leaving the weakened Nola in the cave. Alone. Cold. Afraid. A metaphor for her past.

But what about her future?

CHAPTER TWENTY-NINE

How to tame your beast in a day

GET TO NOLA. *Get to Nola now!* Bane had been tracking her for hours, her note on repeat in his mind.

Dear Bane, aka golden god, aka beasty-boy, aka hot buttered buns,

You've touched my life in so many ways. I've grown to love and hate you, you wonderful, terrible beast! That's right. I love you. But I hate you because I have to leave you and this hurts. This hurts so stinking bad. But there's a reason for it. Are you ready? Here goes. Zion had a psychic dream of the future. He claims I'll stab and kill you. I don't want to take a chance that he's right. You mean too much to me. So, I don't know if this will work, but here goes. I'm ordering you not to come after me or contact me. I plan to kill Aveline and save Meredith. I know you said you're keeping me, but think! You'll have the love of your life back, and you won't remember me. The All War will transpire, but the new queen will send a different Adwaewethian to Earth. We'll never meet, but maybe that's for the best? You can't miss what you've never had, right? Love, Nola.
PS: This is my least favorite day.

Her tears had stained the paper.

Now, he felt skinned alive. Never meet her? *Not a life worth living.* He *breathed* for this woman, and she thought to leave him, because she feared a prediction? She thought to put a new queen in power, one who would send a different warrior to fight in the Terran All War, a man willing to kill Nola at the first opportunity? Nola must have realized the truth, yet she'd planned to sacrifice herself anyway. For Bane. Because she loved him. Loved. Him.

Get to Nola. Just get to Nola.

To give an order life, a royal had to voice it, so he was under no obligation to obey her note. Already he'd attempted to peer through her eyes and speak in her mind, but he'd failed, encountering block after block. He'd decided to track her by scent; all that jasmine and honeysuckle would be a true guide. He would find her. No one kept him from Nola, not even Nola herself. As for Zion's prediction, Bane didn't care. So his little princess might stab him. So what? Whatever happened, they would deal.

Trusting Zion had been a mistake. The bastard had opened a portal and taken Nola away. Therefore, the bastard would die.

Bane increased his pace, sprinting through a tangle of trees. Sunlight glared over a long stretch of farmland, a smattering of homes spaced out between different animal-laden pastures. The animals sensed him and panicked, bucking around. Understandable. With adrenaline plumping his muscles, Bane already partially transformed, his teeth longer and sharper than usual. The beast rammed his skull, demanding blood.

Boom! The ground shook, trees swaying, limbs clapping.

About a mile up ahead, something had exploded.

"Erik," he snarled. Smoke wafted through the air, carrying a strange, sweet scent. *Vale's* scent. The one she'd acquired after killing a female combatant. Nola was with Vale. If his princess had been hurt…

A roar barreled from Bane. The more he inhaled the scent, the more his blood burned with lust. *Focus.* Different sounds caught his attention. Grunts and groans. Clangs. Curses. As he shot past another tangle of trees, he caught sight of at least twenty armed men in the midst of violent combat with Vale and Zion. Knox, too, though he fought on the other side of a scorched field.

Deal with Zion later. The armed men had been snared by Vale's scent. They were more interested in screwing the combatants than killing them.

Nola, where was Nola? No sign of her.

Guess he'd be dealing with Zion now. Bane plowed through the mortal army, tossing soldiers out of his way—after ripping off their limbs, of course. "Girl," he snarled at the male, half-man, half-beast. "Give. Her. To. Me."

"Removed her from your vicinity for your own good. Want to live? Stay away from her." Zion tossed a mortal his way then darted off, disappearing in the trees. Going after Nola?

Frantic, Bane gave chase. He didn't bother tossing people out of his way, just slammed into them, knocking them down. But Knox stepped into his path, and he wasn't so easy to dispatch.

For some reason, the male was just as frantic, frenzied and wild; he threw a punch, and Bane ducked, scraping his claws over Knox's torso, drawing blood. His go-to move.

Rather than strike with his fists, Knox aimed a revolver and hammered at the trigger. *Pop, pop, pop.* Sharp pain and blistering heat exploded through different parts of Bane's body.

Drogo roared and rammed at his skull, and it was then, that moment that Bane realized the beast had been helping him all along, giving him the tools he needed to survive. Claws. Wings. Superior strength. Teaching him to battle through pain and distraction. And, when things looked grim, taking over to ensure their survival. They *were* one and the same.

Bane charged at Knox. More bullets. More pain. He slammed into the other man, who planted his feet and didn't budge. No matter. Bane gripped his collar and shook. "Where. Is. Nola?"

A tendril of smoke curled from the barrel of the revolver. "Help me...kill mortals," Knox commanded. "They must die. Make it hurt."

"Where. Is. Nola?" Bane cared about nothing else.

From a distance, Vale called, "Hey, beasty-boy. Look over here. Look at me. Yo, Bane. You want to talk about Nola? You've got to deal with me."

With a roar, he pivoted to face her. Her words...truth or lie? One way or another, he would find out.

"Come get me, Bane." She grinned and crooked her finger at him, before running off, calling, "This way. Yes, that's it. I've got the one you seek."

"Vale," Knox whispered, his shock clear. "She lives. My *valina* lives!"

When Bane took a step forward, Knox did his best

to stop him. This time, Bane sidestepped him, refusing to engage, and dashed after the woman. Along the way, he scented honeysuckle and jasmine, and nearly wept with relief.

But Vale turned in the opposite direction, moving away from the scent. Did he continue to follow her, in order to catch and interrogate her, or did he follow Nola's breadcrumbs?

Nola. Always Nola.

He veered, sticking with her scent. He would find her. Nothing and no one would stop him. Then, he would begin the Blood Rite.

It was decided. He'd been a fool to wait. She would become strong enough to stab and kill him, as predicted, but he didn't care.

He would rather have a few more minutes with Nola, than an eternity with anyone else.

"HE'S COMING." ZION shot down the ladder, reentering the darkened tunnel. He grabbed Nola and scurried back up.

Her heart sped into overdrive. He—Bane? Dang him! Had he not read her letter? Did he not know she planned to save his wife?

Or maybe he couldn't read English?

Crap! And yeah, okay, he'd once told Nola he didn't want her to time travel, that he preferred a relationship with her, but come on! If Nola and Meredith were standing side by side, both alive and well, he'd pick Meredith, the nonroyal.

Lying to yourself now? You know he's let go of his prejudices. "Where's Vale?" she asked, her voice little more than a grouse.

"Helping Knox."

They emerged into a total nightmare. Smoke thickened the air and formed a canopy overhead, creating a postapocalyptic setting. Throat itching, she coughed.

Zion set her down and took her hand. "This way."

They made it five steps, only five, before a blur of motion plowed into them, knocking them both to the ground—no, not her, only Zion, who released her as he fell. However, momentum sent her stumbling backward, tripping over a rock and toppling. Impact packed quite a wallop, stars winking through her vision, sand filling her mouth.

She blinked rapidly and gasped. She hadn't tripped over a rock, but a body. A man. A human man. There were others, as well. A trail of bodies actually, each saturated in Vale's new innate fragrance.

Sweat dampened Nola's brow, her blood heating with…no, surely not. But, yeah. There could be no denying it. Her blood heated with sizzling arousal, as if she'd spent the past few hours making out with Bane.

Trembling, Nola checked one of the unconscious men for a pulse. Thin and reedy, but noticeable. Maybe the others were alive, too.

If these men had attacked her sister in the lavender field…if they'd helped bomb the house…they might have also hidden in the mountains, shooting at combatants during the assembly. Crimes committed under Erik's command. For payment.

Payment made these men mercenaries. For the right price, mercenaries would attack Vale again and again. And not just Vale. Bane, Zion and Knox, too. Therefore, the mercenaries couldn't be allowed to survive the day.

She eyed their chests, her mouth watering. Finally, she would have the pleasure of eating someone's heart...

Reaching out...

A pained grunt stopped her, drawing her gaze up. Zion and Bane were on their feet, facing off, two snarling predators thirsty for blood. How could she have lost sight of them, even for a moment?

She straightened, taking stock. A veil of smoke protected Bane's sensitive skin from the sun. He seemed to have grown several inches taller and several inches wider, his muscles bigger than ever. He wasn't just enraged; he *was* rage.

And I am desire. Aching... He'd never looked so beautiful. Dark. Monstrous. Bloody. The shoulder wound had opened up again, crimson sluicing down his bare chest.

He pointed an accusing finger at Zion. "You don't take her from me. You don't keep her from me."

"Do you wish to die?" Zion bellowed. "Stay with her, and that is the future awaiting you."

"Everyone dies. I would rather die with her than live without her." Bane kept his gaze on the other male as he angled his pointer at Nola. "If you come between us again, our truce is over. I'll kill you without hesitation." Bane turned his glare on her, snapping, "We do the Blood Rite today."

She wobbled on her feet. *This is truly happening?*

Today? Another life-altering change. One she'd wanted. And yet... *Too many changes, too fast.* "You can't be serious, Bane."

His rage seemed to heat another hundred degrees. "When we first met, you agreed to do it when I believed the time was right. I do. You will keep your word."

But... "What about Meredith? I can save her—"

"You can, yes, but you won't," he interjected. "Listen up, because I will not say this again, because it's too painful. I don't want you to go back."

Tears welled. "You don't know what you're saying. Think! You—" A thought occurred to her, and she glanced between the two combatants. "How are we able to speak of this in front of Zion?" Only an hour ago, she hadn't been able to tell Vale, one of the most important people in her life.

Surprise knocked Bane back. "You are Adwaewethian," he spit at Zion. "A hybrid. Sometime in the past, an Adwaewethian queen sent breeders to your planet. You didn't just dream of Nola. You sensed her royal status, just as I did."

Nola's mind blew into a tailspin.

"You are right. And wrong," Zion said. "I am part Adwaewethian, it's true, but I didn't come from a breeder, and I do not play host to a beast. I was created in a lab, genetic components taken from different races. The best of the best and the worst of the worst."

That made a strange kind of sense. Thinking back, she realized she'd never really experienced mutism with him. She'd assumed she couldn't share, so she hadn't even tried. "Are you subject to the will of a royal?" Why ask? Why not find out for herself? "I command you to heal from Knox's wound."

"That won't work with—" Zion pressed his lips together, going silent. Shock consumed his expression as he gazed down. "It's working. I'm healing. I can feel the muscles weaving back together."

She fluffed her hair and refocused on Bane. "Are you sure you wish to proceed with the Blood Rite? You know about the prediction now. What if, after the Blood Rite, I order you to *let* me stab you?"

"I'm sure you'll have a good reason," Bane replied. "But whatever happens, we stay together. We do not separate. Ever. Understand?"

He'd fought to reach her. Fought to stay with her. Always. He loved her; he must! The next thing she knew, she was running to him. She threw her arms around his neck. "I'm sorry I left you behind. I should have talked to you, admitted everything, but I was so afraid you'd grow to hate me again."

"I will *never* hate you." Cleaving to her, he said, "I am yours, and you are mine."

"But," she continued, "there's no reason good enough to stab you. *I* don't want to risk it."

"Trust yourself, love. You have something the others queens do not. Do you know what that is?"

Had he just called her "love" instead of "dove"? "I have…you?"

A fleeting smile. "You do, yes. But you also have a strong heart." He pressed his forehead to hers and traced his thumbs over her cheeks. "You have loved and lost. You know your mind, and what matters most. You have survived nightmares and thrived. I trust *you*."

His beautiful words tore her apart. But he didn't comprehend the gravity of their situation. "Maybe you shouldn't. I'm merging with my dark side, Bane. We're becoming one."

He did not react. "The only way to assuage your fears about this? Go through the Blood Rite. You'll see I'm right." He gave her a swift kiss. "All will be well, love. I will allow nothing less."

This moody, broody sex machine *had* called her "love." Tenderness welled despite her inner turmoil.

"All right." A little excited, a lot afraid, she nodded. "I'll do it. If anything happens to me—"

"Nothing will happen to you. Nothing!" His civility dissolving, he gripped her arms and shook her. "You won't leave me again and you will survive."

Another nod. She rasped, "I will survive."

"I will help," Zion said.

Bane glared at him, but offered no response. After another swift kiss to Nola's lips, he opened a portal to a motel room with twin beds. Clean but generic furnishing. He'd already secured their backpacks, her gauntlets inside.

Eager to update Vale, she plopped onto a bed and typed a text. Everyone had seen Vale's reaction over Nola's death, giving it an aura of legitimacy, so, they could chat again. Right? Right.

Are you alive and well? YOU HAD BETTER BE ALIVE AND WELL! I'm with Bane and Zion, and we're good. (Sorry my Banie scratched up your Knoxie, but he did it to save your man's life). And yep, Bane is mine! I'm keeping him. We're working together. For real. Equal partners and all that. We'd like to work with you and Knox. Erik made our safe houses hazard zones, so Team Zibanola has no place to stay.

Vale's reply came within minutes: I'm the proud owner of an underground bunker. (Knox gave it to me. A makeup gift for being a douche at the farmhouse.) Come and stay with me. I miss you like a limb. But you gotta ditch the guys first. Sorry, not sorry. They'd be too eager to remove my head.

Nola: I can't ditch 'em. Well, I can but I won't. I love them, V. They're part of my family.

She tried to type more. How she and Bane were a couple, how she'd soon rule a race of beast shape-shifters. Her fingers refused to work.

So. The stupid mutism stopped all communication. Good to know.

Vale: I think Knox has a 2nd safe house Erik doesn't know about. No one does, since no one can see into his cribs. You guys want that one?

She flipped her gaze up. Zion sat at the desk, cleaning his weapons. Bane paced, lost in thought. "How about a truce with Vale and Knox?" she asked. "I mean, you guys are already fighting to protect them. Why not gain their protection in return? To sweeten the pot, they're willing to give us a safe house Erik doesn't know about."

She braced, expecting immediate refusals at top volume.

"Very well," Bane said with a dip of his chin.

Zion persisted, still running the rag over the dagger. "I find the arrangement acceptable, as well."

She sputtered for a moment, confused. "That easily? Seriously? You're not going to make me do up a pros and cons list, or present a PowerPoint presentation?"

Bane squatted before her, his hot, calloused hands resting on her thighs. "At the assembly, Knox put himself into the line of fire to save Vale. I can work with him, because I'm confident he'll do nothing to harm his woman's family."

Nola searched his eyes, knew he'd meant every word. Love for him doubled, tripled. "I'll let Vale know."

She typed, YES!!!!!! We accept. Please and thank you.

Vale: Let's meet in an hour. Somewhere other combatants won't think to look. Let's see, let's see. Oh! I know. The place we swore never to visit—the worst place on Earth.

Ahhh. The spot some of their high school friends had lost their virginity.

Nola: Done and done. See you soon, sis!

"We're meeting them in an hour," she announced.

Bane held her stare and nodded. Expression dark and determined, he said, "Just enough time to prepare for your Blood Rite."

"Welcome to the worst place on earth," Nola said, spreading her arms. "Under the bleachers at the football stadium of my high school rival, Blueberry Hill High." Wrinkled candy bar wrappers, cigarette butts and plastic cups abounded.

Her threesome had just stepped through a portal, five minutes early for the meeting. Knox and Vale were already there, waiting. Overachievers!

Nola rushed to Vale, and Vale rushed to her. They met in the middle, hugging, laughing, then hugging some more.

Vale whispered, "I'm going to find a way to make

you immortal without joining the war. Considering all the supernatural weapons floating around, there's got to be a way."

"The boys are on the case, too," she whispered back, longing to explain the Blood Rite. Trying…failing. Dang it! Maybe, after her coronation, she could share with Vale. A girl could hope, anyway.

Cranking up the volume, Vale added, "You sure you want to stay with Zion and Bane? You're my innocent little sis, and they—"

"She's sure," Zion snapped. Nervous about the upcoming Blood Rite? *Join the club.* He held a backpack, and Bane held the other.

"Watch your tone," Knox snapped back. "You speak to Vale with respect, or you don't speak to her at all."

Clearly fighting a smile, Vale squared her shoulders. "Yeah. Respect."

Nola had to subdue a grin, too. Looked like the two had made up. Not surprising. Vale was just so…at ease with Knox. Most of the men she'd dated had considered her too brash and too edgy, with good reason. She *was* brash and edgy. However, few people dug past the surface to see the vulnerable girl underneath the bravado. A girl whose father abandoned her after the tragic death of her mother. No one deserved a supportive partner more.

Bane arched a brow, the Adwaewethian equivalent of rolling his eyes. "Did she call you innocent?" he asked Nola. "That's like calling a dragon a bird."

Dragon. Ha! Nola elbowed him in the stomach. "I'm not that bad."

"You're right." His eyes glittered with unexpected merriment and a hint of lust. "You're worse."

Mmm. Lust. He looked at her lips and licked his own. Heat sizzled between them.

"You know, if everyone walks away from this expedition with only minor injuries, I'll consider it a win," Vale said. "Who am I kidding? If everyone crawls away, it'll be a win."

Nola picked up the reins of conversation, backtracking to her sister's original query. "Yes, I'm sure I want to stay with these nutjobs. I like having strapping immortal eye candy at my beck and call."

"Well, you're the only reason *my* immortal eye candy offered up his guest home." Vale grinned at Bane and Zion. "Your companions owe us. Big-time."

Knox nodded. "As payment, you'll help us end Erik— but you will not make the kill. Vale will. That is nonnegotiable."

Zion popped his jaw but he, too, nodded. Bane gritted out, "Very well."

"So, we're doing this, then?" Vale grinned and clapped. "We're forming a kick-A alliance?"

"I would like that. I've never before had true allies." With his head high and his broad shoulders squared, pride stamped into every inch of Knox's bearing. "If you keep your word, I'll keep mine. I will fight to save you rather than destroy you. When Erik and his allies have been taken out, we can reevaluate the alliance. With warriors from the other two wars joining ours, we might have to band together longer than anticipated."

Zion filled his lungs and said, "I'll stand with you."

"I'll stand with you, as well." Bane clasped and squeezed Nola's hand.

She all but melted. *My darling man.*

"Let's get you ensconced in your new safe house." Knox opened a rift, then motioned the others to enter.

Zion stepped through first, followed by Nola and Bane. Knox and Vale claimed the rear. Once they were all through, Bane and Zion moved to Knox's side to act as lookouts, guarding the rift until it closed.

Nola checked out their new digs—a cave with limestone walls. A bedrock had collapsed, forming a gorgeous cenote, the water so clear she could see fish swimming below the surface. Crystals twinkled from the ceiling, almost as dazzling as stars, and though the air held a faint musty scent, there was no hint of rot or decay.

"Careful," Knox warned. "The tunnels are vast. I haven't been down here since before our imprisonment, so I have no idea what's happened here. Above the cave is a temple. Around the temple is a jungle. There are no physical exits anywhere down here. You must rift in and out."

"Thank you," Nola said. "We appreciate this." She nudged Bane, then Zion. "Right?"

"Thank you," Zion and Bane grumbled in unison. Nola suspected that, as gung ho as they were to work with Knox, they didn't like owing the man a favor.

Knox went rigid, his dread palpable as he glanced at his ring.

"What's wrong?" Vale asked, paling. "Ansel is requesting a meeting?"

Ansel?

"Can you ignore him?" her sister asked.

Must be a king.

Knox brought Vale's hand to his lips to kiss her knuckles. "We must return home. Now."

Though worry pulsed from Vale, she put on a brave face and winked at Nola. And, though she had no idea what was going on, Nola's heart was breaking. She put on a brave face as well, and winked back. Then Knox dragged her sister into another antechamber to rift home in private, leaving Nola alone with her guys. And her nerves.

One step closer to the Blood Rite...

CHAPTER THIRTY

Always wear the crown!

"THE TIME HAS COME," Bane announced. He'd been in and out of their underground base camp, moving everything he'd gathered pre-meeting to their new digs. By "everything" she meant unconscious soldiers. He'd bound the men with rope and created a circle of bodies around Nola. Finished, he peered at Zion. "You will keep guard. Let no one interfere."

"You can count on me." Zion moved to an alcove, the one with the best view of the cavern, and popped the bones in his neck, ready for anything.

Nerves got the better of Nola. Soon the Blood Rite would start, and she would become queen, experiencing her full power. If she survived. *I will, I will, I will.* But uncertainty threatened to drive her insane. What if—

Enough! Blank your mind.

"You, turn around," Bane instructed Zion. "No matter what you hear, do not look back."

Crap. That sounded bad. "What do I need to do?" she squeaked. *About to be a queen. Act like one. Be, you know, dignified or something.*

Oh! She could think of one way to help her feel queenly. "Hold up."

"Nola—"

"I haven't changed my mind. But there's something I need to do first." She raced to the backpacks and dug out her gauntlets. Once they were anchored to her hands, she returned to the circle. "See? Better." She already felt more dignified.

"Allow your instincts to guide you, and you'll know what to do." Kind, gentle—adoring—he brushed two fingers along her jawline, offering comfort, before moving outside the circle and erasing his expression. All hard edges and unwavering determination, he said, "Ready?"

Her palms sweat, and her stomach protested. Still she nodded. He palmed a dagger and then...he began to move around the circle, performing jumps, spins and crouches—slashing each man's neck. Blood gushed from their wounds, pooling at her feet.

Violence no longer fazed her; the sight and scent of death no longer sickened her. Instead, it helped combat her nervousness, and she began to hum with anticipation and delight.

Instinct kicked in—he'd been right about that—and she knew what she had to do next.

Bane arched a brow, waiting for her to act.

She peeked at Zion. He'd taken Bane's warning to heart, and hadn't turned around. Very well. Trembling, she followed her inner promptings and stripped bare-butt naked, removing everything but the gauntlets. Cool air stroked her skin as she eased to her knees.

Unconcerned about disease, she wet her hands in the pool of blood, and smeared crimson under her eyes, over her heart and across her belly. Droplets slid down, down, streaking the rest of her, blistering her flesh.

Bane continued jumping and spinning, his movements graceful yet powerful. Hypnotic. The air crackled, lightning flashing.

Dizziness invaded, screwing with her equilibrium, but she straightened and moved in a similar fashion. As she danced, the blood attracted the lightning. She absorbed the energy, until her cells crackled, too. Strength infiltrated her muscles…bones…marrow. Glorious strength. And she knew. Those lightning strikes were happening inside her mind, not around her.

Her beasts were awakening!

More. All! Weak? No longer. Never again would someone hurt her or her loved ones. Never again would someone threaten her life or family without suffering for it. Never again would someone make her do something she didn't want to do.

From a distance, she heard a beastly roar, soft but gaining traction. Then she heard another. And another. The sweetest music, sung by thousands of warriors come to life at last.

Connection. Nola felt them, spirit, soul and body, a link forming. Like the one she shared with Bane, but weaker; the beasts fed her strength, and she knew, *knew*, she would never again experience withdrawal, would never have to deal with another disease. The past was the past, dead and gone, a new future forged.

Abruptly, Bane went still. His head was tilted back, streaks of red forking across his throat. When the red bled his eyes, he slipped past the circle of corpses to cup her cheeks and fit his mouth over hers. An action he'd performed many times in the past, trading passion for passion. Now, a river of heat poured down her throat. Too hot, too hot! The pain!

She screamed against his mouth, but she didn't retreat,

not even when pain graduated into agony, the worst she'd ever experienced. *Cannot stop. Stopping equals death.*

Smoke wafted between them, and she breathed it in, letting tendrils fill her lungs. Heating...burning... boiling...melting. Power.

Just as flames erupted over Nola, no part of her left unscathed, Bane leaped back. The blood smeared on her skin courtesy of the slain soldiers acted as some kind of life-giving fuel, providing another dose of strength. Strength she desperately needed as flames overtook her.

Not just burning...old Nola was dying, a new Nola soon to be born. *Let it happen. Don't resist.* Once this was done, she would have everything she'd ever wanted. A man who loved her. A family. A kingdom to rule.

When her body was nothing more than a pile of ash, her spirit—mist—remained in the circle. The pain faded, her world dark and cold. One heartbeat. Two. Three.

—*Come back to me, love.*—

Bane's voice invaded her mind, clearer and louder than ever before.

Determined, she kicked and clawed, tying to fight her way out of the void. A fleck of light beckoned, and she fought harder. Just a little more...

Tingles erupted in her torso, quickly spreading to her limbs. For a moment, her senses got scrambled. She tasted fire, smelled sounds, heard a drumbeat of emotion and felt the soft brush of colors against her flesh.

As the light brightened, the kinks ironed out and her body was remade. Realization struck: her mind hadn't just linked with her warriors. Her mind had also linked to a hive of past queens. Their knowledge, anyway. So much to soak up! And she could. She had time now.

She'd done it, she'd survived! Nola wiggled her fingers and toes, experimenting with motion. No problems arose. Even the coldness vanished from her awareness, the blood gone. Instead, glowing, swirling designs—runes—etched her skin, like tiny rivers of molten gold. When the glow dimmed, a faint outline of the runes remained. *So pretty.*

Bane stood outside the circle, his shoulders squared, his spine straight, his legs braced apart. Concern and relief dominated his features. Love sparkled over their connection…a connection now strengthening, just like her. *Knew he loved me.*

He knelt before her, bowing his head. "All hail Queen Nola."

Queen Nola. Queen. Finally! *Must guard my title at all cost.*

All cost?

Deep down she knew instinct would drive other princesses to try to steal her position. Knew they would use her love for Bane, Vale and Zion against her. Might be better to cut all ties and—

No! She cast the thoughts out of her head. Love was strength. Love was power. Let the other royals try to challenge her. They would not succeed.

"Rise," she said, and frowned. Her voice…her words had weight now, every single one like an armed soldier on a mission. They left her with a purpose, and they would fight to see it done.

Bane obeyed with a growing smile. "You did it, love." Bending down, he picked up the dress he'd obtained for her. He closed the distance and slipped the material over her head. "You survived."

"Something isn't right," Zion announced, disrupting

the moment. "I sense something. Someone. A woman. And I can't stop her approach, no matter how hard I try."

How had Nola forgotten the other man's presence?

"Is she a combatant?" Bane asked.

She frowned and rubbed her chest. "Wait. I sense it, too. A tingle of awareness." Not a combatant, then.

Bane cursed. "Aveline," he snarled.

Between one blink and the next, a blonde woman tele-ported between them. And oh, yes. It was Aveline. She scanned the tunnel, taking everything in, then kicked Nola in the stomach and grinned evilly at Bane. "Hello, warrior. Did you miss me?"

BANE RELEASED A curt oath. "Aveline."

She'd plaited her golden hair into a crown and opted to wear a scarlet dress with mesh inserts to protect her vital organs. Rubies adorned her neck and wrists.

Looking like a live wire of fury, Nola scrambled to her feet, her gauntlets glinting in the torchlight. "You murdered my mother, murdered Bane's wife. You made a mistake, coming here. Today you die."

Aveline flicked her a brief glance and dismissed her as unimportant. "Tsk-tsk," she said, peering at Bane. "Someone has been a naughty boy. Instead of killing the princess, you made her a queen."

Drawing a sword, Zion moved toward Bane to offer aid.

Aveline pointed a finger at the dark-haired warrior. "Stay where you are. Do not move."

The power that laced her words… Though Zion strained to take a step forward, as evidenced by the vein bulging in his forehead, he remained in place.

Bane and Aveline circled each other, Nola seemingly

forgotten. As strong as Aveline was, she had no fear of a newly made queen. "How did you find me?" he asked. *Think!* Best course of action?

"I can find you anywhere, anytime, darling. I am your queen, after all, despite what you've done this day. Once, I was your lover." Aveline gave him another slow smile. "I suspected you had betrayed me, so I came to do your job for you. A quick in-and-out job. No one will ever know what transpired, for I will be the only one to leave this…" She scanned the tunnels and grimaced. "Hovel."

"You are not my queen," he snarled. "Not any longer. I rue the day we were ever lovers."

"Then you're right." Two daggers slid out from under her sleeves, her fingers wrapping around the hilts. "I'm not your queen. I'm your executioner."

NOLA STUMBLED BACK as Bane and Aveline crashed together in a tangle of violence. Aveline's speed and grace surprised her.

Should she interfere? This was what Bane had wanted all along. The vengeance he'd craved from the beginning.

He blocked the queen's parries with mind-scrambling aggressiveness. Fierce and ferocious. But when he'd go to deliver a parry of his own, he would stop just short of contact.

Nola clutched her stomach, confused. Now that she'd earned her full power, he should be able to harm the other royal, right? Or, did he secretly not want to harm his childhood sweetheart?

Oh, he wanted to harm her, all right. His frustration was palpable, his fury growing by leaps and bounds.

Why, why, why did he stop, then?

Answers downloaded straight into Nola's brain. He

couldn't harm her. Her instincts had been right. Only a queen could kill another queen.

The inability to cause harm would be his downfall. Aveline landed blow after furious blow.

Nola *had* to take over. "Bane," she shouted, about to unleash her first command as a queen. Well, the first command he wouldn't want to obey. He might resent her for it—no way; he'd changed—but he would live.

Blood and sweat soaked him. Cuts and bruises littered his entire body. His reflexes were slowing.

Before she could state the rest of her command, Aveline pressed her advantage, working her way behind Bane. She swooped down and slicked her blade across his Achilles tendons.

As he dropped to his knees, facing Nola, the other queen tossed one of the blades.

Too late to duck. The metal embedded in Nola's heart. *Nola* dropped, the pain excruciating. Every time the organ beat, the wound grew longer, wider, tearing through ventricles. Her lungs filled to the brim with blood, drowning her. *Can't breathe. Need to breathe.*

A cloak of darkness creeped through her mind. But she still had a bird's-eye view as Aveline fit her palms against Bane's cheeks.

"Be sure to watch," the other queen told her. "This is the fate that will befall you, as well."

Little lines of black spread over Bane's features, a truly gruesome sight. *We're losing, and Aveline is winning.*

Tears welled as Nola met Bane's gaze. "I'm sorry," she mouthed. Weakness marched through her, gaining new ground by the minute.

"I'm sorry," he mouthed back, and her injured heart squeezed.

What are you doing? Giving up? You are a queen! A leader of dragons, your word is law. You are mighty. Go save your mansel in distress.

Yes. Yes! She wasn't dead. Bane wasn't dead, either, but he would be—soon. Unless she acted. A battle plan formed, courtesy of the hive mind. Actually, courtesy of one queen in particular. Jayne… Nola's ancestor. They *were* related. Some of Jayne's descendants had survived.

What Jayne wanted her to do…it was a risky, terrible, awful, devastating, utterly insane plan. Nola wanted to cry and vomit and spend a few thousand years thinking about every aspect first. If anything went wrong…

Don't let anything go wrong.

Fighting past the deluge of pain—her specialty—she crawled closer to Bane. She had to leave the blade embedded in her chest, lest she bleed out before she completed her mission. Almost there…

Aveline laughed. "You can't stop me, girl."

No wonder Bane had hated queens. The arrogance. The smugness. The hunger for power that ate away at Aveline's humanity.

A fiery dagger lay in the circle of flames, next to Bane's feet. Nola knew she'd have only one shot at this. Hoping to distract Aveline with her words, keeping the other woman's attention off her actions, she said, "I'm going to—" *sneakily clasp the hilt of the dagger* "—kill…"

Still laughing, Aveline flittered to the side, out of Nola's strike zone, *without* releasing her hold on Bane. "You're going to kill me? When you can't even reach me? Tsk-tsk. But go ahead. Please try. This will be fun—for me."

Nola looked to Bane. His gaze remained on her. Black lines forked his eyes. He was dying.

"Love you," he mouthed this time.

He loves me! The confession gave Nola the strength she needed to struggle to her knees.

Took everything she had to remain upright. "Forgive me," she whispered—and plunged the dagger into his heart.

He threw back his head and roared, the flames spreading through him, visible beneath the surface of his skin. His fell over, face-first, hitting the ground with a heavy thud, his eyes staring at nothing.

Nola whimpered. Her beautiful golden god was dead. Killed by her hand. Just as Zion had predicted. The blade she held? Soaked with her lover's blood.

Aveline took another step to the side, putting more distance between them. She wasn't laughing anymore. "Why?" she demanded.

Nola allowed a smile. "Don't worry. You'll never remember this happened."

The color drained from the other woman's face. She charged toward Nola, then. Too late. Nola had already smeared Bane's blood on her hands. She closed her eyes and retreated into her head, fixating on the moments before the Blood Rite.

The foundation beneath her feet vanished. Lightheaded. Dizzy. Traveling back in time...

When a new foundation appeared, she fluttered open her lids. There he was. Bane. Nola raced to him and threw her arms around him, sobbing, "You're alive!"

"Of course I am." He enfolded her with his muscular arms, and she realized she was tangible. That Future Nola had merged with Past Nola. Meaning, they'd been mistaken about the nuts and bolts of the ability.

This? She liked better. It was the equivalent of pressing a redo button.

Zion stood off to the side, watching the proceedings. Which meant Bane hadn't instructed him to turn his back yet.

Should she have gone back further? Probably. But this was a first attempt, and she was learning as she went. Besides, she'd been tired, weak and injured.

"What's wrong, love?" Bane asked.

"Aveline came," she rushed out. "You weren't able to land a blow. She was able to get you to your knees and drain you with her death touch, so *I* murdered you with a fiery dagger, just like Zion's vision. I'm sorry! But I used your death to time travel and reset. I'm sorry," she repeated. "Zion, she commanded you to remain motionless, and you were helpless to obey."

Both males absorbed the news, looking like they could barely contain their dismay and fury.

"*I'm* sorry you had to go through that," Bane said, caressing Nola's cheek.

"Don't be sorry," she replied, aching for him. "You're the one who died in agony by my hand."

"Let us blame the one who is truly responsible. Aveline."

"Agreed." Though she wanted to hold on to him forever, she let go. "We don't have much time. I didn't go back very far." And now Nola was in her pre-Blood Rite body. They had to do the ceremony again. The pain…

Minimal in the big scheme of things.

"This time, we have an advantage," he said. "Get in the circle."

He performed the ceremony again, every motion and word the same. Only, they both demonstrated more stress and strain. No matter. They remained aware and ready for Aveline's arrival.

Must win this time. Must win. Instinct said, *You can't go back to the same moment twice.*

Nola arose from the ashes, more determined than ever. They wasted no time with chatter. She donned the dress and palmed two daggers. He helped her.

"I need you to stand over there with Zion," she said, pointing to the far wall. "Trust me to do this, Bane. Please. I will be the hand of your vengeance, I swear it."

"Your life is all that matters to me," he replied fiercely. "Whatever happens, survive or kill me again to travel back."

Go back to a time even farther back? Risking this future? If anything changed farther back, they might not reach this moment a second—third—time. No, Aveline had to die *this* round.

He waited until she'd responded with a curt nod, then stalked to Zion's side, as requested.

Nola steeled her resolve and—

Aveline teleported into the tunnel, just as before. Before the other woman had time to gain her bearings, Nola blocked out their audience, released a war cry and lunged at her opponent.

Using the skills Bane and Zion taught her, she treated Aveline's thigh as a step stool, swung a leg around her shoulders and hooked a knee over her throat. Then, Nola dropped her upper half forward, swinging down and flipping Aveline to her back.

The second the other woman crash-landed, losing her breath, Nola was on top of her, whaling. The gauntlets protected her knuckles from Aveline's teeth, while the claws shredded her flesh. *Knew I'd need them.*

Aveline tried to buck her off and flunked. *F-, bitch.*

Hold up. No, Aveline hadn't bucked. She'd maneuvered her legs up. Now, she crisscrossed those legs around Nola and thrust her to the ground. Immediately Aveline rose up, reversing their positions. With her knees pinning Nola's shoulders, *she* whaled on *Nola.*

Stars flashed through her vision, and nausea churned in her stomach. Adrenaline surged, helping to obstruct the awful sensations. When Aveline's next series of punches rang her bell, one of Nola's eyes swelled shut. Dizziness consumed her, but so did another idea.

As a queen, she had more power than she'd had as a princess. To teleport, she had only to think where she wanted to be.

Whoa. What was *that*?

Aveline had placed her hot hands on Nola's cheeks. Pain spread, followed by frigid cold.

Understanding dawned. *She's draining me to death.*

Nola attempted to teleport. Failed. Simply too weak. Need strength. How?

Bane!

She retreated into her mind, found their link, as well as her link to the hybrids. She began to draw from their strength. *Something I can do, but she cannot.*

Aveline had made a huge mistake, coming to Earth. She couldn't draw from her warriors back home, couldn't draw from Nola's warriors, either.

Nola grinned. Before she fed Aveline any more energy, she executed a perfect teleport—behind the wicked witch of the hive. The other queen crashed to the floor. Before she could teleport herself, Nola punched into her back, through her rib cage, and ripped out her still beating heart.

As hot blood coated her hand, Aveline went lax.

Nola fizzed with power. *I did it! I won!*

She didn't think about her next actions, just followed those hard-won instincts that had guided her so well and bit into the organ.

The taste was foul, but she didn't care. New bolts of power slammed into her, and she threw back her head to scream.

But all too soon, the power and strength got used up, her body burning through it like fuel. Everything she'd done, everything that had happened had taken a massive toll.

She wheezed and panted, darkness returning to envelop her mind. "Bane," she whispered, her voice slurred. "Heal quickly."

The darkness swallowed her whole.

SHE'D DONE IT. Nola had won! Awe sang within Bane, a melody he would carry for all time. She'd even healed his shoulder before passing out.

He lifted her into his arms, holding her close. Her heart raced against his.

"Will Nola recover?" Zion asked, concerned.

"Yes," he replied, pushing the word through clenched teeth. She must. Aveline had drained much of her life-force, so she had much to recover.

"What about the other queen? Can she regenerate a heart?" Zion stalked to Aveline's body.

"Let's not take a chance."

"I like how your mind works." The male swung a sword, chopping off Aveline's head with a single blow.

A wondrous sight to behold. Once, Bane would have insisted on performing the action himself. Now, with Nola in his arms, he had better things to do.

"I'll give you two time alone," Zion said, opening a portal.

"Thank you...friend. For everything."

The other male nodded, then strode through the doorway.

Bane carried his precious bundle to a wall and eased down. Rocks propped him up as he cradled his love close. "Draw from me, love. Take whatever you need."

How much time passed before she fluttered open her eyes, he didn't know. But it wasn't long, and her wounds healed right before his eyes.

"Bane?" she said. Memories must have flooded her, because she gasped and jerked upright.

"I'm here, love. I've got you." Bane urged her back and kissed her brow. "Never letting go."

"We did it. We won!"

"*You* won. I love you, Nola Lee, my forever queen."

She sagged against him, puffing out a breath. "You do? Still? I mean, I'm a queen now, and I can order you around, like, big-time. That isn't going to change."

"I'm not complaining. I meant what I said. I love you, *all* of you, even your orders."

With a moan of surrender, she snuggled closer. "I love you, too, Bane. So much. I want to rule *with* you, and be with you, always and forever. Nothing less is acceptable."

"Then we will rule together. Always and forever," he parroted. When he'd come to Terra, he'd been eaten up with hate and vengeance. Darkness had shrouded his soul. But this feisty female had teased and tormented him from minute one, steadily pushing him into the light.

"I can't believe Aveline is dead. Can't believe how close I came to losing you forever." A sob left her, causing her entire body to quake, but no others followed. "I *can* believe we did it. We're amazing!"

"You keep including me, but it was you. You did it, I watched. And a more spectacular sight I've never beheld." He laughed with unfettered joy and jumped to his feet, taking her with him. "*You* are amazing, love."

He planted a sizzling hot kiss on her lips. "I can never thank you enough."

"No, babe. Thank *you*. You did help. You trusted me. Now you're giving me the life I've always dreamed of having."

"I trusted you, yes, and I was rewarded for it. You gave me life, period. Before you, I was dead in every way that mattered. But you revived me. You became my heart." He kissed her again. He couldn't *not* kiss her. "You were right before. We will find a way to stop the war so that we all survive. I know we will. Look at all we've accomplished so far. Now that we're working together, we can do so much more. And we will."

"You're right. We've accomplished so much in a very short time frame. You are free of Aveline's tyrannical rule. I gained a crown, powers and an army. But I will. Soon. I think the beasts are searching for me."

"Oh, they are. I have no doubts."

"Maybe they can help during assemblies and battles. You know, do some scouting for us. Perhaps even be trained to ambush the High Council and their Enforcers? Food for thought, anyway."

"Excellent ideas. But right now, I only wish to enjoy you, to keep you all to myself." He brought her hand to his mouth and kissed her wrist, laving her hammering pulse with his tongue. "I don't know if I've ever been this happy, especially during a war."

With a contented sigh, she kissed a spot just over his heart. "After we stop the war, maybe we can visit Adwaeweth and help our people."

"Our people," he said with a smile. "Yes. I'd like that. Wherever we are, we'll work miracles together. But first, I need more of you. A physical pledge of your devotion. Since I'm your king and all."

She smiled up at him. "What my king wants, my king receives."

"What my queen, my treasure wants…" He gripped her hips, grinding her core against his erection. "I will provide."

They peered into each other's eyes, and he knew. They would find a way to work those miracles. The All War didn't stand a chance, and neither did the High Council.

"I hope you're prepared." She ripped off her dress, revealing the body he loved beyond reason. "This treasured queen is going to rock your world."

"You already have, love. You already have."

Nola grinned. "Baby, you haven't seen nothing yet."

* * * * *

*Turn the page for a special preview of
the next book in Gena Showalter's scorching
Lords of the Underworld series
featuring William the Ever Randy,*
The Darkest King.

Coming soon from HQN Books.

SUNNY FLUTTERED A hand over her heart as she stumbled back a step. "You know what I am?"

"I do. Just as you know what I am." A ruthless killer.

Terror darkened her features, and he knew why. Her kind had been hunted for centuries and neared extinction. Different immortal species had different reasons for going after her kind, but many cited their dual-sided nature. One loved, one hated. One spread joy, one killed without remorse. You never knew which one you'd get on any given day. And damn if William wasn't intrigued by the mystery.

His eyes narrowed. "This is the part where you apologize for shooting me in the face," he continued. "Were you anyone else, I would punish you."

"I would apologize for an accident. I *meant* to shoot you. By the way, immortals are supposed to regenerate exact replicas when they lose a body part, but you... Your face..." She exaggerated a wince. "My bad."

Dealing with the dark side today apparently. Noted.

"Listen well." William crossed the room, closing in on the exquisite female who might be the only person in all the worlds with the power to decode his book and break the curse that hung over his life like a sword of Damocles. "I have a message for you."

The closer he came, the more Sunny's breathing quickened, her breasts rising and falling.

Don't you dare look down. He could not let himself desire her...more than he already did.

Finally, he stood before her, only a whisper away, her maddeningly sweet scent and sparkling amber eyes making his erection throb. Voice low and smoky, he said, "You, Sunny Lane, tried to end my life. Therefore, you owe me a life debt, and I'm here to collect. From this moment on, you are my property. Every breath you take is my gift to you. Meaning, yes, I own you now."

As she sputtered for a response, William's darkest instincts surged to the forefront. *Punish. Possess. Protect.*

Protect? From himself? No. But oh, the things he wanted to do to this woman...